The Sol Empire
Volume 4
Power Moves

Vic Broquard

The Sol Empire Volume 4 Power Moves
First Edition
Copyrighted © 2018 by Vic Broquard
ISBN: 978-1-941415-85-6

This is a work of fiction. All characters, organizations, and events portrayed in this novel are products of the author's imagination and are used fictitiously.

What isn't fictional is the work that Humanity and Inclusion (formerly Handicapped International) is doing to help those who have suffered:
http://www.hi-us.org

Published by:
http://www.Broquard-ebooks.com
Broquard eBooks
103 Timberlane
East Peoria, IL 61611
author@Broquard-eBooks.com

For Morgan and L. Ron Hubbard

Table of Contents

Chapter 1 All at Once

Monday, January 23, 2361, Chicago, Earth, Sol Empire

After today, I now hate Mondays. Oh, it began easy enough—the kids' first day back in school from Christmas Break. Matt's in second grade, while Nikita is in third. I expected a little chaos, just not CHAOS.

"Mom, where's my book bag?" Nikita wailed. "I can't find it anywhere. Dad's helping Matt find his. I'm going to look different than all the other kids, 'cause they'll have baby arms like Matt and Dad have."

"But you insisted on being born a telepath," I grumbled, my tall heels clicking on our hardwood floor as I walked around looking for her bag. Without arms, we telepaths depended upon our bags. Last year, terrorists attacked her grade school, unleashing the armless telepath Galactic Doll mutation agent on her class and hundreds of other students. This past year has seen a nightmare of these mutation attacks.

"Here it is, honey," I said. I watched her as she slipped off a tall heel, hoisted her school bag up and over her head, and slid her foot back into her heel. For us, balance is everything. "You look pretty, Nikita. Blue satin suits you. Everyone else is going to look different with their tiny arms. It takes a year for regrowing arms to be halfway normal. Now, get your cloak on. It's freezing outside."

She picked it up, holding it between her head and shoulder. With a swinging toss, it arced over her back and shoulders. I slipped off my heels, sat on the floor, and fastened her cloak clasp with my toes, before kissing her forehead.

"I'm waking them to school as always," Sam said, as he and Matt joined us. Thanks to the late December pandemic virus, their feet were restored so both could wear normal boots, but they'd lost their telepathic ability, and their arms were regrowing, something they both wanted. I watched the three head out the front door, before I struggled to my feet, wobbling some as I slipped into my heels.

"Mom," my eldest daughter called out from our guest bedroom.

"Coming, Isabella." She and her twin brother Bernardo had also been terrorist victims when they were thirteen. Both became linguists on deep space exploration ships, banking millions of credits in salaries. When the pandemic struck late December, she chose to remain a telepath, but Bernardo endured it to get his arms back—the heck with telepathy. Both children had just gotten married, but Isabella was expecting her daughter in late February. She and her husband, Owen, lived with us, while Bernardo and Wendy moved in with her parents.

"Mom, I don't think I can do this." She shrugged her shoulders. "I think maybe I should have gotten the virus to get my arms back like Owen and the others did. I can barely bend over. I have to pee all the time. I don't think I can take care of my baby when she comes. I feel sick, Mom."

I pressed my body into hers, our special hug.

"Honey, sure you can. Stop and think how. We'll all help you. Besides, Nikita is dying to help you practice feeding, diapering, and washing her dolls. You two work on that when she gets home from school. Practice the actions you're going to need. Besides, Sam cared for Matt and Nikita since they were babies, and he didn't have arms then."

"I know," she admitted. "You've told me Dad wanted to be Matt and Nikita's role model while they were growing up. Nikita showed me the fancy three-wheeled bicycles he got for them. I guess I'm just worrying too much. But I'm scared."

"I think all new mothers-to-be get a little apprehensive about it. With the first child, it's all a big unknown. I was nervous just before I had Nikita. Besides, it's only a few more weeks. Then, you'll have a new problem: trying to find anytime to sleep."

Isabella sighed and chuckled. "You keep telling us that. I can't believe that's true. Thanks, Mom. It'll make Nikita happy if we practice together."

"Of course, it will. She adores her older sister."

My phone rang, and someone pounded on the door.

"Get the door, will you?" I asked Isabella, while I sat on

2

her bed, slipped off a heel, and retrieved my phone from my lower dress pocket.

"Hello."

My fancy phone displayed a foot tall hologram of Admiral Skaggs of Azizi-C, the Federation representative sent to Earth to force us to get a handle on this messy armless telepath mutation agent and subsequent viral pandemic. He ordered me to become the Sol Empire's Senior Investigator and Senior Judge. Okay, today was to be my first day on the job. Was he calling to complain I was late? Didn't he have kids?

"Mrs. Parkinson. As you know the Federation of Planets' Tenth Annual Linguist Conference is being held in Chicago on February 14th. Linguists from throughout the Federation are coming. One of those is a Miss Tia Sanchez, from New Amsterdam, Brussels, Tau Ceti. She went missing shortly after her arrival at New O'Hare yesterday. Our own linguist, Bonita Valdez, is due to arrive tomorrow. As the Sol Empire's Senior Investigator, find Miss Sanchez and guarantee nothing happens to Miss Valdez. She's my niece, so I'm holding you personally responsible for her safe arrival. Keep me posted. Goodbye."

I slipped my notepad from my pocket and jotted down the two names. I knew about this conference of linguists. Isabella would be getting the Knight of Language, their highest award, for her groundbreaking work on uncovering the lost languages of the fourth and fifth invaders that she did for her Ph.D. thesis.

Isabella walked in, leading another young woman. Well, after the pandemic in December, every human on Earth looked like a young woman, creating panic and chaos among newly mutated men and boys. Less than a month after hundreds of millions of mutations, Galactic Manufacturing had yet to make enough male clothing that fit their gigantic bosoms and necessary tall heels. Many men had little choice but to wear women's gowns and heels that were plentiful.

She wore her blonde hair up. I gazed into her soft, blue eyes, but had no idea of her gender. I'd never seen her before.

"Mrs. Molly Parkinson. I'm Ashley Peterson, your new

3

Personal Assistant and Chief of Staff for your Senior Judge Office. I know I've only been on the job for a couple days, but I'm working on my law degree. I'm supposed to also be your hands as well as run your office. Guess we can't shake hands. Sorry. I've never been around anyone like you. You'll have to tell me what you need. Anyway, we're late. You have a top priority court case to hear in thirty minutes." She glanced at her watch.

"Oh, and your security guard is waiting outside, a Sherry Cooper from Brussels. Are you sure you don't want male guards, perhaps from Brussels, too? I mean no disrespect to our males, but you know. They're..."

"Rather indisposed at the moment," I interrupted. "No, I know Sherry and trust her with my life. Got two Senior Investigations to handle as top priorities, too. I didn't know I had a court case. Do we have time for a coffee?"

She glanced nervously at her watch. "No. We'll just make it as it is." Her face flushed. "Can you read my mind, too?" she asked.

Ah, a light touch of her mind told me that was what she was extremely worried about. "While I could read your mind, Miss Peterson, an ethical telepath would never do that without your expressed consent. But there are unethical ones out there, so I'd be worried, too. Come on. Help me into my cloak. Oh, and stick my phone in my lower dress pocket."

"Ashley, please. Just Ashley."

She wore a form-fitting, while silk blouse that highlighted her massive endowment, a black skirt, and low, matching pumps—the perfect professional woman look. As we headed out into the living room, she walked much faster than I could and had to stop and wait on me.

"Morning, Sherry," I said, as we stepped out into the frosty day. "Haven't seen you in a while."

"Mrs. Parkinson. Yes, I've been tied up on that other case of yours—the mysterious dead of Ted."

Instantly, I knew what she was hinting at and that she was unwilling to reveal much in the presence of my new Personal Assistant and Chief of Staff. Ted was my first husband who was murdered. For years, all manner of investigations into his killing yielded no clues at all. It became a cold case. As Bishop, she must have uncovered something significant. She was one of five human-form robots programmed to aid us, but in disguise. As far as I knew, I was the only one who knew about her and the four others.

I said, "We must talk as soon as this court case is done. I'm also under orders to investigate a missing linguist and ensure the safety of another one who is coming to the big Federation linguistic conference next week. Why do I feel overworked on my first day? Hey, slow down. I can't keep up."

Ashley set a pace far too rapid for me, but Sherry stayed by my side, used to my pathetically slow, careful pace.

"We mustn't be late. The lawyers'll be complaining," Ashley said.

Well, we were. It took over a half hour to travel the MTES to the Monroe building, mostly because of my slow pace. By the time we walked into the building and past security, my legs felt like ice cycles.

The Investigations Department occupied the lower ten floors, while the Justice Department used the top ten. My official court, Ashley explained, was on the twentieth floor, but there wasn't a thirteenth floor I noted as we stepped into the elevator. She insisted on taking my cloak off before the doors opened onto my floor.

I'd been here once before, only as the "criminal" telepath who wasn't armless. I didn't even get a chance to say one word before the court sentenced me—all without a trial of any kind. Open and shut. I admitted I had telepathic ability and had arms. Ergo, I was an illegal telepath, so the court ordered me to be immediately mutated into the legal form. Well, now that I was the Senior Judge, blind jurisprudence had to change.

A model of efficiency, Ashley already had the original judge's bench removed, replaced by one whose writing surface was close to the floor so I could use my feet to write and handle documents. A large computer station lay to the right of my chair. The smell of lemon polish and wood greeted my nose, along with cologne. An array of ten chairs and a table lay to the left and an identical set lay to the right of my desk.

Already people had taken their seats. A placard on my right read Defense, while a similar one on my left read Plaintiffs. Both sides were present, but I saw only a collection of young women, twenty-five years old at most, though several in the Plaintiff section sported tiny, baby-like arms. I presumed victims of the recent viral pandemic. I took my seat, while Sherry stood beside several armed guards near the doors.

Ashley opened a file on my desk, walked out in front, and spoke loudly. "The Senior Court is now in session and is being video recorded. Senior Judge Molly Parkinson presiding. Official case Number One is being heard: red flag, top priority. Plaintiffs Angelina Flores, Major Kenneth Maxwell, and Doctor Regan Miller of the Enchanter are represented by Carol Taylor. Defendants: Galactic Expansion, Galactic Medicine, the Senate, and the Federation of Planets' Admiral Skaggs of the Kanika, represented by Sam Deckerson, legal representative of Galactic Defense, Earth Division, Moscow, assigned to Chicago GPan."

I stared at Sam Deckerson. "Aren't you the lawyer that forced my sisters to become Galactic Dolls while they were on Brussels so that Deanna could back get her billions of credits that GD confiscated from her account?"

His face reddened; he nodded.

"Wow. You certainly look much better as a Galactic Doll. I take it karma is a bitch. Okay, let's get on with this. I've got two other top priority cases to handle today. Ms Taylor, you have the floor. Please, let's keep this civil. Don't interrupt each other."

"Thank you, Senior Judge Parkinson. I represent these three individuals from the deep space exploration ship the Enchanter, recently returned to Earth for resupply and having discovered a new habitable planet with significant mineral resources. This case presents two very different situations. First, I wish to make certain facts a part of this court record."

"Fine with me. Go ahead," I said, while watching Sam grimacing.

She began, "As we now know, the Sixth Invaders convinced the women of earth to undergo the Galactic Doll mutation—these aliens' ideal body form. The mutation created breasts the size of our heads and distorted our feet forcing the person to wear tall heels. It turned both women and men into gorgeous, shapely Galactic Dolls with people gaining or losing weight to reach this ideal form. But with men, a set of ribs dissolved, their voices rose, their Adam's apple vanished, and their body became indistinguishable from female Galactic Dolls, until you look at their genitals. On the positive side, that mutation both rejuvenated bodies and regrew missing body parts, yielding a body of a twenty-one year old. Further, children born to a Galactic Doll are themselves a Galactic Doll, male or female." She paused.

Sam Deckerson rose. "I object. This is all common knowledge. Let's get to the point of this lawsuit."

Carol Taylor replied, "Your Honor, this has everything to do with this case. If you'll allow me to continue, it will soon be clear."

"You may continue."

"The next mutation version opened the door to atrocities and became the tool of both terrorists and the greedy. That modified mutation produced a normal Galactic Doll but one who lacked arms. Within a few weeks of the mutation, the victims developed telepathic abilities. At once, corporations conducted bidding wars to hire these unfortunate people. Terrorists mutated thousands of unwilling men, women, and children into armless telepaths and then tried to sell them into slavery, often spying for corporations. Vital point: a few lucky ones were hired as linguists on our deep space exploration ships to aid when encountering a people on a new world. It's a proven fact that a telepathic linguist can rapidly learn a new culture's language, supplying the basic vocabulary for our language translators devices."

I interrupted, "Yes, I'm familiar with that. My two older children did just that. For the record, I consider this a very valid use of a telepath's skills. Continue."

"Thank you, Your Honor. As we now know, any child from such a parent will also be an armless telepath; it's a dominant mutation. However, seven years ago, two geneticists created a genetic cure to regrow the lost arms. However, the ruling corporations demanded that any arm regrow cure also remove their telepathic abilities. For the record, their reasoning went as follows. If you see an armless Doll, he or she is a telepath who could probe your mind. But if you see someone with arms, they aren't a telepath and your secrets are safe."

I interrupted. "For the record, not everyone without arms is a telepath. Accidents and birth defects happen. Why not just regrow their arms? Rather, the Senate has ordered them to be given the mutation agent to make them into telepaths."

Sam Deckerson protested. "What's all this got to do with the case at hand? Please get to the point."

"I am nearly finished," she replied. "The Senate's current laws state that any child born as an armless Doll telepath had to be raised as such until they reached the age of eighteen, at which time they could choose to have the cures or remain a telepath. Any adult becoming one, can't get any cures for ten years."

I was acutely aware of these insidious laws. When Nikita came, she insisted she wanted to be a telepath, begging us not to give her the arm regrow cure. So my husband chose to remain an armless Doll telepath so he could show our daughter how to do things and provide moral support.

Sam Deckerson interrupted her. I allowed him to do so, curious about how he'd justify this inhumanity.

He said, "Telepaths are extremely rare; their unique skills, incredibly valuable. Let the record show the going rate for a telepath is a million credits per year. Why those laws? The Senate hoped these new telepaths would desire to remain so and work for them. Give them time to adapt and see how much they could earn as a valuable telepath."

"Miss Taylor, please continue," I said.

"With this in the record, I'd like to begin with Angelina Flores. Angelina, relate your grievance to the court."

The young woman with dark, piercing eyes rose. She wore a red satin, sleeveless gown revealing her regrowing baby-like arms—quite a startling contrast.

"I'm only in my fifth year of being a telepath-linguist on

8

the Enchanter. My contract is for ten years at a million credits per year, paid monthly. All ready I've worked out the basic language of the people on one of the worlds we've discovered, before we had to resupply. We docked at New O'Hare on twenty December last year. Then the viral pandemic struck everywhere. I got sick, too. I've lost my telepathic ability, and my arms are regrowing. This isn't right. I want to continue to be a telepathic linguist. It's a valuable and rewarding career. I'd like this court to order GMed to inject me and make me into a telepath again."

"Next," Carol Taylor said, "we'll hear from Major Kenneth Maxwell, commander of the Enchanter. He'll speak for Dr. Miller as well. Major."

He rose, wobbling slightly on tall heels. At least he had arms to help him keep his balance. His alto voice suggested that he once had been a bass. He wore an ill-fitting man's shirt and equally baggy pants, obviously borrowed. Galactic Manufacturing simply couldn't make Leslie's fancy male Doll apparel fast enough. Most pandemic infected men, I discovered, had to make do anyway they could. His red heels didn't match anything. Dr. Miller's attire was equally as bad. Both men's baby-like arms looked incongruous, poking out of their sleeves.

"We were wrapping up our exploration of the inhabited world called Callie's Place. Linguist Flores had already finalized the basic vocabulary of these indigenous people. Dr. Miller and I stood outside the ship, close to a plant the natives called a bottle plant, awaiting the arrival of the last geological survey shuttle. We didn't know bottle plants explode when they're ready to pollinate. The plant blew up in our faces. Worse, whatever the plant excretes is poisonous to humans. We both collapsed.

"Our doctor said that I was technically dead for two minutes. Any way, before we left on our mission, GPan gave us a supply of the armless telepath mutation agent. Each red packet contained two syringes of the stuff. If anyone on the ship was seriously injured and in danger of dying, they were to be injected with the lifesaving agent. Galactic Medicine had publicized how effective this agent is. One patient had been shot in their head and was pronounced brain dead before she was injected with this agent. Within a month, she was totally rejuvenated."

My face felt hot. He was referring to me. A Sixth Invader put a hole in my head.

"So our ship's doctor injected Dr. Miller and me with that mutation agent. Eight days later, we both woke from our comas—alive and well. Except we were mostly helpless. Thankfully, Angelina showed us how to get by, more or less. What I'm saying is that we would both be dead if it wasn't for GPan's insistence that each ship carry a small supply of that armless telepath Galactic Doll mutation agent.

"He and I consider ourselves phenomenally lucky, since we returned to Earth in time to be infected during the pandemic. While we lost our telepathic ability, our arms are regrowing. And that's what matters to us. While we look—well, like women, in a few months, we'll be able to resume our deep space explorations.

"We beg this court to overturn Admiral Skaggs' orders to confiscate these mutation agents. Having it on our last trip saved two lives. Exploring new planets is one of the most dangerous jobs in the empire. All manner of strange plants and animals have killed many explorers. With this mutation agent onboard, I have a way to prevent some of those deaths. Surely, that outweighs GPan paying out millions of credits for each casualty. If the court needs those statistics, I'm sure GPan can provide them. Please, Your Honor, don't send out deep space exploration ships without this lifesaving agent onboard. And allow us to receive the arm regrow cures when we get back. Thank you."

I nodded to the Defendants and Sam Deckerson. He rose careful to keep his balance on unfamiliar tall heels.

"Your Honor, GPan does not dispute any of the facts presented by the plaintiffs. In fact, we'd like nothing more than to grant both requests. After this pandemic, only a handful of telepaths remain. Major Maxwell is correct. Loss of life on these deep space exploration trips averages 1.5 people per trip. Insurance payouts average six million credits per trip. However, during the last seven years when the ships carried the mutation agent, such deaths have dropped over seventy percent, resulting in enormous savings for the corporations. We wish to continue this program of having all key personnel carry a red syringe containing the armless telepath mutation agent just for these emergencies. Each container has written instructions for its use and is good for a single dose only. At first, the syringes contained the original Galactic Doll agent, but the armless telepath version has now replaced those because this agent is more powerful and can save more lives.

"However, as you are well aware, Your Honor, Admiral Skaggs and the Federation of Planets has ordered Earth to destroy all such samples. GPan's position is that this court must side with Admiral Skaggs."

He sat down. Did I detect a smirk on his face? If so, it was fleeting.

"Okay. I understand all sides. I've been heavily involved in the recovery and rehabilitation of thousands of mutation victims. The crux of the problem is that a true telepath is an extraordinarily rare person all throughout the galaxy. With this mutation agent, any Homo Sapiens Sapiens, if I have my anthropology correct, can be turned into an armless telepath Galactic Doll. In other words, for the first time, a telepath can be made. Hence, we've had all manner of unscrupulous Earth men and women sponsoring these terrorist attacks and attempting to sell the victims into a sort of telepath slavery off-world. Recently, aliens on other worlds have been mutating humans for the same ends.

"What everyone fails to grasp is that the vast majority of the mutation victims didn't want to become a telepath. Thus, in protest they purposely relayed false spy data, for example. Only a few actually wish to be one of us, like Angelina Flores, and for the right reasons.

"The Federation of Planets is right to be terrified of this mutation agent. Not all species of intelligent life in the galaxy are like us and are thus immune to the biological agent, such as our giants and dwarves. However, many are sufficiently close that their people may well be mutated by our agents. Those on Azizi-C, for example, look like normal humans. In fact, so do the Third Invaders who kidnapped many telepath victims. Plus, I would expect any geneticist who knows what they're doing could modify the agent to mutate another species. So, yes, the Federation has every right to be petrified of this biological agent or weapon.

"Our own corporations ignored all such ramifications and have distributed these mutation agents so widely that I can't see how Admiral Skaggs will ever be able to confiscate it. Heck, there are some red syringes in my own home, stuck in a drawer. The problem is corporate irresponsibility with these agents and the Senate's ridiculous laws.

"Yet, as the plaintiffs have said, there are benefits to this agent. Because Angelina Flores endured the viral pandemic, getting her body to accept the mutation agent might not be possible. Something about a body's immune system. Still, if she's willing and signs a waver of responsibility, GMed might try to see if they can re-mutate her."

"I'm very willing. I'll do anything to become a telepathic linguist again," Angelina Flores blurted out.

"This court must make a decision in this case. But I need further information. Let's adjourn for a few minutes while I summon those I need to discuss this with. We'll need Admiral Skaggs, Helen Hugo of GD, the Emperor, the Empress, and the CEO of GMed. Ashley, will you issue the summons and let us know how long we need to recess before they can get here?"

Five minutes later, Ashley announced, "This court will recess for thirty minutes. Court will resume testimony at ten o'clock sharp."

She glanced at her watch. Me, I've never owned one. What's the point. Time is time. Besides, I've always got my phone or computer with me.

Admiral Skaggs arrived before I could even get a coffee or tea. "So have you made any progress on the disappearance of Tia Sanchez? How about security for my niece?"

"Look, I had to deal with this court case first. I'll get on to those as soon as we wrap up this case. Besides, I don't know who to trust in either of these organizations, let alone who is actually working on investigations or court cases. It's only my first day."

He nodded and took a seat on the defense side. Ashley appeared carrying a hot tea. What a lifesaver.

"For the record," Ashley Peterson later said, "Admiral Skaggs, GD CEO Helen Hugo, Emperor Dimitri Leonovich, Empress Natalie Leonovich, and GMed CEO Blanca Ruiz are in attendance. Again, I'm reminding everyone, this proceeding is being video recorded. Your Honor, you may continue."

I outlined the case at hand, making a strong argument for both plaintiffs, before summarizing the situation from the Federation of Planet's point of view.

"CEO Ruiz, your corporation must officially log the death of every person within the empire. Correct?"

"That is correct."

"The defense has claimed there's been a seventy percent reduction in deaths on our deep space exploration ships. Is that an accurate statement?"

"Yes, that is also correct."

"And that drastic reduction has occurred because of the usage of the red emergency syringes containing the armless telepath Galactic Doll mutation agent?"

"That is also correct. If I might add, those syringes have also saved other lives here on Earth. Construction accidents, primarily. We recommend everyone in the empire carry one syringe with them, except for the total boycott of it by all the other worlds and moons."

"What about the pandemic victims' immune systems rejecting these mutation agents? Is that the case?"

"We've had very little time to investigate that aspect. We know that has been claimed, but as yet it's not been verified. Even if a body's immune system fights against a normal dose, there are ways to circumvent the immune system and get the mutation to work."

"Thank you. CEO Hugo, what progress can you report on the confiscation of these agents, per Admiral Skaggs' orders? And how is the detection system coming along?"

Helen grinned. "Can I be perfectly honest, Your Honor?" She stared at Admiral Skaggs.

"Please."

"I and my family were victims of one of the terrorist attacks. Only now are my own arms being regrown, thanks to the pandemic. So as much as I personally want to completely destroy every last trace of that mutation agent, I believe that to be utterly impossible. The corporations have so widely distributed both the Galactic Doll and the armless telepath agents across Earth that we don't have a clue to where it's all located. Heck, average citizens now have one or more of the red packages containing a single dose for a dire emergency. Every lab has tons of samples, including amateur labs. If we send soldiers out going door to door confiscating the agents, I guarantee you that much of it will suddenly appear on the black market and likely off-world, too. Frankly, Your Honor, it's one grand mess. The genie is long out of the bottle, as the saying goes."

Again, she looked at Admiral Skaggs. I also knew how damaging her testimony must be in his eyes. If we couldn't eliminate the agents, he could well be forced to destroy Earth and all its people. I had to avoid that at all costs.

"Admiral Skaggs," I asked, "how goes your project to detect any of the agent being smuggled off Earth?"

"Actually, Mrs. Parkinson, Your Honor, very well. My tech people have created a detection system that can spot even one of those red syringes being smuggled into a spaceship. We're working on making it ten times more sensitive before we give it to Galactic Manufacturing for mass production. With the installation of the Titan World Dome Shield here on Earth, no ship can leave except through the designated, closely monitored entrances. Galactic Expansion is footing the ten billion credit cost of the system which my engineers are currently installing. It should be operational within a week. After that, all incoming and outgoing flights will have to go through specific entry points and subject to search and seizure."

"Great. You've heard that there are specific benefits to this biological agent. If you can keep others from spreading the agent across the galaxy, could we be allowed to continue using it for these two specific purposes?"

"Depends," he hedged. "Look, your terrorists and aliens

14

have foisted this telepath agent off on tens of thousands. How many of those actually wanted to be an armless telepath, eh?"

"Sir, I've helped vast numbers of them, one way or another. I think it's safe to say the number of people who want to live with this disability just so they can be a telepath is a tiny fraction of a percent. Darn few. But those who do are making exceptionally good use of the skill, such as the plaintiff Angelina Flores.

"Empress, do you concur that once this shield is up, we'll be able to prevent anyone from taking a significant quantity of these agents off Earth? Outside of the red syringes, that is."

"If the Admiral's detection system works, then we should be able to finally control the illegal export of the agents and all further versions, I might add."

"Good. Emperor, do you agree that there are two valid uses of the telepath agent?"

"Absolutely. Exploring unknown worlds is fraught with dangerous plants and animals. Until now, we had no way to save lives. We've already seen a significant reduction in casualties."

"Okay then, one final detail before I make my decision. As I understand our new charter from the Federation of Planets, the Senior Judge and the Emperor and Empress can override any law passed by the Senate. Is that correct? And we can reject laws, substituting new ones in their place?"

Admiral Skaggs said, "Yes, that's the intended idea. I have to agree with you. Your previous Senate passed absolutely ridiculous laws regarding telepaths and failed utterly to constrain corporations from exploiting the telepath victims."

"Good. Then, here's my ruling for which I'll ask for backing from the Emperor and Empress. Any previous telepath who wishes to become a telepath again can have the armless telepath Galactic Doll mutation agent, subject to GMed's determination of the dosage required. Anyone who was subjected to that agent can have any and all cures they desire and when they desire them. No time limits. Further, the emergency red packets of syringes containing the armless telepath Galactic Doll mutation agent can be dispensed to those deemed at risk for loss of life. Specific exceptions will be allowed on spacecrafts leaving Earth carrying such doses. They must be accounted for at takeoff and when they land. Any discrepancy in the two counts will force a complete investigation. Anyone caught trying to smuggle the agents off Earth or who is complicit in such an attempt will be subject to immediate termination.

"Will the Emperor and Empress back my decisions?"

Both Dimitri and Natalie agreed.

"Admiral Skaggs, will these protections and exceptions be accepted by the Federation of Planets? We don't want you destroying Earth."

He chuckled. "I will take your arguments to the Council of Admirals and plead your case. If the detection system works, I believe they'll accept this. However, everything hinges on those who take the single dose syringes off Earth. You must ensure they bring them back, except for the ones that were used. Strict accounting by GPan."

Just then, Helen received a phone call. "Hold on, everyone," she called out as the others began to file out of the courtroom. "Galactic Entertainment just broadcast the identify of the person who created the viral pandemic. Some of my security guards went to retrieve her and found she'd just been shot by an angry man who was one of her billions of victims. My forces terminated him and rushed the woman to the med center. Apparently, GEnt got an anonymous tip about this woman, but as of now, it's mere unsubstantiated rumor. Have to run."

"Admiral Skaggs, stick around. We need to talk," I said. Galactic Entertainment would certainly broadcast that information!

Anger swept over me. Admiral Skaggs promised to keep her identity a secret for fear of this very thing happening.

Patricia Ann Gates-Baxter, a virologist and microbiologist, created the virus and set off a pandemic of mutations. Why? Thousands in Philadelphia became the victims of one of these armless doll terrorist attacks. In particular, her husband, a highly skilled neurosurgeon, became an armless telepath, and their newborn son was born as one, too. His medical career came crashing down. Furious over these insane laws that wouldn't let them at least regrow their arms—not for years—Patricia Ann invented a virulent virus that turned every human on Earth into an normal Galactic Doll, regrowing the arms of those who lacked them and rejuvenating everyone to age twenty-five. In the process, many lost their telepathic abilities.

I'd found her before Admiral Skaggs' men did. I arranged for a meeting, saving her life. He'd promised to never reveal who had created the virus and launched the pandemic.

Once we were alone, I said, "I thought we agreed never to reveal Patricia Ann's identity."

"We did. This is news to me. It's as we both figured. Once the world knew who did it, someone was bound to terminate her out of revenge."

"Well, those who knew her identity are my sisters and your aides. Someone blabbed. Someone betrayed us."

"Correct. We must find out who. That person cannot be trusted. I suspect the leak came from one of your people."

I fumed. Hardly. "My bet is on one of your people. I'll check on mine today. If the leak didn't come from them, it had to be your people."

He glared at me, nodded, turned, and left. Ashley rushed back into the room.

"I've got to handle two emergency, top priority investigations and now this happens. Okay, Ashley, get Sherry and let's go visit Deanna Cartwright. Then, we'll tackle these investigations. Hold all court cases for a few days."

"But there's a class action lawsuit case filed by dozens of billionaires on the docket. They want the Galactic Doll mutation undone," Ashley said.

"Billionaires? Ok, they can wait. Let's go."

She gave me a dirty look.

Chapter 2 Spiraling Events

By eleven o'clock, I'd verified none of my sisters had betrayed Patricia Ann. I phoned Admiral Skaggs and told him so, but hung up before he could reply. On my way back to the Monroe building, we stopped at the med center. I wanted to check on Patricia Ann.

I found Vernon in the waiting area, his newborn son in a bag over his shoulder, suckling. He saw me coming and spoke up.

"I thought you said no one would find out."

"The leak didn't come from my people. Admiral Skaggs has a serious problem with his personnel. How's Pat doing?"

Tears trickled down. "They got her on life support. Now they're attempting to inject her with the armless telepath Galactic Doll mutation agent. Apparently, there was a similar case where a woman was shot in the head like Pat was and that agent was powerful enough to fully heal her. But there's a small problem with her immune system rejecting the mutation agent. Right now, they've increased the dose. They told me to be hopeful, but that the arm regrow cure might not work after this much mutation has occurred. I don't know what to think."

"I know the case they referred to. It was me, Vernon. Bullet to the head. Pronounced brain dead, but kept on life support so my daughter could be born. A doctor injected me with that agent. A month later, I walked out of the med center fully healed. So if they can get the mutation agent to work, Pat should recover."

After he thanked me and we hugged, I left him, rejoining Ashley and Sherry who politely waited in the hallway for me.

"Okay, lunch and let's get onto these two critical investigations," I said.

My Senior Investigator office was on the tenth floor, a spacious room filled with six whiteboards, a bank of computers, and numerous desks. Again, Ashley had been a model of efficiency. She'd arranged for a special desk for me, one whose surface was just inches above the floor.

Sherry whispered to me, "They've made some significant upgrades since I ran this office."

The human-form robot had been my choice for Senior Investigator many years ago. That was before she changed her identity into Bishop and then again into Sherry.

Along the north wall stood a fancy coffee maker, an elegant tea set, and a cocoa maker. Ashley noticed my eyes taking that in and commented.

"Thought you might appreciate that. What'll you have?"

"Earl Grey. Thanks, Ashley."

Two others walked into the room, each carrying a folder under an arm. Both wore satin gowns, and their tall heels echoed on the hardwood floor. Of course, I couldn't tell their actual gender. What a nuisance this was becoming.

"Ah, Senior Investigator Parkinson," said the one who had Chinese ancestry. She wore her black hair long and straight, falling to the middle of her back in the typical Galactic Doll style. Shorter than me, her feet weren't distorted, telling me she chose to wear tall heels. I suspected to help the other person not feel so out of place.

"My name is Jie Wu. This is Ward Tilman. Excuse his apparel, but because of the pandemic, we've only been able to find him red gowns. At least his heels match. We're assigned to be your assistant investigators. We both have six years as investigators."

"Pleased to meet you. Just call me Molly. I can use some help. This it turning out to be one messed up day. This is my assistant and Chief of Staff, Ashley Peterson, and my security guard, Sherry Cooper."

Ward said, "We've met Ashley. Incredibly fast breaking news. Glad they uncovered who invented the virus and launched the pandemic. I look and feel awful." He waved his arms about his curvaceous form. "If you would prefer another investigator than me, we can find you several competent female investigators."

I chuckled. "You're fine, Ward. My husband has been an armless telepath Galactic Doll for many years, so I'm used to it. We've got two rush cases to deal with."

"We know. Ashley texted us," Jie said. "I've been gathering information on the missing Tia Sanchez, while Ward has started a file on Bonita Valdez of Azizi-C. She really is the niece of Admiral Skaggs. If you agree, we'd like to post what we have up on the whiteboards."

After I nodded, I watched them rapidly paste large images of each young linguist on separate boards, along with patchy time lines.

"Oh, Ashley, let me know if and when Angelina Flores goes into the Med Center for her mutation," I said. "Now then, let's look at this Tia case first."

Jie said, "She arrived in LA on a commercial transport from New Amsterdam, Brussels, Tau Ceti, two days ago. She's thirty years old, brown hair and eyes, five-eight, and fit. She works out each day. For the past nine years, Tia has held the linguist post on the exploration ship New Light based out of Brussels. Never married. I contacted her ship's major. According to him, the fourth and fifth invader languages always fascinated her, which is why she demanded shore leave to attend this conference. She wanted to meet with Isabella Parkinson to discuss Isabella's findings. So, on the surface, I can find nothing to explain why she's vanished."

"Where was she last seen?" I asked.

"In LA. She had booked passage on a Airliner to Chicago, the next day, but she failed to show up for the flight," Jie said.

"We'll need to locate her in the local surveillance videos and follow her movements," I said.

"I've got a request in with GD LA for access, but haven't heard back yet," Jie said.

"That's ridiculous. My PI license gets me in nearly everywhere. Ashley, get me a computer on the floor so I can use it. Rats. I've just got to find time to get a trim. I'm sitting on my hair again." It reached my ankles.

"While she's getting me setup, why don't you bring me up to speed on the other case, Ward."

"I sound ridiculous, boss," Ward said. His face turned ruddy.

"Who cares about that. It is what it is. We're

investigators." I attempted to make light of his plight.

"Okay. She's scheduled to land in Peking. Something about sightseeing before hopping an Airliner to Chicago," Ward said. "Commercial flight is due to land there at 9:30 local time."

"All right. We'll tap into their live security feeds tomorrow. Meantime, do we have any investigators in Peking or anyone we can send there?"

"Sorry, boss. Right now, all the men have quit. You have us two and some women who handle secretarial duties. The pandemic," Ward said.

He didn't have to spell it out. I didn't pressure him. "How many men quit?"

"Several dozen."

"Shit."

Jie said, "Men. Wish we'd hired more female investigators, but your predecessor wouldn't do that."

I sat down, kicked off my heels, retrieved my phone, and called Helen. "Hi. Molly here. Say, do you have any contacts in Peking's GD? I need to have a security squad meet a commercial flight tomorrow and escort Admiral Skaggs' niece to Chicago."

"Let me check. Yes, I've a contact there. Give me the information. I'll set it up and have them call you when they make contact," Helen said. We chatted a bit before hanging up.

"Your computer is on the floor. Sorry, I should have figured that's where you needed it," Ashley said, as it booted up.

Jie and Ward stood behind me watching my feet do their thing. Soon, Ashley also peeked.

I entered my PI number. It opened many doors. "There, we're in."

Jie rattled off the date and local time. I entered the data and soon had a video stream loaded. Somewhere in the bowels of LA's GD computer system, terabytes of surveillance video began to play back for me.

"I can take it from here, boss," Jie said.

I slipped my heels back on and let her take control of the computer. I could tell that I was going too slow for her temperament. As I watched her, I had to agree. Damn. Main thing, I told myself, is to see how Jie and Ward do on their own. Could I trust them? Were they any good?

The Senior Investigator's office phone rang. I didn't know I had one. Ward answered it for me.

"Senior Investigator's office. Ward Tilman speaking." He put it on speaker phone.

"This is Des Moines, Iowa, GD CEO Thomas Lackley calling. We've a serious situation on Commercial Farm 10956, north of the city. I have the site secured, but I'm requesting a visit from the Senior Investigator at once. Food production has ceased. Get here fast or a food shortage could result."

"Molly here. What's the nature of the problem? I'm in Chicago."

"I know that. If any of us knew what the actual problem was, we could solve it ourselves. Get here quickly."

I had Ward jot down the details. "Okay, Ward. You and I will commandeer a space shuttle from New O'Hare right now."

"Boss, I can't fly one."

"I have my pilot's license. Come on. Sherry, you're with us, too. Ashley, phone Sam and tell him I could be home late. Will Monday never end?"

At the spaceport, Sherry flashed my ID card and got us the exclusive use of a space shuttle, fueled and ready to go. I had the ground crew enter the coordinates for Des Moines and also for Chicago. Then, we walked up the bay ramp.

"Are you sure you can fly this?" Ward asked.

He looked at the myriad controls and then me.

"Don't think an armless person can fly it?" I asked, knowing that was precisely his thought.

"Er, yeah. I can't imagine how you could."

"Don't worry," Sherry said. "I can fly it as well. You're in good feet."

He gave her a strange look before getting the joke. He broke into a smile. "Good one, Sherry."

"Everyone, strap in. Sherry, strap me in to save time."

This ship was capable of flying to any destination as far out as Saturn and its moons. Since the CEO said to rush, this was the fastest way. We lifted off, ascending in a fairly steep arc before descending. The Chicago control tower handled our liftoff, while the spaceport tower in Des Moines handled the landing. Total time: thirty minutes, give or take.

Thomas Lackley, accompanied by a dozen security guards, met us as we carefully walked down the ramp, treacherous in our heels. Again, I saw thirteen very shapely young Galactic Dolls, but presumed most were actually men. They'd cut their hair short, but their apparel was a hodgepodge of mis-matched women's garments, including the heels. Only CEO Lackley wore one of Leslie's fancy men's suits. True, it couldn't hide his massive bosom, but his tall heels were black with rounded toes, more masculine looking. All carried guns and extra ammo clips. This must be very serious.

"Senior Investigator, this way," he said. "I've an EMAC waiting. "Pardon my men. Problems getting male apparel."

"I know. It's a problem worldwide. You can't provide male doll clothing to about a billion men and boys overnight. From what I've heard, the shortage should ease up in a month," I said.

"Okay, here's where we found the body. Clement Farley. This is Commercial Farm 10956. If you're like most people, you've no idea how our synth food is made and processed."

I chuckled. "Duh, I just order from my online store. Stuff is delivered in thirty minutes. More to it than that?"

Thomas saw my tease. We both broke into a hearty laugh.

"Right. Everything is fully automated. These machines you see here, plow, plant, cultivate, harvest, and ship the products to the refineries. Corn in this case."

"Don't men have to maintain these enormous machines?" I asked.

"Not really. Each machine has an automated service box. The machine drives into the service box, where robot arms handle the oil change, grease, tune up, and such. The farmer only has to use a computer to schedule events, such as when to plant. Admittedly, with the weather control satellites, the guesswork has been taken out of that, too. Ah, here's the scene. This entire five thousand acre farm has ceased operations. Since the farms are linked via computer, all Iowa automated farms have shut down. That's Clement Farley or rather what's left of him."

We stood in the middle of a corn field covered with a light snow, though a six-foot wide path of trampled, frozen ground led to the body. All found walking through the uneven field to the deceased quite challenging, though Sherry kept a steadying arm around me.

COD was obvious; someone put a bullet through his head.

"What bothers me," said the CEO, "are the mutilations. He's missing a finger and someone's removed his right eye. Clement is just a farm hand. Yet, all the other farms have shut down until we get to the bottom of this murder."

"It's obvious Clement was more than just a farmer. Someone took his finger and eyeball for biometric purposes. Ward, check Clement's status."

"Boss, says he's a farmer's field operative," Ward replied, reviewing the images on his touchpad.

"Take his fingerprints. We're missing something. This is probably just a cover identity," I said.

Minutes later, Ward said, "Good call, boss. He's really Clement Farley, but his real identity is Chief Computer Control Officer for Iowa Automated Farms, or the CCCO."

"CEO Lackley, where is this computer system? We need to get there as quickly as possible."

"My EMAC," he replied, his face twisted and with a deep frown. "We missed that detail. I'll have words with my staff over this lapse."

Fifteen minutes later, we landed beside a concrete, single story building with dozens of antennae on its roof. No windows. There was a door, but access required a biometric match. As our group approached across the frozen, snow-covered ground, footprints of a single person led up to the door. On the ground lay the severed finger and the grotesque eyeball. I spotted a trace of blood on the finger pad.

"I suppose you don't have an override code," I said.

CEO Lackley said, "No. But obviously someone's inside. No exiting footprints. Guards, draw your weapons. One of you, use Clement's finger and eye to get this door opened. Be ready for anything. You three—fall back in case someone charges out and gets past us."

Sherry, Ward, and I moved way back, preferring to let these GD men handle whomever was inside. Boom! The muffled sound of an explosion from inside the blockhouse startled us.

One of his men activated the door. Guards rushed in. I heard the sound of gunshots and the acrid smell of fried electronics and bomb smoke. The coughing security guards dragged out a wounded giant. He was bleeding from two leg wounds, but in no danger of dying on us.

"Sir, he's blown up part of the control computer system. Several other bombs haven't yet gone off. Calling in the bomb squad now," one guard reported.

CEO Lackley stood before the giant. "Why are you doing this? Why destroy these agricultural computers? You have to eat, too."

The bald headed giant clamped his jaws tightly together, probably not from the pain of his wounds. The CEO pressured him further, only to have the giant spit on him.

I focused and entered the giant's mind, while guards searched his pockets.

One said, "He's a citizen of Liatos-D, not one of the immigrants."

I spotted an image in his mind. A meeting of a dozen giants, several wearing military-like uniforms. One handed him a packet showing this computer station.

I said, "So why is your group of giants on Liatos-D trying to blow up our agricultural computers?"

He jerked violently. "Filthy telepath!"

He lunged forward, breaking the guards hold on him. Even though bleeding from wounds in both legs, he bolted out across the frozen landscape. Even strong human men were no match for the strength of an eight-foot tall giant with rippling muscles. Mutate the men into female-looking bodies and force them to wear tall heels—the guards here had no chance whatsoever of stopping him. Gunshots rang out, dozens of them. I suspected he intended to commit suicide so that I couldn't discover more from his mind. CEO Lackley later told me he held the same opinion.

"Well done, men, Senior Investigator. I'll forward what we've learned about this giant plot on up the lines. I'll get a repair crew out here as fast as possible, but the farms won't likely be up for some days. Machines control the production of eggs, cattle, and hogs. All on automatic. Senior Investigator, thank you for dropping everything and coming as fast as you did. I called you because I learned you were a telepath. I had a suspicion something was going on. Out here in corn country, we never have such things happening—not like you folks in Chicago. Again, thank you."

I nodded. "We should be alert to other giant sabotage attacks on our infrastructure. Please let CD CEO Helen Hugo know all the details. She'll alert all the other local GD offices. You were wise to call me."

He smiled, and we three headed back to the EMAC.

The five o'clock hour approached as we left the space shuttle at New O'Hare and made our way back to the Monroe building. My legs were ice cycles, and I was exhausted. What a long day, but it wasn't over yet.

As we walked in, Jie said, "Ward texted me about what happened. So we have some giants planning to disrupt our food production lines. What next?"

"Don't yet know that or why," I said. "How's the video watching?"

"My eyes are blurry, but I've made some progress. I can definitely say Tia was kidnapped. Here, watch this short segment."

Someone snatched her while she traveled on the MTES. Probably chloroform on a rag knocked her out, while the two men dragged her into an alley out of sight of all video cameras. Professionals, I concluded.

Jie said, "Tomorrow, I'll see if I can pick up their trail."

"Good work, Jie," I said.

"Knock, knock," a familiar voice said, while tapping lightly on the door frame. I looked up to see Casper Hugo, Jr, Helen's husband. Admittedly, his regrowing tiny arms appeared incongruous with the rest of him. As expected, he wore an expensive suit with holes cut so his arms had room. He wore his black shoes, flats, the very ones I'd seen in his clothes closet the night he kidnapped me many years back. The pandemic virus had also restored his feet. Lucky fellow.

"Hi, Casper. What brings you to the Senior Investigator's office at quitting time?" I asked.

He chuckled. "Molly, you never quit. I'm bringing you a very special case, one that's critical to the very survival of the entire Sol Empire."

"Okay. You have my interest. Ward, Jie, this is Casper Hugo, the CFO for GD here in Chicago. Take notes, you two. If he says we have big trouble, we do. All right, let's have it."

"As you know, my skill is finding the billions of credits needed to finance new Sol Empire spaceships. What you probably don't know is that there are perhaps a hundred super-wealthy families that are off the grid, so to speak. They have no corporate sponsorship or affiliations, but these families own much of the stock in the corporations; they're the shareholders. These special people finance our new spaceships—have been for two centuries.

"Now that I have your attention, four of these men in Peking are in deep trouble. Suddenly, they have no idea who they are. They don't know me or their families. Some claim to be prostitutes, if you can believe that. Mei Yang begged me to come check on her husband Chen, who she claims went insane last week. The others within the last two weeks, and it's not from the pandemic. That's long over."

As tired as I was, Casper roused my curiosity. People do go insane, but... Four of the wealthiest men on the planet and all within the last two weeks.

"What exactly do you mean they don't know you?" I asked. Jei and Ward glanced at me, a strange look on their faces.

"Chen Yang and I have been friends for twenty years. I called him yesterday. He had no idea who I was and kept mumbling about where were his satin gowns. Chen managed to get a hold of some of Leslie's male doll apparel around the first of January. Plus, he claims to work for Wang's Escort service. None of this makes any sense unless..."

He let his voice fall off, allowing us to draw our own conclusions.

"Body swap?" I asked.

He nodded. "Would you please come with me to Peking and check on Chen? You ought to be able to figure out what's wrong with him in short order. I've an Airliner standing by."

"Okay. Let me call Sam and tell him I won't be home tonight." I sat down, retrieved my phone, and made the call.

Casper said, "Helen is taking the security for this Linguist Conference seriously. She also told me Admiral Skaggs' niece is a linguist and is arriving tomorrow in Peking."

"Yes, and our hides will be fried if anything happens to her," I said. "Okay, Jie, Ward, you can come with us or stay here."

Jie said, "I'll stay here, boss. I've got to track down the missing Tia Sanchez."

"Coming," Ward said, "but let me grab an overnight bag. Meet you at New O'Hare."

"I'll need to pack, too," Ashley said.

"Okay, meet you there. Casper, let's get our things," I said. "Tell me more about these friends of yours."

Monday finally ended as I fell asleep on the Airliner somewhere over the western part of North America. What a day this had been.

Chapter 3 Shanghaied

Ward headed off to meet the local GD security guards and then greet Bonita Valdez whose flight from Azizi-C was due to land mid-morning. Ashley, Casper, and I commandeered a GD EMAC and a local guide. We headed first to meet with Chen and Mei Yang.

"Wow!" I said, as the EMAC landed beside a huge mansion with its own formal gardens. Oriental evergreens lined one side, shaped like animals in a zoo. I counted twenty of them. Green elephants, rhinos, and camels caught my eye.

"Casper, so good of you to come," the petite Mei said, bowing to us. She wore a typical red satin gown with yellow-brown flowers.

" The pleasure is mine, Mei," Casper said. "Allow me to introduce Mrs. Molly Parkinson and her assistant Miss Ashley Peterson."

"So good of you to come, as well. Aren't you the new Senior Investigator?" she asked.

"Yes, I came to see if I could do anything for Chen," I said, bowing to her.

Mei said, "Chen isn't himself. He's out by the heated pool under the dome. This way."

We walked through the elegant mansion. Their back door opened into another garden and pool, all covered by a gigantic clear dome.

Chen looked like all other male dolls, but he wore one of Leslie's masculine designs, though nothing could hide the massive bosom. He stared off into the blue waters of the pool.

"Let's leave them alone, Mei," said Casper. "How about some tea?" He led her off, leaving me with Chen, who still hadn't noticed me.

I sat down on a nearby garden chair and looked at him. After a time, he glanced at me, noticed my missing arms, and brightened up.

"A telepath? Perhaps you'll believe me. I'm not this Chen person."

"I figured that. How about telling me everything you can recall."

"I'm Mee Sun or I was. An escort woman for visitors at the spaceport. I remember a well-dressed male Doll taking me out. Said he doctor. I called him Dr. Wang. The EMAC sign said so, too. Once seated, he put rag over face. I tried to stop him, but all went black. Then see pretty white light. I wake up. I man now. He said I be Chen Yang. Made me sign paper giving him fifty million credits. I no have. He say I have. I sign. He drop me off here. I crazy person now."

As she talked, I unobtrusively watched the images in her mind. When I saw the white light, I knew what had happened. She was a victim of a body swap machine. Just then, Ward joined me, his face a ghastly white. His hand shook slightly.

"Boss. It's Bonita Valdez. She's vanished!"

I felt sick. "What do you mean vanished?"

"She was on the flight. An attendant helped her stow her bags. When the ship landed a half hour ago, she wasn't on it! The attendant and I watched everyone get off, then searched the whole spaceship. She wasn't on it when it landed."

"Did the ship make other stops on the way here?"

"No, I thought of that, too. Perhaps she got off at another stop. This was a direct flight from Azizi-C to Peking. Boss, what do we do now? Admiral Skaggs will shoot us."

"There has to be a simple explanation, Ward. Go round up all the surveillance video in and around the ship when it landed. I'll join you at the GD headquarters shortly."

Ward nodded and left, while I turned back to Chen or Mee Sun. While I wanted to give her a long round of therapy sessions to help her adjust to what had been done to her, the missing Azizi-C woman demanded my full attention. This could lead to the destruction of Earth.

"Chen or Mee, you aren't insane or crazy. You've been the victim of a body swap machine. Remember what the Sixth Invaders did to Sol's rulers years ago. Swapping themselves into the leaders' bodies?"

"Oh yes."

"That's what this Wang person did to you. I guess they really wanted your Mee Sun body, though the why makes no sense. I will investigate and try to find out what happened to your Mee Sun body and get you swapped back, if I can. Meanwhile, relax and enjoy this incredible mansion."

"You do this for me, me be so grateful."

I bowed and headed back to Casper and Mei. Hastily, I explained to Mei that her husband had been the victim of the body swap machine and that I would do all I could to find out who did it and get Chen back into Chen's body.

With that, Casper and I left, heading for Peking's GD offices in the heart of the city. As he flew us there, I explained what I'd learned.

"Casper, while I try to find our missing Azizi-C young linguist, see if you can find anything about this Wang doctor. His name was on that EMAC he used to abduct the escort woman."

Casper chuckled. "PI work isn't my forte, but I'll see what I can find. Since Chen gave him fifty million, there has to be bank records of that transfer. Follow the money—that I can do."

Now I chuckled. "I'll remember that, Casper."

I found the local GD office in utter chaos. The disappearance of Admiral Skaggs' niece created a near panic. Ward sat in the center of a room filled with monitors displaying the many surveillance videos. At least twenty cameras provided complete coverage of the event, from the landing of the silver commercial transport spaceship to the disembarking passengers and the unloading of the cargo.

Ward spotted me. "Boss, nothing. Nothing at all! Miss Valdez just vanished."

Several other GD personnel—I couldn't tell their gender—nervously nodded their agreement.

"Ward, we both know that's not possible. Not unless someone tossed her body out an air lock."

"Thought of that, boss. There are no air locks. It's a commercial liner."

"Okay, show me the people disembarking." I pushed a chair aside, tossed my hair to one side, and sat down beside him.

He rewound the stream. I watched the bay doors open. One by one, the dozen passengers walked down the ramp. Most appeared to be businessmen wearing suits, though a few also carried briefcases locked to their wrists. The few departing women were all older, at least in their forties. No young linguist.

"See, she's not on the ship. There's the GD men rushing up the ramp to search the ship," Ward said.

"Cargo. Okay, show me the cargo being unloaded."

Presently, I watched as the passengers' baggage rolled out of the rear ramp.

"Freeze it. What's that there? That big crate."

"Supplies, I think the manifest said," Ward replied.

"Zoom in on the shipping label," I said.

He did so. I exclaimed, "Shit! Wang Brothers Foundation. Damn, that's the name of the doctor who body swapped Chen Yang!"

"Molly, I have the information on Dr. Wang," Casper called out, as he entered the room. A dozen GD personnel looked at him.

"What did you find?" I asked.

"There are two of them: a psychiatrist and an electronics engineer—Shen Wang and Yuan Wang. They have a mental research facility here in Peking. They have forced all four of my billionaire donors to give them fifty million credits. All within the last three weeks."

"Damn. Damn. Damn," I said.

He and Ward looked at me, along with the dozen GD personnel.

"They've abducted Bonita Valdez and took her off the ship in that shipping crate."

One of the GD personnel said, "We'll get a security force together and raid that foundation of theirs."

"Hold a second. Casper, can you identify all the other wealthy men you know here in Peking? They could be at risk—"

He interrupted me. "Of being body swapped like Chen. On it. Yeah, there are two others."

"Okay. Get GD security men over to their homes immediately. Let me know if the men have been abducted all ready. Then, let's get over to this Wang Foundation place as fast as possible. I have an awful feeling about this whole thing. I hope we're not too late."

The Peking GD personnel responded. Bodies exhaled and seemed to relax, as far as I could tell, probably relieved. However, to say we rushed would have been an exaggeration. In tall heels, none could race, run, or hurry for that matter. Actually, in hindsight, it looked rather humorous.

As three heavily armed GD EMACs landed close to the two story Wang Foundation building, the reports came in. The other two wealthy men were missing. Their wives were already filing missing person's cases with the local police.

The doors to the building were locked. I nodded, and one of the GD personnel fired his blaster at the door, disintegrating it, leaving smouldering remnants which we stepped over. Once inside, the thirty guards fanned out, searching the unfamiliar building.

Casper, Ward, and I stood near the front doors waiting word. A few minutes later, a guard came to fetch us. "Found them. Basement. Strange. Need you, Senior Investigator."

When we stepped into the basement laboratory, my stomach knotted. Lying on two cots were two women, one of whom was Bonita Valdez. The other was a young Chinese woman. Both were in comas, as far as I could tell.

Casper's two wealthy men lay on cots on either side of the women. Head harnesses filled with wired rested on all four heads. The wired were attached to two crudely made body swap machines that looked much like those used by the Sixth Invaders.

The Wang brothers stood by the machines with their hands in the air, chattering in Chinese with the GD guards. A third man, very robust and with a bushy beard, stood at the back. A language translator box on his waist tried to convert the Chinese chatter into the man's native language. That he came from another planet was obvious by his dress, something akin to what I once saw in our ancient history books from four centuries ago.

As Senior Investigator I took charge. "Okay, Wang brothers, what's going on? I know you've been body swapping. Four of Peking's wealthiest men."

"They refused to finance our research," Shen said. "So we made them do it."

"Why body swapping?" I asked. "And who is this foreign man? Are the women in comas?"

"Don't say a word," Yuan said in Chinese.

However, Casper had his translation box turned on, and we both understood what he'd said, as did the GD personnel.

I smiled. "Come on. Answer my questions."

Both men clamped their jaws and stared at the ceiling.

I focused on Yuan's mind. I saw a stream of images of things that he desperately tried to prevent me from seeing. I pieced together his nefarious dealings.

"So, you've made deals with this man from some world called Blackwell," I said. "Ah, he wants armless telepath Galactic Dolls. No, he also wants their tongues cut out. Gross! Oh, so you kidnapped escort Galactic Dolls. Wait, then you injected them with the armless telepath mutation agent. Have you already—shit! You've already injected these two women with it. Ah, you kidnapped the very men who refused to support your foundation. I get it. You body swap them into these mutating women. Then, it's easy to force the confused women who are now in these wealthy men's bodies to sign over millions of credits. Clever plan."

As I put the pieces together, both Yuan and Shen's faces paled. Even the GD personnel nodded and smiled, probably knowing I must have the story nearly correct. I turned to the alien man.

"What's your role in this?"

His translation unit made strange noises. He smiled and spoke. From the box on his waist, I heard English words.

"I buy these women. Will be baronesses. Queens, in your words. Treated with high respect, but must not speak. Pay one kilogram of gemstones per each new baroness they make for me. Have two more sacks of gems for these two new baronesses. They be very beautiful queens. Will let me have the new baronesses?"

"Take him away for now," I said, knowing that I had to deal with this mess. "I'm the Senior Judge." The GD personnel smiled. I sensed they were very pleased to hand this over to me, but they kept their weapons trained on the two brothers.

I spotted dozens of syringes whose labels stated they contained the armless doll mutation agent and several bottles of chloroform. I focused on Bonita Valdez's mind, but saw only the blackness of her coma. Damn. These men had sold four other women into a hideous slavery. No one has baronesses that I know of. I decided on what to do.

"Chloroform them," I ordered the GD personnel, who readily complied, over the protests of the two brothers. Once silent, I commanded the GD people to inject the two brothers with three dozes of the mutation agent. Why three? Because the men had already been victims of the recent pandemic, becoming male dolls. Thus, stronger doses were needed.

"Unhook these four. Take these two wealthy men away and wake them up. They should be okay. We'll take Bonita Valdez with us. You can handle the Chinese woman, who'll become a telepath after she wakes."

One asked, "What about the brothers?"

"I haven't decided yet. How goes the search of this foundation? Casper, check on their bank accounts."

A guard said, "Senior Investigator, come. We found more women."

Two led me to a side room filled with medical equipment. Two armless dolls lay inside two sealed units.

"Bring a doctor, please."

One chuckled. "All ready did that."

After the doctor arrived, he studied the two women. "They are being kept in stasis. They seem healthy enough. They should be telepaths."

"Can we identify them?"

"If they are in the Earth DNA database. I'll check."

I watched him inserting a toe into a machine. The ID flashed on its screen. I read over his shoulder. She had been an escort woman, reported missing three weeks ago. Minutes later, the other was one, too. I smiled. Now I knew how to punish these two despicable men.

"Bring them out of their stasis pods and hook them up where the two women were on the cots. Put the helmets on the brothers, too.

The personnel roared and carried out my orders. I had watched Holly Ann run her body swap machines several times. These appeared nearly identical to hers. With the Wang brothers hooked up to the two unconscious escort women, I operated the controls with my toes, while others watched.

"That's done. Take the two women to that alien. Tell him if he ever returns to this world, he'll be shot on sight. Bring the two brothers' bodies to Casper and me at GD headquarters."

I imagined the Wang brothers waking up finding themselves armless telepath Galactic Doll women on a strange planet. No way could they ever commit similar crimes again.

Next, Casper and I had to handle the two women who were waking, finding themselves in male doll bodies. We explained to the two what had happened. They knew they'd been kidnapped by the Wang brothers, who said they'd be mutated into telepaths, but they'd dropped into comas and never wakened. Both were ecstatic they weren't armless telepaths, so I knew I'd made the right decision. Few people wanted to become a one for the cost was entirely too steep.

Casper had the two donate most of the brothers' fortune to build a new light cruiser, while retaining several million credits to help them adjust to their new lives, though I suspected they'd get a sex change as soon as possible. And when we left, both hugged me.

"Thank you," one said. "You gave us back our lives."

I wished I could do that for Bonita Valdez, whose comatose body now rested in our Airliner, along with the two confiscated body swap machines, several Wang computers, and a host of documents.

During the long flight back to Chicago, Casper poured over the records. "Listen to this. Last December, the brothers received this e-letter from a giant on Liatos-D. Ambassador Hypnos Kalakos. He says to expect a representative from this Blackwell place who wants to trade bags of gemstones for armless telepathic Galactic Dolls. Now why would an ambassador on Liatos-D want to have the Wang brothers send our telepaths to this Blackwell place? Wouldn't they want the telepaths for themselves? Weird."

"Let's see that e-letter." I looked it over carefully. "It's not a crime to connect this representative with the Wang brothers. But why would a giant ambassador do that? It's certainly unethical."

"Don't know. I agree," Casper said. "It's not a criminal offense to connect two people. But why? What does Liatos-D or this ambassador get out of joining these two parties?"

I shrugged my shoulders.

Ward said, "More importantly, how are we going to break the news about his niece to Admiral Skaggs?"

I sighed. "Not until we get her back to a Chicago med center and get her health and mutation verified. Then..."

"Right. Then..." Ward said.

"Well, she was a linguist," said Casper. "Perhaps she might want to be a telepath like Isabella and Nikita are. Always hope. Can't we?"

Just then, Jie called. "Boss, I found Tia Sanchez, the Brussels linguist. Someone dropped her off at an LA med center. She's in a mutation coma. Armless telepath. I've had her transferred to our Med Center. A giant found her body lying in an alleyway. Surveillance show's he's telling the truth. He just happened upon her. Tomorrow I'll see if I can find out who dropped her off. Got good camera positions."

"Well done, Jei. I'll notify Brussels and her relatives tomorrow."

She chuckled. "Better you than me, boss. Ward texted me about everything. How bad off are we going to be? I mean with Admiral Skaggs? She's his niece."

"Lord, I don't know, Jie. I'm exhausted. Catch you tomorrow. Good work. All three of you." I meant Jie, Ward, and Casper; the latter smiled.

My assistant Ashley was already dozing. It had been a hellish two days. I'd helped Angelina Flores become a telepath again, altering the insane Senate laws. Someone had leaked the identity of Patricia Ann Gates-Baxter, the pandemic creator, and someone else had shot her, but med center doctors injected her with the armless telepath mutation agent hoping the rejuvenation process would heal her life-threatening wound. Giants kidnapped two foreigners coming to the linguistics conference, mutating them into telepaths. And an ambassador of the giants arranged for these Wang brothers to mutate women into telepaths and sell them to some other world. What else could possibly go wrong? I laid back and fell asleep, worrying about the awful phone calls I'd have to make in the morning telling relatives the terrible news.

Chapter 4 Not Again!

My phone woke me. I read the text from my sister, Eve.

```
Someone   tried   to   shoot   Vernon
Baxter.  Failed.  I'm  taking  Vernon,
their son, and the comatose Patricia
Ann  to  a  safe  place.  Lara  and  I  are
working  on  a  cure  and  can  use  her
expertise.
```

With a toe, I entered a "K" and slipped my phone back in my pocket. So much had happened. Once she came out of her coma, Eve could run Patricia Ann through her mutation trauma. I hoped Eve brought along a laptop with the how-to videos.

I needed to do this, too, for Tia and Bonita, making a mental note to request the three life-saving machines and laptops from Galactic Robotics.

That reminded me that Sherry had new clues into the death of my first husband, Ted. I rustled in my seat and got the robot's attention.

Sherry looked up, surveyed the slumbering personnel, and stole to my side.

"I'm certain Ted's killer was one of the five un-programmed human-form robots. It's my theory he was terminated because he was closing in on them." She went on to describe her new clues.

"That makes sense. Ted was determined to find those missing robots. Are they still around? Can we terminate those robots?"

These past years, Sherry had learned to emulate human responses very well. She smiled, then frowned. "Yes, that was Ted's passion. We've been searching for those five for years, but have found no recent traces of them. I believe a blaster shot to their heads would terminate them, but a shot anywhere else would only lame them."

"What are their goals? What do they want?"

Sherry shook her head. "My programming cannot

speculate on that. The three robot laws nullify such speculations."

After a long pause filled with the soft hum of the electromagnetic engines on the Airliner, she continued. "Admittedly, it's most difficult for us to identify another robot. A telepath can identify one in seconds. Until last Christmas, with so many telepaths on Earth, it wasn't safe for them to wander about. Now with so few telepaths perhaps they will come out of hiding. My associates are watching for that."

"Could those robots have played a role in what Dr. Gates-Baxter did with her virus?" I said.

Sherry shrugged her shoulders. "I doubt it. All ten of us had the same basic database installed in our positron brains. We are programmed to learn new things. I know nothing much about viruses and genetics. But I could learn and perhaps one day be a competent geneticist, though that would take several years of study. It is possible one of the five did that and somehow assisted Dr. Gates-Baxter. The elimination of most Earth telepaths certainly helps to prevent our discovery."

"Just because it benefits robots doesn't mean they had a hand in it," I said.

Sherry flashed me a very human-like smile.

I yawned. "Funny, we've only just developed a workable science of the human mind that erases a person's trauma, but our misuse of technology could well get Earth destroyed."

"That's what makes our study of humans so interesting: mental and spiritual advancement versus technological inventions. You haven't had another future vision, have you?" Her serious tone struck a chord in me.

I shook my head, sighed, and tried to go back to sleep. Something didn't feel right. I couldn't put my finger on it, but then I didn't have any fingers.

My phone rang. Sherry retrieved it for me so it didn't wake the others. Helen Hugo's 3-d holo image appeared about a foot tall.

"Sorry to wake you, but I thought you should hear this from me. Our Federation Senior Ambassador Aaron Strawn has been assassinated. Piper is distraught and is bringing his body back here. She said she's resigning her ambassadorial post."

"Did they catch who did it?"

"Not yet. According to her, the authorities believe it was a professional hit. It'll be on the news when you get home. Casper's kept me up to date on your trip. Don't envy the calls you'll have to make tomorrow. If you need something, let me know."

"Could use two more sets of the machines for the women we're bringing back."

"On it. I'll have Galactic Robotics drop them off at your place in the morning. Bye."

That might have been me—they wanted me to become one of the Sol Empire's Senior Ambassador to the Federation of Planets stationed on Bela Prime. But I encouraged the historian and telepath, Aaron, and his wife, a nurse, to take those positions. I felt sick. Then, it struck me. Perhaps he'd been killed just because he was a telepath. I made a note to talk to Piper about it.

As I reflected on Aaron and Piper, something continued to not feel right. Whatever bothered me wasn't his death, but I sensed death. I called Sam. It went to voice mail. Visiting Peking, my sense of time muddled.

"Sherry, what time is it back home in Chicago?"

The robot said, "About three in the afternoon. We'll be arriving around five."

Sam ought to be walking Matt and Nikita home from school. Still, he should've answered his phone. My stomach tightened. I called Sam again and then Matt. Both went to voice mail. "Call Helen Hugo," I ordered my phone.

"Hi again. Say, I can't get a hold of Sam—"

Helen's 3-d hologram face looked taut. "I just heard. Oh, Molly, I'm so sorry."

"Something's happened to him?"

"Yes, a terrorist bomb blew up an EMAC as Sam and Matt walked past on their way home from school. Pretty sure the terrorist timed it or perhaps waited until they walked past it."

"You're saying Sam was targeted? Why? What about

Nikita?" Tear flowed down my cheeks.

"Yes, targeted. Still early in the investigation, but it seems that way. Why? We have no motive yet. Nikita is safe. She stayed after school with Veronica to try out for the cheerleading squad. I sent a security squad to pick up the girls. No one's going to get near Nikita. I also sent a squad to guard Bernard and Isabella, just in case. Both Sam and Matt are in the Med Center in stasis pods. They were pronounced dead at the site of the blast. The doctors are trying to revive them."

"Thanks."

I just couldn't talk anymore. Grief flooded over me. I cried. Sherry cradled me in her arms as though I were her child. I needed that comfort right now. She didn't speak. What can anyone say at a time like this? "I'm so sorry" doesn't do a damn thing.

Later as we approached New O'Hare, Sherry told the others the double news. By then, I could accept their words of sympathy. I'd lost Ted and now Sam, the two loving men in my life. I felt so alone.

Celeste met us at the spaceport. Helen had sent along a security squad with her, and they transported our two comatose women, our bags, and us to my home next to the Hugo mansion.

Isabella directed the men to put the two women into one of the guest bedrooms, while Nikita and I hugged and cried. Celeste also had a nourishing breakfast waiting. Nikita pushed me to the kitchen table.

"Mom," Nikita said, "you're supposed to eat. Aunt Celeste is going to give you a therapy session as soon as you're full. She's already done me. Turns out, I knew Dad a couple lifetimes back. Pretty neat. Oh, and I made the cheerleading squad, along with Veronica."

"Good for you. I miss your dad all ready."

"Me too, Mom. The universe has gone crazy. First, someone released Patricia Ann's identity and revenge seekers got to her, her husband, and baby. Kidnappers got to Tia who wanted to meet Isabella at the conference, as did Bonita. Isabella told me so. Then, someone killed our Senior Ambassador on Bela Prime. And now Dad and Matt are murdered. What's going on? Is someone is gunning for us? Are we going to be safe? Do I get to keep on going to school? I want to be a cheerleader with Veronica. Helen told Veronica, Fritz, and me that a whole GD security squad will accompany us to and from school. We should be safe, don't you think?"

Whew. I finally could answer. "You keep going to school and practicing your cheers. I'm sure the guards will keep you and the Hugos safe."

Celeste shooed her out. "Okay, Molly. Let's handle the emotional loss." She returned me to the moment I found out that Sam and Matt had been killed. Buckets of tears followed. Hours later, I felt relieved. This wasn't my fault. There hadn't been anything I could have done or should have done to prevent their deaths. Yes, I still missed them. Little things reminded me of Sam and Matt, but I could carry on. Life flourished in me.

The next morning, while a Med Center doctor examined both Tia and Bonita, Deanna took me to the Med Center to identify the bodies and arrange for their cremations. On the way, we passed by the destroyed section of the MTES where the bomb had detonated. Already a giant crew worked on making repairs, led by a Galactic Doll, presumably one of our engineers directing the workers.

Dr. Ruiz, the CEO of GMed, met me. "I'm so sorry for your loss. Sam and Matt were officially declared dead at the blast site by the emergency responders. However..."

She led me into a basement room. There, I saw Sam's body attached to the same machine my body had been attached when the Sixth Invader shot me in my head. Beside him, Matt's small body was in a similar machine.

Dr. Ruiz said, "Based on what once happened to you, Mrs. Parkinson, we've taken the liberty to try that same solution on them. We got them into these machines within a few minutes of the blast, thanks to a dwarf in the emergency rescue crew. I had them injected with a substantial dose of the telepath mutation agent on the off chance it'll have the same effect on him as it did on you when you were shot and should have been dead. The blast did blow off their regrowing arms, but thus far, the silver nano graphine mesh is holding."

"They're alive?" I watched the machine making Sam breathe, but saw no outward signs of life.

"Don't get your hopes up, Mrs. Parkinson. We're in an uncharted medical world right now. The machine is pumping their blood, breathing for them, and injecting both with vital nutrients—everything needed to live. Whether the mutation agent will rejuvenate them and repair the damage—well, it's too soon to tell. After all, your body took about a month to heal. We'll let you know the very instant we can say with certainty—one way or the other. No matter what, Sam and Matt are providing GMed with vital case studies that may help other critical cases in the future."

"Thank you. Yes, let me know at once."

"I'll leave you two to watch them as long as you desire. I've got other critical matters to handle. Have you seen the news this morning? A leadership coup is underway."

Deanna said, "I know. I'll tell her about it once we're done here."

I reached out to Sam, spiritually that is. His presence, he the person, clung like glue to his body. I sensed he was unconscious. Accepting that he was still around and hadn't gone off in search of a new baby body, I relaxed. I knew I could find him anytime I wanted, though it was probably best he remain unconscious, especially if this didn't work. Same with Matt.

I sighed. "He's unconscious. I can't do any more for him here. Let's go. Thanks for being here for me."

"Always, sister. All right. About the coup. I'll tell you about it as we head to my office. I've recorded some things that haven't yet been shown on the empire's comm channels. Russell is a clever man. Now that Casper Hugo is back, I'm pretty sure Russell has him in our office, as well."
***
I sat at the head of the board-room style, mahogany table. We sat in soft leather chairs with rollers. Deanna had expensive tastes in decor for her meeting room. GEnt CEO Russell Godwyn, Deanna's husband, ran the meeting. He'd been promoted and now oversaw the Sol Empire-wide Galactic Entertainment. Both Helen and Casper Hugo sat to my right,

while Dimitri and Natalie Leonovich, our Emperor and Empress, sat on my right. I faced Russell and Deanna. High over our heads, a dozen giant monitors blared the latest news, though as I entered, Russell muted them. Behind me, Ashley and Sherry rushed in. I suspected they'd raced down the fast lane of the MTES to get here on such short notice.

Helen frowned and clenched her jaw. "They can't do this, can they?"

Russell said, "We best bring Molly up to speed. First, let me say how sorry we all are about Sam and Matt." I nodded. "Okay, here's the situation as of ten minutes ago." He dabbed at the perspiration on his forehead.

"The billionaire Phillip Soros has just declared himself the ruler of the Sol Empire and Earth in particular."

I frowned. "Who the hell is he?"

"I'll let Casper explain that." He motioned to the CFO.

Casper said, "Most everyone believes major corporations control everything—providing monthly stipends and such. And they do. However, who owns the corporations? Each one has sold stock in their corporation. Around a hundred key families scattered across Earth own all the stock of the major corporations—or nearly so. They and their families are outside corporation controls. None are ever sponsored by any corporation. Each year, the corporations pay these stockholders a percentage of the profits earned. Thus, these fat cats' bank accounts continually grow to obscene levels.

"It's these men that I hit up to finance new spaceships. After all, who can afford to buy a ten billion credit cruiser? Only these men and women. Today, nearly all these men have been mutated, as have all other human males on Earth. To say they are upset is an understatement. Many are furious and quite angry.

"Louis Cho, for example, has just offered a billion credits to the person who can invent a cure to turn male dolls back into normal men. Presumably, he'd be the first one to have it. At least he's also pledged a billion credits to GMed to help researchers find a cure. Russell..."

Russell resumed control of his meeting. "Billionaire

Phillip Soros owns a good percentage of GPan and GD stock. He's hired hundreds of giants and a few dwarves, armed them with the very latest weapons, and has moved to take over these two corporations. Here's his broadcast." He played a recording of that earlier newscast.

I saw a typical Galactic Doll behind a microphone, surrounded by a dozen giants, all wearing suits. His apparel, in sharp contrast, was a mis-matched, ill-fitting collection of male apparel. Galactic Manufacturing simply hadn't caught up to the humongous demand for male doll clothing.

"My fellow Sol Empire men and women, enough is enough. For many decades, we on Earth have had the misfortune to have our corporations badly mis-run, our security compromised on so many occasions that I've lost count. Only a month ago, this happened to all men here on Earth." He motioned to himself and his gigantic bosom.

"Our leaders have consistently failed us. Not once, but many, many times. Even the Federation of Planets has finally had to intervene to prevent the spread of our stupidity to other human worlds, moons, and stations. The ineptitude of our leaders must stop. As of today, I and my fellow billionaires are taking over the corporations that we own. Since I own more stock in GPan and GD than my associates, I am now running both corporations.

"All existing personnel, especially those in charge, such as our CEOs and CFOs are hereby relieved of their duties. Male dolls are hardly capable of fighting or even doing heavy construction work. So I and my associates have hired a number of giants and dwarves to help us enforce our rulings. Hell, as a result of the doll mutation, I can barely walk.

"All leaders including our pathetic Emperor and Empress are relieved of their duties. Vacate your offices or my giants will toss you out. Resistance is both useless and pointless. If you fight my orders, you will be terminated. No need to waste court time. Expect many changes for the better as I lead us forward into a more prosperous empire for all. That is all."

Russell turned the recording off. "There you have it."

"He can't do this!" Dimitri cried, pounding his fist on

the table. At least he wore one of Leslie's male doll suits. I didn't ask him how he managed to get one when this Phillip fellow hadn't.

"The giants tossed me out of my office," Natalie said. "What the hell do we do now?"

Russell said, "I've no idea. But, Molly, no one has made any changes to the Senior Investigator's office or the Senior Judge. Your positions are safe for the moment. What can we do? I've no idea either."

"I put in a call to Admiral Skaggs," Natalie said. "He said he can't intervene; this is a local Sol Empire matter. Thus far, anyway."

I said, "Well, if they haven't messed with my investigations office, I can use it to find out more information. I keep running into giants being somehow involved in crimes here on Earth. Maybe I can uncover some nefarious conspiracy between the giants and these billionaires."

"Hey, that Federation Linguists Conference coming up soon," Helen said. "I can't guarantee their security any longer. But they've said nothing about the army, though the male soldiers are now dolls, too. Still, I bet General Blythe could put together some private security for you. And since we're all out of work at the moment, perhaps we can help in your investigations. I, for one, want to capture the giant who killed Sam and Matt. Just tell us what to do."

I said, "Thanks. I could use the help. There's too many for me to investigate. Besides, I don't think I can stand to watch the video of them being murdered. But I have to notify Admiral Skaggs about his niece. Drop by my old office in the Parker Skyscraper, say around one this afternoon. We'll take it from there."
***

I decided on a face to face meeting with Admiral Skaggs to tell him the awful news. A phone call would be safer, but... An hour later, one of his shuttles picked Ashley and me up, transporting us up to the battleship Kanika in high orbit above Earth.

"Wow, it sure is huge!" Ashley said. "You could put the whole GD skyscraper into it."

The Kanika was just as impressive now as it had been when I was last on it. Back then, I'd been on a mission to save Earth from being conquered by the Sixth Invaders. I hoped today's visit wasn't along the same lines.

Constructed of joined hexagonal tubes, here was a town in space. Ashley fastened the Universal Language Translator devices around our waists, her first exposure to these devices.

A giant of a man in a green uniform stood outside our shuttle's door. The sounds from his voice were undecipherable but the translator box spoke English. "This way. Admiral Skaggs is expecting you."

We walked down a long metal ramp, through a set of giant steel doors, and into a long carpeted hallway. Two other giant guards joined us, falling in behind our group. While we passed many doors, I couldn't see inside them nor read what must have been writing on the wall plaques. We entered a room on our right. Spacious and full of light, the room's gray metal walls gave it a sterile appearance. The presence of a long stainless steel table with matching chairs gave the room a corporation look.

"Welcome again to the Flagship Kanika. I'm Admiral Baba Skaggs. I take it you have some news about my niece?"

He looked much like any human male, wearing a green uniform. Only his had many gold stars on his sleeves and on his shirt pocket flaps. He stood six feet with a robust build. His no-nonsense attitude came across as a stoic, stern disposition. His hair was black and close-cropped. Bushy brows accentuated his dark brown eyes. I sensed no malice in his attitude... Yet, anyway.

"We should sit, sir. I've some bad news about your niece Bonita Valdez. She's in my guest room in a mutation coma— the armless telepath version," I said.

"What?" He yelled and pounded his fist on the table so hard that Ashley and I blinked. When my eyes focused, he'd dented the table!

"She's totally healthy. I've had a doctor examine her thoroughly and verify the mutation. Let me explain."

As I talked, the crimson in his face slowly subsided, but his jaw remained clenched tight. "One of the Wang brothers was on the same flight from your world to Peking." I relayed what we knew and had done, sparing no detail.

"So what punishment did those two men receive? You are the Senior Judge—still..."

"Well," I said with a coy smile. When I told him the pair had been body swapped into two comatose women and were now on their way to this Blackwell world, he finally loosened his jaw—a good sign, I hoped.

"I should tell you something about my niece," he said. "She's thirty-five and a genius with all things electronic. As her thesis, she invented and built a positronic brain from parts. She installed it in a mining machine, and that revolutionized Azizi fuel mining. She went on to study linguistics and stellar navigation, too. Quite why, I'll never know. Bonita wanted to meet your daughter, Isabella. Something about linguistics. My niece is one brilliant young woman and incredibly beautiful. She could have her pick of any man on our world. But..." He hesitated a moment.

"She's never married. Not into men after that accident. What a terrible waste. About ten years ago when she was in college, she was engaged to a handsome man. One night he took her on a joyride in a shuttle and crashed it. She was in a coma for months. When she awoke, we thought it a miracle, except she'd lost part of her memories. It was as if she didn't know us. Anyway, after that, she wanted nothing to do with men. Terrible waste. At least her genius wasn't effected by the accident. She has several degrees.

"However, I know for a fact that she has a crush on you—at least on the holo images we made of you when you were on the Kanika. She's hounded me and my staff for everything we have on you, Mrs. Parkinson. She greatly admires and respects you. So don't let her down.

"But her mutation will cause a total review of Earth's situation. She can never live on our world again. She'll likely be banned from living on many other worlds as well. We on Azizi-C are now under the threat of this mutation. Many have speculated that our species and yours are very close to each other, DNA speaking. Bonita's mutation proves it. I'm afraid that news will cause a panic, not only back home, but on many other worlds. Frankly, I could well be ordered to disintegrate Earth and all mutants on it. Giants and dwarves would be collateral damage."

"Surely, it won't come to that!" I protested. "After all, we now have strict protocols in place."

"Such decisions are out of my hands, Mrs. Parkinson. But since my niece is down there, if I am ordered to destroy Earth and if you marry Bonita, then I'll see that she, you and your family, children, and sisters survive, likely in your own spaceship. If you don't marry her, she'll be the lone survivor. Am I clear? I heard your mutant husband and son were murdered."

"Yes, but—"

"The destruction of Earth, if it's ordered, won't come until after this linguistics conference. Far too many other world's linguists are attending. Besides, I'd prefer to evacuate the dwarves and giants. Hate collateral damage when it can be avoided. So you've got a couple weeks before the decision comes down—one way or the other. That'll be all."

He rose and left the room. Our guide stepped in and asked us to follow him. I glanced at Ashley as we walked slowly back to the shuttle. All color in her face had vanished. She pressed her lips tightly together all the way back.

Once in our shuttle and on our way, I said, "Ashley, don't worry. If I have to evacuate, I'll take you with me. After all, you *are* my personal assistant."

She exhaled. Color returned to her face. "Thank you. Will they really blow up Earth? Murder three billion people?"

I shrugged my shoulders. I wanted to say "not if I can help it," but at the moment, I had no idea what else I could possibly do to help offset the mutation of his niece.

Chapter 5 Investigations

The doctor estimated the two women would come out of their mutation comas by the first of February. That gave me five more days to coordinate these investigations and find answers. Once the women roused, I knew I'd have to run therapy and extensive training sessions for them. With the rulership coup going strong, many others volunteered to help, so I decided to use them.

I tried hard to keep the loss of Sam and Matt from my thoughts by focusing on my job. Didn't work. His scent covered our sheets. Matt's things lay here and there. Little things constantly reminded me of their deaths. But I kept hoping that the mutation agent would heal their bodies, like it had mine. I had to keep those thoughts alive. Still, keep working played a major therapy role for me.

As soon as we got back from the Kanika, I called everyone and arranged for an extended family meeting at my place around nine tonight. That done, I set to work, meeting with everyone in my Senior Investigator's office.

"Ward, you and Dimitri work on finding who and why this Liatos-D Ambassador Hypnos Kalakos wanted to have the Wang brothers sell telepaths to that Blackwell world. Jie, you and Natalie continue tracing that giant who injected Tia Sanchez. Helen and Casper, see what you can discovery why a military group of giants on Liatos-D wanted to damage our food production in Iowa. Bev, I want you to provide security for the Federation of Planets' Tenth Annual Linguist Conference on February 14th. Make damn sure there are no bomb or mutation attacks. This is a critical target, whether others realize it or not. From what Ashley tells me, we're expecting close to five hundred linguists from all over the Federation—a prime target for terrorists."

"What do you want us to do, Mom?" Isabella said nodding towards Owen, Bernardo, and Wendy. Both she and Wendy were expecting their first child in about three weeks.

"Since you four have been out there in space a lot, I

want you to figure out a way to uncover who leaked the identity of Patricia Ann to GEnt. I'm sure someone in Admiral Skaggs crew did it. He has giants on the Kanika."

"What are you going to research?" Isabella asked.

"The death of our Ambassador Aaron Strawn. Piper is due to land with his remains around three this afternoon. I'll meet her at New O'Hare."

"But what are we going to do about the coup?" asked Dimitri.

Many faces stared at me. "Nothing."

"Huh? We can't just let them—"

I cut him off. "Yes, we can. The situation will resolve itself in time. Look, I'll tell you all more at tonight's meeting. Right now, Ashley needs me to play Senior Judge. Some billionaires have filed a lawsuit. I have to hear it."

After glancing at her watch and frowning, Ashley said, "We have to hurry, boss."

As we headed for the elevator, I teased her. "Sorry. I can't hurry, but you can."

Her eyes dropped to my tall heels and then her flats. She cracked a smile and pushed the button. With just us in the rising elevator, she said, "If they destroy Earth, are you serious about bringing me along with you and your family? This is only my fourth day working for you. And honestly, you don't need much assistance."

"As long as you keep on helping me, you're welcome to come if we have to evacuate Earth."

The muscles in her arms relaxed. The doors opened, revealing my courtroom. All ready the plaintiff section was packed with a dozen young Galactic Dolls, but I suspected most were males, the billionaires. Sam Deckerson sat all by himself at the defendant's table. I smiled at the irony. Okay, I intensely disliked that man.

While I took my seat, Ashley opened the documents on my low desk and then started the video recording.

She said, "This session of the Senior Judge court is now in session. Case Number Two: Billionaires versus Galactic Defense Corporation. Plaintiff attorney: Carol Taylor."

I said, "Okay, Ms. Taylor, you may begin."

"Your Honor, eleven of Chicago's wealthiest men are here today seeking justice for the failure of Galactic Defense to protect them from terrorists. As you can see, their bodies have been subjected to the Galactic Doll mutation agent. Against their wills, I might add."

On she went outlining the failures of GD, beginning with the thirty year span when a Sixth Invader had been body swapped into GD's CEO's body. She mentioned the terrible robot war on Brussels, Tau Ceti, and its horrible mistreatment of our soldiers. Then, she presented the discovery of the armless telepath version and the subsequent terrorist attacks and even the misuse of that agent by GD against protestors. On she went for nearly an hour. But we knew she desired to make this part of the official court records.

I nearly cheered when I heard her say, "The prosecution rests."

Sam Deckerson cleared his throat. I'd watched him making notes while Carol talked, but I decided I'd heard enough to make my ruling.

"Excuse me, Mr. Deckerson. You don't have to say anything. This court is ready to make its decision."

He started to protest. I didn't need telepathy to sense he felt I was so prejudiced against him that I'd not let him try to defend the corporation.

"I find the plaintiffs' case to be wholly without any merit. There's no need to even try to defend against them, Mr. Deckerson."

I faced the eleven fuming men. "You aren't part of our society in that you live wholly outside the corporate sponsorship program. You make your living by siphoning off the profits of the corporations you own. Since you own them, this court rules that it is your responsibility to hold the corporations and their personnel accountable. In fact, you did nothing—nothing at all. It's been up to us to fight against the inhumanity and corruption of the corporations. In short, the condition you're in now stems directly from your own failure to take responsibility for your own actions. In short, gentlemen, tough shit. You should know better. I'm throwing this case out entirely. Good day. Try taking some responsibility for Earth and the Sol Empire."

I wished I had one of those gavels. I'd love to have pounded it hard, signaling the end. A shocked look covered Sam's face, but it rapidly turned into a broad smile. The eleven plaintiffs bickered and bellowed as they wobbled out of the room, still unused to the heels they now had to wear.

"Ashley, back down to the investigations, please. Oh, I could use some lunch when we get a chance."
***
Ashley, Sherry, and I met Piper Strawn at New O'Hare. The tearful widow seemed to appreciate us. She had aged since I last saw her. Female Senior Ambassadors always wore these huge dangling earrings, composed of dozens of two-inch crystals hung in a gold layered lattice. Presumably, they helped dampen the emotions of others being sensed or picked up by the wearer or so I had been told. Piper verified that they did seem to dampen emotions. She still wore hers. They draped onto her massive bosom, threatening to pull off her earlobes. Obviously, they didn't do that. Still...

"It's all my fault he's dead," she wailed.

Also, all Senior Ambassadors had their upper lip slit, the fleshy lip loop stretched, and an eighteen inch across disk inserted. Each had their own unique design etched into the outer surface of the disk. Piper's upper lip had a red line across it, suggesting she'd had her lip healed up before leaving Bela Prime. So I had proof that this body modification could be undone. Still I suspected Aaron had had a difficult time with it. I made a note to ask Piper about that.

We spent an hour getting Aaron's body transported to the cremation facility, a funeral service done, and watched as his body slipped into the furnace. Later, his ashes would be spread on farmland, enriching the earth upon his death, just as everyone did. A dozen times, she sobbed telling us that it was her fault that Aaron died.

We accompanied Piper to their old home in North Chicago. While Ashley and Sherry helped her unpack, I took her into her bedroom and gave the grieving widow a therapy session to help her handle the loss of her husband. His death obviously wasn't her fault. Buckets of tears flowed as we went over and over her loss, re-experiencing all aspects of it.

Their housing on Bela Prime lay one block from the Ambassador Building. Walking home that night, a giant stepped out of the shadows and fired a blaster at Aaron, removing the front half of his head. Now I understood why Piper had no chance to use that red syringe containing the armless telepath mutation agent. Aaron was dead before his body hit the ground.

After we reduced the emotional loss charge, I asked her for something earlier that was similar in nature. She fumbled around several minutes before spotting something bluish. As we re-experienced it, slowly the story unfolded. In another lifetime, she and Aaron had been married, though their genders were reversed. Quite by accident, she'd shot and killed him. In an instant, both Piper and I understood why she'd continually wailed that it was her fault that Aaron had died. Piper roared with laughter.

"How silly. It was an accident, but I felt so awful. I never did recover from that one."

I ended the therapy session. "How about some supper? Then, I'd like to chat with you about this and your time as our Senior Ambassador."

Ashley fetched everyone chicken dinners. After eating, we lounged around Piper's living room. We ignored the dust bunnies.

At last I asked the questions for which I needed answers. I began innocently enough. "Do those earrings actually make any difference? Did Aaron wear them too?"

She chuckled. "Actually, they did seem to lessen my experience of other people's emotions. Aaron said he felt they helped him with his telepathy, too."

"I see your upper lip is healing. Weren't those giant lip disks just too much?"

Piper grinned. "That's putting it mildly. Of course, the disk greatly hampered Aaron's abilities. I had to feed him and assist him with nearly everything. Still, they did open doors, as they say. We had no idea at first. As soon as anyone on Bela Prime saw our lip plates, they jumped to help us. Senior Ambassadors are nearly the most important upperclass people on that world. Everyone tries to look after your every need—often for a small tip, mind you. So, yes, the lip plates aided us enormously, especially when we first arrived and didn't know where or what anything was."

"Okay. Before the giant shot Aaron, did the giant say anything?"

"No, not a word. Just stepped out of the shadows and fired."

"All right. What about before that? What was Aaron working on? Had he made enemies? Had he uncovered some kind of plot?"

"Oh, everyone is plotting something. As a telepath, many made use of his skills. Because of that, I think he kept the Circle of Ambassadors honest for the past seven years. But there was one strange thing."

"What?"

"The day before the shooting, he said he'd discovered something terrible, something from Earth. He said he was going to call the entire Council of Admirals and Generals into the Senate the next day. Whatever it was, he deemed it very important. But he never told me what it was. He was killed before he could."

"Damn. Any chance he kept a diary or journal?"

"Well, now that you mention it, he kept a voice journal. He couldn't write. Well, you know that. With that lip disk, writing with his toes just didn't work. It's on his laptop, wherever they unpacked it."

Ashley retrieved it and sat it on the end table by Piper. She booted it up. However, it needed Aaron's biometric and password to activate it.

"He was paranoid about passwords and changed it often. I've no idea what it is," Piper said. "I guess we'll never know if he left us any clues."

"Mind if I hang on to his laptop? I'll see if someone can crack it."

"Sure. If there are any personal photos and videos on it, send them to me."

"Of course, Piper. Thanks. I promise you we're going to get to the bottom of this. There had to be a reason Aaron was murdered."

"You're a dear, Molly. A real treasure. Sorry to hear about Sam's death. You've lost two husbands. That's just terrible."

"Well, if Ted hadn't been murdered, he could probably hack into Aaron's computer right now. Ah well. Thanks. I'll keep in touch. If you need anything, let me know."

Piper said, "And you, too, Molly. You need anything, let me know. I owe you so much. Aaron and I both. Do you realize that no one on Bela Prime knows anything about minds and therapy healing like you and your sisters do. Amazing. The universe is filled with the most amazing technology but knows almost nothing about the our minds."

As we walked home on the MTES, Ashley said, "Could Ted actually have hacked into Aaron's laptop? I mean it's protected by biometrics and passwords. Supposedly, that makes it uncrackable."

I chuckled, remembering my time with Ted. "If anyone could get into any computer system, it was Ted. He was a genius at it. But honestly, I doubt anyone in GD can hack into this laptop. Still, I'll ask Helen and Casper."

Later after my late evening meeting, I asked them about it. Both said it was un-hackable, but Helen promised to make discrete inquiries with some of her contacts at GD.

At nine, my living room filled up with people. All my clone sisters, husbands, children, wives, and close friends such as Lenka and Lea, jammed into the room, many sitting on the floor. Nikita and Veronica took many of the children into the basement playroom. Fifty people crowded in, all staring at me.

"Okay. Thank you for coming. As you know or have heard," I began, outlining my trip to the Kanika, my discoveries with the Wang brothers, and even Aaron's murder. I spent a half hour bringing everyone up to date. Then, I leveled the bomb.

"What does this mean? In short, because of the incredible misuse of the armless telepath agent, the Federation of Planets is extremely worried about their own safety. They've sent Admiral Skaggs here to see if the situation can be contained. If it can't, he's under orders to exterminate all life on Earth. Probably via a series of nukes."

Gasps and cries responded.

"It's worse, gang. As I said, his niece Bonita Valdez is in my guest room in her mutation coma. She's Azizi-C born and bred. She's proof our human mutation can mutate other similar alien species of the galaxy. I presume us humans never founded Azizi-C."

More gasps followed.

"Oh, my god!" exclaimed Leslie. "He's like got no choice but to kill us all."

"That's my greatest fear at the moment," I said. "But he gave me a way out if that happens. It seems his niece is in love with me or rather with my holographic videos streams they made of me when I was on the Kanika. Anyway, he said that if I marry his niece, then he will see that I and my sisters, their families, and associates are saved when he destroys the population of Earth. I presumed he'd provide us with a spaceship of some kind."

As I suspected, the room filled with talk! Celeste sent me via telepathy, 'I let Eve and Randy know what you said here. They said thanks. They're working on a major male cure. They're on the Padella doctors' atoll along with Patricia Ann and her family. Lara says to say hi and that she'll come to help you if you need her.'

'Thanks.'

Deanna whistled and got our attention. "Look. I've got the Friendship. It can take us. I suggest we make plans to depart in a hurry. Each of you, pack up the things you consider vital. We'll quietly move much of that onboard the ship in the ensuing days. Then, if and when things go south, all you have to do is get out to New O'Hare and onto the ship. I'll give everyone here the access code to the bay door lock. Just don't leave the ship unlocked."

"So we'll like be gypsies," said Leslie.

"Right," Commander Lia Johnston said. "Molly, Deanna, and I can pilot. Lenka is a licensed navigator. We'll find a place that wants us."

Deanna said, "If it doesn't happen for another couple months, I'll have a second ship ready. We're building a duplicate of the Friendship. Then, we can take a hundred more. Probably those onboard Earth's other spaceships will be saved, too."

"But where will we go?" asked Lenka. "All other planets, moons, and stations in the empire won't let us live there."

"We'll like be gypsies," Leslie answered. "Like fly around the galaxy seeing the sights."

"Maybe it won't come to pass," I said. "But I wanted you to understand the seriousness of Earth's position. Don't worry. If marrying his niece is what I have to do to save all of you, I won't hesitate. Still, let's continue our investigations. Remember, to have a conflict there must be a hidden party behind it. I can't imagine all giants are evil and want to destroy humans."

***

On Monday, January 30, 2361, I took action on what my investigation team had uncovered. Jie posted an image of the giant who had abducted and injected Tia Sanchez. Ward posted a good image of the Liatos-D Ambassador Hypnos Kalakos who was behind the Wang brothers and their sale of telepaths. Diligent work by others assembled images of the paramilitary group who sabotaged the food production system in Iowa. More importantly, Helen turned in an image of a giant who had murdered Sam and Matt.

Thus, armed with the images and an set of documents outlining all we knew about their crimes, I paid a call on the local Liatos-D ambassadors. Thedra and Biton Demarchis had their offices in Moscow, where the Earth-wide corporation offices resided. In contrast, the empire-wide offices were here in Chicago. Thus, after breakfast, Ashley, Sherry, and I commandeered an official Judicial Airliner to Moscow, arriving there in the afternoon. While the deep snow made walking on side streets challenging, the MTES still functioned normally.

For convenience, the offices of all our local alien ambassadors were in the same building. I had a hunch they were more comfortable with each other than with us Earthlings. Anyway, we entered a large, spacious office. Incense filled the hot, moist air. Giants preferred warm weather.

The bald pair of ambassadors entered the office from a different set of doors, just as Ashley, Sherry, and I entered through the main doors. Ambassador Thedra wore a low-cut gown, rather similar to the gowns we dolls wore. A giant emerald rested at her cleavage. Matching earrings complimented her look. That she stood a foot taller than I did in my heels wasn't lost on me. Inches taller than his wife, Ambassador Biton wore a well-tailored business suit, again similar to those our men used to wear before the pandemic mutations.

The room housed a dozen potted plants, exotic to our eyes, each with a placard with its name on it. They'd brought them from Liatos-D. A pair of high-backed chairs rested on one side of a long, wide desk, while several Earth-sized chairs lined the side closest to the doors we entered. We five politely sat.

"I'm here as the Sol Empire's Senior Investigator. Molly Parkinson. This is my personal assistant, Ashley Peterson, and my security guard, Sherry Cooper. I'm here on official business."

After adjusting their language translator boxes to reflect English and not Russian, they introduced themselves.

"How can we help you?" Thedra said.

I still found it strange to hear a person speaking an unknown language and hearing ours from a box around their waists.

"Ashley, show them the folders." While she opened each case file, I continued talking. "These are documented crimes committed by unknown giants from Liatos-D, presumably ones who've not immigrated to Earth. Let's start with the recent murder of my husband and son, Sam and Matt—that's the folder on your left. These are your copies."

I outlined each case, ending with the best surveillance image of the giant(s) involved. That took an hour. The two ambassadors listened intently and asked some key questions about how the images were obtained."

Thedra said, "Thank you for bringing these cases to our attention. As your Earth expression goes, there are always bad apples in the barrel. Liatos-D is no exception. We've got our own criminal underworld. Our Criminal Investigation Division or CID has a good record of apprehending the guilty. We will send these cases and images to the CID today. First step: identify the men. Second step: apprehend and interrogate them. If they are guilty, what would you like done with them? Sent back here to Earth to stand trial?"

"As far as justice goes, perhaps it would be best if your world handled that," I said. "What we desperately need to know from your CID unit is *why* did they commit these crimes? Who paid them? Who encouraged them to commit these crimes. I don't believe they acted on their own. You don't see people from Earth going to your world and committing heinous crimes. No, someone else is behind these attacks. Someone with a hidden agenda. We need to know who that is and what their objective is."

"I see," Ambassador Biton said.

His expression didn't enthuse me, so I said more. "Admiral Skaggs and the battleship Kanika of the Federation of Planets are here to decide what's to be done with Earth. You know—this telepath mutation agent. We've now proven it mutates other species, ones close to ours. You giants and the dwarves are immune, but many others are not. We've just had the first mutation that crossed race lines. People on Azizi-C can be mutated by the agent.

"So you see this is rapidly getting out of hand. It's entirely possible the Federation will order the compete destruction of Earth. Probably by nukes, making the world uninhabitable for centuries. And that severely impacts the immigration of your people. You'll have to find other worlds willing to accept your overflow population. I need to know who hired these criminals, why Earth, and what their objectives are. Without that, you may soon have to transport all your giants back to Liatos-D. That's assuming Admiral Skaggs will give you enough warning to evacuate your people."

Both giants paled. I made my point. Perhaps a bit too much impingement, but I was desperate. My experience with alien races thus far led me to conclude the giants, though strong, weren't the brightest of people.

I added, "Time isn't on our sides. I don't think Admiral Skaggs will act until the end of the Federation of Planets' Tenth Annual Linguist Conference on February 14th. After that, who knows how soon the admiral will act. So we've got maybe two weeks to sort this out."

Slowly the color returned to their faces. Ambassador Biton said, "You have excellent images here. The CID has good image recognition programs. We should have their identities by tomorrow. I can't say how fast they can be located and interrogated, but I will impress the CID with just how critical this is. I assure you Liatos-D does not want to lose Earth and the Sol Empire as immigration worlds. Your world has given new hope and life to so many of our people."

Both wanted us to stay for dinner, but with so much at stake, I needed to get back to Chicago. We thanked them and departed.

Chapter 6 Crushes

Tia Sanchez woke from her coma to find life completely altered. When she screamed, Celeste rushed to her bedside, as did Isabella.

As soon as Tia saw Isabella, she calmed down enough talk to my daughter. "I am—or was—the linguist on the exploration ship New Light based out of Brussels. I'm from New Amsterdam, Brussels, Tau Ceti. I came to hear you speak at the linguist conference. What's happened to me? I can't do anything anymore."

Isabella explained what little we knew, while Celeste helped Tia stand so she could look at her body in the full-length mirror.

"I really do look years younger, but everything else is awful. Oh," her face reddened, "no offense, Isabella. I couldn't imagine how you did all your breakthrough linguistics. I feel so helpless."

"First things first," Celeste said. "We've gotten you the three robot machines that makes life bearable and the laptop with the how-to videos on it. Let's get you dressed and fed. Then, I'll give you a therapy session which will help."
***

Thus, when we returned home early morning on the last day of January, we entered a hive of activity. Isabella filled me in on Tia's reactions. Only the potential for telepathy to help her with her linguistics kept Tia in control of her terror. Nevertheless, Isabella reported that Tia felt utterly crushed. She could never return to her home on Brussels.

"Mom, I checked with the New Light commander. He says if she becomes a telepath, the corporation will change her contract and up her pay to a million credits per year. He said he'll welcome her back to the ship. I touched his mind, and he wasn't lying."

"Good. That's something. Once Celeste has finished Tia's therapy, Tia will have a tough decision to make. Even if she gets all the cures, they won't let her back on Brussels," I said.

"Yeah. And I took your advice. Nikita and I have been practicing using her toy Galactic Doll. I think maybe I can manage caring for my baby, but I'm still nervous about it. What if something goes wrong? What if I go into labor when I'm receiving my award on stage or giving my speech?"

"Then we'll get you to the Med Center right away. Everyone will understand." We pressed our bodies together—our hug.

She changed the subject. "Are Sam and Matt going to make it?"

I sighed. "Dear, I just don't know. Every now and then, I touch his mind, but he's still unconscious. I lost Ted nearly ten years ago. Sherry thinks one of those un-programmed robots killed Ted. That's the first clue we've had in nearly a decade. Don't suppose we'll ever track that rogue machine down."

"Whatever happened to Ted? I mean the person, the being. Did he get a new baby body?"

"He picked up a baby body, which would make him about ten years old, probably in fourth or fifth grade. Years ago, I totally lost track of him. He might not even be on Earth any longer."

"Well, if Sam's body doesn't survive, he's welcome to my baby's body."

"Thank you. I'll let him know. You can, too. But let's not erase him just yet. Remember, when the Sixth Invader shot me, the rejuvenation process took a month to repair all that damage. We have to remain hopeful. The alternative is..."

"Okay. Say, how are you going to deal with Ms Valdez when she wakes up?"

I grinned—sheepishly I think. "Lord, I don't know. Tell her the truth for starters. Come on. Lend me a hand. We should move Tia's things into the second guest bedroom. A little privacy might help her. Who wants to sleep beside a comatose person?"

She added, "And beside these husks which used to be their arms. Can we dispose of them?"

Sitting on the floor, I held a garbage sack open with my

feet while Isabella rolled four dried out husks into the sack. I lifted it onto the bed and got up. Pinching the sack between my head and shoulder, I carried it out to the kitchen.

Isabella followed after me. Together with our robot maid's help, we fixed a nourishing lunch, heavy on the protein. We both knew when Celeste and Tia ended their session at noon, they'd be famished.

"Oh, thanks, Molly, Isabella," Celeste said, as she walked into the kitchen. Tia followed her.

"You can carry the stuff to the table and dish it out," I said. To Tia, I added, "Carrying things is a challenge."

"Mom," Isabella interrupted, "it's more like a bitch!"

We laughed and watched the tension ease from Tia's face.

"I can't imagine how to carry anything. Trying to eat is beyond awful." She pushed a chair out and sat down. "Isabella, is it worth it? I mean having telepathy and working with an alien language out there? Is that worth how horrible life has become? I feel so helpless."

I glanced at Isabella, wondering if she wanted to field this dicey question. She smiled and gave a diplomatic reply.

"Tia, I think it depends on the person. With me, I got mutated when I was thirteen, so I've had years of practice. Sometimes being handicapped is a real drag, but in our field most of the time having telepathy is a huge benefit. For me, it's more than worth it. On the other hand, Mom has seen thousands of others who wanted nothing more than to get it undone. I think being a corporate telepath spy would make life unbearable. Using telepathy to help learn a new race's language gives me an incredible sense of self-worth. For me, that makes up for the handicap. Like I said, I think it'll depend on you.

"My advice, Tia, is get all the therapy you can from Aunt Celeste. Study all the how-to videos. And practice. I can help you some, more so after my baby comes."

"Thanks. Puts it in perspective. Hell, I'd rather die than become a spy for a corporation. Since I can still be a linguist on the New Light, maybe there's some hope. Celeste said there is an arm regrow cure, but I'd lose my telepathy and still look like one of you Earthling's Galactic Dolls and be banned from Brussels."

Isabella said, "You aren't alone. Angelina Flores was a telepath, serving as the linguist on the Enchanter for five years before she was mutated by the pandemic that swept over Earth a few months ago. She's been re-injected with the telepath mutation agent and is due out of her coma in a couple days. Angelina has had five years experience at it. I'm sure she'd love to help you learn how to do things. I'll make sure she knows about you as soon as she wakes up. Also, Bonita Valdez, Admiral Skaggs' niece, should wake up tomorrow. So there'll be three of you new telepaths here."

"Would you? I feel so helpless right. Everything's changed. Life's become unreal," Tia said, fighting back tears.

"It takes time, practice, and Aunt Celeste's therapy sessions. Oh, she wants you again."

I added, "We can't let external things determine who we are."

***

"Ayuadame! Dónde estoy? Qué me ha pasado?" The voice of Bonita Valdez yelled.

We'd placed her language translation device near her bed. While lacking her emotional tone, the box said, "Help me. Where am I? What's happened to me?"

Even though Celeste and I expected her to wake from her coma anytime, I jumped when I heard her voice. Celeste rushed into my guest bedroom, while I followed behind her. We found Bonita sitting up in bed, staring down at the upper part of her body with its now enormous bosom. Her face, pale. Eyes wide.

"Hello, Miss Valdez. I'm Celeste Sawyers. Can you understand me? We've got your translation unit next to you, if you need it."

She looked up at Celeste as I walked into the room behind my sister. Her brows rose and color returned to her face. Oops. Too much color. She flushed. I also noticed what I didn't hear: screams of terror.

"Sí. Yes, I study your language. Turn it off."

She meant the translation unit, which quietly continued

turning our speech into that of the Azizi-C but in a monotone. Celeste flipped its switch.

"That's better," Celeste said. "You're in Molly Parkinson's guest bedroom."

"Molly? Molly Parkinson? Is this really you?" she gushed, her face almost crimson.

"Yes. Glad to meet you, Miss Valdez. I know your uncle, Admiral Skaggs."

Tears occluded Bonita's vision, and she blinked repeatedly, struggling to wipe her eyes with her missing hands. Celeste dabbed them for her.

I continued. "You were injected with the armless telepath Galactic Doll mutation agent during your flight to Earth. We caught the man responsible. Molly can explain. But first, I expect you need to use the bathroom. Let's get you dressed and fed."

"I'm afraid. I can't do anything." She looked at me. Bonita's face flushed again. "Yet," she added.

"That's partly why I'm here. I'll help you, Miss Valdez."

"Bonita, por favor," she said. "My feet?"

"Yes, distorted. Wearing tall heels helps a lot," I said, while Celeste helped her up and steadied her.

After using the bathroom, Celeste showed her the dressing and hair machines, explaining their use. Then, she demonstrated their use, getting Bonita properly clothed in the usual red satin gown with matching heels. Meanwhile, Isabella and I worked on fixing her a late breakfast of eggs, bacon, juice, and toast. All synth foods, of course.

While Celeste fed her, I explained what happened and the justice we extracted from the Wang brothers. "We're still investigating, trying to find out who put them up to selling telepaths to this Blackwell world. I think there's more to this story. Anyway, you aren't alone. Miss Tia Sanches came out of her coma yesterday. She's held the linguist post on the exploration ship New Light based out of Brussels for nine years. Tia came to Earth to attend the linguist conference, too, when someone attacked and mutated her." I continued to outline what had happened.

"But I can't hear thoughts in my head yet," she

interrupted.

"Usually, telepathy takes a week or two to develop," I said. "Don't worry. I'm sure you'll soon be able to read others' minds."

She flushed bright red. I added, "Don't worry. None of us will probe your private thoughts without your permission. To do that against your will is mental rape."

She smiled, the edges of her mouth twitching. Slowly, the red left her face. Since Bonita took this amazingly well—no screams, no terror, no panic—I continued.

"So, this mutation agent is being widely misused. Your case is critical. It shows that people on Azizi-C can be mutated, too. Admiral Skaggs is right to be very worried about this. Terrorists using this terrible agent could strike on your world at any time." I rapidly outlined what had happened on Earth during the past decade, including the fact that all our men have also been mutated into male Galactic Dolls via the recent pandemic.

"Admiral Skaggs and the Federation of Planets are deciding the fate of us on Earth. He's indicated that perhaps he'll be ordered to destroy everyone on Earth to avoid the spread of this terrible mutation agent—all three billion of us. Don't worry, Bonita. He told me if that happens, he'll save you."

Her brows rose, jaws tensed. "They *can* do that. I know many other worlds in the Federation are very worried about this mutation agent spreading. Like containing a plague."

"Right. However, your uncle told me how much you are interested in me. He said if I marry you, then he would also save my family, my extended family, and close friends—maybe a hundred of us."

When I said this, her face flushed. Her eyes focused on the empty plate of food in front of her.

I added, "And I'm willing to do that. My husband and son, Sam and Matt, were officially pronounced dead after a giant exploded a bomb as they walked by. I say officially, since Galactic Medicine has them in a mutation coma in stasis pods, keeping their bodies alive while hoping the doll agent will heal them. That happened to me once a few years back, so we're praying for a similar miracle. Anyway, I'm prepared to do whatever I have to do to keep myself, family, and friends alive—if they decide to blow up Earth."

Having been honest with her, I figured it was time to let her talk. Celeste had fed her a healthy meal, and I knew she'd soon want to run her therapy on Bonita.

"It's true. Once I saw your holo image Uncle Baba showed me and heard about how you saved his life and ship, I felt this intense attraction to you." She flushed. "I know I'm not a male, but..." She flushed, faltered, and changed the topic.

"I am something of a linguist, too. I so wanted to come to this conference to meet Isabella. She's famous, you know, having deciphered the language of both invaders. I've been practicing your language. This isn't at all how I imagined we'd meet—not like I am. I feel so helpless, so strange, so scared. What am I going to do now?"

"Ah," Celeste said, "it's time to get my therapy. Once we erase all those awful feelings, the fear, the pain, why, you'll feel much better. Molly, you can give Tia some lessons or more therapy while I work with Bonita."

While Celeste helped Bonita back to the bedroom, I headed to the second guest bedroom to see what I could do for Tia. Isabella handled the dishes for us, though I expected my personal assistant and Sherry to drop by anytime.

The brown hair and eyes of Tia greeted me, as I walked up to her door and said, "Knock. Knock." No way to knock.

"Oh, hi, Molly. I heard the other victim waking up. Is Celeste giving her a therapy session?" she said.

"Yes. I'm here to give you more therapy or to help you learn new ways to do things. Your choice."

"Help me learn how to survive. I feel so helpless like this, but you must know what I mean. It's all so strange."

"That's putting it mildly, Tia. Sure. Let's work on that. Remember: stop and think how. There's usually a way. We just have to be smarter than normal people."

She flashed me a grateful smile. I sensed she put on a brave face. Well, she had no other choice at the moment. I worked with her until lunchtime, when Sherry and Ashley arrived to help in the kitchen.

***

Celeste pulled up a chair in front of Bonita, who sat in one of our comfortable chairs.

"I've closed the door so that whatever you and I say in here will remain private," my sister said. After explaining how the therapy session worked, she had Bonita return to when she was attacked while in the deep space transport on her way to Earth.

"It's all so horrible, gone so wrong. A while back, I saw Uncle Baba's holo videos of what happened on the Kanika. When I saw Molly's image, something happened to me. I can't explain it. I felt I just had to get close to her, like we were somehow fated to be joined. I know, it sounds weird. Everyone thought so, too. That's why I was on the shuttle. I just had to meet Molly. I had all these imaginings of how we'd meet, how I'd hold her, even kiss. Silly, I know. But I've never had such strong feelings for another person before. Plus, after seeing Molly's images, I kept feeling this terrible pressure all over my body—like someone was crushing it. Anyway there I was on the ship."

"Okay. So tell me what happened next."

"I walk to the bathroom. As I stepped out, a man is waiting his turn. He smiles. I pass by him. I feel a pin prick in my neck. I turn. He's holding a syringe. It's empty. I try to speak, but can't seem to get my mouth to work. I feel weak. I'm falling. No, his arm catches me. I think he's carrying me somewhere. Then I wake up in this strange bed. My arms are gone. I feel so helpless."

As expected, Bonita bounced over the terrible pain and unconsciousness of the mutation coma. However, after going over it several more times, more details appeared, including the intense pain of her arms withering into dry husks.

However, what so surprised Celeste was just how quickly Bonita recovered and blew the mutation pains, having done that in less than an hour, unlike all the other mutation victims who often took days to erase that trauma.

Since the trauma didn't erase, Celeste asked for an earlier incident that was similar.

"This is a strange one. I've always wondered about it.

Everyone has told me all about it."

"Okay, let's go to its beginning. Tell me what's happening as you move through it."

"An accident. That's what they say. I'm with a boyfriend. I'm told that's who he was. I've no idea if he was, though. We're flying really fast. He's showing off. We crash into the ground. Pain. Massive pain in my head. I'm told he died instantly. They told me I was in a coma for months."

"I understand. Let's go back to its beginning. See if you can find more details. What are you seeing, smelling, feeling?"

Bonita ran though that accident several more times. What Celeste found interesting is that Bonita had no idea who this man was, only what others afterwards told her about it.

"There's something strange about this whole thing. It's like I didn't exist before I was in that coma. Like I was born when I awoke from it. I didn't know where I was, who anyone was. They said I had accident amnesia. But I think it was more than that. I've no memories of her before that point. Plus, remember that intense crushing pressure all over my body? It's really turned on now. I'm being crushed to death."

"All right. Let's go to the beginning of when you are being crushed to death."

"Wow! You're right. I am being crushed to death. A bomb. Oh, I'm sitting at my desk working on robot research. I've no arms, so it's a challenge. Boom. A bomb goes off. I feel this crushing pressure all over my body. Oh! I died instantly. Organs turned to soup. Wow. I'm searching for five missing robots. They look like humans, but haven't had the robot laws programmed into them. They're rogues. Molly and I are trying to track them down. I'm uncovering details of their construction when the bomb goes off. Oh, I'm pissed. I float through what's left of the wall.

"We say goodbye. I get a new baby body. Wait. Then I see one of these very robots I'm trying to find. The one who detonated the bomb. I back out of the baby body and follow him. I'm not letting him go. Maybe I can find a way to stop him, I think.

"I follow him to the spaceport. New O'Hare, it's called. He gets on a small deep space ship and shuts the door. I float through the metal walls. How cool! I see him. He's alone. I try to think of ways to stop him. Without a body, no ideas come. He takes off. I decide to travel with him. If I go back to my new baby body, it'll be twenty years before I can get back on his trail. Molly will understand. We have to stop these rogue robots.

"Hyperspace. Scares me. I latch on to the bulkhead hard. Lord knows where I'll end up if I float off into hyperspace. Time is kind of weird without a body, especially when traveling with a robot that never eats or sleeps. We land. I follow it out of the ship. He's buying lots of electronics parts at a store. Parts one could use to build a robot brain, I think. I stop and ponder what this all means. He's on another world, buying parts to make more robots like himself. Not good. I have to stop him. How?

"I get confused thinking about this. I lose track of him. I look all around, but can't see him. I panic. I need to get a body. I look and look. There's a hospital, I think. I float into it. Yes. Now to find a baby body. Wait. Then I'll still have to wait years for it to grow up. I spot a young woman in a coma. Head is all bandaged up. I look, but whoever had this body wasn't around. I figure she thought she was dead and left the body. Well, it isn't dead yet. Maybe I can fix it up or use it. I latch onto its head. Wham! Intense head pain. I am pulled inside its head in a flash. I wake up. Very confused. Who am I? Where am I?"

Suddenly, Bonita brightened up. "Well, that explains a whole lot. When I woke up so darn confused, I forgot all about who I was and what I was trying to do—stop those robots. Wow! No wonder I'm so attracted to Molly. I'm her husband, Ted. Or was, anyway. Incredible. All that's come back to me. Amazing. So that's why I changed my university major to electronic engineering. I even built a positonic brain and installed it in a mining machine as my thesis. Trying to learn all I can about these rogue robots and their capabilities. I remember you, Celeste. My memories are flooding back! Are the others still around? Leslie? Janine? Deanna? General Bev Blythe? This is so incredible. I remember all these things from my last lifetime—like they just happened. Oh, stop and think how. That was our motto. Is it still?"

Celeste said, "Very well done, Bonita, Ted. We'll end this session now. Let's get some lunch. Yes, they're all around. You can meet them as soon as you want. You'll have to tell Molly all about it. Only recently she discovered that one of those rogue robots detonated the bomb. Sherry uncovered that. Come on."

I introduced the other two victims, Tia, Angelina, along with Ashley, Sherry, Isabella, and her husband Owen.

Frustrated by her fumbling attempts to use her feet and toes to feed herself, Tia said, "This is so damned hard!"

Angelina said, "It gets easier, as long as you keep practicing. It took me ages to get comfortable doing the things I used to do. Then that awful pandemic struck and regrew my arms. I lost my telepathy and job, but thankfully, Molly here got it okayed for me to get mutated again. After the linguist conference, I'll be back on the Enchanter as their linguist. Honestly, I can't imagine a more rewarding job, deciphering the language of an alien race on a new world."

Isabella chuckled. "You can say that again. I don't know how Tia and normal linguists ever figured out an alien language. Say, Bonita, you speak ours very well. I'm still struggling with Azizi-C."

"I studied yours for months so I would be prepared. Given a choice, I'd prefer to have arms."

"Well," Tia said, "I agree, but I'm going to give it a try. If I get mutated again to get my arms back, I'll miss the departure date for my exploration ship, the New Light. I can't afford to lose that job. So I've got a couple of weeks to see if I can somehow adapt enough to get by. If I can't, I've no idea what I can do. They won't let me back on Brussels, Tau Ceti. No mutants allowed. Honestly, I've very little choice right now. Do the corporations on Azizi-C pay your salaries, Bonita?"

"The company that you work for pays your salary. Uncle Baba explained how your corporations work here in the Sol Empire. How screwy. Has everyone had this therapy of Celeste's?"

We nodded.

Bonita said, "After my first one, everything changed. For the better, I think. Now so much of my life makes sense.

You see, last lifetime I was Molly's Ted—Ted Billings."

I gasped. My Ted?

She told us what she'd uncovered in her therapy session. "So when I took over this body, which was in a coma, and awoke, I quickly forgot about my lifetime as Ted. I was on a new world, struggling to make sense of everything. Man, the looks I got until they figured out I must have suffered massive memory loss from that accident. It's like when you lose one body and pickup another, you forget about the old one and that lifetime. Probably because none of it is still around you in the present. At least it was that way for me. Within days of rousing from the coma, I'd forgotten who I used to be, why I was even on Azizi-C, and what my mission was. Now here I am. Say, how soon does the telepathy thing appear?"

"Yeah, how soon?" echoed Tia. "I have to ship out after the convention is over. That is, if I can manage to learn to take care of myself. Do they let you have the machines on the ships?"

I said, "In a week. Two at the most. At least it's been that long with thousands of others. And yes, Isabella and Bernardo took their helpful machines with them. Getting dressed without using them is tough."

"What scares me," Sherry said, "is that Bonita was mutated by our agent. There are many other worlds and civilizations out there with people similar to us. Does this mean they could be mutated too? If so, the Federation really does have a serious problem. Earth can't be alone in having disgruntled people willing to become terrorists to achieve their goals."

"What I'd like to know," Isabella said, "is how come so many of these Federation worlds have people that look so much like us—homo sapiens? It's not like Earthlings moved out and populated the galaxy. We're barely able to explore out some twenty light years from Sol. Senior Ambassador Piper Strawn said many people of the other worlds in the Federation look like us, too. How come?"

"Uncle Baba has noticed that, too. He says it's unlikely human forms always result from natural evolution on distant worlds. It's a big mystery. Me, I've wondered if some of our people migrated to Earth in the distant past. Our language is somewhat close to one of your dialects, Spanish. Not the same, mind you, but really close. I've been studying the relationships of languages across the Federation worlds."

"Have you reached any conclusions?" Isabella said. Her brows rose. Even Angelina and Tia perked up, listening intently to what Bonita said next.

"Well, it's kind of early to say for certain, but it appears that worlds whose inhabitants are close to homo sapiens speak quite related languages. Those, such as the giants, dwarves, and the Sixth Invaders have entirely different languages spoken only on their worlds," Bonita said. "So how long does it take to get arms regrown?"

"It's another mutation process," Owen said. "I was in a coma for eight days, they tell me. It's been about a month now. This is how big they've become—newborn baby arms, not useful for much."

I added, "After six months, regrown arms are those of a teen. After a year, they've become adult arms."

"Oh," Bonita said. She frowned. "Not fast at all."

Owen laughed. "Hardly. Still I'm so glad to be getting mine back. I just hope they will be strong enough to help with our daughter when she comes very soon now."

"You'd better help," Isabella teased.

Chapter 7 Discoveries

After lunch and before Celeste took Bonita back for another therapy session, I took her aside. Ashley and Sherry accompanied us.

"Before you decide to get your arms regrown, there's something I need to ask you and maybe have you do, if you can," I said.

Her brows rose. A smile flickered on her face. I had to admit her smile was infectious. I'd once been at the Miss Galaxy pageant and met two dozen of the most beautiful young women of the Sol Empire. In my eyes, Bonita ranked right there with them. She had gorgeous auburn hair and grey-green eyes. As tall as I was, her hair had grown during the mutation and touched the small of her back. Seeing her, reminded me that I was long overdue for a trim. I kept sitting or standing on my raven locks which now reached my ankles. I'd been too busy to get it done.

"Our Senior Ambassador Aaron Strawn was assassinated by a giant on Bela Prime. He kept a journal on his laptop. Unfortunately, it needs his biometrics and his password, neither of which we have. Is there anyway you can crack it so we can see what he might have discovered? I think it got him killed. I know you don't have hands, but if you can direct Sherry, she'll do what you can't manage. It's really important, Bonita."

"Is it one of those laptops found on Bela Prime?"

"Yes."

"I could have done it in about ten minutes, but not now. I feel so helpless."

"But can you direct Sherry? Or me or anyone? We need to see what's in his journal. I have a feeling it's vital."

"This is the Dingo's Bottoms! I'd so looked forward to meeting you—but not like this. Wait, I was like this before, wasn't I?"

"Yes. Not saying you liked it, but yeah, we both were."

"Okay. I'll try to explain how to do it to Sherry. But we'll need certain tools."

I had her describe what she needed, and Sherry made the list. While Celeste took Bonita for an additional therapy session, Sherry headed off to fetch the supplies. Just then, my phone rang. Ashley retrieved it for me.

"Senior Investigator, your services are needed," a voice said. As I listened, the 3-d hologram of the caller appeared. I couldn't tell the caller's gender, but from the mismatched outfit, I guessed he was a male doll. Women wouldn't be so careless with their appearance.

"Where? What's happened?"

He rattled off an address, which Ashley jotted down, and hung up.

"That's one terse call," I said.

She chuckled. "No kidding. Okay. Looks like an alleyway just at the edge of the Loop. Come on. Let's get going."

I cradled my cloak between a shoulder and neck, twirled it around, and slipped it over my other shoulder. Ashley quickly fastened the front clasp for me, before donning her parka. We stepped outside. Damn. I'd forgotten about the cold and snow. She kept an arm around me while we made our slow way to the MTES. Once on the escalators, Ashley took out her pad and followed the red dot that guided us to the address. For a moment, I wished Sherry was here, just in case.

Her device said, "You have arrived at your destination."

She smiled and tucked it in a pocket, while we stared at a dozen policemen and several GD giant security guards, who stared down into the garbage disposal. In the alleys behind all residential blocks and in the basements of the skyscrapers are the automated recycling garbage disposals. One dumps their garbage, bags and all, into the hopper. It falls down into the subterranean augers which crush everything into fine particles, while moving the bits down the line. Glass, plastic, metal, and organic materials are separated, the latter becoming fertilizer for our farming communities. Everything gets recycled. A larger hopper handles bigger items, such as sofas. These people stared down such a hopper.

"Ah, our Senior Investigator has arrived," one soprano

voice called out. Again, no idea of their gender.

"What's going on?" I asked.

"Have a look, but don't fall in," the person said. "Someone dumped a body down there. The auger did its job on them. We're not sure what should be done about it. We've no idea who the person was or how to best proceed. CP rules require us to take DNA samples, but with everyone on Earth now mutated, a match is unlikely. So we called you."

I chuckled. "When I first started out as a PI, I thought dumping a body down these automated garbage bins was a perfect way to get rid of a body. Someone has finally done it. Okay, take your DNA sample. Someone go through the remains and see if there's anything that can be used to identify the person. The rest of you, check all the security cameras in the area and check if there are any missing person's reports. Someone had to bring the deceased here, alive or dead. You should be able to pick them up on some video feed. One second..."

My phone went off, just as a heavy snow began falling. Ashley retrieved my phone, while the men grumbled, arguing who had to go down into the pit. As I answered it, a 3-d holo image of someone I'd never seen appeared before me, just as I appeared before them. We both had the fancy phones.

"Hello. I'm Josh Pitts, the new head of GD, appointed by Billionaire Phillip Soros, our new CEO of GPan. We need your services as Senior Investigator. Mr. Soros has been kidnapped from his home. Five security giants were killed."

"When did this happen?"

"Hours ago, shortly after breakfast, according to his wife. She heard gunfire before men burst into their dining room."

I called out loudly so the police and security guards could hear, too. "I think we've found what remains of Mr. Soros. His body may have been dumped in a garbage disposal. We're looking at fragments now. I'll get back to you."

I nodded to Ashley, who hung up. "Guys, put a rush on the security videos. You're looking for one or more men bringing CEO Soros here and dumping him in. I suspect he was alive when they tossed him in."

"Why alive?" asked a police detective. I knew the man years ago, but now didn't recognize him since he looked like a Galactic Doll.

"Carrying a dead body around during the daylight hours would be terribly conspicuous. My hunch is you'll find them walking him here before disposing of the man. He was abducted from his home about four hours ago. There's no room for an EMAC to land close to this pit. Blood down there looks wet, so the body was composted fairly recently. How long have you been on the site?"

"The alarm came in about an hour ago," the detective said.

"So he was probably dumped here about three hours ago, around noon. Crap. Another call. Excuse me, guys."

Ashley again answered it for me. No way was I removing my shoes out here. Besides, the cold made my teeth chatter. Deanna's holo image appeared. Russell, her husband and the CEO of the empire-wide GEnt, appeared beside her. Lines creased Deanna's forehead, while Russell looked sober.

He said, "Sorry to bother you, Molly. But we need you at Cartwright Enterprises immediately. Something critical has just come up. As Senior Investigator and Judge, you need to see this before it airs across the empire."

Sighing, I wanted to complain about traveling in the snowstorm, but I knew if Russell thought the matter was critical, it would be. I told him we were on our way.

Twenty minutes later, I warmed up in Deanna's office on the top floor. Russell said, "I received this video about an hour ago. Breaking news. I've no choice but to air it on GEnt news. But I want your opinion first. Mind you, it's gruesome."

A male Galactic Doll appeared in the 3-d holo image. He wore one of Leslie's fancy suits, so he must have had connections.

"Hello. I am the Chief Finance Officer for Galactic Mining, Dr. Kirk Alcott. My job is to handle all the precious metals and gems that are produced each month from all across the Sol Empire. Gold, silver, diamonds, and other precious metals and gems are mined daily, the final products sent to my office for evaluation. My staff appraises the gems and purity of the precious metals. While amounts vary from day to day, month to month, on the average, three billion credits of new wealth passes through my hands each day. Yes, three billion a day. Each month, we add a trillion credits to our empire's wealth.

"Where does it go? Not to you, the citizens of the empire. Rather, it gets divided up among the corporations, who use the funds as they desire. We citizens receive no direct benefit from all this wealth. In the past century, my records show that the corporations received over five hundred trillion credits worth of gold, silver, gems, and so on. None of that wealth was ever passed down to the citizens of the empire, though some was given to these so called owners of the corporations, such as Billionaire Phillip Soros. The fat-cats got richer, the corporations grew wealthier, but us lowly citizens got nothing.

"In fact, wages paid by the major corporations today are the same as they were a century ago. Ignoring the slight change forced on them with the arrival of giants and dwarves. You heard me. Your monthly stipend today is the same as it was one hundred years ago. Yet, during that time, the corporations added over five hundred trillion credits to their bank accounts. Until this recording, almost no one has known the complete picture.

"Here's a bit of history for you. Over two centuries ago when there were such things as countries on Earth, each country had their own paper money. Called fiat money, none was based upon anything of value, such as gold or silver. In the United States, the country that used to occupy our part of the continent, their money began by being based on gold. That was three centuries ago. To obtain more money, rather than obtain more gold, silver, or gems, they dropped that standard, turning their bills into fiat money. Thus, they could print billions more bills backed by nothing of intrinsic value. Three centuries ago, one of their bills called a dollar could buy one hundred cents worth of product. By two centuries ago, they printed so many more dollars, that one dollar could only buy one cent worth of product. They continued printing more bills until truckloads of the bills could buy a cent's worth of product. That's when countries collapsed, and the corporations took control of Earth.

"Today, the corporations continue adding vast wealth in gold, silver, and gems, but none of that is passed on to you, the citizens of the empire. One would think that one of our credits should be able to purchase vastly more product in today's world than, say a hundred years ago. Yet it hasn't. The scale of corporate greed is almost incomprehensible. Who can even count to a million, let alone trillions of credits?

"But the situation is far worse. Our corporations did nothing to prevent the armless telepath mutation agent from being used in countless terrorist attacks. Others have tried to profit off using it to make and sell human telepaths to other worlds. Disgusting? Yes, but it's much worse. With last month's pandemic mutation agent, we see that whole worlds can be affected. Thank god it wasn't the armless telepath agent used in the pandemic or few of us would be left alive.

"A decade ago, the other planets, moons, and stations of the Sol Empire passed laws preventing any of the Galactic Doll mutants from ever settling on their worlds. And they were right to fear these agents. Just look what has happened to the citizens of Earth."

The camera zoomed in on his face. He spoke softly, drawing attention. "From secret sources, I've learned that the armless telepath agent has now infected someone from a totally different civilization, that of Azizi-C. Yes, the Federation of Planets should now be very worried about the spread of this terrible agent. Rumor has it that they may soon decide to blow up Earth, destroying three million of us mutants and all supplies of all these mutation agents, probably by a series of well-placed nukes.

"As I understand it, the final decision hasn't been made, but we can't wait for the bombs to drop to take action. Hopping a shuttle to Brussels or Pylon or any of the moons and stations of our empire isn't an option. None will let you land. In short, there's nowhere to flee to.

"So what do we do? We must retake control of Earth back from the greedy corporations, hold them accountable, and destroy all these awful mutation agents. We'll even have to go house to house, confiscating the red syringes GMed has given to key individuals. We must show the Federation that Earthlings can become responsible people and remove this gargantuan threat to the entire Federation of Planets.

"To that end, as of today, I've declared a Holy War against the greedy corporations of Earth. Wealth must be passed down to the ordinary citizen of our empire. These terrible mutation agents must be destroyed. We must prove to the Federation representatives that we don't deserve to be obliterated.

"As a start, some in Galactic Mining have terminated one of the largest fat-cats, the Billionaire Phillip Soros. He's become fertilizer for our much needed crops. It's time for you to step up. Take arms. Take back control of your world before the Federation blows it up. To prove we in GMine are serious about this, each month after I tally up the newfound wealth delivered to us, I'll divide that up among all citizens of the Sol Empire. Expect to see your fair share of new credits deposited automatically into your accounts later today. More will come each month. It's time to take back your world.

"Finally, a note to those still in power. Don't try to attack me or GMine personnel. For years, I and I alone know where all the incoming gold, silver, gems, and other precious metals are being stored. If anything happens to me, that immense wealth be lost. Further, if I don't send a specific code each day, a nuke will detonate, destroying trillions of credits worth of precious goods.

"Let's work together. Make Earth great, again. That is all."

The video ended. I inhaled. Had I held my breath throughout? No, too long.

"Well, that explains the dead body in the disposal, Ashley. So how soon are you putting this on the news?"

Russell sighed. "Now. I've no choice. If I don't, an accompanying note said they'd hack into the video feeds and display it directly."

He pressed a button, sending it off to all GEnt stations across the empire.

"Of course," he said, "now what do we do?"

"Find out who is leaking critical information about the Federation plans for Earth," I said. "That video could cause widespread panic."

"At least we're still safe," Deanna said, wiping her brow. "I've added even more food supplies to the Friendship. The duplicate ship, the Salvation, is flight worthy, but work continues on the interior. If pressed, we could use it to escape."

"Frankly," Russell said, "I'm worried about riots breaking out. Who's going to be in control? Certainly not the Chicago police. Maybe the Local Defense Force, but who's going to order them into action?"

"I'll speak to Helen. She might still have enough pull to get the LDF into action. I know nothing about Galactic Mining. Is he right about all the gold, silver, and gems?" I asked.

"I believe so. GEnt receives a monthly allotment of credits from GMine. I know GPan authorizes the distributions," Russell said.

With that, Ashley and I headed home. By the time we arrived, many watched the video, which continued to be replayed every hour. Not surprising, I found Helen and Casper waiting for us in my living room.

"Have you seen—" Helen said, her face quite pale.

I interrupted her. "Yes, Russell showed it to us before we headed here. Shocking. Is Kirk right about the enormous wealth coming in each month?"

Casper smiled. "You bet. But I had no idea it was this large. Each month, GMine used to send me as the CFO of the empire-wide GD a voucher for our share of the credits. I'd then break it down into the shares for each planet-wide GD corporation, who in turn would parcel it out to all the local GD corporations. Each month, I usually wrote out a vouchers for around one hundred twenty-five billion credits, sending one to each of our two dozen empire worlds. Earth's Moscow's GD took theirs and divided it into smaller vouchers for around ten billion credits for each local GD corporation. So Kirk's numbers add up."

I shook my head in disbelief. What I hadn't known!

"Helen, can you get the LDF mobilized? We should post

constant guards around all GMed facilities and all medical centers," I said.

"I'll see what I can do about it. Soros appointed a new head of GD. If I were him, I'd abandon the post and go into hiding," she said.

We laughed, and I said, "Okay. Do what you can. If you can't, I'll check with General Bev. Maybe she can post some infantry soldiers. I know they disbanded the army, but..."

"Hey," Casper interrupted. "How about finding out who leaked the fact Admiral Skaggs is considering destroying Earth?"

"Yeah, that's what I intend to do. I thought Mondays were bad, but now maybe Wednesdays are even worse!" I exhaled deeply.

They left. Ashley and I headed to my Senior Investigator's office. Once there, Jie and Ward had seen the news. Between them, they had many questions for me.

"Look, right now, our most important action is to find out who is leaking information. I'm certain someone on the Kanika is responsible. Both of you, drop all else and see what you can uncover. I've got to see to new security measures. Unless I'm completely wrong, we're about to see all manner of civil unrest and riots, particularly against the major corporations and the medical centers."

"You got it, boss. But Ambassador Commander L'Grina is waiting in your office. She says it's urgent. Arrived two minutes before you did," Jie said.

Without asking, Ashley removed my cloak. I smiled and headed on into my side office, where the Sixth Invader ambassador waited for me. As usual, she didn't use her disguise device. Her light grey skin, massive bosom, and six-fingered hands were plainly visible. She rose when I entered.

"You're looking a bit haggard, Molly. So sorry about Sam and Matt. I've talked to our science officers about it. They think the mutation agent will revive them. Still, what a mess your world has."

"Ambassador, good to see you, too. God, I thought I hated Mondays, but now I hate Wednesdays, too. Soon, I'll be hating all days!"

We both laughed, breaking the ice.

She asked, "Has your people reached any decisions about how to deal with the mass mutations? We see your society as being now very similar to ours, an optimum one, where males know their place at home and women are in charge."

"It's a fricken mess, L'Grina. One grand mess. Have you seen the latest news?"

"Yes. I warned you about the Federation of Planets. Your world is facing annihilation at their hands. Honestly, I'm amazed it took them this long to strike you. Is it true that a citizen of Azizi-C has been mutated?"

"Yes, Admiral Skaggs' niece, Bonita Valdez. She's at my place recovering. So yeah, our mutation agent affects other aliens, but likely only those whose race is close to ours—DNA wise."

"I thought so. I took the liberty of informing Home World about this latest development. Expect Sixth Invader support. Within the hour, three Sixth Invader battleships will arrive to support Earth. If the Kanika tries to obliterate you, we'll destroy them. That's what allies do for each other."

I chuckled. "I didn't know we were allies."

"As I said, your society is now almost a mirror of ours. We've traveled the galaxy extensively, and your world is the only one similar to ours, if only we can get your men into their rightful roles. And your women into theirs, too."

I shook my head. "I best let Admiral Skaggs know about this."

Ambassador L'Grina grinned. "Don't bother. I've already notified him. Don't want him opening fire on our ships when they arrive. Not unless he launches an attack on Earth."

"Thanks. God, what a day. What else can go wrong," I joked.

"Oh, just so you know, when our ships arrive, one of our negotiators will be contacting this Kirk Alcott fellow and seeing what kind of arrangements can be made. I'd like to keep violence to a minimum, if we can. Why fight if you can reach agreements, eh?" She grinned.

"Keep me informed. I've got to arrange protections for

all GMed facilities around Earth."

"With that, she left, while I dug out my phone. Soon, the image of my sister appeared.

"Hi, Bev. You're looking good."

"Hey, back at'cha. Heard the news?" I said so. "I figured ya'd be callin' us. Gail thought you'd wait until tomorrow. So I win. You want me to mobilize soldiers?"

"Yeah, Bev, I do. Helen's trying to mobilize the many LDFs, but we both know your soldiers are ten times better, even if they're all male dolls now."

She laughed. "Yeah, they're complaining about the boobs and heels. All hated that we got disbanded. Still, I can reach many of them. I plan to have a hundred guarding your linguist conference, but I'll see if I can't get them to watch over GMed facilities in as many cities as we can cover. Can't watch them all, though. Oh, Gail says hi. We're both hoping Sam and Matt pull through. Any word on them? If this all goes south, we'll make damn sure we get their stasis units brought onto the Friendship. You don't have to worry about that."

"Thanks, sis. I appreciate all you're doing. Oh, plan to drop by tonight. Bonita Valdez is out of her coma. She has quite a story to tell everyone. Say, can you call all our sisters and invite them over tonight? I'm so damn busy I best not take time off to make the calls."

"You got it. Cya tonight. Bye."

For a moment, I wondered how my extended family would take the news that Bonita used to be Ted Billings. I checked on the other investigations.

Ward had no news about who and why the Liatos-D Ambassador Hypnos Kalakos wanted to have the Wang brothers sell telepaths to Blackwell. Jie traced the giant who injected Tia Sanchez with the agent to a visiting transport. He'd come and left within three days. I already knew that Helen and Casper had no further news on why a military group of giants on Liatos-D wanted to damage our food production in Iowa. Three strikes. My only hope now rested on our two Liatos-D ambassadors, Thedra and Biton Demarchis. I decided to give them another day before I hounded them further.

Ashley and I headed home. Deep snow slowed me way down. She kept a steadying arm around me. After that pandemic, most of Earth's men had to wear similar tall heels. As I slipped along, I wondered if being annihilated might not be so bad after all. I could see L'Grina's point. Hobbled, our men would have a much easier time handling domestic duties, while women who wore flats took over. I shook my head, banishing such alien thoughts.

At home, Ashley headed into the kitchen to make supper, while Sherry and Bonita summoned me into my home study.

"We're just about to get access to Aaron Strawn's computer," Sherry said.

"Okay, unscrew the bottom," Bonita said. "Easy does it. We don't dare jar the mass storage device. Good. Now see that. Dingo's Bottoms, I can't point."

"You mean the storage cell? Yes, got it," Sherry said.

"Right. Unhook the connector but do it very gently. Okay. Now on your computer, download the replacement code you wrote down. Got it off the Dark Web. Right. That one."

To me, Bonita said, "We're just replacing the code block that handles biometrics and passwords at login time. Good, Sherry. Copy it onto that thumb drive. Now, go over to the other opened up laptop, insert the drive. No, don't turn it on yet. Where's that special long cable I asked for. Yeah, that one. Hook one end onto Strawn's storage unit, but be gentle with it."

I watched Sherry skillfully following Bonita's orders, but I sensed her intense frustration at not being able to do this for herself.

Bonita leaned over, picked up a pencil between her teeth, and used it to point to where Sherry was to connect the other end of the cable. "Yeah, that's the spot. Carefully, though. Good. Now power it up. We're going to copy that replacement code block over to Strawn's storage block, wiping out his stored biometrics and password. When it then boots up, it'll ask if you want to install your own biometrics and passwords. Always say no."

Sherry carried out her instructions efficiently. We three

watched as Aaron Strawn's laptop booted up. Sherry replied "no" to both requests. No biometrics. No password.

"Say 'No password' when it asks for your password. That's the initial default on all new laptops from Bela Prime. Lame, if you ask me," Bonita said.

We watched as the computer booted up. Aaron wasn't much on security. Nor was he a big computer user. He had one user file on the machine. My Journal.

"Open My Journal," Sherry said.

Up came his diary, positioned to the last entry he'd made. Our eyes scanned the text, looking for clues.

"Oh, my god!" Bonita said. I glanced at her face and saw her brows had risen while her eyes, huge. "He's found one of the missing rogue robots. Maybe even the one that killed me!"

```
At  the  combined  ball  with  the
admirals  and  generals.  Bored  and
avoided  by  all.  So  made  a  game  of
sensing  the  minds  and  emotions  of
each     person     there.     Fun.
Entertaining.  Amazing  crap  these
people  are  thinking.  Wait.  One
admiral  had  no  thoughts  at  all.
Strange.  Spent  the  rest  of  the  night
trying  to  sense  his  mind.  Nothing.
Got  to  thinking  about  something  Ted
once     told     me.     About     robots
indistinguishable  from  humans.  Could
this   be   one   of   them?   Gotta
investigate  this  admiral.  Asked
around.  Such  robots  don't  exist
anywhere  in  the  Federation  of
Planets.  Hey,  got  news  for  them.  One
does.  He's  an  admiral,  too.  Or
should  it  be  an  it?  Plan  to  bring
this  up  at  the  next  full  Senate
session.  Maybe  someone  knows  about
this.  Still...
```

"I wish he'd mentioned which admiral," I said. "He asked around. That's probably what alerted the robot who killed him before the next session. As if we don't have enough problems... I'm not sure if I hate Mondays or Wednesdays more."

Chapter 8 Chaos Arrives

At supper, we exchanged news, mostly mine. Bonita's complexion look healthier, her smile, bright. I knew her therapy sessions benefitted her, but I longed to be delivering them instead of my empire duties. Naturally, the discussion then centered on the challenge given by Galactic Mining.

The sheer amount of new wealth being added to our combined empire each month amazed us.

"Wish we had some of that, Mom," Isabella said. "That would have sure helped. Then, we wouldn't have had to accept these high paying jobs just to save enough for the future."

"Hey, by Azizi-C standards, Isabella, your salary as a telepath and linguist is tremendous," Bonita said. "Try more like fifty thousand credits a year."

Tia said hesitantly, "I'm still not sure being so handicapped is worth the million credits a year. Life is still scary, even with all your therapy, Celeste."

"Super challenging's more like," added Bonita. "But hey, we're alive. That's what counts. Stop and think how. But I'd like to get all the cures, just not until the conference is over. No way am I going to miss it. Right Tia, Angelina?"

"That's what I came for," Tia said, "but I had no idea what it would cost me."

"It's not so bad," Angelina said. "With the salaries we make, I can retire in a few more years and live comfortably on my savings. Get the cures then. I hope..."

A loud explosion shook the tea cups on the table.

"What the hell?" I said.

"What was that?" asked Bonita, whose face paled instantly. "A bomb?"

"Are—are we under attack?" asked Tia.

I sensed how fragile her grip on life without arms actually was. The explosion amplified her fears. From experience, I knew it took lots of time, patience, and practice to get used to such a life.

"Bet my phone will ring," I said, trying to lighten up the

suddenly somber mood. I dug out my phone, plopping it on the floor, a toe waiting to accept the call. Everyone watched me, before several chuckled.

Ashley played with her phone, announcing, "A half foot of new snow is down. More is expected tonight and tomorrow. Then the deep freeze comes. Hey, supposed to warm up in time for the conference. That's something."

My phone rang.

"Hi, Helen. What's up?" I put it on speaker-phone.

"Explosion in the GMed skyscraper downtown. Bev's soldiers are just now arriving there. Police are on the scene along with some first responders. You best head there and lead the investigation. I'm still trying to get our LDF activated, but the men say they can't walk in this snow in their heels. Wimps."

We both nervously chuckled. After ending the call, Ashley appeared with my cloak, and Sherry had their parkas in hand.

"Best wear my boots tonight. Ashley will be my hands. Let's get going."

"Hey, keep us informed," Celeste called out as we headed to the front door.

My fleece lined boots kept me warm, though I needed their arms around me to keep me upright. Once on the MTES, travel improved. Few were out in this snowstorm. As we approached the fifty-story GMed building, I observed a hive of activity. Two army EMACs landed, their green-clad soldiers fanning out forming a perimeter. I watched them slipping and sliding in their heels, too. I didn't need telepathy to know these men cursed their mutations.

Emergency workers trained two spotlights on the north side of the building. There, a blacken hole on one floor attracted everyone's attention. I relaxed a bit. The whole complex hadn't been destroyed. As we neared the soldiers, one recognized me.

"Ah, Senior Investigator Parkinson. Good to see you. Someone detonated a bomb on the pharmacy floor. Probably trying to destroy all the mutation agent samples. That's all we know so far."

"Thanks. Any injured? Any culprits?"

"Two night orderlies are dead, four nurses wounded. That's what they're telling us. They found what remains of the bomber. According to one nurse, he or she walked up to the pharmacy which was closed and locked. They said nothing, but blew themselves up while facing the pharmacy doors. That's all we know. Too bad we couldn't have gotten here sooner."

"Had you, why, you might have been blown up too," I said.

"Say," he said, "is what we're hearing from that GMine CFO person right? All that wealth and we got none of it?"

"Yeah, I checked with other local CFOs. Everything he said is true. Greedy corporations, but hell, we always knew they were corrupt and greedy," I said.

"You got that right. I didn't want to be a solider, but GD insisted. Can't live on nothing in this world."

"I understand. I lucked out and got to be a PI, only I had to have a little computer hacking help."

We both chuckled. Ashley gave me a funny look, which I ignored. Sherry already knew that Ted had hacked into GD's computer and changed my career to PI from soldier.

Since the bomber was dead, I had nothing I could do on the site. We headed home. After telling the others what we'd learned, I called Helen and told her. Most, she already knew.

"No one is now in charge," she said. "Expect more chaos until someone regains control."

Even though it was a school night, Nikita wasn't yet in bed. I found Isabella and her practicing diapering Nikita's Galactic Doll. My youngest daughter asked, "Mom, will Dad and Matt be okay? Will some madman bomb the Med Center where they're at? Can we bring them home? Aunt Deanna says if we have to evacuate in her spaceship, we'll bring them with us. Can't we do it now?"

"I don't think anyone will bomb a Med Center. Besides, they are better off there, where doctors are watching over them. Would you like to go see them tomorrow after school?"

She brightened up. "Oh, yes. Let's." She frowned. "But I expect they are still in their comas. I keep trying to talk to them, but no luck yet."

"I miss them too, honey."

"Are you going to marry Bonita?"

"If I have to, I will. I'll do anything to keep you kids safe. Now it's way past your bedtime."

I tucked her in and kissed her forehead.

The next day over breakfast, I watched the news along with everyone else. Several other GMed facilities in other cities had also been attacked. In each case, the perp tried to get access to the mutation agents. I learned that GMed and the Med Centers kept these mutation agent in a secure vault, one that was fire proof and bomb proof. I smiled when images of Chicago GMed's vault was lifted out of the ruins via crane and opened, only to find no damage had been done.

In Budapest, someone had left their vault ajar. So while the bomber died, the explosion released the agents, putting forty doctors, nurses, and aids into mutation comas. Since the various forms of the agent were stored in this vault, speculation suggested the dominant form would mutate these victims, the armless telepath version. Sad, since these were the very medical personal dedicated to saving lives. Ah well.

Just as I was about to turn it off and head to work, live images appeared. Hundreds turned out to protest the greed of the corporations. Some carried signs demanding a cut of all new wealth. In a way, I found the protest comical. The protestors kept slipping in the deep snow, some falling. Thus, I knew most were male, since the pandemic repaired most women's feet.

GEnt then panned away. "Protests have sprung up in all major cities around the world. The larger Galactic Medicine facilities are now being guarded by ex-soldiers from our First Infantry Division, reactivated by General Blythe. Further disruptions are expected."

With that, I turned it off. Ashley slipped my cloak over me. Sherry arrived, and we three headed to the Senior Investigations office. I appreciated their support, as we trudged through even deeper snow, as the snow continued to fall.

"I believe it's warming up," Sherry commented as we struggled to reach the MTES.

We'd just gotten to my office and switched my boots for my pumps so I had access to my feet when Ambassadors Thedra and Biton Demarchis arrived, stomping the snow off their boots and shaking their large parkas free of the white stuff. He carried a briefcase.

"Ah, there you are. We have the information you requested," he said formally, though the words came from his language translation box on his waist. I couldn't understand his speech. For a moment, I marveled at Bonita, Tia, Isabella, Bernardo, and Angelina. They had a knack for languages, something I certainly didn't.

They followed me into my office, furnished in standard stainless steel table, chairs, and desk. Modern LED lighting added to its sterile appearance. In its defense, my office was outfitted just like most all corporation offices, save I didn't have a fancy desk.

"Pull up some chairs. I can't do that easily for you. Thanks for coming out in this miserable weather," I said, tossing my head from side to side to get my long hair out of the way so I could sit down. I really needed to take time off to get a substantial trim. My jest brought a brief smile to their faces.

He placed several files on my desk, opening them for me, before speaking.

"First, the paramilitary group that sponsored the assault on your agriculture system in Iowa. They were hired by an elusive human male, who went by the name Blackheart—from Bela Prime he claimed. He gave them a complete schematic of the computer system and paid them five hundred thousand credits to carry out the sabotage. They were supposed to knock out all Midwestern agriculture computers, creating a severe food shortage. Why? Who knows. This Blackheart person doesn't seem to exist. Our CID unit can find no trace of him. He paid the militia group in untraceable credits. We hit a dead end. So it's back to you on this one.

"Next, we found the giant who detonated the bomb that killed your husband and son. Again, please accept our deepest sympathies. He was apprehended and interrogated. That's an image of him after our CID unit finished getting him to talk. He was hired by Senior Ambassador Sanura Fenuku of Zahra-

C. She gave him a complete dossier on you and your family, complete with when best to strike. He was supposed to have killed Nikita, too, but she wasn't with the two. As you requested, our CID unit handled justice. He was terminated, to use your terminology. Again, we have no dealings with this Zahra-C Senior Ambassador. Back to you, as well.

"Ambassador Hypnos Kalakos was approached by an ambassador from Blackwell-C, who had heard Earth had armless telepath Galactic Dolls. He asked for images of some. Of course, all Dolls are very attractive, so this ambassador explained that the various barons who controlled Blackwell-C wanted to purchase some of these women to become their honored wives and baronesses. I'm afraid Hypnos didn't find anything amiss with this request and forwarded it to the Wang brothers, whom he'd once met. He presumed everything was legal and acceptable to everyone. Our CID unit is convinced he is otherwise blameless in this matter. He received no remuneration for his go-between efforts.

"Our CID unit apprehended the giant responsible for injecting Miss Tia Sanchez and then dumping her body in the alley. Under interrogation, he confessed that Major Bertrand Blumenthal, the commander of the New Light deep space exploration ship based out of Brussels, Tau Ceti, hired him to do it. The major paid him ten thousand credits to do it while she was Earth-side to attend the linguist conference. The CID unit also terminated the giant. Her own commander had her mutated. Therefore, the rest is up to you."

"Incredible. Thank you both very much. Yes, I'll take it from here. I'm glad there isn't some grand conspiracy going on, mostly greedy people," I said.

Ambassador Biton smiled. "Indeed. I, too, was worried. I do hope this doesn't affect our relations with Earth and the Sol Empire."

I grinned. "No, I can't see how it could. Thank you. What a relief to know we're not enemies."

Both returned my smile. Thedra asked, "All these protests—is this normal? What's going to happen? Will everyone's salary be raised? Many of our constituents have been asking about that."

"Normal? Heck no. As Senior Judge, I expect to soon have to make a ruling on the salary-wealth issue. Our corporations have been greedy."

She laughed. "Aren't all corporations greedy?"

With that, they rose and left.

"I've texted Ward," Ashely said. "He's filled out an arrest warrant for Bertrand Blumenthal." Her phone beeped. "He's off to make the arrest now. Taking a large security force with him. Next?"

"Make an appointment with the ambassadors from Zahra-C. Thema and Mert Makalani, if I remember right. Make copies of the file on Senior Ambassador Sanura to give to them. I need to talk to Tia right away."

"To figure out how to punish her commander?"

"Yeah, something like that. Sherry can assist me. Back as soon as I can. Have Ward put him in a holding cell until I get back."

Back out into the snowstorm trudged Sherry and me. I found Isabella working with Tia, practicing using her feet as hands.

"Hi. Tia, we've found out who hired the giant to inject you with the mutation agent."

"Wow! Who did it?" she asked suddenly perking up.

"Major Bertrand Blumenthal, the New Light commander. Ward is off arresting him as we speak."

"My boss? This can't be possible. He's offered me a million credit per year contract if I return as the ship's linguist. There must be some mistake."

"Well, I'll find out for sure. That's my job. If it does turn out to be him, then I'll have to pass judgement on him. The question becomes what sort of punishment fits this crime? Ideas?"

"No, none. It's awful trying to live like this. Isabella has been working with me, but it's awful. No disrespect to you, though."

I laughed. "None taken. It's the pits being like this. But never give up. Never let external things control our lives."

She flashed a fleeting smile, but I knew how hard adapting to a life without arms and hands was. Sherry and I headed back to my office, while I pondered the fate of this major. Should I consult GPan on Brussels? Or perhaps our Admiral Aldo Rossi? I decided to contact our admiral.

Back at my office, I place the call, but had to wait nearly a half hour before he appeared on my comm center monitor.

"Hi, Admiral Rossi. I've a serious question for you. Has to do with a judicial matter. Suppose one of your majors who commands a deep space exploration ship hired a giant to inject one of his crew members with the armless telepath mutation agent—against her will, of course. Is this a matter for the Senior Judge to determine the penalty for the major or should it be up to the space force—you guys?"

"That's a serious charge. But yes, if proven, the space fleet has jurisdiction. Why? Has this occurred?"

"Yes. I will investigate it on this end first. If proven, I'll send you the details and the major. Right now, I'm helping the poor victim learn to adapt. Not fun."

He saluted and ended the call. Now I waited. Mid-afternoon, Ward ushered Major Bertrand Blumenthal into my office, sitting him across from me.

"What's the meaning of this arrest? How dare you!" he blurted.

I observed him. Proper military uniform and discipline. Slightly overweight, but tall. His stern face probably struck fear in his underlings, especially his eyes that tried to burn holes in my face.

I had Ashley slide the folder of proof over to him. This time, I touched his mind as he looked over the incriminating documents. I probably didn't need my telepathy to ascertain his guilt. His face flushed. He fidgeted and squirmed in his chair.

"My only question, major, is why do this to your ship's linguist?"

"Damn woman wouldn't have it done. Everyone knows how incredibly valuable having a telepath as a linguist is when meeting aliens on new worlds."

"Thank you for telling me. I'll let Tia know the reason. Ward, take him to New O'Hare along with this folder. Admiral Rossi will send for them. That is all."

97

Ward ushered him out. Security guards bolted restraints on his arms and legs, before leading him out of the building. I placed another call to Admiral Rossi.

"Yeah, they'll be at New O'Hare in about a half-hour. Documents, too. Would you let me know what his punishment is? His victim would like to know."

He agreed to that. One down, one to go. The arranged appointment with our local Zahra-C ambassadors was set for three o'clock. So out into the snow we went. Ah, the snow had stopped; warmer air started the melting process, particularly on the MTES canopy.

Ambassadors Thema and Mert Makalani welcomed us into their office. At first, I thought we entered a greenhouse. High humidity and green plants covered their office. Both were my height, so without my heels they probably stood six feet. Both had black hair, though hers was held in a tight bun. She wore a green dress with a forest of trees embroidered on it, but she also wore the nylon hose that Ambassador Sanura Fenku tried to get me to wear. Mert's head was elongated and tall, as though someone had sort of squished it upwards twice its normal size, indicative of his upper class status.

"Welcome, Mrs. Parkinson. Your aide told us you've proof of a crime?" Mert said.

Ashley undid my cloak and laid the folder on the desk. Unlike the sterile offices of corporations, their mahogany desk welcomed me. Plush, soft chairs rounded out the room, though there must have been a hundred or more plants competing for this office space.

"As you've probably heard, via a bomb, a giant killed my husband and son. I had our ambassadors track the culprit down on Liatos-D. Their CID unit arrested and interrogated him. This folder documents what they uncovered. It says Ambassador Sanura Fenku hired him to kill them. She provided a complete dossier on my family, including the best time to kill them."

Thema inhaled sharply. "Mert, she's one of our Senior Ambassadors on Bela Prime!"

"Can we trust this information?" Mert said. "If I know the giants, they beat a confession out of him. Still, thank you for bringing this to our attention. We'll forward it to the proper Zahra-C authorities, who will thoroughly investigate these charges. If they prove correct, they will handle her punishment, unless you wish her to be brought here to stand trial."

"No, I think it best for your people to adjudicate her guilt and punishment. However, I'd like to know what happens."

"Of course. It may take some time, but you can be assured we will keep you fully informed," Mert said.

"Quite a lot of plants in here," I said.

"Indeed. A bit of home for us," Thema said, a broad smile on her face.

"Might I ask," Mert said, "what's happening with these bombings and protests?"

"Exposed greedy corporations. They've been keeping trillions of credits of new wealth to themselves, passing nothing on to the citizens of our empire. Until recently, none of us even knew about it. Now people are protesting against that practice. As far as the bombings go, some want to handle the widespread availability of these terrible mutation agents by destroying them via bombs. Honestly, better ways exist."

We chatted a bit longer before Ashley and I left. By the time I got home, I was starving, having missed lunch. While others worked on making supper, I had to tell everyone the news of the day, which was quite a lot.

"So there's no giant conspiracy against us," Isabella said.

"No. Each attack seems dis-related from the others. In a way, that's a blessing. However, all these bombings and protests aren't likely to sit well with Admiral Skaggs. We've a very volatile Earth, not conducive to preventing the spread of these mutation agents to other worlds."

Only the call for supper altered that somber thought.

Chapter 9 Follow the Money

On February 9, Ward called me at breakfast.

"Boss, I'm in, thanks to a little help from Ambassadors Thema and Mert Makalani."

"In? Not following you."

"Trying to find the leak in Admiral Skaggs' people. We needed a complete list of all personnel currently on the Kanika. Well, they used their connections and sent me that huge list. Are Piper Strawn's access codes on Bela Prime still valid? If so, I ought to have the leaker pinned down today."

I promised to check with her on my way to work. Escorted by Ashley and Sherry, I headed out into the frosty morning. According to the weather report, a warm front promised to remove the last of the snow in time for Valentine's Day and the big linguistic conference.

"I can't divulge those codes." Piper explained the situation to us. I'd explained why I was there and what we needed. "I can only give them to the next Sol Empire Senior Ambassador. But there's nothing to prevent me from coming along with you and using the computer terminals for you."

"Oh! Thanks." My face must have reflected the sudden change from gloom to relief. She smiled and grabbed her parka.

Later, we entered my investigator's office. Ward and Jie had several computers correlating the thousands of names of those onboard to known criminals and such.

"Ah, Ambassador Strawn. Good morning," Ward said. "Molly filled you in on our project?"

"She has. I can't release the passwords, but nothing prevents me from helping. Tell me what you need," she said.

I let Ward handle this. After all, I did assign this project to him.

"Okay. I've got this list of all personnel currently on the Kanika. What I propose to do is search finance records looking for any one of these people who has recently had a large deposit to their account. That should narrow down the suspect pool."

"Now that's something I can help with. Where do I sit? What computer? Has to be a secure one. Protocol Ten. Top secret," Piper said.

After getting started, I saw a light in Piper's eyes. She smiled and said, "I feel useful again. Thanks, Molly."

Ashley brought me a tea. I sat and watched the three automating the search process, narrowing down the suspect pool from over four thousand to a few, I hope. This gave me time to think about the actual situation. Would Admiral Skaggs actually destroy Earth just to prevent the spread of these mutation agents? Yes, some uses were unethical if not illegal, but these same agent might be saving the life of Sam and Matt.

Then, I realized that these mutation agents themselves were neither good nor evil. People's use of them dictated the result. Memories of my initial attempts to convince those in power that these weren't a deterrent swept over me, reminding me of past adventures. How could I argue the survival of Earth with Admiral Skaggs and the Federation of Planets? Instinctively, I knew it had to be along this line. The agents themselves were neutral.

I couldn't put off letting him know that I would marry his niece. And soon. Before the linguist conference. As soon as the three-day meetings were done, the five hundred attendees would board flights for home. At that point, my guess is he'd have to act—one way or another. Best be married and secure before then. Besides, with all the protests going on, ignoring the scattered bombings of GMed facilities, there might not be time to do that after the convention.

Trouble was Bonita. She'd only had a few days to get used to being handicapped and to start learning alternate ways. I knew months of practice, failures, and encouragements were needed. While in her last lifetime she'd been similarly handicapped, that was then and with a different body.

Taking Bonita up to visit Uncle Baba Skaggs and getting married in his presence required both confidence and competence on her part. Right now, she didn't have either. And that ignored any fear, nervousness, embarrassment, or terror she might feel while facing her uncle. Yet, this had to be done. And soon. I promised myself I'd talk to Bonita tonight about making the trip to the Kanika.

Ward pulled me out of my thoughts. He said, "Well, this is no good. It'll take us months to check all these. Boss, we have to find the planet on which the person banks before we can enter their ID and access their records. We don't have that kind of time for this many."

"Agreed. So let's make some assumptions," I said. "First, let's look at all the officers. If that doesn't yield clues, broaden it to the top dignitaries onboard, like ambassadors. Save the enlisted personnel until last. In all likelihood, the leaker must be someone who has access to the information—his top people."

Late afternoon, the searches finally yielded a possibility. Eleven days ago, Captain Cesaro Luna received a two hundred thousand credits deposit. The back trace on the funds showed it came from Senior Ambassador Sanura Fenku via the local ambassador currently on the Kanika, Ambassador Godana Obote, also of Zahra-C. This wasn't actual proof of collusion, but sufficient for me to bring this up before Admiral Skaggs, which I vowed to do tomorrow.

That evening, I held a frank talk with Bonita. "Look, tomorrow, I'm going to have to pay a visit to your Uncle Baba. I've got a potential spy in his crew that needs to be investigated. I know he wants to see you and be reassured you're doing okay. Also, I know he wants to give the bride away at our wedding. Things could get very hectic right after the linguistic conference, so honestly, we best get married before Valentine's Day and the conference. We could do it tomorrow when I visit him, if you're up to it."

Bonita sighed and slumped into a chair. "I'm scared, Molly. I feel so helpless. It's going to be humiliating to have him see me like this, especially when I can't do much for myself yet. Embarrassed or not, I have to do this, especially since he's promised to spare your entire family and friends along with me—if he has to destroy Earth, that is. I don't really have other options. Just realize I'm freaked out by it."

"Hey, you'll have me by your side. We can do this

together. Six months from now, why, you'll be an old pro at doing everything. But right now, it's frightening."

"Dingo's Crap! You've a penchant for understatement. Frightening? Nah, try terrifying."

We laughed, breaking the tension she'd built up.

"So who should we bring to our wedding on the Kanika?" I asked.

"I'll be nervous enough with Uncle Baba there. You pick, just not too many, please," Bonita said.

"How about Bev and Gail? A little protection for us, just in case."

"Good thinking. They're like we're going to be. I like that. Won't feel so—well, you know."

"I know. Not the traditional marriage. Okay, I'll call them now and set it up. Deanna will probably want to come along as our pilot."

I called Bev. She said, "Well, it's about damned time. Gail and I had a pool on how long it would take for you two to get hitched."

I chuckled. "So who won? Or should I ask?"

"Gail. Say, Leslie'll want to dress you both up. I'll check with her and work your gowns out. Probably bring them with me when we come by tomorrow. Bye."

Bonita flushed. "I hope she brings easy to handle gowns. I can barely function in these. But I do like how they encase our shoulders. No chance of accidentally pulling it down off our boobs. We don't dare wear strapless gowns, right?"

"I'm not that gutsy." I laughed.

The next morning, I called Admiral Skaggs and told him I might have found his leak and that Bonita and I wanted him to marry us. His frown changed to a grin. He set the time for one o'clock.

Given his okay, I called Leslie and Deanna, both of whom came over to fuss over us. So did Nikita and Isabella. Bernardo came by to congratulate us as well.

"I like figured you two would like get hitched, so I like made these specially for you," Leslie said.

She'd outdone herself this time. We both wore white

satin gowns and matching heels. As expected, the top covered our shoulders completely, guaranteeing the gowns couldn't be pulled down by any kind of accident. Glittering rhinestones covered the bodices. The gowns fit tightly down to our waists, where many pleats allowed us complete freedom of motion with our legs and feet. Giant bows fit securely around our waists.

Once dressed, I looked at Bonita and said, "I think I'm getting the better deal here."

She flushed and giggled. After hug presses from Nikita and Isabella, we bundled up for the trip to New O'Hare. Ward joined us, bringing along the documents he'd put together. Ashley and Sherry met us at the spaceport. After Leslie said goodbye, our small group boarded the Friendship, Deanna as pilot.

As the giant Kanika came into view, Bonita said, "I'm getting really nervous! What if I stumble? It's so hard to get back up. My stomach is a complete knot. I don't think I can do this. What's Uncle Baba going to think seeing me like this?"

"Like his gorgeous niece. If he doesn't, I'll kick him where it counts. You look beautiful, Bonita. Together, we'll be fine."

A soldier met us at the docking bay, which dwarfed our ship. Over a hundred transports could dock here. Several held various types of deep space transports. He took us to the same conference room that I'd been in before when I'd had the premonition of the Sixth Invaders triggering bombs.

"The admiral will be with you shortly," he said and left us alone.

Bonita whispered, "Did you see all those people staring at me, at us? I feel so embarrassed, so scared, so helpless."

"We do look very different from them, especially because these gowns broadcast our lack of arms. I used to slip my long hair over my shoulders, hiding empty shoulders. It's all right to be scared. In time, that helpless feeling will evaporate, but not anytime soon. Look, you spent what thirty-five years with arms and just a few days without them. These feelings are natural. And let's face it, people will stare at us. Our bodies are very different from theirs. It's the damned sympathy we can do without."

Admiral Skaggs knocked and entered. Today, he wore his official dress uniform. Various medals contrasted with the stark white.

"Uncle Baba!" Bonita gushed.

She rose and a giant grin formed on his face as he moved close to her. He hugged her tightly.

"Butterfly, you look years younger and even more beautiful."

"Thanks Uncle Baba."

"But are you doing okay? Surviving?"

"Perfectly healthy, but I'll admit I'm nervous about what you'll think of me now. I feel so helpless, Uncle Baba, but Molly says to give myself time to adjust. Have Mom and Dad heard about me?"

"I can't imagine how you must feel, Butterfly. Yes, we had a conversation about it three days ago. They're shocked, of course. While Azizi-C law prevents you from moving and living there any longer, you are allowed to visit. I know they'll want you to visit them as soon as you can. I had your apartment cleared out; your things packed up and shipped here. The transport is due to arrive the fifteenth. So you'll have all your possessions. Your parents charged me with making damned sure you are going to be all right. I told them she's marrying the best possible partner."

He turned to me. "You treat Butterfly right or you'll answer to me. Got that?"

I grinned. "Aye, sir. Before we have the ceremony, we have something for you. Ward, show him what we've uncovered."

The mood in the room changed, particularly as he scanned down the incriminating document.

When he finished, he said, "Damned sneaky Zahra-C people. Scoundrels. All of them. Big heads with tiny thoughts. We'll look into this immediately. If you'll excuse me, I want my people on this right now. Then, I'm going to give away my Butterfly. Mrs. Parkinson, you have to realize Bonita's been as close to my own daughter as can be. I'm so proud of her achievements, though I admit I lobbied long and hard to get her to join the space fleet. Now, she couldn't. But I do hope she can somehow continue to put her incredible knowledge to work. She's an electronics genius, too. Top of her class."

Bonita blushed. "Uncle Baba helped pay my tuition, too. My folks aren't wealthy."

"Good people, though," he said, as he left us alone again.

Ashley and Bev fussed over us, adjusting our hair and gowns. As our nervousness grew, Admiral Skaggs returned, this time with the Kanika's chaplain with him.

The minister spoke, but we listened to the monotone voice from the small box at his waist. "We'll conduct the ceremony in the CCC room. Everyone knows just how much Admiral Skaggs admires his niece. This is the highest honor he can do for you. After the brief ceremony, the reception party and dance will be in the ship's formal ballroom. Questions?"

Admiral Skaggs leaned towards my ear. "Remember what I said. No decision about Earth has yet been reached. If it goes south, what I promised still holds."

He put his arm around Bonita, escorting her to his CCC, while the chaplain and us followed them. I could tell he wasn't used to walking so slowly, but Bonita and I had no choice.

As we entered the room filled with his top executive officers and walls of monitors, I became nervous, too. Dozens of eyes stared at us. Even though I wasn't focusing my telepathy, I could sense the overall feeling of pity for Bonita and the Old Man. For her sake, I hoped Bonita's telepathy hadn't yet manifested itself.

That Admiral Skaggs cared deeply for his niece wasn't lost on anyone present. I also sensed many of his officers felt pity towards him—that he'd somehow lost his favorite niece— that she'd have a no more useful life. I felt like screaming, but smiled instead as Bev led me up to the two.

The ceremony didn't last long. After sharing a kiss, everyone clapped, while the chaplain led us off to the ballroom and reception. All his officers couldn't be off their posts at the same time. They came and went during the hour long event. Admiral Skaggs, however, spent the entire time with us, rather like a proud father I thought, though I could sense the pity and sorrow he felt. From his point of view, Bonita's promising live and career had just ended. Still, he danced with her and with me. Awkwardly, I might add, because none had ever been around or close with someone like us. So I was thankful for my sisters, who broke the ice by dancing with us first.

When Uncle Baba danced with me, he whispered. "I can give you at most two hours notice to get to your ship and lift off. Keep my Butterfly safe or I'll hunt you down."

Okay, it isn't everyday that I got a threat from an admiral. "She's now my butterfly. I won't let anything happen to her. Promise."

As the dance ended, the chaplain brought us our marriage documents and papers transferring Bonita's bank account on Azizi-C to the Sol Empire. Awkwardly, he tried to hand them to her.

Hastily, Bev stepped up and took them. "Thanks. I'll take them."

A bit later, I relaxed in the comfort of the Friendship, while Deanna handled the flight back to New O'Hare.

"I've never been so embarrassed in my whole life!" Bonita admitted, leaning her body into mine. "Everyone kept staring at me. Like I was a freak or something."

"You done good, kid," I said. "Relax. It's over. You're never going to have to go through something like that again."

"Good point. But we will, you know. Whenever we visit my parents. I don't know if I can face that."

I saw a change of topic would help. "So tell me, how come he calls you Butterfly?"

That brought a smile to her face. We chatted all the way home.

Once safely inside my home, Bev and Gail handed us a box of wedding presents—the kind that two women could use. As we looked inside at them, Bonita flushed and my face felt red hot, while Gail and Bev just giggled.
***

The next morning, Admiral Skaggs called. "Mrs. Parkinson, you were right. I owe you, again. Under questioning, he broke down and admitted everything. He's being tried for treason and will likely get life in prison. Once again, thank you."

"Welcome. I just hope you don't have to pay up anytime soon, if you know what I mean."

He chuckled and the call ended.

Chapter 10 Escalation

On the thirteenth while many deep space transports arrived from many Federation worlds brining hundreds to the linguistic conference, a dozen Sixth Invader cigar-shaped battleships and cruisers dropped out of hyperspace close to the Kanika. Admiral Rossi had been notified of their arrival time. In response, half the Sol Empire's fleet appeared around the Sixth Invaders' ships, protecting the Kanika. But within minutes, more Federation ships appeared. All this was carried live by GEnt.

I watched the display of arriving warships while eating breakfast. The contrast in shapes caught my eye. Grey cigars versus the silver delta wings of our fleet played out against the hexagonal tubes of the Federation ships. Earth wanted to survive. The Sixth Invaders wanted to help our unique society develop along the lines of their own. And the Federation? Lord knows what they had decided to do with Earth.

I doubt Chicago had ever had such tight security before. General Blythe pulled in around a thousand of her soldiers to guard the Convention Center and spaceport. The LDF continued to patrol all GMed facilities, but protests had died down some, particularly after Bev's soldiers killed two would-be bombers.

GEnt carried the arrivals live. For the fledgling Sol Empire, hosting the Federation of Planets' Tenth Annual Linguist Conference put us on the galactic map as a significant player. Isabella's deciphering of the Fourth and Fifth Invader languages guaranteed the entire Federation of Planets had to pay attention to our empire.

Isabella fretted over her speech. Her discoveries were to play a central role in the three day conference, along with her lengthy description of her finds. She planned to chair a discussion workshop on it as well. But her due date was Valentine's Day. Worry, nerves, and physical discomfort combined to undermine Isabella's state of mine.

"Mom, what am I going to do if I go into labor while

giving my speech? Should I try to finish it first? Maybe I ought to mention it right away or do I try to hide it. Make light of it?"

"Don't ignore it, honey. There'll be other telepath linguists watching you as their role model. If Isabella can manage this, maybe I can, too. That sort of thing. I know Angelina certainly does. Now Tia is in the same position. She's going to have to make a big decision once the conference is over. Do we even know how many telepathic linguists there are?"

"The pandemic wiped some out. Like Bernardo. He's coming anyway," Isabella said. "I think at last count, there's a dozen of us telepaths. Thirteen counting Tia, if she doesn't get the cure when the convention is over. You think others are going to want to be like us?"

"Don't know, dear. Just do your best. Let's hear your speech again. Practice makes perfect."

She laughed and recited it once more. "I've got it memorized by now, Mom."

"That's a good thing. That way, no matter what happens, you can just carry on."

"Hum. I suppose you're right. What'll I wear?"

And so the day went. I didn't go into the office. She needed my support. I did keep the comm center monitoring the news, just in case. Often, the cameras showed images of the arriving linguists, baggage in hand. Five hundred and their guests stayed in the attached hotel, making it easy for the GEnt crews to record the pre-event activities.

Well armed soldiers stood in the background. Nearly every arrival stared at them. They sported giant bosoms and wore tall heels—neither of which blended with their green uniforms, ill-fitting at best. A very few managed to acquire Leslie's new male doll apparel. I suspected a few had no choice but to wear women's gowns. Galactic Manufacturing hadn't yet caught up to the tremendous demand, thanks to the pandemic.

Late that afternoon, I accompanied Isabella to the center. The hosts introduced her to the layout, showed her where she'd be speaking from, and where us guests would sit. Walls of giant monitors ensured everyone would be able to see her video presentation of what she'd deciphered about these ancient alien invaders to the Sol system.

That evening, Tia also developed a case of nerves. Isabella told her and Angelina that all thirteen armless telepaths would be seated in the front row as the most honored linguists.

"God, everyone will be staring at me. I still feel scared and nearly helpless," Tia wailed.

Isabella said, "I know. But think of me. They'll really be staring at me. I'm worried I'll pop right there on the stage."

"Hey, the hosts will handle that if it happens," Angelina said. "Look, Tia, we're special. Life is a real challenge for us, and yet we live it to do our jobs as linguists. It's only right that others look up to us. Still, I know it's scary. But we can do it. What's more important will be the discussion groups. Everyone will want to know just how much easier it is for us to decipher a new language. They'll be comparing us to themselves."

"But I've not even gotten my telepathic abilities yet," Tia said. "What'll I say?"

"The truth," Isabella said. "That your telepathy hasn't yet developed. You can certainly tell them about your linguistic experiences in the field onboard the New Light. You can speculate about how telepathy could have been a benefit had you had it."

"I suppose I can do that. Still, I feel so embarrassed, so vulnerable. I can't do much yet on my own," Tia said.

Bonita laughed. "Isn't that the truth. I can't either. We're in the same boat, Tia. I can't begin to tell you how embarrassing it was for me on the Kanika. But I survived. You will too. Just don't let all the stares get to you. I'll be there and take some eyes off you."

The big day dawned. We arrived at the center early. The hosts wanted the armless telepath Galactic Dolls to come early and take their reserved seats. Plus, they wanted to queue up Isabella's presentation and test the system. Bonita and I watched the others take their seats. We and they wore the same style gown, Leslie's design that totally enclosed shoulders, which prominently displayed the unmistakable absence of arms.

The hosts had Bernardo and five others, whose arms were regrowing and baby-like, sitting on either side of the thirteen. A partial honor, since they'd already been telepath linguists, but now had lost that gift.

With front row gallery seats, Bonita and I had a great view of the attendees. Ashley and Sherry accompanied us, though our relatives chose to watch it via the GEnt broadcast. Seating was limited.

As the attendees filed in, representatives from over a hundred Federation worlds, or so the brochure claimed, I observed many alien races. What so shocked me was at least half of the linguists looked human-like. That is, they could pass as homo sapiens. True, their languages, cultures, and dress varied widely, but dressed in Sol Empire clothing, they'd appear to be normal humans.

Yes, half didn't. Some had skin that resembled fish scales. Lizard heritage, perhaps. The man from Zahra-C stuck out from the others with his very elongated, tall head. One couldn't tell aliens from skin color alone. They varied as much as the people of Earth did. Rather the foreign aspects caught my eye. Some had claw-like hands. A few had a rather bird-like beak for a mouth and feathers instead of facial hair. Half the attendees provided me with an inside look at much of the Federation population. But I couldn't shake the gnawing fact that at least half could pass as homo sapiens sapiens. Okay, Bonita was one of these, too.

As I watched the parade of linguists before me, I realized just how much about our larger galaxy I didn't know. Duh. Try most of it. Looking back, I think this was the point I decided to expand my horizons and knowledge. I'd put in to be our next Senior Ambassador to the Federation's Senate.

Finally, the hosts took the stage and gave the welcoming speeches. Isabella was first on their agenda. As my daughter walked slowly on stage to the speaker's podium, I felt a surge of motherly pride. I sensed the buzz among the attendees, who realized just how pregnant Isabella was. A hush then fell. The lights dimmed. Her presentation began, a myriad translation units converting her English into many other languages.

"I became an armless telepath when my twin brother and I were barely thirteen," she began. "Yes, like so many, we were the victims of a terrorist attack. Our birth parents committed suicide. Bernardo and I were very fortunate to be adopted by Molly Parkinson. I owe her everything. She helped me get my position as a linguist on the Star Voyager. She insisted I study and take all the university courses I could. As you all know, we linguists usually have nothing but idle time on these trips. So I took her advice.

"I needed a thesis. We hadn't encountered a new species and language to study. But who isn't aware of the undeciphered Fourth and Fifth Invader documents? I chose to study them. This presentation demonstrates how I made my discoveries."

The video stream appeared on the myriad monitors while Isabella continued to describe the scenes. This was the first time I'd actually seen these alien documents and writings before. Watching it unfold captivated me. The true genius of my adopted daughter overwhelmed me. I had tears in my eyes, but with the dim lights, no one noticed.

Isabella received a standing ovation when she finished. Then came the presentation of her award: Knight of Language, their highest award. Whistling and cheering accompanied the host as she placed the medallion attached to a purple ribbon around her neck.

Once the noise died down, the host explained the next discussion group. "As you can tell, we have a number of current telepath linguists sitting in the front row, along with some who used to be before the pandemic caused them to lose their telepathic gift. We know one of the hottest topics at this convention focuses on these telepaths. If and how telepathy aids in deciphering a new language is on everyone's mind, along with the physical side. Obviously, life can be challenging for them. Isabella's due date is today, so I've moved this discussion to right now. She might not be available tomorrow or later this afternoon."

Several chuckles responded. "We're going to have the stage hands move their chairs around into a circle on the stage, facing you. One at a time, you may direct your questions to any of these telepaths and former telepath linguists. The questions flowed.

"My question is for any of them. Isn't life nearly impossible without arms?"

"I got this one," Isabella said. "Yeah, life's a bitch without them. But our motto is stop and think how. We use our feet and toes in clever ways. We have to become smarter people. Lack of arms hasn't stopped any of us up here. We do our jobs well. But yes, life's a challenge."

Another asked, "So how much help is having telepathy when making first contact?"

"I'll take this one," Angelina said. "This is my seventh year as our exploration ship's linguist. I can say with absolute certainty that being able to see the concept in another's mind makes deciphering those initial five hundred words a breeze. Honestly, I don't know how the rest of you can ever figure out those beginning words."

Many chuckled, while several actually laughed.

Another asked, "Doesn't the inability to gesture with your arms and hands severely restrict your ability to make that initial communication? I point and gesture constantly."

"You can still gesture using heads and feet," Angelina said. "But yeah, it's harder at times. Still, we can touch their minds and latch onto the concept they're trying to communicate, so that more than makes up for it."

A man asked, "What changes does this mutation agent do to you, besides giving you telepathic ability? Can you be specific?"

"I'll grab this one," Bernardo said. "First, it turns all bodies, male or female, into what we call Galactic Dolls. Giant breasts, tiny waists, and warped feet that force us to have to wear tall heels. If one's overweight, it's lost. Underweight people gain. Hair thickens and grows longer. Male bodies lose ribs and Adam's apples. Our voices rise, and we don't have to shave. So much for a mustache. One can't tell a male or female Galactic Doll by looking at them. We appear similar. Yet males still function as males. Further, the mutation resets the biological clock. It's estimated that we're rejuvenated back to our early twenties. Kind of like the fountain of youth. Oh yeah, arms wither and fall off while you're in the eight-day coma."

A woman asked, "Doesn't the obscene salaries of a million credits a year entice you to being a telepath?"

"Hardly." Isabella laughed. "Still, for all the challenges we endure and difficulties, it seems reasonable that we make enough to be able to one day retire. Until recently, there wasn't any method to get one's arms back. So our job possibilities used to be quite limited. Unless you have no ethics and want to be a corporate spy."

A man asked, "If you had a choice, would you chose to be an armless telepath again?"

Isabella said, "I think that's a personal choice. Me, absolutely. The feeling of accomplishment I get when I help develop the basic five hundred words of a new language is something I live for. I can't imagine life without that. Being a telepath makes it easier for me to do that. So we telepaths have an additional tool to use to make this job that we love easier to do.

"I know my brother took this job so he could earn enough credits so he could open his own restaurant. Angelina here was a pandemic victim and lost her telepathic gift. Thankfully, she was able to get mutated again and has regained her skill. So some of us would and have done it again, while others probably wouldn't. It can be a frightening experience, no doubt about that."

"But don't you feel helpless, sometimes?" asked another young woman.

Tia laughed. "Damned right! I just became one—a terrorist attack victim on my way to this conference. So I'm often terrified and feel really helpless, until I see Isabella and Molly doing everything. I've got a lot to learn and practice. But yeah, I feel very helpless at times. Damned frightening, too."

Similar questions occupied the next half hour, before someone asked a key question. "We've heard that this armless telepath Galactic Doll agent has mutated someone from another world outside the Sol Empire. That any species whose DNA is sufficiently similar to yours could be mutated. Hasn't this agent been widely used as a terrorist weapon? Isn't that the reason the Federation is considering Earth's destruction?

To prevent the spread of this agent."

A confused look illuminated Isabella's face. This wasn't supposed to be common knowledge. If the average person on Earth knew the Federation was about to destroy them...

"Well, yes, someone from Azizi-C has been mutated like us. And yes, unethical people have used this as a terrorist weapon. Earth has had thousands of such victims, though the recent pandemic has cured many of those who survived. Like all good governments, the Federation must do what Earth hasn't been able to do on its own: prevent the spread of these mutation agents. You see, the agents themselves are neither good nor evil. It's man's use of them that is.

"The unethical misuse them. We've had a lot of those kind trying to illegally make telepaths and then sell them to the highest bidders. We think we've stopped most of those plots. I hope the Federation can help us find a way to prevent these agents from leaving Earth. On the other hand, these same agents can save people's lives. My dad and brother were killed in a bomb attack, but their bodies were put into stasis machines and injected with these agents. We believe in time they'll be healed and alive again. These agents have restored lost limbs on thousands of soldiers. These agents have cured many diseases, including dementia. They have rejuvenated elderly people into young adults. The drawback is that they're now Galactic Dolls. None that I know of are complaining about that. So there are many uses that are incredibly valuable. We just need to keep them out of the hands of the unethical people."

What a diplomat Isabella would make. She deftly sidestepped the key question and focused people's attention onto the positive benefits these agents have had. Clever woman.

"Isn't it true," that same person continued, "that the other worlds of your own Sol Empire prohibit Earth's mutants from living there? Isn't Azizi-C doing the same thing?"

"Yes, and there's a good reason for it. These Galactic Doll mutations are dominant, particularly the telepath version. So yes, my daughter who's wiggling now will be like me. When we had terrorists making thousands of us in their attacks, yes,

116

this was a good policy for the other worlds to follow. Any children we have would be like us.

"Do the math. Begin with a pool of say a thousand mutants. Each has a couple children who in turn are mutants. They marry and have children. In a few generations, any world would have a big problem, particularly with us telepaths. What's needed is a way to undo these mutations by those who were mutated against their will—which is almost ninety-nine point nine percent of telepath victims.

"What's really needed here is a way to prevent these agents from leaving Earth, except for those in the exploration process. We just had a case where the ship's commander and chief scientist got poisoned by a plant on the world they were exploring. By injecting them with the mutation agent, they survived certain death. Again, there are valid uses of these agents. I wish geneticists would develop mutation agents that did their thing without all these other side-effects."

At this point, the meeting broke for lunch. I wasn't surprised to learn that dealing with dining was what the telepaths dreaded the most.

"Everyone kept staring at me," wailed Tia that evening. "I was so mortified."

I took her aside and asked her to return to the first moment when she felt that way. Presto. A needed therapy session began. As a younger schoolgirl, she had to recite before the class and messed it up badly. Since neither had erased, I asked for something earlier and similar. Whoa. Did trauma ever show up. In an earlier life, she'd been raped by a gang of boys, stripped naked, and paraded around the school before authorities intervened. That one did erase, leaving Tia amazed and feeling cheerful again. At least until the next time.

Call me a mother hen, but I continued to go to the convention. However, mid-afternoon that second day, Isabella and I went to the Med Center. Within a few hours, a healthy Maria was born. Mother and daughter did fine. Grandma, not so much. I worried and fretted. Bonita and Owen, the proud father, joined us. Later, I brought Nikita by to see her niece. Naturally, she and Isabella chatted on endlessly, making all manner of plans to care for Maria.

One by one, our extended family dropped by to see the pair. So I headed home, but on my way out, I stopped the basement to check on Sam and Matt. Bonita got her first look at the pair. A nurse spotted me and came to talk.

"Molly. Good news. The mutations are healing their wounds. Dr. Schmidt thinks they'll be coming out of their comas in a few days. Then, we'll know if there's been any permanent damage."

As we walked home, Bonita said, "What's he going to think of me when he wakes up?"

"One sexy young woman. That's what."

We laughed breaking her building tension.

Chapter 11 Breaking News

Sunday, the nineteenth of February, the conference ended with a huge banquet. Bonita and I attended along with many other family members who had come to be with their linguists. Most of these lived on Earth. Isabella didn't attend, naturally, but we were there to back Bernardo and also Tia and Angelina.

Thankfully, a coat person took ours for us, as the five of us entered. Bernardo's regrowing arms were still too small to me of much use to him.

"Thanks for being here with us," Tia whispered. "I feel less self-conscious with you by me. They're going to stare at us.

Angelina chuckled. "Yeah, they always do. After all, most of these people have never see anyone like us. They're curious. I'd be staring, too. Try to not let it bother you."

"Easier said than done," Tia whispered back.

We found our table. They'd put us telepaths at the same long table. At once, Angelina started chatting with other veteran telepaths from other deep space exploration ships. She attempted to pull Tia into the conversations. Though still shy, Tia joined the chat. Soon, the conversation turned to Bernardo and how he felt about losing his telepathy and his regrowing arms.

After the meal, a dozen other linguists joined us. They wanted to know just how hard life was for us.

"You're thinking about becoming one of us?" I asked.

Several blushed. One said, "Yes, Isabella is an inspiration to us. But, well, it's..."

"A difficult choice to make," I finished her sentence. "Of course it is. And it should not be taken lightly. No other world in the Federation will allow you to live there. You'll have to make Earth your permanent residence."

"We know. But the benefits of being a telepath are huge," one said.

Tia said, "Hey, I'm terrified still. You can't imagine how helpless I felt when I awoke from the coma. I can barely function. Probably not at all without those machines. If you guys decide to do it, make sure you have your own hair-nail machine, dressing machine, and housemaid robot machine."

"We feel bad for you, Bonita," another said. "We heard you can't go home to your world."

Angelina changed the topic. She asked, "So why are you ladies thinking of becoming a telepath? Surely not just for the money."

Flipping it around, she cleverly deflected the embarrassing questions for Tia and Bonita. They chatted about their lives until people began leaving. Angelina wasn't shy about answering their specific questions, much to the relief of Bonita and Tia. The questioners were all women, which I thought interesting. No man wished to look like Bernardo. Not for a million credits per year. Not for gaining telepathy.

When we got home, the Med Center called. Sam and Matt showed signs of waking from their comas. Deanna, Ashley, Sherry, Bonita, and I headed there. Nikita also demanded to come with us. Even though the hour was late, I agreed. The six of us found a flurry of activity in the basement of the Med Center.

A nurse explained. "Wonderful news. Their bodies are alive. We're unhooking them from much of the life support apparatus now. I must caution you. We're in uncharted waters here. Who knows what permanent damage has been done? They might still be mostly vegetables. Don't get your hopes up too high just yet. That we've brought them back from the dead is huge."

They brought us chairs. Now, we could only wait and watch as their bodies continued to stir and fidget.

"Dad will be all right. I just know it," Nikita declared. "Come on, Dad. Wake up. I need you."

An hour later, Sam's eyes opened. "Matt! Bomb!" he yelled.

A nurse helped him sit up. "You and Matt are safe. You're in the Med Center." She yielded to a doctor, who took over, while she helped Matt, who was also waking up.

"Do you know your name? Where do you live? What's your wife's name?"

The doctor began running down a checklist of questions they'd prepared to help detect and diagnose any serious brain problems. They had no idea of minds and beings. Still, I paid close attention to Sam and his answers. Was he my Sam? Or had some other being taken over his body as had happened with Bonita?

"My head is throbbing. Matt, are you okay?" Sam asked, at first ignoring the doctor's questions.

"Think so, Dad. My head hurts. I feel awful," Matt said.

I nearly cried to hear my son's voice again.

Sam rattled off his name and address. "Molly Parkinson. Molly, you're here. Tell them I'm me. We got caught in a bomb blast. I tried to shield Matt. Is Nikita okay? Oh, she's here, too."

"Sam, let's get these questions answered and let me check your vitals. Then you can have your family reunion. You've been in a coma for nearly a month. Plus, you and Matt were declared dead on arrival at the Med Center."

"Dead? I'm very much alive, but with a throbbing headache. How?"

"We took the liberty of experimenting on you and your son. We injected you with a massive dose of the telepath agent. It's saved both your lives. Now, next question. What's two plus two?"

He carried on with what I thought were silly questions, but I finally grasped what the doctor was doing. Checking Sam's analytical facilities and then his motor skills. Finally, he had Sam stand up and be dressed.

Then, we all plowed into Sam and Matt, pressing our bodies into theirs, our way of hugging.

"I told them you and Matt would be all right," Nikita declared. "They said you were dead, but I knew differently, Dad."

We chatted for a bit. Then Sam asked the question I dreaded. "Who's this gorgeous golden haired woman?"

"Bonita Valdez from Azizi-C. She's Admiral Skaggs' niece. She's now married to us. Long story, Sam, but not here."

"When can I go home?" he said.

"Look, we'd like you to stay overnight. Just to be sure.

You were pronounced dead. Let's make sure you're perfectly okay, shall we?" the doctor asked.

We hugged and kissed, before departing, promising to be back in the morning.

"You'd better be," Sam said.

'Are you really all right?' Sam sent me telepathically.

'Yes, dear. Lots to tell you, but get something to eat and a good night's sleep. I'll be here in the morning. God, I'm so glad you're all right!'

I lay awake that night, thinking of Sam. The next morning, Ashley and I waited at the discharge desk for Sam and Matt. Soon, their smiling faces appeared.

"I need a bath," Matt said. "I smell like a hospital."

"I thought I'd lost both of you."

Sam said, "We're harder to kill than most might imagine." We laughed. Ashley fastened their cloaks, and we headed home.

Once there, Nikita had to show Matt little Maria. "You're an uncle now, Matt."

Sam and I slipped into our bedroom.

"Okay, what's going on?" he asked.

I explained just how critical the situation had become. "So Admiral Skaggs promised me that if I married his niece, Bonita, then our huge extended family and friends would be spared, if and when he destroys Earth. I had to do it. Not about to let us all die. Plus, Bonita was Ted Billings in her last lifetime."

His eyebrows rose. I explained in detail what had happened.

"So, are you okay with having to wives," I asked. "Not mad at what I did to save us?"

"No, good thinking. What about the terrorist who bombed us? That bothers me even more."

"Senior Ambassador Sanura Fenku paid a giant to kill you and the kids. We're still trying to get to the bottom of that one."

Just then, my phone rang. It was Admiral Rossi.

"Turn on your comm center. I'm sending a shuttle to pick you up at your home. Crap is really happening this time," he said. "We need you up here."

I did. GEnt news showed one of the Third Invader flying saucers hovering near the Kanika, closer to that ship than the cigar-shaped Sixth Invader ships and our own delta-wings. I sighed and got ready to meet the shuttle. Ashley and Sherry decided to come along with me, which I appreciated.

As we headed out the door, Ambassador L'Grina walked up. "Mind if I join you? I've got to join this discussion. Can you believe this? A Third Invader saucer. Impressive. Everyone wants to know what these raiders want."

I laughed. "But many perceive your people as the raiders."

She teased me back. "Perception isn't what it's seen to be."

A shuttle arrived, landing on the snow of our front yard. Minutes later, we climbed aboard a transport at New O'Hare for the trip into high orbit where the multitude of battleships, heavy cruisers, and cruisers hung in suspense. I hoped not for a battle! We couldn't win. Or had Admiral Skaggs made his decision? Probably not, since many convention visitors hadn't yet left. Thinking about that aspect, I wondered if some of the linguists were planning to undergo the telepath mutation. I put that silliness out of my mind, but I had a hunch I wasn't done with that.

"Don't get out," Admiral Rossi said. We'd docked and found him at our bay door. "We're heading over to the Kanika. Big conference. Ah, good. The Sixth Invader ambassador is with you. We need her, too."

He and some staff came onboard. As we departed, I asked what was going on.

"The Third Invaders have demanded a conference with us and with Admiral Skaggs. No one has any idea what they want, but if we can get any clues about their technology, we're taking it. My people are using all available sensors on that saucer. Maybe we'll get lucky."

Ambassador L'Grina said, "This can't be good. These nasty aliens make us look like your best friends. Treachery factorial."

Admiral Rossi chuckled. "That's a good one. Gonna

remember that one."

My math is weak, but I finally got the jest.

Before long, soldiers escorted us to the large, stainless steel meeting room on the Kanika, the very room we'd used years back when they made us the offer to join the Federations of Planets as a way to avoid being conquered by the Sixth Invaders. I wondered if we were about to get Federation notification of the destruction of Earth. But why were the Third Invaders here? A lone flying saucer, despite its advanced technology, probably wasn't a match for fifty ships from three civilizations.

Admiral Rossi, Ambassador L'Grina, and I took seats at the long table. Ashley and Sherry sat against the wall behind me. I heard boots clicking together just outside the opened door; the guard jumped to attention as Admiral Skaggs arrived.

He brought two Third Invaders with him. I knew that's who they were the instant I saw them. Both reminded me of those who had captured and mutated Isabella's deep space exploration ship and Bernardo's, too. We'd killed several of their guards and turned the surviving female leader over to the local tribesmen who wanted their own brand of justice. They'd kidnapped hundreds of their women to become the arms and assistants to all the telepaths the invaders had made out of our people. My jaw clinched instinctively. Twisted treachery defined these people. What was going on? Memories of Edyta Iakob-Ra returned. I wondered what happened to her.

The two aliens took seats across from us, while Admiral Skaggs shut the door, turned on a recording device, and sat at the head of the table.

"Rashidi and Mosi Omari of Gamma Orionis-C, otherwise known as Third Invaders in these parts. They've demanded this formal meeting and wished it to be broadcast live to all citizens of the Sol Empire," he said. "This is Ambassador and Commander L'Grina, the Sixth Invaders' representative to the Sol Empire, Earth in particular. This is the Sol Empire's Admiral Rossi. And this is the Sol Empire's Senior Investigator and Senior Judge, Molly Parkinson."

"More like just for Earth," I spoke up. "I've never been

to all the other many worlds of our empire. But I have met other Third Invaders and defeated them. Shouldn't we have other Sol Empire leaders here?"

With glistening tan skin, Rashidi sat erect, his perfectly muscled arms and torso visible through the gauze-like vest. He wore brown pants that ended at his knees, shorts I'd call them, with brown leather sandals on his feet. Perfect desert apparel, I thought. She wore similar shorts and sandals, only with a thin brown bandeau that matched her shorts. Both had black hair, but hers lay draped across her right shoulder. Both wore enough gold and jewelry to make a jewelry store envious. Their wrist bands, rings, and necklaces probably cost more than my lifetime's salary as a PI.

Rashidi spoke first. In English. That impressed me, since we'd forgotten to bring along translator devices.

"We're conducting this meeting using your English, since here that is the most commonly spoken language. Everything we say and do is being broadcast to all parties of your fledgling Sol Empire. For official record, I am Rashidi Omari, Emperor of we Jafari from Gamma Orionis-C. Our Empress, Mosi."

Both bowed slightly, jewelry glistening in the lighting. Had they'd oiled their skin so it shone, too?

"We have spies everywhere. Thus, we know Federation of Planets sent Admiral Skaggs to Earth. He awaits their orders to destroy Earth's human inhabitants. Why? Obvious. Remarkable invented mutations. Well, that's not entirely correct. Is it Ambassador L'Grina? Didn't your Chief Science Officer invent Galactic Doll mutation agent? One that gives them giant breasts so admired by your people. One that makes them wear tall heels. One that turns all female forms into ideal Galactic Doll shape. One that eliminates both overweight and underweight women."

Ambassador L'Grina interrupted him. I suspected she demonstrated she wasn't about to be intimidated by him. "Quite true. But it also regrew missing body parts, such as arms and legs. It rejuvenates older people. All can be youthful once more. There are many positive aspects of our mutation agent."

"Of course," he said, but not after attempting to stare her down. That failed as she glared right back at him.

"Real problem came later, didn't it." L'Grina shut up and let him talk. "Second agent—one Earth's men were supposed to have received—one now called armless telepath Galactic Doll agent. Pardon me. Telepathy became unexpected side-effect."

He looked at me for a moment. "Didn't Mrs. Parkinson try to convince those in power to destroy agent?"

How did he know that? How had we missed their spies? I said, "Yes, I did. But they didn't believe it would ever be used as a weapon. A deterrent perhaps."

"Precisely. Instead of destroying it, didn't rulers of Earth widely distribute that and other agents? Isn't it available in quantity in every Med Center and GMed facility on Earth?"

He sure had precise details. I answered. "I believe so, but I'm not an authority on those details."

"Precisely. Further, didn't they provide syringes of armless telepath agent to people that those in power considered important? To save their lives in an emergency."

"Well, yes, they did. It's saved a number of people from certain death. The armless telepath agent is the strongest one. In fact, it's recently brought back to life my husband and son, who were pronounced dead from a terrorist bomb attack paid for by Senior Ambassador Sanura Fenku." I imagined gasps from some of those who were watching.

"Yes, we're aware of her actions, Mrs. Parkinson."

Okay, my turn to be surprised. I had never suspected a Third Invaders connection to her.

"For the record, hasn't mutation agent been used in many terrorist attacks on Earth?"

"Yes. Thousands were mutated against their will."

"And haven't numerous others, including some of your own Earthlings, plotted to make and sell telepaths from Earth?"

"Thousands. Including your people, Rashidi. Call me Molly, please. Whatever happened to your own Edyta Iakob-Ra who kidnapped our people, mutated them, and attempted to sell them as slave telepaths? I know quantum entanglement allowed you to retrieve her flying saucer from our people."

I hoped to get a flush or rise out of either of these aliens, but neither gave any outward sign that I'd hit a nerve. On the contrary.

"Quite true, Molly. Like many other aliens, we attempted to, as your saying goes, jump on bandwagon, whatever that object may be. A failure. Naturally. Through all this, Federation of Planets looked other way, since your mutations here on Earth didn't affect them, though I know many were concocting their own schemes to make and acquire telepaths. Through all this, hasn't all other member worlds of your fledgling Sol Empire passed laws forbidding any of Earth's mutants, male or female, from ever residing on their worlds?"

"Yes, that's true. The twenty-three other members flatly refuse to allow that, not even their own senators who were victims of a terrorist mutation attack," I replied.

"And because of that, Federation watched these others in your empire. They've stuck to their law and haven't allowed any Galactic Doll mutants to live on their worlds. But..."

He paused a moment. I sensed a master of manipulation.

"Why is that? Simple. Original Galactic Doll mutation agent alters person's DNA. This alteration is dominant during reproduction. In simple terms, children born to parents, one of whom is Galactic Doll, will have Doll body themselves, whether male or female. Worse, armless telepath mutation is dominant over all other forms. Isn't that right, Molly?"

"Yes, my daughter just had a daughter who is like her mother, an armless telepath."

He raised a fist as though he'd just won a contest. "Yes, this is why other worlds of your own empire and other worlds are so afraid of these agents. It's dominant. Run through any breeding population simulation and you'll see this mutation eventually becoming dominant portion of population of any world. Eventually, everyone in that population would be one of those mutants. Frightening. So I commend other worlds, moons, and stations of your Sol Empire for having wisdom to prevent such a calamity on their worlds. But..."

Again, he paused before releasing his next argument, making us lean forward expectantly. Damn. I leaned back.

"However, Federation has now concrete evidence your armless telepath Galactic Doll agent mutates other people on other worlds outside your Sol Empire. Hasn't Admiral Skaggs' niece, Bonita Valdez, become armless telepath Galactic Doll? Haven't you married her, while your husband was dead?"

My face felt hot. How dare he bring Bonita into this? I saw Admiral Skaggs flush.

"Yes," I admitted through clenched teeth.

"Admiral Skaggs, hasn't this event shaken foundations of Federation? Are they terrified this mutation will rapidly spread to many other worlds throughout Federation of Planets?"

He mumbled, "Yes."

"And that brings us to why we're all here. Isn't Federation of Planets seriously considering destroying every human on Earth? Not giants or dwarves, if they can help it, but even them if there's no other way. Genocide of mutants."

Again, his face reddish, Admiral Skaggs said, "Yes."

This time, Mosi spoke. Smiling, she said, "We Jafari simply cannot understand history of Earth. Back in early 1900's, Chicago shone as gangster capital of world. Corruption wove the very fabric of society. Mobsters bought police and judges. In early 2000's, corruption still ruled Chicago, now murder capital of country. Three thousand murders a year, ignoring other crimes. Rampant political corruption then as it had been century before.

"Then, came Big Collapse. But again those in Chicago regained control of Earth and beginnings of its empire. Corrupt men now ran most powerful corporations on Earth, forcing their will on all citizens of Earth and new empire. They pay your salaries and demand loyalty. Don't you have to do what corporations order you to do? Why hasn't your world wiped out Chicago and its eternal corruption? That's what we haven't figured out."

I wished Janine's husband Hank accompanied us: a history professor. Once again, I felt amazingly ignorant. I'd never paid much attention to history. It didn't solve mysteries and crimes.

"Now then, another critical piece must be revealed," Rashidi said. "Normally, we Jafari would never admit this, especially to you humans. But we feel we must. Why do you suppose so many of your Federation worlds are inhabited by humans who look very much like you do, Admiral Skaggs?

"Earth just held a linguistics conference, but what was missing was how come so many of these alien worlds speak languages so similar to those found on Earth? Or how come so many of Earth's languages are akin to those on many other Federation worlds? In fact, Admiral Skaggs, wouldn't you say sixty percent of Federation worlds are inhabited by humans, whose DNA is so closely related they could interbreed? Ignoring dress and speech, couldn't a citizen of Azizi-C pass as an Earthling—before their mutations that is? Even Zahra-C people could pass as Earthlings, just not those with big heads.

"Why is this? No one asked that key question at linguist conference. Isn't this why Federation so fears these mutation agents? Sixty percent of Federation worlds could be wiped out by use of these agents. That's ignoring damage terrorists might do with them, such as extorting money and concessions from world leaders. Yes, your Federation ought to be extremely worried about spread of these mutation agents, enough so nuke Earth to eliminate them."

"I can't argue against that," Admiral Skaggs said. "We've long known people of many worlds are very similar. I'm not a galactic-anthropologist nor archaeologist. I think the general thinking is that human beings are the most logical result of genetic evolution on most planets, with exceptions, such as the giants and dwarves on their heavier gravity planets and such."

Mosi laughed, the kind that cuts to the quick. "Just like humans to believe they are center of universe. Ha. No, there's very good reason why homo sapiens inhabits so many of your Federation worlds and speak similar languages."

She paused, riveting our attention. "We put them there. Yes, over millennia, we Jafari have been transplanting members of one world to another world that we've prepared for them. Azizi-C is one of those, as is Earth and many, many others. If homo sapiens lives on a world, it's almost certainty we put them there. Only exceptions are worlds your people colonized, such as Brussels, Tau Ceti.

"Jafari have been doing this for at least ten millennia, as far back as our records go. Call us Galaxy's Society Experimenters. That's what we do."

She let this bombshell sink in. Now I truly wished others from Earth had come along with me. I had no idea what questions I should ask her. This was almost unbelievable. These people had been tinkering with the populations of more than half the known worlds, if I believed her.

She said, "I can see you are dumbfounded by this revelation. I suggest we adjourn for lunch. We can resume at one o'clock, to use your time."

With that, she and Rashidi rose and headed for the door. Admiral Skaggs jumped up to open the door for them.

"Escort them to their cabin or to the mess hall," he ordered, before turning back to us. His white face spoke volumes. "I'm going to have to relay this back to Bela Prime. The guard will escort you wherever you wish to go." He turned and left, nearly running.

"Well, that's a shocker," I said.

"You think?" L'Grina said. "She might be right. My people have visited a large number of these Federation worlds as well as others that aren't. There's a race of lizard men on one, and a race of snake people on another. Don't recommend visiting either. Both like hunting humans for sport."

Chapter 12 The Offer

We broke for lunch. The guard escorted the five of us to the mess hall. I was thankful Ashley came with me. She handled our trays. Already I was the object of many stares. People everywhere are curious. How could I eat without arms? I slipped off my right heel, and dug in, ignoring the many eyes.

We ate in silence, each grappling with their own thoughts over what the Third Invaders just revealed. Afterwards over tea, Admiral Rossi spoke up.

"Well, I suppose I should contact my fleet. Presumably, the morning's session was broadcast to all. While interesting data, we've no way to prove their hand in the settlement of the galaxy. I think we've been fortunate in not running into other worlds onto which they've put homo sapiens. What bothers me more is what *is* the real purpose of their meeting with us? I don't trust them, not remotely. Molly's proof of that. Look what that woman did to the two exploration ships' crew and later to Molly and her people. Diabolical traps. Why are they here?"

I grinned. "I don't disagree. These are treacherous people. I wish Isabella were here to question them about the language situation. Languages evolve over time. I learned that much at the conference."

"Boss," Ashley said, "what are we going to do if these aliens make some kind of proposal? We don't have any leaders up here, excepting our space fleet admiral, that is."

"I don't know. Worse, who are the leaders now? That coup more or less failed. Things are mostly continuing on automatic at the moment. Who can we call for help or for approval or disapproval?"

Blank stares greeted me. We sipped our tea in silence, before the guard returned to escort us back to the meeting room. Yes, we needed his guidance. I still had no idea where anything was located on this ship. A map might have been helpful.

"The recording has started again," Admiral Skaggs said.

"Okay. Now we get to heart of matter," Rashidi began. "First, we should point out positive aspects of these two types of mutations. Original Galactic Doll mutation regrew missing appendages, rejuvenated recipient back to a biological age of early twenties, and in few cases prevented or circumvented person's death, even curing diseases and forcing optimum body mass. Drawbacks included what many humans consider to be too large breasts, distorted feet, and that mutation genes dominant over normal human genes. Further, it reduced variability of physical traits and turned men into Galactic Dolls as well.

"The second mutation variety does that, but it removes arms, substituting telepathy in their place. Value of telepaths need not be mentioned. New drawback is also obvious; most consider it a handicap.

"Given these facts, question facing everyone today is what to do about Earth's human population and widespread mutation agents. Let me begin this discussion by pointing out that currently Earth and Sol Empire has lost top leadership positions, though as I understand it, they acquired those positions using by nefarious and forceful means. Currently, Earth and Sol Empire is represented by single remaining top position, that of Senior Investigator and Senior Judge, Molly Parkinson. Our position is that she can make judicial rulings, which is what we need.

"We've seen that rest of Sol Empire is content with status quo, namely not allowing Earth's mutants to settle on their worlds, moons, and stations. Federation may wish to take further restrictive actions, based on mutation of Azizi-C citizen, who has been forced to remain on Earth.

"At this time, let's hear from the Sixth Invader Ambassador L'Grina. Earth's human population is currently similar to your world's population. What advice would your people give Earth?"

"Well," the grey alien said, "on our world, males and females look similar, just as Earth's humans do. On our world, men generally remain in the home, handling the family domestic duties, though a few take other positions while they are youthful. They handle nursing our young, freeing up valuable time for our women, who run everything. Men wear the dresses and try to look as attractive as they can, while women have short hair and usually wear suits or other work clothing.

"I will admit that this is the state that my deceased Commander R'Ina had attempted to create here on Earth. She failed, as we all know. However, right now, Earth could adopt such a society. There are other worlds on which women run everything and men are the domestics. I am authorized by Home World to offer Earth our complete assistance in converting your world into a female run one. Officially, I am giving you this offer to consider, Molly."

Everyone looked at me. I knew I had to respond. "Well, I can say that most men are very upset with what's happened to their bodies. And frankly, many have committed suicide rather than to continue living. The path we take depends upon whether men can have their masculinity restored or at least lose the mammoth bosoms and distorted feet. If the pandemic results can be undone or partially mitigated, I'm sure men would take advantage of that and wish to continue running Earth and the Sol Empire. If a cure can't be found, then I will present your offer, L'Grina, to our people."

I tried to be as diplomatic as I could. She certainly had been.

"Accepted," Rashidi said. "As for cure. I've learned brilliant geneticist and microbiologist who created the pandemic's virus has been attacked and turned into an armless telepath. A prime example of how Earth treats its most valuable personnel, its geniuses. This woman is now so handicapped that her career and usefulness as geneticist is over.

"The question before us: is there a cure or can one be found?"

I didn't like where this headed. Time to speak up. I said, "My sister and others are working on cures. They did invent two minor ones that are useful: breast size reduction and foot repair. Patricia Ann Gates-Baxter, a virologist and microbiologist, created the virus and pandemic. After she was mutated, as Rashidi said, we had her join my sister's group, hoping to make headway on undoing what her virus did to men. We just need more time."

"Ah, so that's what happened to her," Rashidi said. "At least she still has her mind. That might ultimately be of some use to your sister. Next, we come to Federation's desires. Correct me, Admiral Skaggs, if I mis-speak. Primary fear is unscrupulous people will steal quantities of mutation agents, particularly telepath-making version, and then either use them on member worlds in terrorist attacks as has been done on Earth or in extortion attempts. This is very serious threat to continued existence of Federation of Planets. A solution must be found."

"Of course," Admiral Skaggs said. He maintained his stone face. I sensed he wasn't about to reveal anything to these aliens.

"Genocide is option, but political fallout from killing all humans on Earth could well be immeasurable. Such could foment unrest on other member worlds. So you are looking for alternative solutions. But..."

Again, he paused at just the right moment for just the right amount of time to grab everyone's full attention.

"But lack of leadership on this world creates diplomatic problems. After all, how can you reach agreements if there's no one in charge?"

Admiral Rossi's jaw tightened perceptibly. Ah, so this was a sore point with him, too. I wondered if I might make some use of this fact.

"Well, we agree with you. You can't. Only stable position is Sol Empire's Senior Investigator and Senior Judge, and only because same person holds both positions, Molly Parkinson. Nevertheless, Admiral Skaggs, you have proceeded down viable path: detection of mutation agents. How is this project coming along? Will you be able to guarantee with absolute certainty none of these agents could ever leave Earth?"

Admiral Skaggs smiled. "Yes, my people have developed highly sensitive sensors that can detect minute traces of these agents. We're in the process of working out how best to deploy them in all spaceports on Earth. Admiral Rossi's staff is working with us to carry out these measures. Anyone trying to smuggle these agents off-world via a spacecraft will be summarily executed on the spot. No trial. No lawyers. Just bang!

"How sensitive are these devices? By actual tests, it can detect the presence of one of those emergency syringes given to Earth's more valuable people, an injection designed to save their lives through the armless telepath mutation."

He paused, glanced around the table, his eyes lighting on mine and then Admiral Rossi's. "Absolute certainty? No."

"Ah ha. And that's problem, isn't it, Admiral Skaggs. Higher authorities on Bela Prime are not satisfied, are they? Genocide is still possible," Rashidi said.

The stoic admiral flushed ever so slightly. "Yes."

Rashidi continued, this time looking at me. "On the other hand, because of benefits, Earthlings aren't willing to destroy these agents, assuming someone could ever find them. They've saved lives on some of your deep space exploration ships. By the way, how are that major and his crewman whose lives were saved by injection of telepath agent doing?"

I answered. "Major Kenneth Maxwell, who was the commander of the Enchanter, and Dr. Miller are alive though they wouldn't be if it weren't for the mutation agent in the syringes they carried. Today, they are telepaths, but I admit both are struggling to live. Their lives have become challenging as is the case with any of us. Neither can return to their former work. The last I saw of them, they were very happy to still be alive. Whether that will continue to be so remains to be seen. I think both are scheduled to get the arm regrow cure as soon as it's available."

"So you aren't willing to have these mutation agents destroyed?" Rashidi said.

"Me personally? I don't know. The agents themselves are neither good nor bad. They have saved lives, regrown missing limbs, cured dementia, and rejuvenated the elderly. Hell, it's just saved the life of my husband and son. That's right. They were pronounced dead at the scene. At the Med Center, the doctors put their bodies into stasis pods and injected with massive doses of the telepath agent. They just walked home from the Med Center yesterday. So could anyone convince Earth to destroy these agents? I doubt it."

Rashidi smiled. I didn't like the sense of covertness he radiated. "What if something could be done to those sensors that would guarantee no volume of these mutation agents could be missed in any ship leaving Earth?"

"That would help," Admiral Skaggs said. "Smugglers will try just about anything to get samples off Earth."

"Is it safe to say that as of this moment, fate of Earth's humans still hasn't been decided? Even with your detection sensors?"

"Well, yes. I've relayed the facts and test results up to High Command on Bela Prime. But I've not received any orders, one way or the other."

"Good. This brings me to why we are here."

Ah, finally, we're getting somewhere, I thought. What an incredibly long preamble. But I suspected much had been said to convince us that he had current and relevant knowledge of the situation on Earth. The more he explained, the more certain I was that was the case. He needed to have his proposal taken seriously.

"Our people have been around this galaxy for tens of millennia. Our scientists are experts at genetic modifications. I'd like to offer our services to your sister and others working on cure.

"As I see it, cure should result in your male bodies returning to roughly what they used to look like. Everyone's distorted feet should be repaired and females have smaller breasts. Results of this new mutation ought not be dominant so offspring wouldn't inherit your original two types of mutations. Or since original Galactic Doll mutation was sold to women as a beauty enhancement, we could devise one so it wouldn't be inherited by their offspring, unlike present situation. We should outline precisely your desired changes and then engineer them into cure.

"We can assist you in total destruction of all current mutation agents. These new ones could be designed to also regrow missing appendages, cure serious illnesses, and even rejuvenate as current ones do. In other words, we offer you replacement set of mutation agents that are only helpful to humans, not harmful as both versions currently are."

"What about telepathy?" asked Admiral Skaggs. "Telepaths are extraordinarily rare in the galaxy."

"For everyone's sake, that modification should be eliminated. Then, no one will want to steal agents or misuse them, as has been done. Your earthmen can look much as they used to. These mutated traits don't have to be inherited by your children. Sixth Invaders' mutations can be undone," Rashidi said.

"And what price do we have to pay?" I asked. Okay, I was cynical. No one offers a magic bullet for free. What was the catch?

Mosi answered. "We want to have one thousand of your humans. We're constructing new civilization on newly discovered habitable planet. These will be the seeds of new civilization. We'll be discrete in our choices of people. So, Admiral Skaggs, if this comes to pass, then your Federation will have no reason to kill all humans on Earth. Everyone wins."

"These thousand," Admiral Rossi said, "will they be given a choice? Will they be allowed to return to Earth if they don't like what they find? Will they be mistreated? Where is this new world? Can it be added to the Sol Empire? If so, that would go a long way with us."

"We'll pick those we feel best suited. Once we have them, they won't be able to return to Earth. Of course, we're not going to mistreat them. What's point in that? Perhaps in time this new world may wish to join Sol Empire. Can you honestly say as of today any new world would want to join, considering mess you have on Earth?"

She continued. "Real problem here is no one running Sol Empire. So we're making their Senior Judge sole person who can negotiate this deal. Molly, you speak for entire empire and Earth in particular. You decide. But this is a one time offer. After we leave, we won't be back. As it stands, you're a hair's breath from termination. Choose wisely. We will adjourn for a week. Meet with those you desire. Construct your list of what genetic modifications are wanted in cures, changes which will avert Federation's desire to nuke Earth."

"If we go along with this offer," I asked, "will the genetic changes satisfy the Federation? What good will it do for us to get mutated again if the Federation still insists on wiping out the Earth?" I stared at Admiral Skaggs.

"As long as these new mutation agents can't change men into women or vice-versa or make the victims handicapped as you are, then most likely the Federation will be satisfied. But all existing mutation agents must be destroyed. That is mandatory."

Mosi said, "Molly, choose well. Fate of Earth rests on your shoulders. This meeting is adjourned for a week, after which we'll resume and hear Molly's reply. Thank you."

The two rose and headed for the door, but Admiral Skaggs beat them, opening it for them. "Take them to their ship," he ordered the guard just outside the door.

As we filed out, Admiral Skaggs whispered to me. "How's Bonita doing? Is she coping well enough?"

"She's fine. I think she wants to get her arms regrown and give up telepathy."

"Okay. Wise choice. Give her my regards."

With that, another guard led us to our ship. When Admiral Rossi went his way, he said, "Molly, stay in touch. If you need something, call."

Reassuring. But once in our own shuttle, I cursed for an entire minute. "Why the hell does all this fall on me? Damn it!"

Chapter 13 What to Do?

Once home, I slumped on our couch. Sam said, "We watched the meeting. GEnt broadcast it live. What're you going to do? Are they really going to nuke us just to get rid of us?"

"More and more, I think so, Sam. Frack. The fate of three billion people is in my lap. Damn."

"I can't think of a more level-headed person than you," Sam said.

Bonita joined us. She looked rather pale. "Are you doing okay? How's my uncle taking this?"

"Oh, he said to say hi. He asked about how you were doing. I said as well as can be expected. Guys, let me lie here in quiet a while. Ashley, you can fix supper if you want. I need to think."

After supper, Deanna and Russell dropped by to offer assistance.

"Can you have your Airliner ready to take me to that South Pacific atoll again?"

"You got it. Be ready to go first thing in the morning," Deanna replied.

"I'm going to visit Janine and Hank yet tonight. I wish I wasn't so darn ignorant of things."

"Hey, don't chide yourself," Russell said. "No one knows all about everything, excepting maybe Sam here with his mind. You know more than I do about PI things. That's why you're our Senior Investigator."

"History. I didn't pay attention to that in highschool. Duh. Now it haunts me."

"I'll walk you there," Ashley said.

"Not without me along as your security person," Sherry said.

"Can I go too, Mom?" Nikita asked. "I haven't seen Aunt Janine and Uncle Hank in weeks."

"School night. You and Matt do your homework and practice your cheers. Besides, Hank and I will be talking adult stuff."

She frowned but headed off to do her homework, Matt trailing behind her and groaning about how much he had to do to catch up. He'd missed a month of school.

When I entered their home, Janine gave me a big hug. She headed off to make us tea, while Hank and I sat around their dining room table.

"Hank, I'm a history dummy. Were the historical facts that these aliens rattled off today correct? Chicago has had a long history of crime?"

He sighed. "Yes, dead on. What I don't get is how these aliens know so damn much about Chicago's history. But yeah, mobsters ran the city in the early 1900's and had the police and judges on their payrolls. By the next century, while the gangsters were more or less gone, the corruption spread into politics. So looking back, it's no wonder you and Ted found so much corruption in GD when you were the temporary CEO of GD. This is corruption city. At least the once-huge murder rate is under control these past two centuries.

"But the aliens didn't mention what happened when the corporations rose to power in the first quarter of the twenty-first century. Islamic terrorists sprang up all over the world. Local governments couldn't stop them. That's when the corporations stepped up, beginning here in Chicago. They outlawed the Muslim religion and then a year later, all religions. They invented the microwave boiler, something you never read about in the usual history books.

"They attached them to low-flying fleets of drones. In the areas they flew over, the microwaves boiled the brains of humans and animals. They swept the entire Mideast and North Africa clear of all people, before hitting selected spots elsewhere in Africa. The result: no more terrorists and a lower population. Within two generations or forty years, all traces of organized religions vanished. Anthropologists, though, still look for religions in superstitious people on the new worlds we discover. I sometimes wonder if that's what's missing in our modern world: religion.

"But then, look at all the good the corporations have done. I guess we can't say the corporations were entirely bad."

After getting over the shock of hearing this and

realizing once more how ignorant I really was, I continued. "Okay. Next question. What the hell do we do for rulers? They got rid of the emperor and empress. Now the self-appointed stockholder billionaire is gone. No one is leading, except me in my small areas."

Hank chuckled. "It's all on your shoulders."

"What if they don't support it?" We laughed.

"I've been thinking about this for weeks, ever since the takeover began when he ousted Dimitri and Natalie. What we need are leaders elected by the whole empire. A popular vote thing. Call them the President and the Vice-president. But make them elected officials and for a specific term. That used to be the way things were done over two centuries ago."

"Best idea ever. So how do we get this implemented?"

"Hey, you're the Senior Judge. Make a judicial ruling to that effect. Perhaps they'll fire you, and then you'll be free of this yoke. Lord, I don't envy you. Nothing like the fate of three billion people on you."

"Thanks. Just remember, if things go south, Janine and you and your kids are going to survive with me and our other sisters."

"Because you married Bonita?"

"Yeah. I would have anyway. She used to be my Ted."

"I heard that. Impressive. Best of luck."

"Tea's like up," Janine said, bringing it in on a tray. "So are you two done?"

"Yep. Hank's a history genius, you know."

Janine laughed. "You like can say that again."

***

The next morning after seeing Sam and the kids off to school, Ashley hung my laptop bag around my neck and then draped my cloak over me. Sherry arrived, and we three headed to New O'Hare where Deanna waited with her fancy Cartwright Enterprise Airliner.

"I certainly don't envy you, Molly," Deanna said once she'd set the nav controls and joined the others in the plush passenger seats. "Plus, it's strange flying back to this island where I first picked up you, Ted, and our three younger sisters so many years ago. You didn't have arms then, too, and honestly, I worried about you for weeks after we got back to Chicago."

"Yeah, that was scary, but I learned firsthand what these victims would feel and respond. I can't complain."

"But are you going to take the Third Invader help?" Ashley asked. "Undo the mutations?"

"Don't know yet. That's why this trip. Most don't know this, but my sister Eve and good friend, the dwarf Lara Axe-head, are on this atoll. Both are geneticists working on cures. They've also kept Doctors Janet and Nelson Padella with them. Actually, it's the Padella's secret research lab. Patricia Ann and her family are there, too. Eve is brain-picking Nelson, Janet, and Patricia Ann, since the three are now armless telepaths. Yeah, the Padella's got caught in one of the terrorist attacks when they visited the mainland a while back. Still, with five of them working on the problem, I'm hoping they've already made good progress so we don't need these aliens."

Deanna laughed. "Well, isn't that something. I hadn't heard that about the Padellas. Serves them right for what they did to you, Ted, and our younger sisters. Payback can be a bitch."

I knew she was venting her long held anger with those two doctors. In the past, those doctors always seemed to be heroes in the public eyes and yet carried out inhumane experiments in secret. When I was rescued from their clutches years ago, I, too, would have cheered to have heard the news the Padellas had become armless as they did to me. Today, that anger had long evaporated. I felt sad for them, since their handicap would make them next to useless in the critical search for cures.

Four hours later, we landed on the atoll. Memories flooded back of my six months here and just how terrified I'd been to have awakened to find I'd lost my arms. Ted was so right. It felt like my space had collapsed from around three feet around me down to my head and chest. I was thankful for the minute that Deanna needed to shut down the Airliner.

With a deep breath, I followed them down the steep exit stairs made challenging by my tall heels. I didn't need convincing that these mutations had to be cured.

"Molly! You look great. We saw the live broadcasts," Eve said. She rushed up and hugged me tightly.

Then, Lara got her turn. She hugged me, picked me up, and twirled me around. "I'm so glad you're okay. What an adventure you've had. How's Sam and Matt?"

"They're back from the dead. Literally. None the worse for wear. Celeste is handling their therapy. They've got to erase being blown up by a bomb. Thankfully, I've not had one of those to erase."

We laughed. Then, I saw Patricia Ann timidly walking towards us, followed by Vernon carrying their son in a baby sack. His tiny baby arms looked strange.

"Hi, Molly. I'm like you now, darn near useless as a virologist and anything else. But I'm trying," Patricia Ann said. "Never give up. The Padellas mostly have—given up, that is. Those Third Invader aliens sure look weird. Do you trust them? That's what we've been discussing here."

"I don't know, Patricia Ann. Come on. Let go inside. I've got plenty of questions for you three."

I found the Padellas already sitting at the discussion table in their lab. While they looked up at me as I entered, their eyes had a blank, not there look. I sensed both were in apathy. I ignored them for now.

"Okay, Eve, Lara. You probably know why I'm here. Progress report, please."

Eve sighed. "Well, it's not very good yet. We think we can turn a partial cure into another virus, maybe. Patricia Ann was good at what she did, making our bodies build up an immunity to these mutations. That's why you've seen the Med Centers having to give people huge doses of the agents in order to have them function as they once did.

"I knew you'd be visiting us. So we've discussed this at length. Molly, we think you should accept the help these aliens are proposing. Even if we're eventually successful at inventing more partial cures, we're years from being able to widely implement them. Earth hasn't got that long to wait."

"That grim, eh?"

"We're being ethical about it," Lara said. "Unlike others. That necessitates a slower pace, since we don't just experiment and see what happens to the test subject. I certainly hope these aliens won't be doing that."

"If I agree to have them help, can I bring them here and have you watch their every move? I don't want them doing unethical experimentations either."

Dr. Nelson grumbled. "That'll slow your progress down to that of a small Gastropoda."

"Huh?" I said, looking over at him. Janet cracked a momentary smile.

"A snail."

I countered, grinning. "Didn't the tortoise win the race with the hare?"

"Fairytales. Bah." Nelson said.

"Back to business," Eve said. "The problem will be coming up with the specifications for the cures that Earth desires."

"We all want normal feet," I said.

"Yes, that's probably the one aspect everyone would agree to," Eve said.

She explained her reasoning. "Look, the original Galactic Doll mutation was designed and sold to all women as a beauty enhancement. The Sixth Invaders implanted the desire to become enhanced into everyone's mind. Still, there's no arguing the healthy side-effects that original mutation had. Beyond curing diseases and rejuvenating bodies, it also enforced proper body proportions and weight on women. As far as we can tell, a good percentage of women love their large bosoms, while the rest of us hate them."

"Duh. No kidding. I'd love having them smaller. But I see where you're heading. We can't even say definitively that we don't want our female children inheriting mother's Galactic Doll mutations. The beauty thing again, right?" I said.

"Precisely. But for the sake of survival, we probably can sell that one. So put it on the list of desired cures," Eve said.

"Ashley, start a list for us. Normal feet. Galactic Doll mutation not inherited by our children. So how about a Galactic Doll mutation for women only that has all the usual healthy side-effects and give women a choice on breast sizes? Is that possible?"

Lara smiled. Patricia Ann grinned.

Eve roared and said, "Who knows what's possible with these aliens. Go ahead and write that one down. Maybe two versions based on breast sizes. This mutation would be very useful if children don't inherit it from their parents. Gives women a choice. Considering the implants the Sixth Invaders gave to women, unless you run therapy on every woman on Earth to erase them, women will insist on having the Galactic Doll mutation, which they see as a beauty enhancement.

"Now as far as men are concerned, the female Galactic Doll mutation ought not modify males. Further, we should have Patricia Ann's male mutations undone. As far as is possible. Her mutation basically implemented the usual Galactic Doll mutation onto male bodies. So perhaps just say turn male Galactic Dolls back into normal males."

Patricia Ann said, "One catch. A few men loved the change. The transgender men. They won't like waking up to find their dreams shattered. How do we handle those few men who welcomed this change?"

"We could stipulate the female Galactic Doll mutation also work on men, but then we're right back at the starting point. Terrorists could use it on men," I said.

"What about making a special version of the female Galactic Doll agent, one that requires a sample of the male's DNA to activate it? Then, terrorists couldn't use it as a weapon, since it would alter only that one person's DNA?" Lara suggested.

"Add that one to the list, Ashley," I said. "We're making headway."

"But what about male rejuvenation and disease curing? That positive aspect can't become the sole province of Galactic Doll women," Patricia Ann said.

"Good point. The current ones are being used to save lives like Sam and Matt. The agents saved lives on one of our deep space exploration ships," I said.

Eve said, "How about having a male agent that cures diseases and rejuvenates bodies like the female Galactic Doll one does?"

Patricia Ann said, "So the female version wouldn't

modify males and vice versa. The two syringe versions could be colored blue and pink."

"Good point. Write that down too, Ashley," I said. "Wait a minute. Part of this whole mess is that these agents are being stolen and used against other humans on other Federation worlds. If we keep the rejuvenation aspect—"

"Others might still steal it just to get their hands on potential immortality." Eve finished my thought.

"Never sell that." Nelson mumbled. "I want to be cured and youthful again. Janet, too."

"Point taken. We'll leave rejuvenation on the list," I said. "What about the current telepaths? Some definitely want to be telepaths and have accepted being handicapped as the price they need to pay to have it."

"Don't want it," muttered Nelson.

Janet countered. "Yes, you do. Now you know how to please me in bed."

"Too steep a price," he said.

"Do we want to leave a path open to make new telepaths?" I asked. "Or do we want to allow existing telepaths to remain so until they desire to get the new cures?"

Eve said, "We got into this mess primarily because telepaths are so rare that the unscrupulous saw ways to get filthy rich by making and selling them. The galaxy doesn't need people who can spy into other people's minds. Molly, you know this as well as I do."

"Yes, yes, I do." I bit my lip. "Okay, the cures should undo whatever was done to give them telepathic abilities. Still, I think the few who are still armless telepaths deserve to have a choice. I know Sam and Matt would love to get their arms back, but Nikita has wanted to be a telepath since before she was born. Not sure if Isabella wants to remain a telepath or not. It should be each person's decision. Some might like to take advantage of the get rich offers they signed on for before they get the cures and lose their telepathy. This will work well if none of these mutations end up being inherited by their children. No propagation of mutations."

Eve said, "Yes, that has to be in there or the Federation will likely veto it."

Patricia Ann sighed. "You know, it still isn't perfect. Someone could acquire a lot of the new female Galactic Doll mutation agent and unleash it on a city. They could do the same with the male rejuvenation agent, but much less likely. However, it takes only a tiny tweak to turn the female version into unisex in effect. We'd be right back where we started. It didn't take much for me to turn it into a virus and cause a pandemic."

I tensed and ground my teeth. "The only way out of that box is to entirely eliminate these mutation agents. I doubt I can sell that one at all, not with the implants the Sixth Invaders inserted into our women. All right. I'll make two plans. The first with all we've discussed. The second will be to undo all modifications to everyone and nothing else added or changed. That'll be my fallback plan if the Federation doesn't go for the first one because it could still be potentially abused."

"But what about their side of the deal?" Eve asked. "Taking a thousand of our people. Why? To where?"

"I don't trust these Third Invaders. Not even a little bit," I said. "Yet, if we don't do something—I can't believe this is laid in my lap. Three billion dead if I don't accept their help."

"Well, it's not a certainty yet, is it? Maybe the Federation won't do it," Eve said.

"Do I gamble on a maybe with three billion lives at stake? What a pickle."

"Just get our arms back," Dr. Nelson Padella said. "Do anything to get them to cure Janet and me, somehow, someway."

I ignored them. Their ideas of cures had been to change hair and eye colors via a mutation.

Deanna and I spent the rest of the day chatting with Eve and Lara, whom we'd not seen for ages. They wanted to know all about what had been happening back in Chicago. I felt sorry for them, stuck on this atoll with only the Padellas for company and now Patricia Ann and her family.

That night, we headed back, the Airliner on autopilot while we slept.

Once back at her Cartwright Enterprises office of the fiftieth floor, we met with Russell, the CEO of GEnt. He made arrangements for me to make an empire-wide broadcast outlining my idea for a democratically elected president of the empire. With that arranged for one o'clock, I went home to clean up and prepare my speech.

Ashley dolled me up for the cameras. I wore a shiny, red satin gown. Deanna sat me behind her corporation desk. Thus, I looked as official as I could.

"Hello everyone in the Sol Empire. I'm Molly Parkinson, your Senior Investigator and Senior Judge. Today, I'm speaking to you as your judge. At this time, the empire lacks a leader. It's obvious that we need an honest, dedicated person to execute the laws of our empire and to guide the corporations.

"I propose that we democratically elect a President and Vice-president to oversee the daily operations of our empire. As many candidates can run for these offices as desired, as long as there are at least two for each position. Each world, moon, and station holds free and open elections. Every citizen of that world gets an equal vote. Whoever wins the total votes on that world, moon, and station becomes that world's nominee, yielding twenty-four winners. Those twenty-four votes are then added and the candidate receiving the most of these two dozen votes becomes the next President and Vice-president.

"It can't be he or she who receives the mot empire-wide votes. Why? What chance would our smaller populated colonies and moons and stations have? None. They'd have no real say or power in who gets elected. This total empire-wide vote count would only determine the winner if there is a tie vote among the two dozen worlds and moons.

"I'd like our Senate to reconvene and legislate how long their terms of office should be and similar details. For now, anyone interested in running for these offices should contact your local GPan corporation and get your name approved. GEnt will air speeches and help disseminate facts about the candidates, even hold debates.

"Let's hold the election on May Day. That gives us enough time to get candidates, hear what they have to say, and get the election process established. By summer, the Sol

Empire will not be leaderless any longer.

"Finally, on the matter of these mutation agents, I've reached a decision and will explore its implementation before I announce it. My goal is to avoid genocide of our people. Thank you. Good day."

The floodlights ceased melting my face.

"You did a good job, Molly," Russell said, as technicians bustled about dismantling their equipment.

"But will this be accepted?" I asked.

"I hope so," he said.

Chapter 14 Take Back Our Empire

"Give me an 'R'," yelled Nikita. "Come on, Matt. You have to help out."

After supper, Nikita insisted on practicing her cheers. I had to listen.

"Go Rockets," Matt muttered. "This is dumb. Guys trying to play basketball in their heels is a joke. Everyone knows it. There's nothing to cheer."

Ashley yelled from the living room. "Hey, Molly, everyone, something big's happening. Come quick,"

With our heels clicking on the hardwood floor, we three joined the others, plopping on couches and chairs to watch.

"It's originating from Brussels, Tau Ceti," Sam said.

"Again, I am Oz Rankin, the CEO of GPan for Brussels, Tau Ceti. With me is Vassily Nevsky, the CEO of GPan for Pylon, Epsilon Eridani. Behind us are the other twenty-one CEOs of the other GPan corporations on our smaller worlds."

The camera panned across the men sitting in two rows behind the two podiums. We could see they were in a corporate conference room, filled with stainless steel tables and chairs.

"We twenty-three CEOs have met and reached a decision. We are taking back our empire. The era of Earth running our empire is over. Ended. Caput. From now on, Vassily and I will share those duties, as will our other major corporations. Earth can still have its own worldwide corporations, but they'll have no say in the running of the Sol Empire. Why?

"By now it should be obvious why we've had to dump Earth. Ignore the fact that for over thirty years Sixth Invaders occupied the bodies of Earth's top CEOs and ran the empire, nearly destroying it. They forced a war here on Brussels, a war against their own homemade robots no less. Earth's women have been mutated into exaggerated Galactic Dolls. Then came the severely handicapped armless telepath Galactic Dolls mutation.

"We all know how that worked out. Vassily's own daughter, Mila Nevsky, was turned into one while she was attending the Miss Galaxy contest. Thousands of lives have been ruined by Earth's continued bungling. Now, they've pulled the Federation of Planets into their mess. Admiral Skaggs is likely to soon exterminate all humans on Earth. Even if they don't, that world is full of freaks—men who look like Galactic Dolls. Hell, you can't tell an Earth person's gender by their looks or voices. You have to pull their pants down to see if they're male or female.

"Do we want people like this making the critical decisions that impact our ever-growing empire? Hell, no! Enough is enough. Today, we're taking back the control of our empire. Earth can rot in its own cesspool of corruption and mutation.

"We've established a new Senate located here on Brussels. Already the twenty-three worlds had elected new senators. Beginning next week, they will meet and begin making the new laws that govern the Sol Empire. We've taken Molly Parkinson's suggestion about having a single elected leader to run the empire. We've seen corporations fail to handle events. In a conflict or tense situation, you need a single leader to deal with it. We've seen what happens when an issue is turned over to a committee. Nothing gets done or it takes forever to reach a consensus.

"We like her idea about the election process. So at this time, I will be the new Sol Empire President, and Vassily will be the new Vice-president. The Senate's first actions will be to define precisely what our positions will consist of and how elections are to be handled. We anticipate that new elections will be held next year. We have vacated our CEO positions and will remain so while we are your president and vice-president. The Senate's second action must be to work out a compromise on the distribution of acquired wealth from the exploitation of new worlds. Citizens must receive some benefits, as Galactic Mining has said.

"We thank Molly Parkinson for all that she's done for the Sol Empire. However, as of today, she is no longer the Sol Empire's Senior Investigator and Senior Judge. Vassily, the

Senate, and I will fill those positions as soon as possible. At this time, Molly Parkinson remains in those positions, but serves only Earth.

"Also, with the death of our Senior Ambassador Aaron Strawn and the retirement of our other two senior ambassadors, the Sol Empire must appoint three to these critical posts on Bela Prime. In view of her unfailing service to the entire Sol Empire, we hereby appoint Molly Parkinson to be our newest Senior Ambassador. We still have to choose the other two. If you have a desire to fill that position, let Vassily or me know. This is our way of thanking Mrs. Parkinson for her many years of service to the empire."

He stepped back, allowing the camera to zoom in on the other podium.

"Hello, I'm Vassily Nevsky. Yes, some of you may remember my beautiful daughter Mila who went to Earth for the Miss Galactic Doll contest last year. She became Miss Galactic Doll 2360, but has paid the ultimate price for her crown. Mila was turned into a helpless armless telepath Galactic Doll. She can never return home to me. I've lost my only daughter to the bumbling incompetence of Earth's leaders."

A bitter man, I thought, and rightly so. I was there. Mila was gorgeous and deserved to win, but all got mutated into armless telepaths, part of Jill's scheme to get rich quick making and selling slave telepaths.

He continued. "The total ban of Earth's mutants on other worlds of our empire still stands. They messed up their own world; we're not about to let them start in on ours, big boobs or not. Further, it is now a high crime for anyone to employ an armless telepath, but with one exception. We do recognize the invaluable work said telepaths perform in translating languages on newly discovered worlds. Thus, these telepaths can be employed as linguists on the deep space exploration ships, but only those ships. Anyone else caught using one will be summarily terminated. There's no place on any of our worlds for these mutant freaks.

"As of now, Admiral Rossi and the entire Sol space fleet is under our control. We recognize that a number of these ships belong to Earth, but their crew members are un-mutated and may wish to immigrate to other worlds in our empire. Hell, who wants to return to Earth and live among those freaks? No one. Still, those ships that do belong to Earth will remain under Earth's ownership and will help in the defense of Earth. However, they will not be controlled by the freaks inhabiting Earth. Admiral Rossi has been granted Pylon citizenship, for example. We aren't stealing Earth registered ships, merely guaranteeing that the freaks on Earth can't control them and that their crew members can immigrate to sane worlds.

"If Earth and its freaks can somehow manage to build more space ships, they can crew them with their own mutants. A new infantry division will be formed. Obviously, Earth's original infantry division can no longer fight a battle. We will morn the loss of General Blythe, though; she was the finest infantry general in the last two centuries. But as a mutant, she's hardly capable of fighting a real battle any longer.

"Earth and its corporations will be allowed to function as they wish. They will receive their fair cut of the profits, as long as they continue to meet their usual financial responsibilities to the empire as they always have done.

"The corporate chain of command for Earth still goes through Moscow group, who represent the Earth-wide corporations. They in turn will report to their Brussels or Pylon counterpart. New orders to be followed will originate not from Chicago, but from either Brussels or Pylon and be sent to the Moscow corporations, who will send them on down to the thousands of local corporation offices.

"Finally a word to the giants and dwarves who have immigrated to Earth. If the Federation decides to nuke Earth, you will be asked to immigrate to any of the other twenty-three worlds of the empire. You bank accounts will follow you, and you'll be remunerated for any physical losses you may suffer by abandoning Earth. We value your work and lives.

"Oh yes. All Earth-registered ships that are out in deep space have been notified of these changes and given their new directives. Like other crews, they don't wish to become mutants either. So Earth, you are officially on your own. You can send senators to the new Senate, if you desire. Trading arrangements are unaffected, unless you wish to change them. In short, you no longer run the Sol Empire; we do. You and your mutants can be a part of the empire or not. Your choice. That is all."

The transmission ended. Sam spoke up. "Can't say I blame them. Surprised it took them this long to bail."

"Mom, are you really going to be the Senior Ambassador and move to Bela Prime?" Isabella asked.

"But then I can't be a cheerleader," Nikita said.

Matt rolled his eyes.

"First I've heard of it," I said. "Something like that should be a family decision. Everyone gets a vote on that. Right now, I'm trying to prevent the Federation from killing everyone."

Someone rang our doorbell. Ashley answered it. In walked the Hugos followed by Dimitri and Natalie Leonovich—our ex-emperor and empress. Veronica and Fritz headed off to play with Nikita and Matt, while Helen and Casper joined us in the living room.

"I can't believe they've abandoned Earth, after all we've done for them," Casper said.

"Earth founded all these other colonies, moons, and planets. How dare they?" Dimitri said. He slapped a fist into his hand.

"For these past thirty years, Earth hasn't exactly been—well, I don't know," Helen said. "We've stopped a war with the Sixth Invaders. How short are their memories?"

"Yeah, well I don't like being called a freak," Natalie said. "Or a mutant. But I guess we sort of are, especially our men."

Ashley answered the knock on our door. She called out, "Molly, best come here!"

When I got there, my mouth opened. I recognized the Chief Finance Officer for Galactic Mining, Dr. Kirk Alcott. He had been in hiding and had threatened to blow up the stockpile of precious metals, though only he knew its location. I suspected others also knew where it was—hence the bomb threat.

"Come in, Dr. Alcott."

"Kirk, please. I need to see you as our Senior Judge."

I led him into our living room.

"Am I interrupting something?"

"No, we're just talking about the cessation of twenty-three other worlds. Have a seat. Everyone, this is—"

Natalie interrupted. "We know. Dr. Kirk Alcott. CFO GMine. Join us."

"Dimitri, Natalie. Casper, Helen." He sighed as he sat down. He wore one of Leslie's new male doll suits. Bags under his eyes told much.

"I came to see our Senior Judge, but it's good our emperor and empress are here too. Galactic Mining isn't taking this lying down. Chuck Riggs, our CEO, has issued orders to all Earth-owned mining ships. I should say that we own twenty-nine out of thirty-eight of the largest ships. The other worlds own many more smaller ones. Anyway, Riggs told the ships' commanders that if they bring their raw products only to Earth, everyone on the ship will receive double pay and double any bonuses due.

"We've changed signatories on bank accounts. No other world's finance officers can have access to the Galactic Mining accounts. They can only have what we specifically send them, which after their action today will be none. Riggs is also discussing this with other CEOs, in hopes all Sol-wide corporations will lock these renegades out of our banking. We're hoping Galactic Manufacturing will cease all exports of refined metals. We've setup storage depots for both raw ores and refined metals in the abandoned desert regions of the Mideast. The smelters there don't have enough capacity to handle all the anticipated raw ores coming from so many large mining ships."

"Way to go! Great thinking," Dimitri said. "All right. Hit them where it hurts."

"Senior Judge, is what we're doing legal? We had to act fast before they could drain Earth's accounts. Originally, I wanted to bring this up as a lawsuit in your court. But there wasn't time. De we have the legal rights to do this? They are *our* colonies, after all."

Shit. Was I ever on the spot! "Honestly, I have no idea of the legality of your move or theirs. I need time to research the agreements made when these corporations were setup and what ones were made with the other worlds and moons. I can't see their move to abandon Earth as right. You did need to act fast. I will begin research on the legal side tomorrow. It'll be some time before they figure out the extent you've gone to isolate them. I suspect they'll eventually want me to get involved. Otherwise, it's civil war. They've got control of our space fleet. Not so good, I expect."

Natalie said, "We should get all major corporations working together on this. But everything hinges on whether the Federation is about to nuke Earth. Molly, you should make that your top priority. This civil war can wait."

Casper said, "Have each of the empire-wide CFOs withhold monthly stipends to the other off-Earth CFOs. That will get their attention. I like your plan to destroy the empire's wealth if anyone tries to harm you. We should get something similar set up for the other corporations."

Dimitri asked, "Do you think it'll come to a war? If so, we're going to lose. Our men can barely walk. What lousy timing to have men mutated into Galactic Dolls."

I laughed. "Dimitri, when would have been a good time to have men turned into dolls?"

That brought chuckles to all, lightening the somber mood. Casper, Helen, Dimitri, Natalie, and Kirk left, discussing further steps to take and how best to coordinate Earth's response.

When we were alone in bed, Sam said, "This is only going to give the Federation more reasons to nuke Earth. We can't fight a civil war, at least not physically. Can we even win a financial war?"

Chapter 15 Make a Deal

"So that's what we'd like."

I finished making my short presentation onboard the Kanika the next day. The same people were there, when I listed off what mutation changes we desired to have made. The Third Invader ambassadors took notes.

"So let me make sure I've got it right," Rashidi said. "You want optimum healthy bodies for both men and women, but women should continue to have their Galactic Doll shapes. All should have normal feet, and males should look like males again. None of these changes should be inherited, and diseases and missing appendages should be cured and regrown. What about telepathic abilities?"

"They can go. That's what mostly caused this mess in the first place," I said.

"All right. And should each mutation not affect opposite sex?"

"Yes, that would also help. If no one can use the Galactic Doll agent on men to turn them into male dolls, that'll also help prevent misuse. So is this even possible? Our geneticists believe they might accomplish some of these changes in the next few years. But we don't have that kind of time."

I looked at Admiral Skaggs, but couldn't read any expression on his stoic face. The ambassadors whispered; their faces, serious. I had Plan B ready to go.

"We'll have to look into this," Rashidi said.

"Okay, if that's not doable in a short amount of time," I said watching Admiral Skaggs' face, "then we have an alternative. Make men and women normal again. Nothing else, just normal male and female bodies. Forget all the rest. We'd rather be alive than nuked."

A flicker of a smile creased his lips. He said, "What's happening with your civil war? I heard your empire has revolted. All twenty-three of them."

"We're working on that, sir. This threat of

annihilation..."

He grunted. I couldn't tell if that was positive or negative.

Rashidi said, "Okay. Give us day to consult with our scientists. If we agree to do this, are you prepared to give us thousand humans?"

"Do we have a choice?"

Rashidi smiled, but didn't answer. The meeting broke up. Ashley and Sherry said little on the journey back to New O'Hare. So much for the day.

The next day after the kids were off to school, I joined Sam at the University of Chicago Library. I needed his help. What exactly had been the agreements between Earth and the other twenty-three worlds, moons, colonies, and stations? I understood why they wanted to separate themselves from Earth, but was that a legal option for them?

An hour later, Sam found me slumped over the pile of books, sound asleep.

Yawning, I said, "Only a lawyer could ever understand all this mumbo-jumbo. The words don't seem to mean anything. God, I hate lawyers and their lingo. Gotta be a linguist to read this stuff."

Sam laughed. "Could have told you so. So what're you gonna do now?"

"Make a ruling that's based on common sense and what's right for the most involved. Not much else I can do, except hope for the best."

I headed home, glad for the cold wind in my face, fully waking me up.

Boom! An explosion shook the MTES, which stopped so suddenly that I was tossed down onto the conveyor belt, knocking the air out of me. Deltawings. Our own spaceships fired their weapons, aiming at the many skyscrapers of Chicago. Boom. One struck the GD building close to me. I struggled to get back onto my feet, wishing for arms once more. In slow motion, I watched the entire hundred story building lean over. As it fell, it gained speed. My god! I couldn't get out of the way, not even if my feet were normal. Wham! A wall of steel and glass hit me. Blackness flashed.

Then, there I was moving along on the MTES, the cold wind in my face. "What the hell?" I said, looking around. Everything seemed perfectly normal, a cold day in late February.

As I looked between buildings into the distance, I saw a flash of intense white light. No sounds, just a light so bright I had to turn away. Then, a wall of grey came rushing at me. The MTES stopped, tossing me and others onto the ground. I lifted my head. What is that grey cloud? Wham! It hit me. The debris from a nuclear bomb. The Federation had just nuked Chicago. My death was instantaneous. Wait! But I was supposed to be spared.

No, I was still moving along on the MTES. I blinked. "What?" I cried out. Several passersby looked at me as though I was a crazy lady. I swallowed and closed my eyes.

When I opened them, I sat at the controls of the Friendship. We were flying through a dust nebula. I could hear "oohs" and "ahs" coming from others. I slipped out of my X harness and looked down into the passenger area. There were all my sisters, their spouses, children, and even some of our close friends. Bonita waved at me, and I smiled back. When I turned back to slip into my seatbelt, I found myself moving along on the same MTES ride. "What's happening to me?"

I shook my head to clear my thoughts. That was what was supposed to happen to me and us, if and when the Federation decided to destroy Earth. Was that first the colonies declaring war on Earth? Must've been. An overhead noise from a two-man shuttle distracted me. I looked up.

What planet was I on? This wasn't earth! Tall buildings, giant causeways connecting buildings like bridges a hundred feet in the air, strange small shuttles darted about like flies. The sun was redder than ours. The air smelled foul, a mixture of fuel fumes, oil, metal flakes, and rot. Bela Prime. I was in the capital of the Federation of Planets, walking somewhere. Huh? I shook my head.

And there I was, still moving right along our MTES. Purposely, I faced the cold wind. What was happening to me? Then, it dawned on me. I was once again seeing multiple possible futures. Only this time, I had no idea which one I needed to choose or what I had to do to choose it! Shit.

Was Earth going to be destroyed by our other empire worlds or by the Federation nuking us without warning or letting me and my family escape in the Friendship only to travel endlessly around the galaxy or was I to be our Senior Ambassador on Bela Prime? Didn't I have any choice in my future? What it all being chosen for me?

"No, no, no!"

Okay, I yelled, causing others nearby on the MTES to stare at me. My face felt hot, and I let the cold wind blow directly on it until I felt better. At the next intersection, I turned around and headed for the lake and the park benches lining the beach. I needed to think. I sat with the wind off the lake in my face.

Suppose these Third Invaders could make these new modified mutation agents, designed to set things right. We'd have to confiscate all existing quantities of the two major mutation agents, the Galactic Doll and the armless telepath. "Not realistic," I said to the waves lapping onto the shore. Every Med Center in Chicago, to say nothing of every hospital and Galactic Medicine facility in the city, had countless samples. Usually, large containers held the bulk of the substances; yet I knew the staff usually filled up small working bottles from which the required amount could be withdrawn via a syringe. And there were the countless syringes that had been given out for emergencies, particularly those on our deep space exploration ships. Thousands of other cities around Earth duplicated these widespread quantities. How could we ever be certain we'd disposed of all these agents?

Worse, as soon as we began confiscating them, surely enterprising individuals would confiscate some for the black market. They'd likely fetch a high price off-world. No, the time to have destroyed them was way back when we first killed Commander R'Ina and took possession of that initial batch. Only the corporations hadn't done as I asked. Damn them.

I sighed. No matter how I looked at it, some of these agents, the armless telepath one in particular, were sure to be smuggled off-world. Admiral Skaggs meant well with his super sensors that would detect the agents, but smugglers were sure to find loopholes in protocols. Just look at history. No matter what we did, some of these terrible agents were bound to wind up in the wrong hands off-world. In a way, I pitied the Federation of Planets. Years from now, other of their worlds were sure to be experiencing what Earth was undergoing now. Hell, I'd bet my life on it.

In a flash, I realized that whatever we finally agreed to wasn't going to matter much in the very long term. Someone was bound to smuggle this stuff off-world, if they hadn't done so already. That simplified my choices. In fact, what I did didn't matter all that much, not in the years to come. That brought a smile to my chilled face and relief to my mind. I headed home. No freaky images hit me this time.

The next day, the aliens summoned me to the Kanika. Ashley and Sherry accompanied me. In the conference room, Ambassador Rashida discussed what could be done.

"My scientists tell me they can produce agent to undo male modifications and repair all feet. None of existing modifications would be inherited by offspring, and no lost appendages would be regrown, but telepathic ability would be lost. Allow four months for that one to be produced. Allow eight months to produce agent that meets all your requirements. Your Plan B version of simply making men and women normal again could be done in one month, maybe less. Nothing regrown, though.

"Admiral Skaggs, do they have eight months left before you take action or should we go with fastest possible one?"

"Hey, don't put the decision on me," he said. "Still, Mrs. Parkinson would want me to answer this question. Eight months? No, that's far too long to wait. If you're talking a month or less to get everyone more or less normal, I think that's the safest route. I can pretty much guarantee you have that long—what with the Federation bureaucracy. I'd say it's risky to not do something in say the next month."

"Okay then. We'll take the one month or less version. But what do you really want in return?" I asked.

"One thousand humans, evenly divided between men and women between say twenty-one and thirty," Ambassador Mosi said. "We'll pick and choose. Discretion at all times. In fact, you won't even need to let your people know you're giving them up. They'll become colonists on one of the new worlds we have prepared."

"Yeah, but," I countered. "We're only getting a partial mutation agent fix, not the full one which might take eight months. Shouldn't we get a break on what we're supposed to pay?"

Her shiny hand brushed across her lips, as though in thought. "Well, yes, I suppose that's true. We can't take a lesser number, but what if we promise those that don't like it can return to Earth."

"If we aren't choosing them, how will they know that's part of the agreement? We don't want to lose our top scientists and engineers. We don't want to lose our brightest people."

Admiral Skaggs interceded. "Look, ambassadors, the Federation and the Sol Empire both have guidelines on just who can be considered for a colonist position. We recognize that not everyone is a good candidate to help build a new world."

"Quite true," she said.

Here was another area I knew nothing about. Now that he mentioned this, I could see the truth in it. Criminal types wouldn't fare well, for instance. I imagined candidates had to be hardy souls.

She said, "We will agree to take only those suitable for colonizing new world. Brochure will outline terms of this agreement and circumstances under which they can return. We can have that prepared for you in day or two."

"Will any of us know who has been taken? Those you take will be missed by someone. They could file a missing person report. Authorities could waste valuable time searching for them."

"We'll provide you with list of their names. Will that be satisfactory?"

"Yes. Can I have a private word with Admiral Skaggs?"

Everyone left the room, including my assistant and security person.

"What's the real situation with Earth, sir? Are you really about to nuke us?"

"Frankly, this civil war has just tipped the scales. I probably can buy you a month at the very most. Beyond that, I'm sure they'll issue the genocide orders. Whether they'll let me get the giants and dwarves evacuated in time isn't known, but no matter what, I promise you'll get a couple hours warning so you, Bonita, and the others can escape. Look, they need colonists. You need mutation cures. The Federation needs this mutation threat neutralized. We all win."

"Okay. I don't have much choice except to agree to it. I don't want to see three billion people murdered."

The others rejoined us. I agreed to Plan B of simply making men and women normal again but with nothing regrown and no rejuvenation. I knew this would be a hard sell, since regrowing lost appendages and organs was a crucial aspect of either agent, along with the fountain of youth. Still Earth didn't have enough time left to get a better agent. The possibility existed that Eve and Lara could invent one that did both, given time.

I returned home with the news and met with Russell Godwyn, Deanna's husband and CEO of Galactic Entertainment. After telling him about the deal, I asked him whether I should make a worldwide announcement or just leave it be.

"Wait until these Third Invaders actually produce the cures. Time enough to tell others at that point. They might not succeed," he said. "I'm thankful the admiral let you know he'd give you warning so we could evacuate if needed."

"I'm not about to lose everyone I love. Thanks," I said.

We then shared an ale to toast my new agreement, one that probably saved three billion lives.

Chapter 16 Choices

"Mom, you know I've always wanted to be a telepath," Nikita said.

I'd just explained the deal struck with the Third Invaders to undo the mutations, saving Earth's three billions from the genocide of the Federation of Planets.

I said, "Look, the mutation agents we have are going to be confiscated and replaced by these new ones that aren't going to rejuvenate bodies or regrow anything missing. If we don't hurry up and get the existing arm regrowing cure, you'll be stuck like this for the rest of your life."

Sam said, "Matt and I should get it done right away, if it's possible in our cases. Bonita, you too?"

"You bet, Sam. I'm with you. I don't enjoy being so incredibly handicapped. I know given enough time I can make do—at least I think I did so last lifetime. But it's so damned hard for me right now. And if Earth's going to lose its regrow mutation, I have to take it, unless Molly says I shouldn't."

"Hey, I'm never going to tell you what you should do, Bonita. If you want it, then get it. This could be your last chance."

"Yeah, well, you certainly didn't give the people of Earth any choice," she said. "What if some men don't want to be 'normal' again? What if some women don't want normal feet, but love having to wear these tall heels? They are only a major hurdle for those of us who don't have arms. What if an existing man or woman who is a telepath doesn't want to lose that ability? You've given them no choice."

"Complete sex change operations have been around for two centuries. I remember one boy had it done while we were in highschool. Tall heels?" I flashed back to when I first met my sister Leslie. Dolled up in a tight latex fetish gown and wearing tall heels, she could barely walk from the club where the shooter fired at her. I had to agree some women loved tall heels. "But now women will have a choice," I said.

"As far as telepathy goes, I didn't have much choice. We

here know because I had enough hours of Celeste's therapy, I developed telepathy. Others can, too. But beyond this household, we know what telepathy has brought us. The Federation and all other worlds are terrified a person who looks perfectly ordinary having telepathic skills. With us armless telepaths, we stand out. See an armless person around, most likely he or she is a telepath, so guard your secrets. Just look at the gigantic salaries corporations are paying telepaths. If we're ever going to have any chance of normalcy as a planet, we've got to eliminate this armless telepath mutation agent."

"Mom, Isabella and I don't disagree with you. Neither of us wants to be kidnapped and sold into slavery. But I still want to be a telepath like I am today. So does Isabella and Maria. Don't you, too, Tia? They are offering you your old job back as a linguist, only you'll make a million credits a year instead of twenty thousand," Nikita said. "People should have a choice."

Tia, who had been silent, said, "I'm afraid, Nikita. I can barely function; I'm not skilled at using my feet like you or Isabella are. And the way it's looking, if I don't get my arms back now, I may never get them back. That's what scares me. I want to make a million a year being a linguist, but I'm afraid I will never get them back. I still have bouts of helplessness. I want to be a telepath and linguist, but I don't want to be this helpless and really did want get them back when my contract ended. I'm terrified I'll be like this forever. So I don't know what to do. I can't even choose."

Nikita said, "Well, I suppose being born this way and not having a choice but to learn to use my feet properly has made a difference, Tia. But I know you can get skilled, too. You just need to practice more. Isabella wasn't born without them, and she got used to living without them, didn't you, Issi?"

"I was young, Nikita. Thirteen. Had a crappy life. Parents were—well dumb and killed themselves after we got mutated. So I had no choice but to learn. Still, I've had so many benefits from being a telepath. Meeting up with Owen here being one of the best."

Nikita giggled. Owen had helped her learn to adapt

while studying and being the linguist on their deep space exploration ship.

Isabella continued. "My brother got his wish. Be a telepath, earn lots of credits, get his arms back, and open up his fancy restaurant. Me, I still just want to be out there in space looking for new civilizations and languages to learn. But now I have Maria, my family, to think about. There's not really a place for a baby on a deep space exploration ship." She sighed. "So I don't know what to do. I want Maria to have a choice, since she's already developed telepathy. The way it's looking, once Owen and I decide, there's no turning back. She's too young to make that decision for herself."

"So, Mom, why can't I just sit in the Friendship and ride out the mutations like we did the pandemic? Then, I won't lose my telepathy," Nikita said.

"If that's what you really want, dear, we can do that."

Sam said, "Hold on a second, Nikita. Since you were born, either me or your mom has been like you and Matt to help you learn ways to do things, be moral support, and so on. You're making Mom miss her chance to get her arms back."

"But you don't have to do that," she said. "I do love having you around me, but I'm grown up now. I'm eight, going on nine. I don't need you to be like me anymore. Not really. Mom should get hers back. If she wants to."

The doorbell rang, interrupting our family conference. I'd given Ashley the night off, so I had to deal with the door myself.

"Special delivery for Isabella Parkinson," the deliveryman from New O'Hare said. He awkwardly tried to hand me a small brown envelop filled with official stamps.

Cradling it between my shoulder and head, I carried it back to the living room, dropping it into Isabella's lap. "Special delivery, he said. Sure has a lot of strange stamps on it."

"Oh! Who's it from, Issi?" Nikita said. She moved to look over Owen and Isabella's shoulders. "From Bela Prime. Oh! Open it!"

"I'm trying, Nikita." Isabella chuckled, while manipulating it with her feet. "It's from the Federation Linguistic Institute on Bela Prime. Dear Mrs. Isabella

Parkinson, bla, bla, bla." Her voice fell silent as her eyes scanned the page. "Good god! Mom, Owen, they're offering me a position as a full professor of linguistics. Whoa! Look at this. If I remain a telepath, my salary will be one million credits per year, but with summers off. If I'm not a telepath, my salary will be a hundred thousand credits per year. Holy cow! What an offer. What do you think, Owen? It's only the most prestigious linguistic institute in the galaxy!"

Before Owen could say anything, Nikita said, "You just *have* to take this job, Issi! Imagine making a million a year for like forever. You'll be wealthy. Owen and Maria can do anything they like. Oh!" Her face turned pale. "You'll be far from here. But wait!" Her face brightened back up. "Mom's going to be the new Senior Ambassador, so we'll be moving to Bela Prime, too. So we'll be there with you. Isn't that the coolest?"

I roared. Just like my precocious daughter to make both our family's decisions for us.

"Mom, are you going to take that position?" Isabella asked. "If you do, then I will take this one. Our families will have each other on this strange new world."

"I probably will have to take it, but for entirely other purposes." I looked over at Bonita. "Have a murder mystery to solve. I owe it to Aaron Strawn to find his killer. So yeah, I probably will take it, Isabella."

Owen said, "Go for it, honey. Even if I get cured, I'm not about to ship out on another deep space exploration ship. Too dangerous when you have a family. I can look after Maria and see what other opportunities are available. I'm sure I'll find something of interest for me. You've got to take this offer. No danger this time."

"Okay. I'll send them my reply in the morning. Gosh, I have to tell all my aunts and uncles about this," Isabella said.

"Don't worry, Issi. I'll be there to help mentor Maria," Nikita said, a giant smile on her face.

"Okay then. Tomorrow let's get Dad, Matt, and Bonita to the Med Center,"I said. Purposely, I didn't mention myself. In spite of Nikita's enthusiasm, I wasn't about to take her to Bela Prime as an armless telepath without either Sam or me being like her for support and guidance. I knew what it's like being socially very different from everyone around you.

***

Events progressed. Admiral Skaggs made a worldwide announcement that they were confiscating all mutation agents and that the new Third Invader replacements would be available by mid-March.

In general, the agents were kept in well marked containers, either ATGDMA or GDMA, the latter being the Galactic Doll Mutation Agent for example. Large volume containers held a thousand doses. From these, hundred dose jars filled the workrooms. Individual syringes held single doses. All were appropriately marked and kept in sterile, cool safes. Thus, squads of security personnel merely had to gather up all the supplies from each Med Center, hospital, GMed and research facilities, and smaller private practices and researchers, such as Eve and the Padella doctors.

Once gathered and logged, Admiral Skaggs had them shipped off to crematoriums to be destroyed.

Edgar Gascon, owner of Able Cremation Services, a small company that operated out of Toronto, had a lucrative contract of disposing of deceased humans. He'd made a fortune some years back when terrorists struck. Many of the mutated people refused to live, and their bodies arrived at his loading docks to be disposed of, their ashes shipped off as fertilizer to Ontario farms. But there hadn't been serious terrorist attacks for almost seven years. He missed the steady income he'd made for several years. Thus, he submitted a bid to burn up these mutation agents being collected by Admiral Skaggs. He won one of the contracts.

EMACs arrived daily, bringing boxes of the agents for him to destroy. Accurate records were mandatory. Each box was scanned as the crew unloaded it into his factory. Additionally, Edgar's people had to scan each box as it rolled down the ramp into the furnaces. Thus, every scrap of these mutation agents was tracked from collection point to destruction point. Admiral Skaggs wanted to be thorough and certain all these terrible agents were destroyed.

Back when hundreds of bodies were being dumped at

his crematorium for cremation, his doctor injected the heavily sedated people with a lethal drug before rolling them down the ramps into the furnaces. However, a giant offered him a small fortune for a number of live bodies. He couldn't turn down that amount of cash. So he scanned them as they came down the ramps to the furnaces thereby logging them as having been properly cremated, but instead slid them outside into the giant's waiting EMAC. Shortly after that, a human had made him a similar offer, which he eagerly accepted. For a time, Edgar reaped welcomed extra cash.

That source of extra income had vanished. Worse, he, too, had been a victim of the pandemic and looked like a female Galactic Doll. For a time, he wished he might just die, but then came the news these Third Invaders were going to undo what had been done to men during the pandemic. Enheartened, he gladly put in his low bid for the destruction of the mutation agents.

However, when the EMAC loads of boxes arrived for him to destroy, Edgar thought about what he was doing. "These could be valuable. Someone is likely to pay handsomely for these agents, especially if there's no rejuvenation or appendage regrow agents around. Or ways to make telepaths. I heard many millionaires made fortunes off making telepaths." He laughed.

Secretly, he rerouted one box in ten from his fiery furnaces. He opened the boxes and kept one thousand dose bottles along with a fair number of individual syringes. These, he moved into his secret basement vault, kept locked via biometrics. When the last of the boxes burned, his vault held a hundred boxes of the agents, an equal amount of each of the two mutation agents. His future looked bright indeed. Someone would eventually pay handsomely for his stash and foresight.
***

In Kiev, another crematorium owner had the same idea. While he destroyed nine out of ten boxes delivered to him under his new disposal contract, he stashed the other box away for a rainy day. When the last delivery occurred, he'd set aside eighty boxes, again about equally divided between the two agents.

Years later, investigators discovered these two men had done this. In all likelihood, I suspected many others charged with the destruction of the agents had done the same thing. Only these two were ever caught, and then only long after the fact of the sales.

***

A week after Matt, Sam, and Bonita entered their mutation comas to have arms regrown, Tia received an official letter from the Third Invaders. She showed me their offer.

```
Miss Tia Sanchez,
     We are amassing around a thousand humans
from Earth to help colonize a new world we've
discovered. We are accepting only those we
deem to be valuable colonists, people who can
add significant expertise to these original
settlers.
     We would like to have you join these
select thousand as their sole linguist. There
are  ancient  records  that  ought  to  be
translated,  much  as  Isabella  Parkinson  has
done with Fourth and Fifth Invader documents.
Here's your chance for fame.
     If you agree to join the colonists as
their linguist, we will make sure your body is
fully prepared for the tasks at hand. No need
to waste time regrowing arms. We'll take care
of that for you and in much less time...
```

The letter continued with cautionary notes and how to accept to this offer.

"So what do I do now? They want me as a linguist. There must have been an ancient race living on this new world. How can I turn this chance down? I guess they'll regrow my arms faster. What do you think?"

"I don't know, Tia. I'm not sure what 'We'll take care of that for you' means, but it does imply they'll regrow them for you. It's just I don't trust these Third Invaders, but then I'm biased based on what they did to the crew of Isabella and Bernardo's exploration ships. I guess you'll have to make your own decision."

"Being a colonist—that would help save three billion people, too," Tia said. "The way things are now, the whole crew of my exploration ship are mutated and out of a job. Maybe they'll get re-employed once the mutations are undone, maybe..."

"Yeah, I know. You've got your own future to think of. You can't just wait and hope they'll rehire you."

"My thinking. But if I went ahead and joined Sam and the others, I'll miss my chance to be a colonist and study that ancient language. I'm damned if I do and damned if I don't."

We shared a cynical laugh. Later, she made her decision and became a colonist.

True, I hadn't really given people a choice. In my push to save us from being killed, I'd sacrificed individual choice. I hoped others would understand why I did it. Otherwise, I might be cursed forever.

Chapter 17 The Undo

For the next two weeks, I received phone calls and dispatches from the "new" leaders of the Sol Empire. Each communication encouraged me to accept my appointment as one of our new Senior Ambassadors. I stalled a little by asking who our other two would be. After all, our population allowed us to have three Senior Ambassadors. What about housing and schools for my children?

I didn't need their official responses. Rather, I asked Piper Strawn who gave me realistic details. The influence and power wielded by a Senior Ambassador awed me a little. I could get anything I wanted merely by asking.

Rachael Berg from New Haven, Brussels, Tau Ceti, and Arne Eschenbacher from Baden, Pylon, Epsilon Eridani became the other two Sol Empire Senior Ambassadors. I looked them up on the internet. Rachael had been a history professor, while Arne was a wealthy businessman. I relaxed, thankful one of the three knew our history and could better represent us. A businessman would provide a solid footing for deals. I could only offer investigative powers and a sense of what was ideal for people. Thus, on March 1, 2361, I formally accepted, subject to completion of the Third Invaders' mutation cures.

Finally on March 15, 2361, the curing of the mutations began. Rather, I should say further mutations began, which appeared to undo some of the existing mutation effects. Third Invader shuttles from their main saucer dropped off batches of the new agents to Med Centers, hospitals, and GMed facilities of Chicago. The medical personnel had spent the last two weeks gearing up for this massive distribution and thus were ready when the supplies arrived. Chicagoans became the first guinea pigs

Two days after distribution began, our turn came, via phone calls that specified a day and time to report to a specific facility, one that was closest to where we lived. The Hugo family and mine reported to our Med Center, where Sam,

Matt, and Bonita were staying as their tiny arms continued to grow. Scheduled for release in a week, the three wanted out of the center. A month's confinement had all three clawing the walls.

A nurse checked my name off her list and gave me a shot in my right thigh. "Is that all?" I asked.

"Yes, in a day or so, your feet should return to normal. Theoretically, your Galactic Doll mutations should not be inherited by any children you may have in the future. That's not been verified yet. Your arms won't be regrown. Telepathic ability isn't affected. Only your feet. Women must look good, so breasts aren't going to be changed either. Once your feet alter, you can still wear your tall heels if you desire."

"Not much is changing for us women, is it?" I asked.

"No. Mostly, these changes impact our males. It's supposed to undo what that pandemic virus did to them last December. We'll see," she said. "Oh, yes. Sam and Matt have already been given their shots, as has Bonita. We'll release them this time next week."

As I walked out of the room, I ran into the Hugo family. Helen said, "Well, that was simple enough. Nothing much for us, Molly, but the world for Casper and Fritz."

"They don't have to stay in the Med Center?" I asked. Normally, a mutation coma lasted around eight days.

"No, she said they'll have aches and pains for the next month as their bodies change. Unlike regrowing appendages, they don't have to be here or in a coma. I guess that's a good thing."

"Absolutely a good thing," I said. Memories of the intense pains people endured while they were in their mutation comas flooded my mind for a moment. Of course, the pain could only be recovered and erased via Celeste's therapy. I wondered how Sam and Matt would fare. Celeste and I planned to take them into therapy sessions the moment they got home.

"Gee, Mom, the nurse said my telepathy isn't going away. If we can wear flats, that'll help lots, but I still want to wear my tall heels when I dress up. I can, can't I, Mom?" Nikita asked, as we walked out the door and onto the MTES.

I rolled my eyes, while Helen chuckled. She said, "Veronica already asked me that. Best say yes or you'll never hear the end of it."

"Yes."

Both Nikita and Veronica smiled and held their heads high as we moved along. Casper merely shook his head.

When I got up the next morning and stood on the dressing machine, both feet suddenly cracked and went flat on the floor like normal feet. Pain shot up both legs, nearly causing me to fall down. I cried out, but then I heard Nikita cry out as well. Her feet had returned to normal, too.

'My feet are fixed up, Mom.' Nikita placed her thoughts into my mind, obviously testing her telepathic ability to make sure it was still there.

'Mine, too. What a relief.'

'Way cool, Mom. Still got my telepathy. Yeah!'

We looked at each other making sure nothing else had changed. I relaxed. Nikita looked just as cute as she always had.

"Mom, heard something at school. Is it true?"

"Is what true? Or am I supposed to guess what you heard?" I teased.

"Oh, Mom! They say a GMed report says women look alike. Veronica and I don't look anything like each other."

"Aunt Eve and Aunt Celeste showed me that report. GMed carried out a huge study of Earth's men and women before the invention of the Galactic Doll mutation. They measured the ratio of the height of your face to the width, distance between eyes, height, weight, and on and on. Hundreds of measurements. Then, they graphed each type. Of course, they found wide divergences within each one. You know from school that heights vary widely. How much they vary is given by what they call a bell curve.

"Originally, that curve was very wide. They redid the measurements after most women had become Galactic Dolls. With most measurements, that wide variability shrunk by about a factor of a hundred. Meaning the variations between women's physical appearance are drastically less than they used to be. Of course you and Veronica don't look alike. Only us clones are identical, but statistically you two are closer looking than you would have been had you not had the Galactic Doll mutation. That's what that means. Less diversity in appearances.

"I wonder if that's happened to our men. Already they've had the Galactic Doll mutation via the pandemic, but there's not been enough time for GMed to collect the measurements. Then what's the Third Invaders' undo cure going to do? I highly doubt it will restore the men's original appearance. But we'll see."

I learned much later that men also had a hundredfold reduction in the variability of their key physical attributes just as women had. This belated finding didn't surprise me.

After Sam and Matt returned home, for over a week, they complained of pain. We went through a bottle of pain killers in six days. When I tried to buy another bottle on line like we did with our groceries, I got a sold out message. I guess everyone undergoing this undo cure needed them. However, after that first week home, both ceased complaining.

Each day, Nikita examined Matt, looking for changes.

"Mom, make her stop staring at me!" Matt said.

"I'm just looking to see if the mutation is changing you. Don't you want to know what's different?" Nikita protested.

"No. I don't look any different except my feet work right. My arms are growing. It's Dad who's changing. Stare at him," Matt countered before storming off.

"Matt's young, and most of the Galactic Doll mutation effects haven't yet become apparent on him, Nikita. He's right. Sam's the one to watch."

He walked in. "Yes, I'm the one to watch and listen to. My voice is deepening already. Breasts are reducing. The pain is from regrowing ribs, I think. In time, I'll look like I did before I ever met your mom. I wonder if Molly's going to like how I used to look?"

I laughed. "If you were an ugly looking old fart, then probably no."

"Oh, I came to ask you if anyone has seen Tia today. She's gone, but her clothes and the machines are still in her room. Bed's not been slept in," Sam said.

Focusing, I attempted to touch Tia's mind just to make sure she was okay. Nothing. "Strange. I can't contact her. Let me try again."

"Thanks. Matt and I have lost our telepathic abilities."

After two intense minutes, I gave up. "Nope, no trace of her. I think she must not be on Earth any longer. I hope she is okay being a colonist for the Third Invaders. I don't trust them."

"Do you have a bad feeling about the deal?" Sam asked. "I'm elated to get my body more or less back to that of a man."

"Not exactly a bad feeling. I can't dispute the positive effect this is having on our men and on keeping the Federation at bay, but..."

"Yeah, know what you mean. She's entirely too vulnerable. I hope they regrow her arms, too. Can't imagine her being a colonist without them," Sam said.

During the next week, Celeste gave us some additional therapy sessions. I found no new traumas to handle and felt wonderful, if a bit apprehensive about going to Bela Prime. Nikita also had nothing to erase, but Matt and Sam had quite a lot to handle. Both had to view the current mutation pains, the coma and pains from the mutations to regrow arms, the massive dose of the agents just to save their lives, and the bombing's affects on their bodies and themselves.

I had no intention of leaving until my men were fully handled. Sam's situation took the longest. By mid-April, Celeste pronounced him trauma-free. Neither Sam nor Matt regained their lost telepathy, but they didn't mind that detail, which I found interesting. People are different. Nikita demanded to keep hers, while the fellows could care less.

On April 20, the Third Invaders and their flying saucers vanished from Earth orbits and from Sol Empire space. However, that was the day the great shock came.

Sam's voice woke me up. "Molly, get up. Something's wrong with me."

His tenor voice had again shifted into the soprano range. His bosom had grown back over night. I blinked and got up, looking him over, as did Bonita.

"It's like his mutation is undoing itself," she said.

Later that morning, calls flooded both my Senior Investigator and Senior Judge's offices. All over, frantic people reported men's bodies begun reverting back to what they'd been before the alien's supposed cure. Scared men flooded into the Med Centers and GMed facilities around the Chicago area. During the ensuing days, men who'd been injected later swamped other centers. Within days, everyone realized we'd been had. The cure the Third Invaders gave us only lasted about a month. So by late May, all those who had had it found their bodies back the way they'd been before the injections. With one exception: everyone's feet were normal.

Worse, the Third Invaders had vanished. We had no way to contact them to protest and demand the return of our thousand volunteer colonists. In my own defense, I didn't specifically specify that the mutation changes should be permanent. I felt betrayed and used, but I also felt I'd let Earth down by not discovering the Third Invaders' treachery sooner.

Hank, Janine's husband and history professor asked me to come by. I figured he wanted to tell me how upset he was over the failed mutation. Partially right.

"Molly, I'm going to tell you something that these days few people know. Over two centuries ago, when the corporations purged the world and took over total control, they handled the terrorists in a unique way. Yes, they also wiped out the Islamic religion, as well as all organized religions. Ever wonder why the arid middle east is virtually empty of civilization?"

"I figured who would want to live in a hot desert like place."

"True, but there's a real reason long lost to us, though if you search ancient volumes, you'll find it. The people there were constantly fighting each other and the rest of the world, a holy war against everyone who wasn't them. They brutalized women, too. Their constant terrorist plots finally caused the corporations to act."

"I figured they sent them off to colonize a moon or something."

"Nope. They had the space fleet utilize the experimental MW1. That was an unmanned drone that carried a nuclear powered microwave broad area ray."

"Huh?"

"As I understand that ancient and obsolete technology, it flew overhead and boiled all living matter below the machine. They used several in tandem, sweeping over a city, leaving everything living thing below it dead. They eliminated the terrorists and everyone else in the Middle East and much of Africa. They called it terrorist elimination, but I'd call it genocide."

"How could anyone tolerate that? Didn't the others in the world protest it?" I couldn't believe what Hank was telling me.

"The rest of civilization was sick and tired of terrorist attacks and bombings, so no one objected much at all. My point is this. After that only use of the MW1 system, it was put into storage at a secret lab in western Nevada. Until a couple days ago."

"What do you mean? Has it been stolen?"

"Something like that. I've still got contacts with members of the Infantry Division. One sent me a message that someone broke in and stole it. Borrowed it, or so the note left behind said. I thought you ought to know."

"Okay, just what I need right now. It's not bad enough these Third Invaders betrayed me and all of us, but now someone's stolen a doomsday machine. Are they going to use it on us?" I asked. Yes, I'd become cynical.

Hank laughed. "Now that I leave up to you. I sure as hell hope not. Guess you're going to have to find out who stole it. On another note, since we're not cured, it's a bummer all the old mutation agents are gone so we can't rejuvenate, restore lost limbs and organs, and so on."

"Yeah, true, but no one can continue to make and sell telepath. So maybe that's a good thing. But I see your point. Now people could well want those agents back for a number of reasons. I'm in the pickle barrel, aren't I?"

"You bet you are."

When I got to my office, I gave Jie and Ward a new investigation to handle: find out who stole that mothballed invention and why. Where it was at—if they could find it. That gave them something positive to do instead of dwelling on our situation, particularly that of Ward, who had just lost his male appearance.

Next, I called Eve and Lara, who were still on the Padella's atoll in the South Pacific. Eve said, "Boy, is Dr. Nelson Padella ever angry. He hates looking like a Galactic Doll. Both hate being disabled, too. Any idea why the Third Invaders did what they did?"

"No clue. Any chance you and Lara can make any use of what they gave us to make the male mutations permanent?" If I had any fingers, I would have kept them crossed.

"Well, actually, Molly, we do have an idea. Lara and I've been studying the genetic markers in their mutation agent. We think we can couple that with our own work. We're going to try it on the Padella's. Normally, experimentation on humans is unethical and criminal, but they are desperate for us to try it on them. That's how badly they want to become normal people again. So we're going to give it a try. If it works, then we need to get it mass produced and everyone injected. We had thought of making a new virus and setting off a pandemic like Patricia Ann did. We're using her breakthrough work and could use her help. But she and her family were taken by the Third Invaders as colonists."

"Okay. Keep me posted. I'm sure I can convince GMed people to work overtime to get it implemented. Before it's too late, that is. I best see what Admiral Skaggs intends."

"Buy us more time," Lara said.

So I requested a time to discuss the situation with the admiral. Late afternoon, he called. I outlined what I knew and that Eve and Lara believed they had a solution, if only we had a little more time. I didn't tell him about the stolen doomsday machine.

"You've also got another problem. My people have been monitoring the Federation Dark Web. It seems someone on Earth is trying to sell the mutation agents to the highest bidder, but with the caveat they have to come and get it."

"Crap! So much for destroying the lot of it. Want me to investigate it?"

"I'm putting my people on it. Obviously, we can't trust

Earthlings. If we can't put an end to it, I've no choice but to make sure nothing is left on this world. So you've maybe a little time left before I have to act to safeguard the rest of the galaxy."

"I understand, but give me time to evacuate as you've promised. Bonita doesn't want to die, especially now that her arms are regrowing."

He didn't reply, but ended the call. At least, he smiled at that last. I hoped his love for his niece was enough to allow us to escape the destruction of Earth. Now I could only wait and see what developed.

Chapter 18 A Race Against Time

I couldn't sleep that night. Turmoil. Science and technology had left humanity light years in the distance. Hardly no one studied history. Hank proved that to me. But I couldn't help pondering what else he'd told me. Combined with Sam's vast library experience, people had completely forgotten religions. Before the corporations took over control of Earth, many religions flourished: Christians, Jews, Muslims, Buddhists, Hindus, for example. I admit I knew nothing about any of these, except how to spell these words. Religion meant nothing to the people of Earth and our fledgling Sol Empire.

But it was worse than this. Philosophy—I had to look up its meaning: the study of the nature of knowledge, reality, and existence—hadn't been studied in over a century and a half. According to Sam who'd read many ancient books, sociology had evolved into how to predict and control populations of people. It had more or less merged with what ancients had called the head-shrinkers, the psych-studies people. Knowledge of the human mind hadn't progressed beyond how to compel behavior in populations and people so corporations could more readily control them.

Man: a living biological organism made from mud, returning to mud upon death. Upon cremation, one's ashes fertilized next year's crops on the vast automated farms. Proof of man from mud. So I wasn't shocked or surprised that Admiral Skaggs fully expected to terminate three billion humans on Earth to prevent the spread of this nasty mutation agent to other worlds in the Federation. He'd do it in a flash and think nothing of it. After all, men, women, and children were merely biological organisms made from mud. Besides, if he did it right, other overpopulated worlds could then dump their excess on Earth, assuming he didn't leave the planet radioactive.

Yet, I knew we were more than flesh bodies. Via Celeste's therapy, I handled minds, specifically erasing painful traumas and unwanted emotions and attitudes. Totally real to me, I am something else, a spiritual entity with personality, intelligence, and potential that has a mind and inhabits a fleshly body. For me, man is spirit, mind, and body. More importantly, while bodies grow old and died, the spirit lives on, moving to another baby body when the old body passed away. Yes, I'd lived through many cycles in which I'd inhabit a new baby body, live a life, upon body death depart it and begin again with a new body. On and on, seemingly endless. I'd lost count of the number of deaths I'd encountered in my many therapy sessions.

Few people had any reality on this, only those few who'd received our therapy sessions. Yet, if one knew that the pain given to someone would be stored in their mind and thus carried by the person on into their next lifetime and that it could adversely affect them in their next lifetime, hopefully, one would think twice about inflicting such. But our entire empire believed you only lived once, and when you died, that was the end of it. Given that premise, it didn't matter what you did to a person. There were no long term consequences, except terminating that person. Well, maybe someone would miss their loved one, but that's all.

No wonder our high technology empire, including the Federation of Planets, could contemplate genocide as a solution. Only now was our GMed people beginning to realize what Celeste and I showed them: that giving older persons the dementia causing drug so they could be terminated by age sixty-five eventually after five such lifetimes resulted in people with moron IQs. Shipping them off to be miners for the Sixth Invaders became their solution.

And here I'm right in the middle of it again. I could do nothing. In that case, Admiral Skaggs would probably destroy Earth. That was the easiest choice for me. Especially since I had his word that I, my family, and friends could fly away before it happened. But what would we do then? Fly around the galaxy until we ran out of fuel and food? Find an uninhabited planet and colonize it?

Hey, that didn't sound so farfetched. We could establish our own civilization, not one in which technology ruled and that man was an animal to be controlled and used. But I knew

I couldn't turn my back on Earth and my people. I had to do something to get these mutation agents destroyed. Plus, I wanted to scream. I had wanted them destroyed the day we discovered them years ago.

I knew nothing about the Dark Web, let alone how to find it. So I called up Ambassador L'Grina.

"Hey, tough break with the Third Invaders. I told you not to trust them. So how can I help you?"

"Yeah, I know. I need help. Like I suspected, someone or someones secreted away a quantity of those mutation agents and are now trying to sell them on the Dark Web. I've got to get to them before they sell them and spread them around the galaxy. Only a couple days at most before Admiral Skaggs is forced to take action to prevent that spread. Ideas?"

"Yeah, two. Home world isn't going to let the Federation exterminate the people of Earth. Period. Second, I think I know a way to uncover those who kept some of the mutation agents. Need some credits, though. Like a million for starters."

I laughed. "Good thing I've got that kind of money. Let's make it happen. Are you going to pose as a buyer?"

"You called it. You're good. I'll make some Dark Web inquiries. As soon as I get a bite, we'll nail the perp. I do like some of the idioms your language has. Catch ya."

With that, she left. I wondered how the Sixth Invaders could stop Admiral Skaggs if he received orders to wipe us out. Would they start a spacewar? That'd alienate us even more. And if they wiped us out, how could I be one of the Sol Empire's Senior Ambassadors to the Federation of Planets? I wouldn't.

Quietly, Sam and Bonita started packing personal possessions we didn't want to leave behind. Just in case. Once a day, Sam took an EMAC of boxes to the Friendship, parked in the long-term lot at New O'Hare Spaceport. My sisters and their families, along with some friends also took similar precautions.

Me, I just continued to go to work, checking on the progress Ward and Jie made tracking down the MW1 system that had once wiped out all living things in the desert regions of North Africa and the Mid-East.

"We've gone over all the surveillance videos around the underground mountain storage facility," Ward said.

Jie added, "Nothing, boss. They wore masks and knocked out the video cameras as their first action. We think twelve men heisted the drones."

"Right," Ward said. "One man per drone. We think their nuclear reactors are still operational, though it's possible new fuel rods might have to be added. Some are still being made to keep several ancient satellites operational, like the climate control systems."

"So we're watching those sites. Just in case. Trouble is, we don't even know what these drones look like or their size or anything much about them," Jie said.

Ward said, "Back then, corporations took a lot of heat for their destruction of millions of people. That action ended all the terrorist attacks, so people eventually believed it had been justified."

"I think that was the high point of microwave technology," Jie said. "Kind of like the end of its evolutionary path. Like those fossil fuel engines when the orbital solar power plants came on line."

"Is someone planning to use it on us?" That was the key question in my mind. After all, if someone used that system to obliterate whole populations two hundred years ago, they could certainly use it again. Was this the way Admiral Skaggs intended to wipe out the people of Earth? Nukes would render the planet inhabitable for centuries. But microwave boiling of bodies would leave the infrastructure intact. It seemed plausible. My phone rang interrupting my speculations.

"Hi, Ambassador L'Grina. News?"

"Different kind. Strange. I just got word that one of our cruiser cloaking devices has been sold to an Earth-based group calling themselves the Justice League. I've never heard of them, but I thought you ought to know. As far as our little project goes, I hope to have results by tomorrow."

I thanked her. "Ward, Jie, what do we know about an Earth-base Justice League? They've just bought a Sixth Invader cruiser cloaking device."

Blank looks didn't promise much.

"Sorry. Never heard of it," Ward said, entering it into his computer system. Jie followed suit. "Hey, a dozen fuel rods were sold last week to this Justice League. The records just came through. Someone's activating the MW1 systems."

Now I was worried. Powered up, they could be used nearly anywhere. I had no choice but to call Helen Hugo at GD to warn her. I knew she would put Earth defenses on high alert. Probably with shoot to kill orders. Five minutes later, that's what happened. Damn, my predictions were still dead on.

An hour later, I got a call from our Admiral Rossi. "Senior Investigator, I have to officially alert you to a new crisis. It seems one of our cruisers has been stolen."

"What? How can someone steal a cruiser? And all its crew?" I stared at his holo image on my phone.

"The whole ship has gone missing. It's the Bolt."

"Isn't that Commander Lia Johnston's old ship?" I asked, recalling how she'd come to our rescue when we first discovered the Third Invaders.

"Ex-commander. Remember, she was mutated and lost her arms. I had no choice but to relieve her of her command."

I wanted to shout, to scream, to protest. We're not helpless invalids. We can do most anything, just that it takes us longer to do tasks. Okay, sometimes a lot longer.

"The Bolt has a crew of a hundred. It's vanished. Commander Petrov is here with me. He took a week of shore leave to check on his family in Moscow, helping them adjust to the mutation reversal. The Bolt was in orbit above Moscow, but it's vanished."

"How can a ship vanish? Doesn't it have to have its commander with it? To do something like this?" I asked.

"Cloaking device, we suspect. But the Bolt never had one. And yes, unless the crew mutinied, the commander must give orders to carry out any operations. I know Commander Petrov wasn't liked by the Bolt's crew. They demanded I reinstate Commander Lia Johnston, but of course I'm not able to do that. We can't allow mutants and Galactic Dolls in the service. You understand that."

"So what so you want me to do?" I bit my lip hard to keep from giving him a piece of my mind. Lia could have continued to command her ship, especially now that she'd had her arms regrown.

"Just be aware of the disappearance. Let me know if you hear anything about it or anything strange happening."

He hung up. Strange happenings? God, the world was full of them of late. What could her former cruiser be up to? I called Lia. Voice mail. "Lia, it's Molly Parkinson. Give me a call when you can. It's about your old cruiser, the Bolt. Thanks."

"Hey, Ward, could a cruiser carry all those drones?" I had one of those Molly hunches. Stolen drones. Missing cruiser. Not rocket science.

"Yeah, pretty sure it could. You don't suppose..." Ward said.

"Their former commander might be able to give us some ideas. What's weird is the Bolt's commander is on the ground in Moscow while his ship has vanished."

My assistant brought us lunch. By early afternoon, I still hadn't heard back from Lia. Worried, I called her husband, Senator Bill Fennel of Brussels, Tau Ceti. Both had been mutated into armless galactic dolls, though both had their arms regrown. Still, Brussels prohibited any mutant from returning there. They were outcasts from their own world, but had known each other from high school. And they'd gotten married.

"Hi, Senator Fennel. Molly Parkinson here. Say, I've been trying to get a hold of Lia, but my calls keep going to her voice mail. Is she okay?"

"Yes, she is just fine. I'll tell her you called and to call you back as soon as possible."

He abruptly ended the call. That wasn't like him either. Something was definitely going on with them. But what? Crap, I didn't have time for another crisis.

"Ward, let's see what video you do have on the robbery. Maybe I can see something you and Jie missed."

As the sun set, I noticed two details they'd failed to mention. "Look, those two there," I pointed with my toes. "Those are arms regrowing. They have to have been armless telepaths who've had the cures. And the rest of the masked men—none have been mutated. No monster breasts or distorted feet. Those are normal men."

"But there are no more normal men on Earth," Ward protested.

"Exactly. They aren't from Earth or if they are, they've not been planet-side in years. But those two definitely have. I'd say one was male and one was female—maybe. Based on clothes. Pants and dress."

"Yeah, we saw that, but what does it mean? We had no idea. Figured it wasn't relevant."

"Probably isn't. I'm heading home. We'll pick it up from here in the morning."

After dinner, I tried Lia again. Nothing. So I called Senator Fennel. Stranger still. Voice mail, too. I decided to drop by their home tomorrow on my way to the office. Sherry promised to tag along for security.

***

While the Bolt hovered in orbit high above Moscow, Commander Petrov took a shuttle craft down to visit his relatives and help them over the shock and turmoil of becoming normal and then reverting back to Galactic Dolls. When he left, Lieutenant Commander Marcus Leon took another shuttle craft down, not to Moscow but to Chicago.

"Marcus! I never thought I'd see you again," Lia said, her large blue eyes gazing on the man who had been her second in command. "What brings you to my door? You haven't been mutated, have you?"

He laughed. "No. No time for that on the Bolt. Can we talk? I'm not sure how long I can stay planet-side."

Seated in her small living room, the thin man explained. "Commander, we of the Bolt want you back as our commander. Commander Petrov is okay, but he's no Lia. Anyway, the crew is furious about the betrayal of the Third Invaders. Many of us have relatives here on Earth, Petrov included. We're infuriated that Admiral Rossi isn't going to do a damned thing about it. Plus, some of us have lost relatives to the agreed upon Third Invader colonists. After their betrayal, we want them returned. But no one's doing anything about it.

So we're taking matters into our hands."

"Hey, it's quite a shock to the men of Earth. Bill's taking it hard, too. But what can we do?" Lia said.

"Make the Third Invaders pay. Pay until they tell us where our thousand colonists are and return them."

"I agree. They need to pay for their treachery. We must have our people returned. But how? A war?"

"No. There's another way. In the underground mothball facility in Colorado, there is the means. It's called the MW1 system, a group of unmanned drones that carried a nuclear powered microwave broad area ray. The corporations used it to eliminate all life in the Mid-East and the deserts of North Africa, back during the height of the never-ending war on terrorists. We snatch those drones, fly them to the Third Invader world, and boil a few cities. That'll get their attention. Make them negotiate."

Lia chuckled, then frowned. "I like it. But how can you get close to their world without being seen? They'll shoot you down on planet approach."

"We buy a Sixth Invader cloaking device. Probably have to get some new nuclear fuel rods as well. It's doable. But we need a reliable commander, one we can trust. You, Commander Lia Johnston. Will you help us obtain justice?"

"What about the hundred crew members?" she asked.

"We took a vote before I came down to find you. Ninety-nine for this: zero against. We didn't ask Commander Petrov. But we gotta act fast. The window is closing to snatch the Bolt. We're calling ourselves the Justice League. Will you join us and lead us to victory?"

Lia laughed. "How can I refuse that vote? Okay, I'm in. Probably Senator Fennel is in, too. Hell, he and I can't ever return home to Brussels."

Lieutenant Commander Leon visibly relaxed. "Here's the details your CCC has worked out." He brought up the plans of the underground facility on his computer. "We can snatch these easily. There isn't even a guard on duty. Only cameras. This is the easy part. The hard part will be getting funds to buy a cloaking device and how to do that."

Lia said, "I've a connection to the Sixth Invaders. Let

me see about getting it. Bill and I will accompany you to snatch these drones. I have to see if they'll even fit in the cargo hold or the fighter bay of the Bolt. You don't know their dimensions, do you?"

"Er, nope. How the hell did you know that? Ah, you're Commander Johnston, that's how come." Both laughed.

"The only flaw in your plan," Lia said, "is that we don't have the precise coordinates of their home world."

"But we do know the star. We can cruise around it, looking for habitable worlds. Can't be that hard, especially if the Bolt's invisible," he countered.

"And the whole crew is with us?"

"Absolutely. We want justice. They betrayed us all. Lord knows what they've done to our thousand colonists, but I bet it isn't good, considering their betrayal. That's why we're calling ourselves the Justice League."

"Wouldn't it be easier to nuke one of their cities?" Lia asked.

"Yes, but we figured that'd start a war. This way, no one will have any idea what caused the damage. The drones have been stored away ever since their one and only use over two hundred years ago. From what we've seen, no one even remembers them. For once, the Third Invaders won't know everything or who to strike back against."

"Okay then. Let's go over these plans. Take out the security cameras first. Wear masks. In and out fast." Lia took charge.

Later that day, Ambassador L'Grina told her who to contact about purchasing a cloaking device. Lia used some of her mutation settlement money to purchase one with rush shipping, since they couldn't make a move until it was operational on the Bolt. That took several days to build the interface and make it work. When they winked out, the whole crew cheered.

Lieutenant Commander Leon ordered, "Lay in coordinates for Chicago. Let's pick up Commander Johnston." More cheers.

Minutes later, he escorted Lia back onto her cruiser. A thunderous applause and cheering overwhelmed her, as she set foot in the Bolt's docking bay. She did get many stares, though. Her huge bosom and tiny regrowing arms looked strange to all, including herself.

"Thank you all for having me back as your commander. Even when I lost my arms, I worked out and trained hard so I could come back and be your commander, but you know what the Admiral had to say. I'm back. Let's go get justice for our friends and relatives. Lord knows what they've done to the thousand colonists. Nothing good, I'll wager."

More cheers echoed around the cruiser.

"Set coordinates for the underground storage facility in Colorado," she ordered.

Senator Bill Fennel, who had accompanied her onto the ship, followed her to her old cabin.

"Now comes the tricky part," he said. "We've no idea how big these drones actually are. I do hope they come with an operator's manual."

Hours later, a dozen men, led by Lieutenant Commander Leon, and accompanied by Lia and Bill, landed just outside the entrance to the underground storage facility. All wore masks and clothing that couldn't be used to identify them. Systematically, they shot out the video cameras as they came to them. Of course, their intrusion sounded alarms back at GD headquarters in Denver, but by the time someone came to check on the facility, they planned to be long gone.

Corporations excelled at meticulous record keeping. Thus, even though this tunnel complex stretched for miles and held countless relics from a bygone age, they knew the precise location of the drones.

When Lieutenant Commander Leon pulled the tarp off the first of the dozen drones, he relaxed. "We get a break. These will fit nicely in our landing bay, Commander."

"Okay. Let's get them out and into the Bolt before GD sends a security squad to investigate," she ordered.

"It's so well balance I can push it myself," one soldier said.

One by one, each slipped their blasters over their shoulders and pushed the next drone along, like a line of penguins. Lia and Bill led the way, alert for incoming security guards. Outside the fence, fighter pilots waited, prepared to tow a drone up to the Bolt, currently cloaked in a low orbit above the site. Lia's crew worked well together, and thirty minutes after pushing the last drone outside, it, too, was onboard the Bolt, which headed back to Chicago. However, on their monitors, everyone in CCC saw the arrival of a dozen EMACs checking on the break in.

By morning, technicians concluded the nuclear power plants had to have new fuel rods. The drones' power supplies allowed full diagnostics, but not flight. Next step: find several dozen fuel rods. That took several days. Meanwhile, Senator Fennel returned home to deal with Senate business. He introduced a bill asking for Admiral Rossi to do what was necessary to force the Third Invaders to return their thousand colonists or make good on their mutation promises. While the bill passed, Admiral Rossi fired back.

"Just what would you have us do? Their flying saucers out maneuver us and their top speed vastly exceeds ours. Nice bill, but I've no way to implement it," the admiral fired back.

The next morning, Senator Fennel called Lia. "Hi. Molly Parkinson has been trying to call you. Left a dozen voice messages. I think she's on to us. Maybe you've better call her back."

"Okay. I will. I'm sending a shuttle down for you. We're ready to head for the Third Invader's home world. We've got the drones activated. The Justice League is about to do what's necessary," she said.

"Molly? Oh, hi. Yeah, this is Lia. Been kind of busy lately. Everything is all right. Better than all right, actually. I'll call you in a couple days with some more news I think you'll like."

Chapter 19 Power Play

"Okay, make the jump," Commander Lia Johnston said. To her second, she added, "I never expected to be able to say that again. You've no idea how much this means to me. My whole life has been dedicated to the fleet and the Bolt. That bitch of a Third Invader took this away from me in that instant when she released the mutation agent on us."

"I can't imagine, Commander. But you married Senator Fennel?" Lieutenant Commander Leon asked. "We weren't allowed to even talk to you."

"Yeah, we were highschool sweethearts that drifted apart after graduation."

"Commander, estimated arrival to Gamma Orionis-C is ten hours," an aide said.

"Excellent. Notify me a half hour before then. Lieutenant Commander, care to join me in inspecting these drones? I want to discuss their operation with the dozen drone operators."

The two headed to the docking bay. As they walked along, various crew paused to smile at Lia and salute her, even though that wasn't required.

She found the eight men and four women working on the controls. When she entered, they stopped, saluted, and grinned.

"At ease. So how's it going? Archaic systems?" she asked.

One man said, "Understatement. Amazing these could even work. But we've already replaced their control electronics with modern game panels."

"Game panels?"

"Yes, we operate these drones identically to how we play many video games. Piece 'o cake. All of us," his arm encompassed the other eleven, "are the top gamers on the ship. That's why we're chosen to fly these babies. Elaine, show her our simulation runs."

A woman who Lia recognized as one of her fighter pilots

pivoted and activated a monitor display. She explained what they saw.

"This shows how the dozen are flown, a staggered formation as best we can tell from the ancient records and our best estimates of coverage. These babies are almost totally silent. Their minimalist shape and coloration make them hard to spot, invisible at night when we intend to strike. Less chance of discovery and being shot down."

"How high up?" the commander asked.

"The design specs suggest two hundred feet with a horizontal cone spread of eight hundred feet. Allowing for some overlap, each flyover should sweep an area about a mile and a half wide. Plus, their non-metallic construction makes them stealth drones. Undetectable. We hope."

Another man added, "The sheer microwave output power is mind boggling. That's why they need a nuclear power plant."

"Flight time?" she asked.

"That's the only iffy thing," another man answered. "These drones almost hover, damned slow moving. The operation manuals suggest a speed of two miles per hour for maximum damage. What we need, Commander, are the operational parameters. How far, how fast, when."

"Okay. What's their flight duration?" Lia asked.

"At operational speeds, ten hours. But their top speed is a hundred fifty miles per hour. We've been looking at the ancient flight operations logs. Sometimes, they flew them operationally for five hours before swinging around and coming back, thereby covering a path three miles wide and ten miles long. Other times, they flew them for nine hours out and then flying back at top speed, covering a path a mile and a half by eighteen miles. According to the manuals, every living thing in these paths would be terminated."

The original man said, "What we found amazing is originally the corporations built a fleet of a dozen of these systems. If they operated together, multiply the coverage area by twelve on each pass. What's so interesting is an idiot could operate these. You don't need a hot shot video gamer to fly them."

One of the women interrupted him. "Unless they come under attack. Then you need us, unless you want them shot down."

Lia smiled. "Well done, all of you. We're going to get some measure of justice for our people and maybe recover the thousand colonists ripped off by these fiends. I'll be sure to pick a juicy target path."

The dozen cheered her. She and her second returned to the CCC. Later, she joined Senator Fennel in their cabin. He'd been dozing. Her arrival roused him.

"All okay?" he whispered.

"Yes, just inspecting the drones. So far, perfect. Ten hours before we get there. So get some sleep, dear."

"You coming?"

She disrobed and slipped into the cramped bed beside him.

"I keep getting stares at my tiny arms," he said.

"Yeah, I do, too. Still, this is a million times better than having none."

***

"Are we sure we want to kill so many people?" Senator Fennel asked Lia. "These Third Invaders haven't actually killed any of ours that we know of."

"They mutated two entire exploration ships crew, trying to create telepaths to sell for profit. Molly found a hundred more. Lord knows how many they actually kidnapped, made, and sold off. Then, they come to Earth promising a miracle cure and helping us destroy all our mutation agents, even though some save lives. But their cure undoes itself after two months. And they run off with a thousand of our people as supposed colonists. Bill, if you believe that, you're foolish. I'll make you a bet right now. Those thousand colonists have become a telepath breeding population somewhere out there in the galaxy."

"Good lord! You think so?" Her eyes and taught face answered him. "Well," he sighed, "all the signs of that being true are there. Maybe they had something to do with ancient Egypt and that civilization. But every modern encounter has dealt with the telepath mutation in some way. So, dear, I'd be a fool to bet against you. Still, we'll be killing many people."

"I'd rather be dumping the armless telepath mutation agent on them, but we know their DNA is sufficiently different from ours so it wouldn't harm them. I'm hoping one pass will convince them to reveal the location of the thousand colonists and let us rescue them," Lia said.

Bill's tiny hands rubbed his face. "What'll we do if we find them and they've been mutated into telepaths? We can't handle a thousand of them, can we?"

"No, we can't. Probably ferry a dozen back with us. The Bolt's got a full crew plus the extra weight of the MW1 system. I'll call Molly Parkinson and ask for help. She always knows what to do."

"What if they don't divulge that location? Are we going to risk a second strike?"

She rubbed her face with her tiny hands. "We'll see how the first one goes. Never commit to a second plan when you don't know the outcome of the initial plan."

Both chuckled. When Lia received the half-hour notice, they both headed to her CCC, where the night skeletal crew yielded their posts to the fully staffed day crew.

Someone barked, "Commander on deck." Everyone looked up at her and saluted. Then, cheers arose. Lia stood tall and returned their salute.

"Activate cloaking device," she ordered. "Drop out of hyperspace. Be alert for trouble."

Bill grabbed a railing and held on tightly. He felt the slight lurch as the stars reappeared on the giant view screens. Ahead, Gamma Orionis or Bellatrix blazed the ship in blue and ultraviolet light, a blue-white giant star. Eight times larger than Sol, this type B2 star formed twenty-five million years ago and thus was young. For a moment, the entire CCC froze. How could an advanced civilization, the Third Invaders, have developed around this blazing sun?

Lia shook her head. "Okay. Obviously, these aliens didn't evolve here. Look for a habitable zone and planet. They must have established a colony here."

"Ah, so this isn't their home planet," Senator Fennel said. "That makes sense. That sun is so bright. I can't imagine living around here."

"Commander, picking up flying saucers. We're tracking them. Maybe they'll lead us to their world," an officer called out.

"Good observation. Nav Officer, enter Sol coordinates. Be prepared to drop us into hyperspace on a second's notice. Stand by. Okay, astronomers, how's it coming. Need a planet in the habitable zone."

"Rocky planet found. In the right place. Saucers around it."

"Okay. Head for it. Sub-light speed," she ordered.

All eyes drifted to the forward monitor as a bluish planet grew from a dot to a large sphere.

"Saucers on landing trajectories."

"Comm officers, see if you can pick up any of their broadcasts. Try all frequencies," Lia ordered.

Soon, facts about this new world appeared. About the size of Earth, its oceans covered about fifty percent of the sphere. Two giant continents floated on the magma core about equidistant from each other and with nearly the same area. The flying saucers tended to land on the eastern continent, from the Bolt's point of view.

"Take her closer to the eastern land mass. Be alert for the saucers. Remember, they can't see us. We don't want a collision," Lia said. "Magnification at max."

From her post, Lia operated the scrolling controls. She studied the surface below.

"City. Pyramids. More city. Ah. Farmland, I think. How do we determine which is their capital city or most important one?"

"Have a comm channel working," one aide reported. "Putting it through the translation unit. Thank the stars for linguist Isabella Parkinson. Ah, tower chatter."

For the next six hours, they studied this eastern land mass, eventually deciding to strike what appeared to be the largest city complex and adjacent to a massive spaceport. Since ships continued to land and depart, Commander Lia decided to launch their strike a safe distance from there, avoiding any possible chance of a collision with the drone system. She hoped a black night would hide them. They watched the dark shadow of nightfall creep across the continent.

Since they had no estimate of a day's duration, Lia waited until four hours after full dark to launch her strike. Torn between her command post and her desire to be in the docking bay to watch the dozen fly the drones, Lia sighed and chose to remain at her post, content to watch them via video stream.

"Launch drones. Position them for an optimum spread. Notify me when ready to activate. Nav, stay alert. We may have to jump on a second's notice. These are highly intelligent people with ships that can run circles around us."

She watched as the drones flew down the bay and out into the air above the city. Currently, the Bolt hovered two miles up. After a hectic ten minutes, her drone crew finally got them properly positioned and themselves used to the live controls. Now they awaited orders.

"We don't know how quickly the drones will be discovered. I don't want to lose even one of them, so we play it safe. Set for optimum operation, two miles per hour. Be prepared to abort and return to the Bolt at top speed. For now, we'll set the distance traveled to be two miles. Execute," Commander Lia ordered.

A bit later, she said, "Are they working? I'm not seeing anything up here. Are we supposed to see something happening?"

Shrugs answered her. A drone operator said, "All systems seem to be operating. No way to tell. The microwave cones are pointed downward. We can see the buildings and stuff, but no people. Glad these drones have a vid camera attached. Wait. There's a figure down there. Zooming in. Wow!"

All eyes watched as a person covered his head with his hands and slowly sank to the ground, obviously writhing. Then, the body ceased all motion. In the dark, very little else could be discerned.

Playing extra safe, Commander Lia allowed the drones to fly out five miles and then back at top speed. Only once did a flying saucer's path come near the position of the Bolt. With the drones safely onboard, she ordered the Bolt to climb above the atmosphere and the many satellites in orbit around the planet.

Everyone listened to the translation unit, anxious to hear the Third Invaders' reactions and what, if anything, the drones had done.

Down below morning arrived, bringing the specter of death with it. Emergency personnel rushed into the affected sections of the spaceport city. A government reporter said, "Over ten thousand dead. Every person, animal, and even plants in this zone are dead. While autopsies are needed, it's apparent they died from extreme heat of some kind. Some speculate a new death ray. But the Federation of Planets doesn't have such a weapon and neither do the Sixth Invaders. The High Council is searching for other civilizations which might have such technology. The Guards are examining all video surveillance recordings made last night in hopes they'll catch a glimpse of the enemy who unleashed such death upon us."

Commander Johnston said, "Now we wait. Did they detect us or not? Stay alert and let me know."

"Are we going to ask them for the location of our colonists now?" an aide asked.

"No. We wait. Let them stew some. Patience. This is the tricky part. We don't want to start a war between them and our empire or the Federation, for that matter. Which means I must choose my words with great care."

Hours later and after learning the Bolt hadn't been spotted, though surveillance video briefly captured the drones in flight, Commander Johnston acted.

"Scramble my voice, and open a channel on the frequency they're using."

"Done and open," came the reply.

"This is Commander Fliegel of the Starship Bonnan. Now that I have your full attention, I want only one thing from your world. I've learned you've established a colony using a thousand people selected from the population of some world called Earth, apparently in the system known as Sol. Doesn't matter how I've discovered this. What I want to know is the location of said colony of humans. If I find them, you'll never see me again. If you provide me with bogus coordinates, you'll definitely see me again, only it won't be a couple miles of boiled people. Send coordinates on this frequency."

She signaled. Her aide broke the connection.

"Now we wait," Lia said.

A hush fell over the ship. All ears waited.

Lia thought we've got justice for the mutation betrayal, but will we find the thousand colonists?

Just under an hour later, a different voice came over the comm channel. It gave the coordinates. Hastily, the astronomer entered them and reported.

"Commander, that's Iota Piscium. A yellow type F7 star, slightly variable and about forty-five light years from Sol."

"Scramble my voice. Open the channel."

"You're live."

"Acknowledged your transmission. I'll return if coordinates are wrong."

She signaled, and her aide broke the connection.

"Hyperspace jump now."

When she felt the lurch, Lia finally relaxed. They'd not been shot out of the sky. Probably not even detected. No one had any way to track a ship through hyperspace. She opened a long distance comm channel to Earth. She sent the information to Senator Fennel's office. If the Third Invaders somehow followed them, the data wouldn't be lost. Someone would eventually listen to his voice mail.

"Okay, enter the coordinates for this Iota Piscium. Let's see if they told the truth," Commander Johnston said.

Chapter 20 The Colony

The Bolt dropped out of hyperspace over Colorado. While the Earth now had a defensive screen to keep unwanted spaceships from landing without clearance, the force barrier could be defeated by this action. Of course, one had to know the precise coordinates or risk materializing within the Himalayan Mountains, for example. Arriving this close to the Rocky Mountains begged for a crash, but they used their original landing coordinates at the site of the underground storage facility. Even so, the Bolt appeared barely one hundred feet above the rugged mountainside, pushing the accuracy of hyper-spatial coordinates.

An hour later, crew members finished rolling the drones back inside. Again, they wore masks to confuse the surveillance cameras, which had already been repaired. This time, they didn't bother to damage them.

"Liftoff," Commander Johnston ordered. Once the Bolt rose a few feet into the air, she barked, "Make the hyperspace jump now."

The Bolt cleared the ground and then vanished from Colorado. With the coordinates of Iota Piscium entered, she brought the Bolt up to cruising speed.

"Fifteen hours until we're there," an aide called out.

Lieutenant Commander Leon took over, and Lia returned to her cabin and her husband.

Bill said, "You pulled that one off, but I worry about the consequences. It could have caused a war between us and the Third Invaders."

"Hey, if anything goes wrong and they capture this ship, they won't find any drones or anything that could point to our involvement. I left the cloaking device with the drones, and I've had the electronic logs and records of our trip erased. So no physical proof. Of course, they could torture us and get us to admit to having done it, but without any real proof, they'd not start a war. Confessions under duress are worthless."

"Still, I'm worried," Senator Fennel said.

"Don't be. We're safe now. Look, they couldn't see the Bolt, so they've no idea what kind of ship hovered over their world. They've no idea what kind of device was used to terminate their people. A thorough search of the Bolt will show them we can't be invisible and have no weapon that could have caused the damage. We got away with our revenge."

"But how will their leaders know this was retaliation for their mutation betrayal and theft of our people?" Bill asked. He rubbed his face. "As a diplomat and senator, I'd see thousand dead via an unknown ray gun done by an unknown and invisible ship. The connection to our actions with Earth wouldn't enter my thinking—your request for the coordinates of the colony, not withstanding."

Lia changed the topic. "I've also let Molly know what we did and are doing. Just in case."

"Won't she let Admiral Rossi know?" Bill asked.

"Not yet. I left it on a remote send. Each day, I have to send it another hold signal. If something happens to me and I don't send it, then the system will forward that lengthy message to Molly. Just covering all our bases."

"I feel better knowing that. But what if they have a huge fleet guarding this new colony of theirs?" he asked. "We're going to be almost double the distance from Earth that our deep space exploration ships have ever traveled. About twenty-five light years is their latest distant search radius—last time I checked."

"I factored that into my decision to abandon the cloaking device. If they capture us, I wanted them to find no physical traces that we could have been that ship over their world. We can't cloak. We don't have the drones. Not us. But yeah. They could have many flying saucers hovering around that colony. It's risky. The moment we drop out of hyperspace, my navigator will enter Earth's coordinates, so we can jump out of harm's way in seconds. Look, while they might suspect we're coming, they won't know when. We'll take them by surprise. All we need is a few seconds to look for their saucers. What I really want to know is if that colony is really here."

"You think they lied to us?" Bill asked. "From their behavior so far, lying seems to be their modus operandi."

"Honestly, Bill, I just don't know. I can argue that point either way. The trouble is that we don't have hyperspace coordinates of anything that far out in that direction from Sol. Pity. Even the Federation hasn't mapped all of this side of the galaxy and its swirling arms. What we know is only a tiny fraction of what's out here in these arms. Sometime, I'd like to go to Bela Prime and see what being closer to the center of our galaxy is like. Meanwhile, we should get some sleep. Need to be alert when we arrive."

Hours later, Commander Johnston stood at her post on the bridge, calling out orders. "Is the streaming video recording? Automatic send if we do nothing?"

"Aye, sir. Recording now. It's set for two hours. If we don't do anything to stop it, the recording will be broadcast to the Senior Judge," an aide said. "It'll record everything we see and hear in this CCC, plus the exterior monitors. Bases covered."

"One minute until arrival," another called out.

"Gun crews armed and ready," the combat major said.

The bustling activity in the CCC died down. A hush fell. The moment arrived. An aide called out, "Three. Two. One."

The Bolt dropped out of hyperspace. The navigator entered Earth's coordinates.

He said, "Laid in and ready for activation, Commander."

The two astronomers studied the star field, while the two battle majors surveyed the surrounding space for enemy saucers. Commander Johnston focused on the brilliant blue-white star, somewhat larger than Sol and a little hotter.

The supplied coordinates placed them just inside the Oort cloud surrounding this star system, far out from the sun. To find the colony, they'd have to waste time trying to find the habitable zone and search for potential planets. That meant delay.

But her two hotshot astronomers rapidly zeroed in that zone. For the moment, they had the controls.

"We're flying up and inward," one said. "Get a bird's eye view down on the planetary system. Calculated the habitable zone. Now scanning for planets."

An aide said, "No sign of enemy saucers. Yet," she added.

In the bowels of the Bolt, Airman Recruit Nain Hammerhead swept up the dirt and metal filings left behind by the work crews that had modified the Bolt's controls to utilize the Sixth Invader-built cloaking device and the hastily fabricated fittings to adapt the drone systems to utilize the modern control devices. The youthful dwarf of fifty-five years had enlisted two months ago, hoping one day to be on the bridge, preferably giving orders. He'd immigrated to Earth. Why? Over-population of his home world guaranteed he'd never get into their space fleet.

The fledgling Sol Empire offered immediate hiring, though sweeping dirt and lugging heavy loads wasn't exactly what he had in mind. Always jovial, Nain had endeared himself to the crew of the Bolt. That he was more than twice as strong as the strongest man had something to do with his acceptance. He followed the action via the intercom system, imagining himself in the CCC.

A voice said, "There it is. Found a rocky planet in the proper zone." He paused and punched a fist into the air. "Has an atmosphere. Has an ocean." Nain grinned and continued sweeping.

Commander Johnston said, "Good work. Take us down to that planet. Stay sharp. Could be a trap. Navigator, hand on the Jump button. Gunners, stay alert."

The pilot took over from the astronomers, who continued using their remote telescopes to look for additional potential sites or moons. One reported, "Planet has two moons. Both small. Estimated planet diameter: nine thousand miles. Moon's diameters: eight hundred miles and seven hundred miles."

As the bluish planet grew in size on the monitors, Commander Johnston said, "Okay. Bring us down on its equator. Scan for land masses."

"One large continent. A very big ocean," an aide reported. "We're at its geosynchronous orbit position. Holding for long range scans."

Lia's attention turned to the giant monitor on which displayed the scans in real-time. Lush equatorial forests dominated the images, along with a tall mountain range on the eastern edge of the continent.

"Scan northward," she ordered. Lia realized it was a fifty-fifty proposition. The colony would be very small, either north or south of the hot zone. A new colony would never be established in such a zone. Rather, they'd use the more temperate zones just as on Earth.

"Holy crap!" an aide cried out. "Civilization. Wait. Make that ancient civilizations."

All manner of cries echoed in the CCC.

Down below, Nain sighed. He'd have to wait and review the recordings later on. "Dingo's dog!" he muttered.

Giant spiral-like buildings rose, but nature had already recovered the ground levels of this once large city. Grasses, shrubs, and trees reached skyward, though the spirals dwarfed them.

A few miles later, the edge of the city gave way to forest lands. More long abandoned cities came into view and dropped behind them. When they reached the temperate zone, the encroaching nature hadn't completely covered the ground levels. Individual dwellings dotted the cities. Giant transparent domes covered these cities, quite unlike the equatorial cities. The telescopes looked down and through the domes.

That the tops of all buildings were transparent struck Commander Johnston, reminding her of the flying saucer she'd captured with Molly. The ship's metal domed roof opened up, revealing a transparent dome over the habitation zone of the ship. Each cabin and its occupants were visible from above. Had the Third Invaders gotten their plans from this world? Had this once been a Third Invader civilization?

Commander Johnston took the Bolt lower so they could get a closer look at these towns. Inside the domes, the vegetation grew with abandon, implying these dwellings had been abandoned long ago. They spotted some four-legged animals roaming the countryside outside these domed towns.

Lieutenant Commander Leon said, "Anyone of these towns would make a great place to start a colony. From this height, all the infrastructure appears intact. Question is: where is the colony? Lots of land to search."

"Maybe, maybe not. I'd expect the Third Invaders to have some screening saucers around this colony. If this is actually where the colony is located," Lia said. She frowned and continued to watch the monitors, the tiny fingers of her left hand crossed.

"Flying saucer at twelve o'clock," an aide called out.

"Gunners stand by," the gunnery major ordered.

"Back tracking the saucer. We can probably estimate where it lifted off from," the pilot said, maintaining the Bolt's heading, one that shot toward the saucer.

"Here's what we need to do," Commander Johnston said. "Slow us down, as though we're planning to meet this saucer. Meanwhile, calculate where it likely lifted off from. When we're close to the saucer, use maximum sub-light speed and get us to that liftoff position. Gunnery Major, buy us the time to get there."

"Aye, sir."

A minute later, a Third Invader commander hailed the Bolt using normal Sol Empire frequencies.

"This is restricted planet. You are not authorized to be here. Turn back now. If you persist, we have instructions to shoot you down. Over."

"Reply?" an aide said.

"No. Full speed to that saucer's liftoff point. Let's see what they're hiding," Lia said.

Her move took the speedier saucer by surprise, as the Bolt shot past the saucer. On a rear monitor, others watched as the saucer arced around and shot towards them. However, the alien move was too little, too late. The Bolt reached the location.

"Oh, my god!" and aide said.

"Wow!" Lia said.

"Below them rose the largest domed city they'd yet seen. She estimated its diameter to be fifty miles. Plowed fields and new growth planted fields dotted part of the encapsulated land. A rough guess suggested a million people once lived here. A landing field with numerous parked flying saucers lay at the northern edge, where a domed entrance reminded Lia of a giant transparent igloo. The Bolt shot past the city. Now what, Lia thought.

Commander Johnston barked to her pilot, "Immelmann turn now!"

That was a reference to an ancient World War I biplane aerial maneuver
in which the plane did an ascending half-loop followed by a half-roll—all of which resulted in flying level but in the opposite direction and at a higher altitude.

In the bowels of the Bolt, Nain grumbled. His pile of swept up bits scattered in several directions. He'd have to re-sweep.

"Have a lock on the saucer," the battle major reported.

"Fire at will," Commander Johnston ordered.

The Bolt's cannon blazed.

"Five hits. It's going down," the major reported.

"Any signs of other combatants?"

A series of "no's" echoed. The other saucers remained on the surface near one edge of the domed city.

"Okay. Take her down near that igloo-like entrance," Lia ordered. "But stay alert. Marines, prepare to depart and secure our perimeter."

The Bolt slowly descended, making a perfect landing. Still no enemy counter-fire. Six armored marines charged out, blasters at the ready, and took up securing positions. Still nothing.

"Landing party: prepare to disembark."

She gave the order she hoped to give. Were their thousand colonists here? Inside this dome? Lia felt the familiar adrenalin rush and wished she could go with the dozen men and women.

"Oxygen levels a bit higher than Earth's. Gravity is also slightly lower," one of her planetary scientists reported. "Humidity at forty-five."

Outside, one of the marines said, "Kind of a funny smell out here."

"Must be all those rotting forest trees we saw coming in," another said. "Stay alert. Where are all those Third Invaders?"

He yawned. His arms lowered his heavy blaster. One by one, the others lowered theirs, before slumping down to sit on the ground. The landing party walked down the bay ramp. Their movements gradually slowing down.

"Hey, what's going on out there?" Commander Johnston asked. "Why do I feel... Tired." She slumped over in her seat in the CCC. All around her, others either slumped or dropped onto the floor.

One of the crew manning a gun asked, "Hey, is everything all right up there?" She meant in the CCC. She received no reply. Something didn't seem right, so she rose to go find out, but slumped back into her seat instead.

Bit by bit, the noise onboard the Bolt died down, leaving Nain still sweeping down below. Finally, he realized things were too quiet. He used the intercom. "Hey, what's happening? I've got the mess swept. What should I do next?"

Silence. Utter silence. He swallowed. Best check it out, he thought. Nain climbed out of the lowest level only to find other mates unconscious, sitting or lying on the metal floor. "Dingo's rats! Something's up." He headed on up to the CCC. More and more crew lay in awkward positions in the hallways, forcing him to step over their bodies. They were alive, just unconscious.

Everyone in the CCC slumped over their workstations. On the monitors, he saw their landing party and marines also lying on the ground, unresponsive. Nain swallowed hard. "I'm the only one alive? Can't be. What do I do? I've only been on the job two months. Best go find my regulations manual."

He turned to head to his tiny cabin in the lower deck when he saw movement on one of the monitors. A dozen of the brown Third Invader aliens wearing some form of battle armor and carrying large weapons resembling blasters marched out from the dome. One paused to examine an unconscious marine, while the others headed for the bay ramp.

The Third Invaders stood six-six. Beautifully tanned, their bodies and torsos looked much like humans. Their heads shocked him. Flattened faces seemed squashed, while their heads curved back like a giant bird's beak, the tip of the head's rear nearly eighteen inches behind what would have been the back of a human head.

Nain swallowed hard, again. *What should I do? Not get caught, that's what.* He dashed down into the lower levels again. *Hide. Where?*

The translation units in CCC activated automatically. The intercom system was still on. Thus, the monotone words from the device echoed throughout the ship, while the aliens examined the captured Bolt.

"This can't be ship that murdered ten thousand on home world. It's just one of Sol Empire's lowly cruisers. It doesn't have cloaking ability," one said.

He added, "Check engineering. Also, stay alert for some horrible new weapon. Home world said victims were boiled alive. Hideous."

After a pause, Nain heard him say, "Okay. Cart these humans out. If memory serves me, there should be about hundred in its crew. They are all in mutation comas. Strip them of all apparel and take them to Implant Section. We've got eight days to prepare these new arrivals. Now colony will have eleven hundred armless telepaths. Oh, don't forget to count number of each sex. Rha needs that data."

Nain swallowed hard again. *Mutation comas? Armless telepaths?* He felt sick. He could do nothing to save any of them. Everyone onboard the Bolt would be mutated, excepting him. Dwarves had different DNA. For now, his only option was to hide. He didn't need to be a commander to know these aliens would kill him if they found him.

He climbed into a food conveyor that lifted supplies from storage up six levels to the kitchen. Only a dwarf could fit inside the small opening. His knees up against his chest and arms around them holding them secure, Nain waited, the translation units still occasionally echoing the alien's conversations throughout the ship. Finally, someone turned them off, leaving Nain in the silence and dark. He waited.

Later, he felt the ship being moved, dragged perhaps. Still, Nain remained cooped up, his legs, numb. Finally, he could take it no longer.

As quietly as he could, he opened the door and climbed out, only to collapse on to the floor. He rubbed circulation back into his legs. No one came. All lights were off. Fumbling, he made his way to his own cabin. There, he found a flashlight. He took a deep breath and headed off to see what he could discover.

The Bolt had been powered down. The aliens parked it on the landing pad, but as far away from the igloo doors and saucers as they could. He recalled what he'd heard about the number of parked saucers. Only two remained. Nain concluded the others must have brought the soldiers here and had now departed, having captured the Bolt.

"This is not how I envisioned my life in the space fleet," he whispered. "I'm stuck here with no way to get home. Dingo's rats. I don't even know how to operate any of the Bolt's controls to call to get help. Plus, I'm hungry. Ah, well. There should be plenty of food for me to eat."

Later as he ate a cold meal, he estimated he could live on the supplies for at least a year. After that? He didn't dare think.

Nain didn't know that the overall video recording of what happened in the CCC finally ended. Since Lia didn't enter the counter-code, the ship compacted the video and automatically sent it via a long distance message to the Senior Judge on Earth.

Chapter 21 The Adventures of Nain

Nain stole back to his cabin and strapped on his translation device. Now he'd not be dependent on the ship's units. Besides, he didn't want to be heard, just understand what these aliens said.

A voice said, "We covered every inch of Sol Empire ship. No cloaking device. Can't be ship that attacked home world."

A female voice said, "What about this new weapon? One that murdered ten thousand in their sleep?"

"There's nothing like it on this ship. I swear, Commandant Iakob-Ra, this isn't ship they're looking for," the original male voice said.

The woman said, "So either this ship just happened upon us—"

"Hardly likely. We're twice most distant location of any Sol ship from their home worlds. It's more likely this Commander Fliegel of Starship Bonnan just relayed coordinates to this Sol cruiser. If so, my troops have guaranteed they will never report back to this Commander Fliegel person. But don't worry. We'll stick around longer. Just in case Sol sends out search party or better yet, this Fliegel person comes."

"That would be wise. This time, nothing can be allowed to interfere with my experimental program," the woman said.

Nain listened to the footsteps of someone leaving. Then another voice spoke up.

"Now there goes one pathetic psychwoman. Why Home World didn't just populate this world with normal humans is beyond me. Whoever lived here left all their infrastructure undamaged. We could move in at least billion people and still have towns left over."

"Pathetic? You're being kind about it. Still, Home World backed her latest experiment. But I've heard this is last time, unless she gets spectacular results," the original man said.

"Rather we should be out there looking for that alien butcher, that Fliegel man, not hiding underground on chance he'll come here. Look, why would any reasonable person bother with these mutants? They're darn near helpless. And they don't have slave servants like Commandant Iakob-Ra has."

"No argument from me. You'd have to be nuts to want to rescue these colonists. Except for one thing."

"You mean telepathy?" the second man said.

"Yeah. Her goal is breeding telepaths. But we both know they're as helpless as she is. Who's going to want someone you have to look after their every physical need, eh? Edyta Iakob-Ra failed once, but Home World has given her a second chance. Why? Only gods know. But I heard if she doesn't get definitive results, they're pulling the plug on this whole mutation mess."

"So we sit on our butts underground and wait?"

"Yeah, that's right. Wasn't even battle today. We best head below. Not supposed to let helpless cripples see us."

Their footsteps faded away. Nain relaxed. For the moment, he was safe. He set about seeing just what the aliens left on the Bolt. He found the armory hadn't been looted. Though none of the armor fit his four-foot stature, he armed himself with several pistols, two blasters, and a ammo tin. Next, he stowed a pair of knives in his pockets, along with two flashlights and night vision goggles.

When night came, Nain crept out of the Bolt, using the emergency escape hatch in the bowels of the ship where he'd been sweeping when they landed. Satisfied no one could see him, Nain studied the landing pad. The saucers sat close to the igloo doors, but in the dual moonlight, he spotted pipes protruding from underground. He crept to the nearest one and sniffed. Mutation agent. Now he knew where the mutation agent had come from.

Clever. Let a ship land. Seeing nothing threatening, they open the ship's doors and some exit onto the pad. Out comes the colorless, airborne mutation agent, striking humans down. Commander Johnston and the others had no chance at all. Nain concluded they must have a storage tank and injection system underground, probably where the soldiers stayed.

Nain wanted to do something, but what? The odor of rotting vegetation filled the air. Perhaps that's what reminded him of a conversation he'd overheard between Commander Johnston and Lieutenant Commander Leon, the man who had given him this chance in the space fleet. She'd talked about someone's therapy that erased trauma and even nasty implants, but knowing the words of the implant greatly helped the therapy.

Their arms must be rotting off. I need to see if that's happening and if the thousand colonists are inside the dome. But if they are implanting the people, I need to record what the aliens are saying to them. Plus, it'd be a good idea to destroy those flying saucers, too.

Nain crept forward toward the igloo-like protrusion which housed a set of very wide doors, the main entrance inside the giant dome. He spotted two surveillance cameras in operation and stay out of their way. *Foolish aliens. Guards should patrol the area.*

The doors were locked, but Nain picked the lock in under a minute. He slipped inside. A long tunnel had two side branches that led to stairs to the underground facilities, along with two elevators. These, he passed by, choosing to enter the domed city proper. Once inside, the air felt fresher and warmer, perhaps too warm. He stood on a wide street. On either side, buildings rose, but had no roofs. He heard voices coming from the first of these and crept up to it. Someone spoke English.

After a minute, he realized he was listening to a recording. Emboldened, he slipped inside and into a hall. Ten rooms opened off this corridor and their doors weren't even shut. He peered into the first one. The voice grew louder, but also he spotted several of his fellow crew members lying naked on cots. An inspection yielded what he presumed. They were in mutation comas and listening to this recording, which must be on a continuous play loop, since this was the third time he'd heard the current bit.

After checking on several more rooms, he headed farther into the town. The identical homes had no actual doors, so he slipped into one. Kitchen and pantry held typical goods; the odor of fresh baked bread still hung in the air. He crept into a bedroom and saw several naked humans sleeping. None had arms. *That's why there's no doors.* Quickly, he fled the town, locking the front doors on his way out.

Once safe in his cramped crew cabin, he sighed. "Well, the Earth people got fooled again. The Third Invaders turned the thousand colonists into armless telepaths. They must be planning on raising and selling telepaths. Nasty business. How can I stop them? Should I stop them?" He fell asleep before he could think of an answer.

The next day while the sunlight provided some illumination within the Bolt, Nain hunted for a recorder, finding one in the CCC. He tested it to make sure he could make it work. Next, he found several wireless units and hooked them up to relay sound to his translation unit in his ear. Satisfied, he prepared himself for the night's work.

Long after full dark, Nain slipped out, picked the door lock, and spent two hours positioning his spy microphones around the igloo tunnel and doors as well as just outside. Then, he crept into the home which held some of his fellow crew. Although only in their second full day of their mutation comas, already their bosoms had grown while their arms withered. As before, a recorded voice on a continuous play loop reached all ears in the room. Nain turned on his recorder.

While he waited, he noticed something else. A wire harness rested on their heads, an intense light coming from it. Not a normal kind of light that illuminated the insides of the Bolt, but something else. In a flash, he realized he wasn't seeing it with his eyes, rather his mind somehow saw this intensely beautiful light. He shook his head, breaking the semi-trance it held on him.

What the heck is that? Must be part of this mess. He stepped out of the room, still shaking his head.

He recorded the entire sequence twice before leaving. While he had no experience with mental phenomenon or electronics, he suspected what was said probably had some relationship to keeping the victims here and content. The entire sequence:

"I love myself just the way I am. I don't want to change

anything about my body. I just love how I look. It may take me longer to do things and sometimes it's much harder, but I'm very pleased with myself and my abilities. I'm strong, smart, beautiful, and powerful. I'm always cheerful, totally happy and content, though I have to learn new ways to do things. My life is precious to me.

"I am very happy to be here. I am part of a wonderful group. The colonists are the very best people. I want to always do my part for the colony. I must help other colonists, just as they help me. I love being here. I'm honored to be a member of this colony. I never want to leave. I'd rather die than leave this colony. I must follow the orders of the Council. They know what's best for us.

"I must have many, many children and with as many fathers or mothers as I can to help promote genetic diversity. I must have sex when I wake and at night. I will only be sexually satisfied after I've had a child by everyone in the colony. Having many children is vital for the survival of our wonderful colony. I promise to do my part.

"I will never forget any of these words. I will repeat them several times each day."

As far as Nain could tell, this sequence repeated endlessly all the time the Bolt crew members were in their comas. It played during the night while the colonists were sleeping, further reinforcing the desired behavior pattern.

During the next day, his remote microphones captured many conversations. He concluded Home World and Commandant Edyta Iakob-Ra had different views on the significance of the murderous nighttime attack that killed thousands.

"I'm sure they plan to come here and attack me," Edyta Iakob-Ra said. Apparently, she was talking over the Long Distance Communication Array, since the time lag of responses was nearly fifteen minutes. "You must keep defense forces here to protect valuable experiment in progress. Over."

A male voice replied, "Look, other than that random cruiser—which has been reported as having been stolen or lost—there's been no action. That cruiser could not have been involved in attack. No cloaking device. No unknown hideous weapon, just usual ineffective disruptors and blasters. We think it was fluke that ship found you. Over."

"But I've been promised security force. Not like last time. I was defenseless when Sol Empire found site. Over."

"Yeah, well you did a good job in taking out two of their deep space exploration ships. Over."

"But not larger cruiser-like ship. It's guns could have damaged saucer and ruined experiment. Hell, they did ruin it. Over."

"In part, that's why Home World has agreed to give you another chance to prove your theory. Besides, not only have you gotten your requested thousand key humans, Home World has moved all other mutated humans to Iota Piscium-C. What's your official population tally now? Over."

"One thousand six hundred ten. But that's not point. I need these dozen saucers with their fighters here to protect base and experiment. Over."

A cynical chuckle began the reply. "Don't you mean to protect yourself? You're as helpless as those telepaths you're raising. You'll get to keep squad another week. After that, Home World wants them redeployed to help protect Home World from another murderous attack. Over."

"But that'll leave me with only one saucer and three fighters. You can't mean that. Does Home World really want me to fail? If they could just see results I'm getting. This time, everything is working flawlessly. Twenty years from now, we'll be able to sell telepaths throughout galaxy and at incredible prices. Over."

"Yes, yes. But you have gaseous mutation agent spreader installed. Didn't it just wipe out entire crew of that cruiser? Your soldiers didn't have to fire even one shot. Surely, that is more than enough to stop any humans who come calling. Over."

"But Earth humans also have dwarves and giants living there. We both know mutation agent doesn't affect either of those races. My forces will have to kill any of those who might be part of rescue fleet. And I heard Earth is furious about fake mutation agent we unloaded on them. What's Home World going to do when Earth and perhaps even Federation demands we return colonists? They could send armada here, ruining everything. Over."

"You are over estimating just how valuable your experiment is to Home World, Commandant Edyta Iakob-Ra. True, they discovered Iota Piscium-C and its lost civilization whose infrastructure is in pristine condition. For now, they've given it to you for your experiment. Just between us, they did that because it cost drastically less for you to run your tests there than to build new, large facility on some other uninhabited world as you had them do on small scale for your small hundred person bands. So you should consider yourself incredibly lucky, Commandant. Incredibly. Over."

"Lucky? Those humans killed my husband and my son. They cut my arms off, leaving me disabled. That's not what I call lucky. But this planet is perfect for this experiment. More than perfect. Temperature inside domes is such that I can have them all go naked, which removes barrier of getting dressed and undressed. Just try that without arms. I can't live without my assistant to help me. Plus, with them all running around naked, it encourages them to have frequent intercourse, which is key factor in this project. We've already proven that adults who lose their arms have very hard time adapting, if at all, while children born without arms adapt very well. It's this next generation here that will provide telepaths we need. So I demand protection for at least twenty years. Besides, if humans attack here in force, we haven't any way to evacuate them, let alone any place we can take them. Home World must protect us for two decades. Over."

More laughter preceded the reply. "You're dreaming if you think Home World is going to keep those saucers and their crews on Iota Piscium-C for twenty years. They are probably incredibly bored already. Bored crew makes mistakes. Besides, keeping that many saucers there is too costly. Your experiment isn't that important to Home World. Yeah, I know you're famous and that you've lost your family. In part, that's probably why they agreed to back you in this next phase. But there are limits. You're exceeding yours. Expect to have them recalled soon. Over."

"Is there nothing I can do to convince you to argue on

my behalf? Please, I feel so helpless. This project promises to make Home World untold millions when we can finally market telepaths. Over."

"You'd be better off figuring out how to make telepath with arms and is indistinguishable from ordinary human people. Your telepaths are instantly identifiable. So much for espionage or secrecy. I've done all I can do. Over and out."

Another female voice spoke up. "Commandant, that didn't go so well, did it?"

"No, I'm afraid it didn't. You don't know how awful it was when those humans came and killed my family, ruined my experiment, and turned me into a helpless cripple. Every day, I face how mutilated I am. In part, that's why I included what I did in these humans' implant. That's also why I insisted doctors use arriving males to impregnate all new females. Get head start on producing offspring—children who will know nothing about arms and who will adapt and be quite content with their lives."

"But can't these thousand plus be sold, too?" the other woman asked.

"No. In my initial experiment, mutated adults weren't implanted. Results were dismal. In end, I had to round up some sub-human women and train them to care for telepaths' needs. You know how that ended. Implants can alter behavior. But."

"But what?"

"But they cannot go against that programming. They'd be unsuited for general work as telepath on some other world and culture. Implants won't let them adapt to ever-changing life situations. In this experiment, plan is to have these thousand plus be utterly content to live their lives here, independent of any outside help. Grow their own food and so on. That way, their children will grow up in such environment and be just as independent as their parents are, only without restrictive implant that would prevent them from being marketed successfully across the galaxy."

"So we stay invisible in background—underground in this case. I can see why. But they're so helpless. And having them not wear clothes is brilliant, Edyta. Sometimes as I watch them, I so want to help them like I help you."

"But you can't. You mustn't. We remain here underground and let them work out their own solutions to life. It's crucial. They have to learn to be independent. Well, mostly independent. Having them assist each other was brilliant notion I had based on results of earlier experiments."

Her assistant chuckled. "That's also brilliant. They're always helping each other do something they couldn't do alone."

"Just don't go getting ideas I could learn to do things with my feet like they are. Not going to happen. I'm Home World aristocrat. Don't forget it," Edyta whined.

That same day, Nain overheard her commenting on the colonists' progress.

"Perfect. They have crop planting completed. Ahead of what I predicted. Implants are working better than I anticipated. They have enough acreage planted with enough crops that come harvest time, they will have over-abundance of food."

Her assistant said, "And nutritionally balanced. Without any animal or poultry products, that's real challenge. I did rise to the challenge to get it right for them. I didn't expect their nutritional requirements to be nearly same as ours, though we do need ten percent more B vitamins."

Edyta chuckled. "In part, that's why I hired you to be my assistant. You are Home World's top nutritional expert."

After a pause, she said, "This town, this civilization must have been amazing. Domes control climate and provide proper rainfall, too. Those solar panels in orbit provide more power than they need or can use. Yes, took true geniuses to built these domed cities. I'm hoping that linguist I brought along can decipher their writing. Maybe we'll learn who they were and what happened to them. It's like they just abandoned everything. Got up and left."

Her assistant said, "I read original report. Our explorers didn't find any corpses. So yeah, giant mystery. What happened to these people who had idyllic civilization?"

"Perhaps this Tia linguist will answer that for us. Did you know that before you came, our scientists dated these cities from some found organic material."

"No. Probably can't be more than couple hundred years, though."

Edyta laughed. "Our city here was built five thousand years ago. Dates back to when our people were setting up various human colony experiments on many worlds."

"Wow. Expected more decay or something. Any idea when these were last occupied?" her assistant asked.

"Forty-nine hundred years ago. Carbon-14 dates. More curious, though, they believe all domes abandoned at roughly same time. Lack of bodies or skeletons suggests migration. Perhaps if this Tia can decipher their language, we can learn more."

"Yeah, but probably more rather useless facts. Does Home World even care?" her assistant asked.

Edyta snickered. "Nope. But this keeps some of elite happy. Rather, they wanted to put these ready-made towns to good use. Resettlement. New colony. Our usual long term societal experimentations. But I convinced them to let me make use of them first. Made to order for this test. Still, I worry about Earthlings' interference. Especially that Molly Parkinson woman. She's caused me huge problems. Royal butt pain."

"Don't worry. We have long distance comm set. Even if saucer fleet leaves, we can call for help," her assistant said.

"True, but we'll have to hold them off long enough for help to get here. And that's what I'm afraid of. Bureaucracy. Might take them too long to agree to respond."

"You think these Earth people will cut off my arms, too?" her assistant asked.

Nain didn't hear a reply. Sitting in his cabin on the Bolt, he decided what he needed to do. "If Earth people are coming, that long distance antenna must be destroyed. Those three soldiers will just activate their gas device like they did to us, so those three men have to go. Plus, I need to get into that basement and wreck the gas device so no one can use it. Tall order, but it must be done. But I don't know when Earth ships will arrive. How much time do I have?"

Through Day Three and Four, he watched and studied

the soldiers movements. A great forest lay around this domed city. Nain had no idea how big it was or how far away the next domed town lay. However, often a soldier merely appeared on the tarmac, and he swore the man hadn't come out of the igloo doors. That meant they had another exit from the underground complex. Curious, that night Nain crawled across the landing pad and into the nature-gone-wild woods.

After getting disentangled from a briar patch, the moons rose. In the pale pink light, he spotted a trail through the thick underbrush. The well-worn, easterly path ended about eight hundred feet from the dome. A man could navigate the path from here to the dome. While the path didn't end here, it narrowed, becoming some animal's trail. He'd seen deer on Earth, but he'd also seen other hoofed animals on other worlds. The flacot on his home world could tear a man apart with its razor-sharp horns just because one looked at it.

Were there wild animals on this world? Even though he was heavily armed, Nain saw no purpose in following what had to be an animal. Rather, he wanted to find the entrance the three soldiers used. The moons rose higher, but here the canopy blocked much of their light. Nain moved off the path, fighting the brambles, until he dropped down and crawled. *Much better.* Like a slithering snake, he burrowed into the underbrush, before turning around to watch. With luck, he'd spot one of the soldiers as they came out of their secret tunnel.

He fell asleep.

Noise of trampling feet woke him. Ten feet away, he saw a soldier's legs moving westward down the path. *Damn!* All he could do was wait and hope the man returned this way. Ants crawled under his clothes, but he dare not move. As dense as this brush was, he'd draw attention to himself. He clenched his jaw.

Other strange wildlife appeared here and there as he waited. Animals for sure, the soft furry kind, as well as others with claws and teeth. At least no snakes. Nail hated snakes, thanks to a childhood encounter.

Dusk found a starving dwarf still lying on the ground, his clothes soaked in moisture raised from the humus. But the soldier returned, crunching small sticks beneath his boots while humming a tune. Oblivious to Nain, he paused, pulled down his pants, and watered the underbrush barely ten feet from the dwarf. Then, he turned and pulled on a concealed door latch. When the trap door opened, light from inside flooded the area, temporarily blinding Nain. He blinked. With just the faintest sound, the door closed, though the footsteps of the soldier descending stairs thundered until the door fully closed, bringing back the dusk.

Hastily, the dwarf crawled out of his hiding place and scampered down the path to the Bolt. Once inside, he allowed himself a shower to wash the creepy crawlers off his body. Dressed in a fresh uniform, he made himself a large meal, before heading to bed. Time to figure out his next move.

Before dawn, Nain lay perched behind the trap door. Made of composite materials similar to the dome, the door looked just like the ground around it, save for the almost indistinguishable handle. It opened so silently that Nail almost missed the event. Once opened, the footsteps of a soldier thundered upwards, breaking the stillness. In that moment, Nain wondered if there were birds on this world.

The head of the soldier appeared. Nain acted. His hands grabbed the man's head from behind. His powerful muscles twisted the head. Cracking noises replaced the footsteps. Nain paused, but heard no further noises. The soldier was alone. He dragged the dead soldier out of the hole and shut the door. Next, he pulled the man eastward along the faint animal path for about five hundred feet, before shoving the corpse into a bramble patch. Backtracking, he did his best to cover his trail before returning to his hiding place.

He knew he dare not make a daylight return to the Bolt. Anyone looking could see him. Besides, another soldier might come looking for the missing one. None did. After full dark, he slipped back to the Bolt.

The next day, he heard voices through his ear translation unit.

"No, we haven't found any trace of him. I know he's been missing a whole day, but there's no sign of him out there."

A female voice said, "Well, look again. He can't have

disappeared. And our saucer is still here. Maybe wild animal got him. Stay on this comm channel."

"Aye, sir. Okay, you heard her. Let's search again. He's got to be here somewhere."

Nain headed to the CCC where he could see the men via the video system which continued to function. The two soldiers headed eastward along the path, muttering to themselves. He resisted the urge to follow them.

Hours later, the men walked out from the igloo doors. Their tone had changed.

"Something out here tore his body apart," one said.

"Yeah, he probably didn't see it coming. The undergrowth is so dense between these towns. Who knows what vicious creatures roam this abandoned world," the other said.

"Keep your eyes open. This boring assignment took nasty detour."

"Right. Ought to send her lordship out here. See how she likes it," the other said.

Both men laughed.

"Say," the first man said, "how about you covering me from here when I patrol the back entrance tomorrow morning. Blast crap out of anything that moves. Except me."

"You got it. This crummy assignment can't get any worse."

Nain smiled. Late that night, he crept back to his hiding place behind the trap door and waited. Just after dawn, the door opened. A blaster barrel appeared first. Then the head of the soldier. Nain responded in a flash, snapping the man's neck. This time, he let the man's body lay sprawled on the ground, its feet keeping the door from closing. Nain crawled into the brush just a little westward and waited.

After a time, the third soldier came charging along the path, yelling the name of his buddy who failed to appear out of the woods.

"Hey, this isn't funny. Where are you?" he yelled, sweeping his blaster right and left as he thundered through the underbrush. He cursed and paused when he saw the body lying mostly out of the door. He whirled around three times, but saw nothing. Calmed, he bent down to check on his buddy. Nain struck.

The soldier rose and turned to see what made the noise behind him. Nain was faster, his fist upthrust into the soldier's arms. The blaster flew out of the man's hands. Then, Nain lunged onto the man, his powerful arms encircling the soldier's torso. Like a giant vice, the dwarf squeezed, crushing the breath out of the man. A hideous cracking sound announced the rupture of the soldier's back, followed by another neck twist mercifully ending the soldier's life.

Nain dragged both further east along the animal path, depositing the bodies. Perhaps those animals would have a feast, he thought. As far as the dwarf knew, only two aliens remained, the helpless leader and her assistant. Thus far, he'd not see the assistant. Armed with a blaster, she could be just as dangerous as the soldiers. Nain couldn't afford to be careless.

He blatantly walked back down the path to the dome. Their long distance array attached to the side of the transparent dome pointed skyward. Cables led through one of the many holes in the composite dome on up to the antenna where it attached to it. Nail ripped the cable from the antenna array and then strained his muscles to stretch and pop the cable itself, removing a ten foot section. Now this assistant person couldn't come out and reattach the cable. She'd have to re-string a whole new cable, if they had one.

Confident they couldn't call for help, Nain headed inside. However, he didn't go in the igloo-like hallway. Rather, he ran back eastward and entered their backdoor.

As before, bright lights illuminated the stairs heading below ground. Like everything else in this dome complex, they were made from a composite material. His footsteps echoed, too, despite his attempts to be stealthy.

He entered a realm filled with composite pipes painted in a rainbow of colors. More like a surreal maze, the hidden infrastructure confused the dwarf. Shaking his head, he decided to follow the floor and ignore the pipes, some of which were overhead and some floated just above the ground.

He checked each side room, of which there seemed no end, often finding control valves or actual controlling electronics with strange writings on them. These, he ignored. Some contained what he suspected might be repair materials, again covered with the weird symbols, the ancients' writing he surmised.

Nain came across many junctions, the majority leading away from the landing pad and deeper into the town. Obviously, this infrastructure lay beneath the entire town. And thus was just as large as the town. He might have to search for weeks to find the aliens. At that though, his stomach growled.

Thus far, he'd continued traveling in his original direction, not following any of the side spurs. That's when he noticed faint chalk marks on the floor. Little arrows pointing the way he'd come. Nain smiled. The aliens faced the same problem. Their solution: a simple one. He followed the arrows.

Eventually, he walked into a huge room. Two elevators and two stairs led upwards. A giant gas cylinder rested in the middle of the room, metal pipes led out through the walls. Ground up composite material lay on the floor beneath the holes that allowed the pipes through. This had to be the gas mutation agent trap and the stairs that led upwards to the igloo doors. A large lever controlled the release of the gas. Nain studied the device, knowing he had to disable it. If he couldn't get to the assistant, she could release the gas herself.

He could turn it on and release all the gas, but that might alert the two women. Or. Nain smiled. Or he could bend the metal level back and forth. Grunting, the stocky man pulled the lever towards his body and then pushed it back to the pipes. Back and forth. Each time, it bent easier, until it simply snapped. He smiled. *Now they can't mutate more victims on the landing pad. Not unless they can replace that lever. Bet the assistant can't do that. Now to find them.*

Four hallways led from this large room, along with four other doors. He checked the doors first. Inside one, he found cots and some belongings for the three soldiers. The other three contained tools and materials, but one held food reserves, labeled in strange writing, likely that of these aliens he guessed. Satisfied the rooms held no surprises, he explored further. Besides finding the women, he wanted to discover the source of the recordings being played into people's minds at night.

Down hallways he went, frustrated that he had no idea of the maze's organization. After a time, he knew he was lost and hungry. He pulled on his chin. *What to do?*

That's when he heard the women.

Edyta yelled, "Where are you soldiers anyway? Why aren't you answering your comm sets? Men?"

Though the sounds resonated up and down the halls, they clued Nain into the women's location. Jogging, he headed toward their voices, pausing at junctions to determine which one to follow next. Their yelling grew louder.

Suddenly, he dashed into another large room. All kinds of electronic equipment lined one wall, while two plush beds lay opposite them. A kitchen, table, and a wardrobe sat against another side. Edyta sat before a microphone, yelling for her soldiers. Her assistant fiddled with the remote video cameras that covered the landing pad and entrance. The women's hair were styled up in a sort of elaborate turban affair. A gauze-like robe draped over the women's shoulders. Both wore sandals.

"No sign of soldiers anywhere," the assistant said.

As she turned to Edyta, she saw Nain dashing in and screamed. She tried to draw her own blaster, but Nain fired first, drilling a three inch hole in the woman's chest. She died instantly.

Edyta cried out. All color drained from her face. "What have you done?" she shrieked. Then, she tensed up. Nain didn't need telepathy to sense the helpless woman's terror. She reeked of it. Fear's odor he knew well.

"So how do I turn those recordings off?" Nain asked.

Edyta's face twisted into a blank look. "I can't understand you. I'm helpless and can't change the translator to your language."

He switched to English. "Can you understand me now?" She nodded. "So how do I turn the nighttime recordings off?"

"You can't do that! You're ruining everything. My experiment. Please don't ruin it."

"I sure can. If you don't tell me, I'll fire my blaster into that whole mess of electronics."

Edyta shrieked. For a second, Nain thought he's

mortally injured her.

"No! Don't. You'll ruin everything and harm thousands, particularly those new arrivals from Bolt."

"What do you mean?" He rubbed his forehead. *I'm not trained for this.* Believing what she was saying might be important, Nain activated his recording device.

"You came on Bolt?" she asked. He nodded. "Well, they're being mutated into armless telepaths and will join sixteen hundred others like them in my colony. Those implants are vital for their very survival. They will awaken in another two days."

"Huh?"

"Look, everyone knows those who wake from their comas and find themselves armless Galactic Doll telepath are terrified and believe they are helpless. Most find ways to die. By implanting them with all these positive suggestions, I've proven they can awake to this and learn to adapt and not want to die. If you turn it off now, when Bolt's people awake, they'll freak out and find ways to die. I want them to live."

"Why? So they can be sold as slaves?"

"Hardly. We've proven those who are mutated against their wills make terrible telepaths. You can't trust them. Not remotely. No, it's their children who are born this way that are valuable. Future generation—they who won't know any difference. It's those who will be able to be valuable telepaths. I'm creating galaxy's first telepathic society. This is huge breakthrough. If you'll help me, I'll give you cut of profits later on. Or let me call Home World to have them send me new assistant and more soldiers."

"Hardly. I've destroyed your antenna, so you can't call."

Her face paled. Jaw slacked. Her body slumped. She exhaled slowly.

"Do you realize who I am? I'm Home World's greatest human psychologist, best in the entire galaxy. That's my specialty: human pyschology. Most famous, too. What I've achieved here is gigantic breakthrough in human psychology. You can't even imagine how incredibly important this is. Do you realize, dwarf, that my people, Third Invaders, have been manipulating various human populations for last ten millennia? All over this galaxy. Ever wonder why so many worlds have human-like populations and not dwarves or giants? What I've achieved here culminates ten thousand years of experimentation and study. Perfection of human psychology."

Since Nain didn't interrupt her and did seem to be listening, she continued. "Sixth Invaders attempted to take over Earth by series of genetic mutations. Those people are idiots. They had no idea how or what to manipulate in human genes. Monster breasts, crippled feet—absolute silliness. Humiliation finally has played role, when they mutated Earth's men into similar Galactic Dolls. Still that's hardly worth mentioning. What benefit did Earth's men receive from being turned into Galactic Dolls, indistinguishable from female Galactic Dolls unless you pulled their pants down? None. None whatsoever. But there are always flukes, random wild mutations. That's what happened when they accidentally turned on telepathic abilities when they were only trying to make all males not only Galactic Dolls, but also armless and helpless.

"Sixth Invaders wanted Earth's men to be so disabled they couldn't fight back, making Earth very easily conquered. Their accidental discovery of how to make telepath, I must admit, is of incredible importance throughout galaxy. I've traveled extensively and can honestly say other than these from Earth, I've never met real telepath.

"At once, many people tried to turn unsuspecting humans into what are now being called armless telepaths. Terrorists. That's what Sol authorities called them. They unleashed mutation agent on unwilling people. Have you heard what happens to victims when they awake from their comas?"

"Well, I heard some wild stories. Did they really shoot thousands of the GD and GPan victims in their heads?" Nain asked.

"Ah, you've heard of that one. Yes, they did. When victims awake from their mutation comas only to find themselves incredibly helpless, just like I am mind you, they freak out—to use Sol word for their behavior. Fear and terror strike with incredible vengeance. I know. When redskin natives chopped off my arms and returned me to humans— fear, terror, utter helplessness I felt was more than I could bear. Yes, dwarf, I too went insane, cackling like some feathered 'kin bird.

"So I know from personal experience just how awful it is to wake up and find your world crushed beyond recovery. Yet because of our superior technology, our fabulous flying saucers and their quantum entanglement recovery system, as insane and utterly helpless as I am today, I and my ship escaped to Home World, where they provided me with personal assistant so I could continue my valuable experiments.

"You see quite by accident, Sixth Invaders gave me incredibly valuable concept. Implant technology. Even the Earth humans in Moscow realized its true importance. Behavior modification. They tried to rehabilitate criminals with it, though its use soon became banned on Earth. Humans never were too bright, eh, dwarf?"

"Anyway, I tried to grab some humans and mutated them into armless telepaths. I tried to establish group of hundred, but that failed utterly. None could rise above their terror. They simply succumbed, laid down and quit living. So I tried providing personal assistants for each one, including providing sensual stimulations designed to make their lives more enjoyable. Just as I was nearly achieving my goal, that Parkinson woman interfered, ruining everything.

"But actually, her intervention, while it cost me my arms, forced me to ponder all known evidence. Even her own children have played key role in development of my theory."

"Huh? What are you saying?" Nain asked, scratching his forehead. He'd heard only positive things about this woman, rumors spread by Commander Lia Johnston.

"She has had children who were born or raised from an early age as armless telepaths. Those who have grown up without arms and who were shown many Sixth Invader compiled videos of how to do things with their feet and toes have learned to adapt and survive well. They've accepted their disability. Probably because they've never had arms. Gone entirely is all that fear and terror. Gone is insanity and total lack of will to survive. No, those children are just like all other normal children, only they have telepathic skills. You see where I'm going with this?"

"Sort of," Nain said. He rubbed his chin. Evidently, she didn't believe he did and continued.

"Armless telepaths who are born this way grow up as normal humans. They've learned ways to compensate and still live independently, more or less. But they have telepathic skills. Look, one of her daughters, this Isabella, she's become top linguist in galaxy. She's deciphered writings of both Fourth and Fifth Invaders. For humans, that's incredible achievement. Of course, we Third Invaders already had done that centuries ago. Anyway, these children are perfect telepaths.

"So while I was on Home World recovering from what Parkinson had done to me, I realized what had gone wrong. You cannot successfully make and armless telepath from unwilling adult. Even willing adults undergoing mutation have horrible time adapting, as Earth people have proven many times over. No, for person to be successful telepath, they must be born that way. Raised to be independent, educated properly, and trained, these children mature into responsible adult telepath, people whose skills are in demand throughout entire galaxy, people who can work for ten years and retire multimillion credits richer.

"That is my incredible breakthrough. That's why Home World has given me this new world for my experiment. They went to much trouble to acquire just right Earth people to be my initial colonists, handpicked for their unique skills and knowledge. These thousand have abilities to make this colony rapidly flourish and prosper. Home World had also brought all others who've survived earlier failed experiments here, adding them to colonists, just as I've added humans from your cruiser.

"The initial results are just fabulous, dwarf. As I expected they would be. During their long mutation comas, I continually implanted them with positive thoughts and drives, replacing negative, destructive ones that I and others had always awakened to. By subjecting them to eight days of these positive suggestions, when they awoke from their comas, instead of terror and giving up, they're adapting and doing well, making go of this colony. Each person is doing their best every day and is cheerful and happy about their new life. Marvel to behold.

"In few more days, crew of Bolt will waken and you'll see how they react. They'll be cheerful and want to become contributing members of this new colony. None will commit suicide or slump into apathy or even shriek in terror. My behavior modification is only giving them positive and reenforcing survival tendencies so they want to learn to adapt, live, and become productive members of colony.

"Now don't misinterpret these results. None of my implanted colonists will ever be allowed to go off-world as telepath. I believe their implanted behavior will prevent them from ever doing that. No, ultimate goal rests with their children, who will be born as armless telepaths. It's children who will grow up independent people, highly educated, responsible people, but with telepathic abilities they can share with galaxy.

"Twenty years from now, first five hundred telepaths will be ready to expand outward into universe, aiding their employers. Century from now, this world of Iota Piscium-C will have become heart of all civilizations in this galaxy, richest, most powerful world ever. But only if I'm allowed to continue my breakthrough work here. Help me, dwarf, help me achieve this miracle of evolution. This vital experiment will make you wealthier than you can ever imagine. If credits don't move you, think of how invaluable these future children will be. No longer can others keep critical secrets that can bring about wars. This colony is most important group of people in galaxy."

She sighed. "And now that you've killed my assistant, I need your help. Even if long distance antenna wasn't damaged, I don't have hands to operate controls and make call. If you don't want to help me, at least help me into my flying saucer. It responds to my voice, so I can fly to Home World, get new assistant, and return to continue my work here. Surely, you can see just how vitally important my work is, how dependent this colony is upon me."

Decision time. Nain knew he had to choose and choose wisely. These Third Invaders had betrayed Earth twice. Once with mutations that undid themselves after two months and once with this colony whose people had been mutated against their wills. Nain acted.

He threw a punch at Edyta's head, stunning her. As her body slumped to the ground, Nain caught her. He carried her up and out into the dome, going from room to room. The dwarf found an unoccupied cot and laid her on it. He placed the electronic harness on her head, comparing it to the ones on the others of the Bolt's crew in the next room. Satisfied, he then examined the single switch control. The switch was down with the crew and he could heard the voice, which he now recognized as Edyta's, playing back in their ears. So he flipped the switch on Edyta's set. He heard a distinctive humming sound as the white light appeared surrounding her head. Then, the recording began playing. Nain smiled.

"So it's all right for you to make all these sixteen hundred people learn to use their feet to survive, but you don't even try and demand an assistant. Ha. What's good for the hees is good for the ander, as we say on my world. I wonder if Earth has a similar saying? Ah well. I'll keep her under for eight days, just like she does for the others. I've got to get ready. Two more days and my fellow crew members will be waking from their comas. I've got to be able to help them. But how can I handle over a hundred of them? Best try to get some help. I wish they'd trained me more. One thing, though, I best not turn off the implant recording thing. She's right. I heard horror stories about humans killing themselves when waking up to find themselves helpless telepaths. If I unhook them, I could lose the whole crew. Best play along with her, since the colonists look to be doing okay. Food and then figure out how to call for help. That's the plan."

Chapter 22 Actions and Reactions

As April ended, I felt frustrated. Things continued to become increasingly mixed up. My sisters and their families along with some friends continued making preparations to abandon Earth. Ambassador L'Grina worked the Dark Web trying to make a deal to buy some of the supposedly destroyed mutation agents. Ward and Jie worked long hours trying to find out who stole that ancient weapons system and why. Then, there was my friend Lia, who wasn't returning my calls, and when she finally did, I sensed something very different in her tone. Was she more enthusiastic or cheerful or what?

The next morning, Ambassador L'Grina called. "Molly, go get a hundred thousand credits and meet me at your old PI offices in the Parker Skyscraper. We got a hit on the Dark Web. I'm arranging transportation to Kiev, of all places. Dress for winter. Cya in a couple hours."

I thanked her and promised to do so. Ashley and Sherry accompanied me to a bank, where I took out the credits in large denomination notes, printed on demand for me. Hardly anyone ever carried around physical credits. Sherry thoughtfully brought along a sack so I could carry them around my neck. With fleece lined boots, fur hat, and heavy cloak, I and my friends took the EMAC to my old PI office. I'd kept it, hoping one day I might return to just being a PI and running therapy sessions. If I were to accept the Senior Ambassador post on Bela Prime, I intended to still pay the rent for this office. I just couldn't bring myself to abandon it. Something about losing a part of my past.

We boarded an Airliner rented by Ambassador L'Grina. Once airborne, she explained her plan.

"I out-bid several others for these mutation agents. We're to pay a visit to Rostov's Crematorium in Kiev. I checked. That was one of the mutation agent destruction sites. So the owner probably got a bit greedy. Instead of destroying the agents he was given, he probably secreted some away. We're buying his entire supply. Once we see the goods, if we encounter any trouble, I'll activate this signal. A squad of our soldiers will swoop down and assist. Good plan, eh?"

I laughed. "Yes, ambassador, very good. I wonder how many other crematorium owners had the same idea?"

Hours later, while Ashley and Sherry oversaw the transporting of the dozen crates of the mutation agents onto the Airliner, I chatted with a very pleased Mr. Rostov.

"With this money, I can afford to buy my family's safety. You know, don't you. Soon the Federation will terminate everyone on Earth. But some of us are going to become space gypsies. Those of us who can pay, that is. A hundred of us from Kiev can survive. That's what they said. I know how badly my body looks, but we so want to live. I've heard there are others who are buying passages on deep space ships, becoming gypsies. Check your city. Probably a wealthy person has bought a ship for gypsies, too."

When we arrived home, Ambassador L'Grina hauled the crates into one of my bedrooms, while I discussed with Deanna what we'd found from the Kiev man. She chuckled and explained what had been happening here.

"Two wealthy Chicagoans purchased new deep space exploration ships and are taking on a hundred chosen people each. Space gypsies. That's what's being marketed. Not sure how their passengers are being chosen. But it's a way to survive, just as we're doing with my Friendship and its sistership."

We chatted while Ambassador L'Grina checked her Dark Web email.

"Hey, got another hit, Molly. This one is close by—in Toronto."

"How much this time?" I asked.

Deanna sprung for the cash. Two hours later, we headed out again. This time, Edgar Gascon, owner of Able Cremation Services, sold us his stash. While he wanted to take a long term wait and see approach, if he could raise the funds, he, too, could purchase the survival of his family as space gypsies.

Once home and these crates stacked in the bedroom, I thanked Ambassador L'Grina for her impressive assistance.

She grinned.

The next day, I checked with Ward and Jie. They'd found no further clues on the stolen weapons, except that now they'd been returned to the underground mountain storage facility. The perps had broken into the facility, mirroring their initial methods, leaving no clues to their identity. Both my investigators cursed. With nothing new in my Senior Investigator office, Ashley and I headed up to my Senior Judge office.

Ashley hung up my cloak, while I sat at my desk. No new folders meant no new cases to judge, for which I thanked the gods. With those who could flee Earth making arrangements to do so, I had a sinking feeling I couldn't save us this time. The unethical had gone too far. Ashley checked our mail.

"Hey, Molly. You've got a secure voice mail waiting for you. You'll have to enter your code to retrieve it. It's the first password-protected voice mail we've ever received. So it must be important. I suppose I should leave while you listen to it. What do you think?"

I walked over to our large communications system and looked at the meta-data of the call. Damn. Top secret. For your eyes only.

"Yeah, I suppose so. I've never received a top secret message before. I've no idea who it's from. Best be safe. Just hang nearby in case I need you to hear it."

Ashley nodded and stepped out of the room. I slipped off my shoe and punched in my ID code. Then, the message played. I saw a 3-d holo image of Lia Johnston, but she wore her blue officer's uniform, similar to the one she wore when I first met her when we found our two missing deep space exploration ships and the Third Invaders' flying saucer. The message was days old.

"Molly, Commander Lia Johnston here onboard the Bolt, my old cruiser. They've invited me back as their commander. Look, everyone on this ship wanted to get some justice from the lying Third Invaders. Admiral Rossi isn't doing anything, so the Bolt is and did. By now, you've probably discovered someone broke into the ancient equipment storage site in Colorado. That was us. We stole the ancient MW1 drone system, bought new fuel rods, and modernized their control circuits.

"We bought a cloaking device from the Sixth Invaders and installed it on the Bolt. We just returned from the Third Invaders' home world. That ancient system worked perfectly. The Bolt remained cloaked the whole time we flew the drones. Initial reports suggested we killed about ten thousand of those lying fiends. They still have no idea who did it. That's only a small part of our justice for their treasonous mutation scheme. We did it so that they'd give us the location of the colony where they took our thousand people."

She rattled off the coordinates, which I jotted down, repeating that portion of her message several times, triple checking them.

"So now we've put the MW1 system back along with the cloaking device. We're on our way to this Iota Piscium-C. We hope to rescue our colonists, but we doubt we'll find our colonists in one piece. These are treacherous beasts. I'm leaving you this message just in case something happens to us. If you don't hear from us, we wanted someone to know the supposed location of this colony of a thousand of our people taken in bad faith. To justice, Molly. Justice. Bye and thanks for everything."

Lia's image faded. Since the message had the top secret marking, it destroyed itself when I hit Finish. I could have replayed it, though. I called for Ashley.

She saw I'd jotted down some coordinates and gave me a curious look. "Someone just gave me the coordinates where the Third Invaders took our colonists. A ship is going there to see if our people are there."

"Wow! That is news. Where the heck is it? I don't recognize those coordinates."

"No idea yet. I need to make some other secure calls. How do I do that?"

Ashley, ever the efficient assistant, knew how to set that up on my phone. Once she did, again, she left the room, though I sensed she was dying of curiosity. First, I called Sam and gave him the coordinates.

"Please see if you can find out where they lead to, Mr. Navigator. Call me back. Secure call."

I called Celeste and told her what I'd done about the mutation agents, about many becoming space gypsies, and what I'd just learned from Lia, though I didn't mention any names. I sighed. "What do I do?"

"Wow. Space gypsies. Honestly, we're running out of options. Worse, so many others are going into agreement that Earth is about to be destroyed that it'll be increasingly difficult to alter that future. The more people agree it's going to happen the harder it is to change it. With these space gypsies, we might have just passed the point of no return. Still, I'll check with Eve and see if she can hurry up a cure. I'd say sit tight and wait for your informant to call you back with news about the colony. It could be a trap and not our people."

My mood was dark when I returned home. Celeste's words struck me like a hammer. I'd never considered other people's agreements as having any appreciable affect on any future path. Always before, when I saw possible future paths, I was able to find a way to nudge the one I desired to come into being. That other people agreeing to some aspect of a potential future could help bring it about rattled me. More than I dare admit. Now, all I could do was wait for Lia's next call. Wait and fret.

Twice, I checked with Admiral Rossi to see if he'd heard anything from the Third Invaders. He hadn't. But he did report they hadn't found the location of the missing cruiser, the Bolt. Given the resources of our space fleet, I found that very curious. Could the admiral be hiding something from me? Possibly, but my telepathy didn't reach off-world.

I even checked with Admiral Skaggs but with the same result. If Lia had killed ten thousand of the Third Invaders, they sure weren't blaming Earth. Maybe she'd gotten away with it. If so, she may have been the first to ever do something like that to those all-powerful aliens. Well, Earth deserved justice for their treachery. But was that really justice? Especially if they didn't know who'd murdered their people or why.

Days passed with no word from Lia. I had her call

236

frequency logged in my computer. On the sixth day with still no word from her, I decided I needed to act. I called Deanna and Bev. Deanna agreed to come with us, along with two engineers. I asked General Bev to come and bring a dozen ex-soldiers. I needed a navigator, but I also didn't want to pull Matt and Nikita out of school just so I could have Sam come with me. In the end, Bonita convinced me she could walk the kids to and from school.

"Look, I'm sort of their second mother anyway. It's the least I can do for our family," she said.
***

Hours later, the Friendship departed New O'Hare bound for this unknown world. We had no idea what to expect, except trouble. Since Lia still hadn't responded to my messages or called me back, I concluded she'd run into problems. These Third Invaders had a knack for being deceitful, which reminded me of the mess we'd had some time back with that Edyta Iakob-Ra woman. Deanna wanted to study her flying saucer, but the men of the various space commands had denied her that chance. She still carried a grudge.

"We'll arrive in about fifteen hours," Sam said, reading his nav system display. "When we get there, we'll have to try to find habitable planets. So it might take us longer."

Deanna said, "Iota Piscium, here we come. I'm going to try to raise the Bolt when we drop out of hyperspace. If I can get a fix on the ship, that'll save us a lot of time. Until then, let's get some sleep."

"When we land," General Bev said, "my force will be ready for anything. Even gas attacks. Not like when you got mutated by that Third Invader woman."
***

The Friendship dropped out of hyperspace right on time. Sam verified we were safely inside the star's Oort Cloud. While he studied the star looking for habitable planets, Deanna and I tried to raise the Bolt. No one answered, but the cruiser received the signal, meaning the ship had to be in this system, relatively nearby. Before Sam could even identify a planet, Deanna activated the Bolt's homing signal.

She said, "All our ships have a built-in homing beacon.

In case of a disaster, others can locate the ship. I just activated it. Heading there now."

Sam complained, "She's put me out of a job." We all laughed.

But once more, I felt ignorant. I knew nothing about such things. While I could pilot the ship, that's about all I really knew about flying. Who was I kidding when I thought about becoming the Sol Empire's Senior Ambassador on Bela Prime?

"There it is, the planet," Deanna announced. "I'm playing it safe. We'll circle it before zeroing in on the Bolt. Everyone, stay alert for Third Invader flying saucers. Sam, you be ready to jump us into hyperspace. The Friendship can't take the damage that a cruiser can."

I watched monitors that showed what was on our left side, while Bev studied the monitors showing what was off to our right. Deanna watched our front. I even had one of Bev's soldiers watching the rear view monitor.

"I see domed cities or towns down there," Deanna called out.

Sam said, "Sensors don't show any warm bodies. Uninhabited towns, perhaps."

"There's one heck of a lot of these domed structures," Deanna said.

"Where are all the people who live in them?" I asked. "Still nothing on our left."

"Weird. I'm not picking up any flying saucers," Deanna said. "If this is that new colony, I'd expect lots of shipping, many saucers, even a control tower contact. But I'm getting nothing at all, just the Bolt's homing signal. You guys spotting anything?"

No's echoed, but we remained vigilant. I think we all expected to be attacked by one of their flying saucers at any moment. After all, we were invading their space, their new colony.

"I don't get it." Deanna complained over the intercom. "Coming up on the Bolt's location. Get ready everyone. Ten. Nine."

She counted down, but I sensed the Friendship

decelerating with each second.

"Flying over the Bolt now. There's a dome town by it. A landing pad? The cruiser is on our left. Molly, how badly damaged is it?"

"It looks like it's parked on the tarmac. Don't see anyone around. Can't see any visible damage, but that's not saying much."

"Saucer off to our right. Just one," Bev said. "Third Invaders must be here. Time to kick some butt!"

Deanna said, "I'm still not picking up any outgoing signals or any other ships. It's quiet as a mouse. So where is Lia and the entire crew? Why isn't someone in the Bolt answering my hail? Setting us down. Be alert for treachery."

"Nice landing," I said. "I see a door. Kind of looks like an igloo, only it's transparent ice. No one's rushing out with blazing guns."

"Oxygen levels a bit high. Humidity is ninety. Temperature's eighty-five," Sam read off his dials.

"Okay, we're heading out," Bev said. "Donning breathing masks. We don't want to risk running into mutation agents. Sealing off the cargo hold now. If we get gassed, it can't get to you guys. Let's kick some butt!"

She and her crew charged down the ramp, members fanning out to the left and right, establishing flank coverages. General Bev marched boldly down the center toward the doors.

"Weird. Nothing at all. No, wait. Doors opening. Get ready," she said. "What the..."

Her group halted, while safely inside we stared. A dwarf armed with several weapons including a blaster strode out of the dome. He wore a space fleet uniform.

"Who are you?" he asked.

"General Beverly Blossom Blythe. And who are you? Where's the Third Invaders? We're looking for our missing colony of a thousand."

The dwarf dropped his blaster and sat down on the landing pad. "Am I ever glad to see you! Airman Recruit Nain Hammerhead, at your service. I've only been in the fleet two months, and now I'm the only one left. Oh, you found the colony, but I don't think you're going to like it. I've killed the Third Invader soldiers and have taken their leader out of action. And you can take off the gas masks. If only our people would have taken that precaution, they might be okay today."

"Save the explanations for the Senior Investigator and Senior Judge," Bev said. "Molly, it's safe for everyone to come out. Guys, take up a perimeter defense, just in case company comes. Stay alert."

I and the others joined Bev and Nain. He said, "Glad you've come to rescue us or at least me. I've only been in the fleet two months. Not had enough training to know how to call for help. Anyway, I've terminated four of the five Third Invaders and taken the remaining one out. There are one thousand six hundred ten of our people here. My ship's whole crew are in mutation comas. Armless telepaths. I've also recorded many conversations. Maybe that'll help."

With Celeste at my side, I toured the facility, at least the small portion Nain had visited. I recognized the unconscious Edyta Iakob-Ra. So she was behind this hideous plot. Then, we took Nain onboard the Friendship and had him tell us what had happened.

Celeste and I listened to the recording he'd made of the implant words. Edyta's lengthy discussion of her grand experiment and its goals shocked us both. We discussed what could be done for the victims; Celeste crushed my hopes.

"Look, she's given them a comprehensive maniac implant. She's covered all angles. We can't take them back to Earth. They must remain colonists. It's much worse. While we've handled Sixth Invaders' implants, Edyta's are a hundred times stronger. She's given them that implant for eight continuous days while they were in their comas. Likely we'll never be able to reach their buried pain and unconsciousness. If that weren't enough, she's reenforced the implants every night while they sleep. Honestly, Molly, I've no idea how we can possibly help them recover. We can end the nightly re-stimulation of the implants, and perhaps after sufficient time has passed, we might be able to undo the enforced behavior patterns. Maybe. But we're talking years."

My heart sank. Many others also sighed. We wanted to

rescue our people, but...

Based on Edyta's explanation of her precarious position within the Third Invaders, I decided upon another approach.

"Look, we can't take them home. We'll have to leave them on this world working together. No choice there. But we can claim this world as the newest world in the Sol Empire. Invite others to immigrate here. Bring some fighters and cruisers to protect us from Third Invaders counterstrikes. Maybe a year from now we can reach them and erase their trauma and enforced behavior patterns. Anyone have any ideas how we can do this?" I asked.

"I want to study this alien technology!" Deanna said. "What we could learn. Do you realize this dome is some kind of composite material? Not metal. And it's stronger than metal. Maybe Isabella can figure out what those symbols mean. Their writing. If we can find a library in one of the hundreds of domed towns we passed over and if she can translate them, think of what we could learn. A bonanza!"

"Okay, I can take a hint. I'll call Helen and see what can be arranged," I said.

An hour later, Admiral Rossi called me via the long distance set on the Friendship.

I explained what we found. "So we've got a new planet to add to the Sol Empire, along with all this exciting ancient technology. Plus, there's a Third Invader flying saucer here that you can have. Just be extra careful of traps. It's Edyta's ship. Over."

After a fifteen minute delay, he replied. "Expect a fleet to arrive there in fifteen hours. We'll check this out. Well done. Over and out."

Deanna said, "I bet he can't wait to get his hands on the saucer. Still, if he brings a sizeable fleet, then we won't have to worry about other Third Invader ships dropping by. In a fight, the Friendship can't take on even a light cruiser. I presume these saucers have weapons. Anyway, let's go exploring."

Chapter 23 The Decision

Frustration and disappointment. That's how I would describe my feelings when I found Lia and her crew and the thousand volunteer colonists who went willingly with the Third Invaders in order to save the Earth from destruction. As I watched them struggling just to accomplish normal life tasks, their maniac cheerfulness couldn't counter the suppressed tears and fright. Edyta's implants eliminated shrieks of terror and death wishes from these newly mutated people. I have to give her credit for that. After all, I'd seen what had happened when Dimitri's parents and associates woke up as mutants and flooded the skyscraper with screams of terror before begging for death. Still...

I didn't doubt these sixteen hundred would succeed. A dozen formed the leadership council, who planned and organized the colony and the work the colonists did. When the crew awoke from their comas, the council welcomed them and explained how the colony worked. Then, they led them off to find their new homes, which had already been prepared for them. Obviously, Edyta had informed them about these hundred arrivals. Workers had eight days to prepare the new homes. The council insisted eight live and work together as a team with each sex equally represented whenever possible. When they discovered the skills the Bolt's crew had, they assigned jobs in their fields, whenever possible. Plus, they invited Lia to join the council and help lead the colony.

Edyta joined them. I anticipated they might kill her, but instead, thanks to her own implant, she rattled off her implanted mantra, feigning a sort of manic cheerfulness just like the Bolt's crew, and fumbled to help out using her feet like everyone else. That, I found curious and perhaps fitting. Beyond making sure the colony was functional, for now, I could do no more for these sixteen hundred.

We returned home with Admiral Rossi whose battleship towed Edyta's flying saucer. He left ten warships guarding the planet. I laughed when once again the quantum entanglement feature of the flying saucer ripped the ship from his tractor beam and jumped into hyperspace, presumably returning the ship to their home world.

While Deanna and I wanted to remain on the new world—so much to explore, so much new and unknown technology—I had to come back. Admiral Skaggs ordered me to the "Final Conference" to determine Earth's fate. Considering the mutation mess, I figured the Federation had made its decision, but I intended to hold him to his agreement to allow my family, my kin, and my friends to evacuate before the annihilation began.

Hence, mid-May, accompanied by Ashley and Sherry, I headed up to the Battleship Kanika in high orbit above Earth. This time, Admiral Skaggs met me in the docking bay.

"Mrs. Parkinson, congratulations on discovering the new planet and the colonists the Third Invaders took," he said. "This way. The decision about Earth has finally been made. Your sister, Eve, and dwarf friend, Lara Axe-head, will join us shortly via another shuttle."

"Have they found a mutation cure?"

"I'm not entirely sure."

He led us into the same conference room as before, replete with institutional white walls and stainless steel tables and chairs. An aide brought us tea while we waited on the second shuttle. Before the tea cooled, Admiral Skaggs ushered Eve and Lara into the room. Both women's wide-open eyes darted about.

"Amazing. Wow!" Eve whispered to Lara. "Oh, hi, Molly. Ashley, Sherry."

Lara gave me a hug and whispered in my ear, "We've had a breakthrough."

She didn't have time to tell me more. Admiral Skaggs entered, leading two Federation personnel. The man wore a brown business suit. His beady eyes and black moustache suggested an aura of power or perhaps influence. The woman had to be one of the Senior Ambassadors. Her giant upper lip disk with crossed hands embossed on it told all. She wore a white satin jumpsuit, appropriate for space travel. Her brown hair rested on her shoulders. She wore long and huge earrings, while each finger sported a gemstone encrusted ring. Both wore translation units around their waists and sat across from us. Admiral Skaggs closed the door and took his seat.

He said, "This is Dr. Tye Westby, the Federation's top geneticist, and Senior Ambassador and President of the Circle of Ambassadors Heidi Le Blanc."

He introduced our small group to them, before turning the meeting over to the Senior Ambassador. If she hadn't worn her language translation unit, I couldn't have understood what she was saying, though the language was akin to some dialect of English.

She began, "We have much to discuss. The Circle of Ambassadors has finally reached a decision regarding the Earth situation. However, two other Federation worlds now have a stake in this decision. Quite unexpectedly, I should add. So let's begin. I understand you were developing a mutation cure, since the treachery of the Third Invaders. Report, please," she said.

Eve looked at me and then said, "Yes. First, let me give you some background. The Sixth Invaders managed to implant Earth's women into believing that the ideal physical form for a woman was that of the Galactic Doll. We've developed a mutation to reduce breast sizes. Unfortunately, only those women who received Molly and Celeste's therapy and who have erased those implants desired that cure."

Senior Ambassador Heidi Le Blanc interrupted. "What are you talking about? Everyone knows implants cannot be erased."

"Our sister Celeste has developed a mental therapy that does just that."

"Wait! Are you that Senior Ambassador Lara Axehead who left the Circle of Ambassadors because she had been implanted, declared insane, and scheduled for termination?" Senior Ambassador Heidi Le Blanc's eyes opened wide finally recognizing just who Lara was.

Lara replied, her voice soft. "The very one. Molly here saved me and erased every trace of that vicious implant."

"Fascinating. We'll have to talk more about that later one. Now then. Please continue, Eve."

Eve said, "We went ahead and had the Third Invaders undo women's distorted feet. Today, women can wear flats or heels. Unfortunately, Galactic Medicine is receiving millions of calls from women demanding their Galactic Doll mutation be redone, since they don't want normal feet. So with Earth's women, we're pretty much stuck with keeping them as Galactic Dolls. However, we have undone the dominant angle. Their children will not inherit their mutation.

"As far as the men go, we have developed two potential cures. One is based on replicating what the Third Invader mutation did, only we've corrected the flaw that made the changes temporary. All that must be done is to manufacture this mutation agent and then get it injected into the men of Earth. The second version is more promising, but will take much longer to implement. Lara and I've been working on this one for a long time. Earth established a DNA database. We've worked out a way where we can input a man's name, retrieve his DNA profile, merge it into the fetal regeneration sequence, and then inject him with it. In principle, it should return his body to normal. We estimate that version will take several decades to reach every man on Earth. Of course, there are some from other worlds and some who's DNA isn't in the database."

Dr. Westby said, "Fascinating. So you're saying that we can't restore Earth's women. That they insist on remaining Galactic Dolls?"

"Correct. Their implants dictate they have giant breasts, wear tall heels, and have well-defined curves. Sorry," Eve said.

"But the women who've had this therapy—"

"Have erased the implant and so wish to be more normal. Still, peer pressure forces many to keep their large bosoms," Eve said.

Senior Ambassador Le Blanc asked, "Has all the original mutation agents that weren't initially destroyed now destroyed?"

"As far as we can tell," I answered. "However, some men kept some, hoping to make future profits by selling it on the black market. We've recovered much of that. No way to say we're retrieved all of it. But right now, I'm fairly confident we've gotten the vast majority of those agents."

"All right," she said. "I hope and pray you've not yet destroyed what you've recovered. It's vital that those agents still exist."

"Well, yes. Ambassador L'Grina packed them into our spare bedroom. Why? I thought they were to be destroyed."

"I'll get to that later," she said. "Let me begin by saying initially half of the Senior Ambassadors voted to destroy Earth the moment we heard these mutation agents could affect others whose DNA is close to yours, such as Admiral Skaggs's niece. A hair's breath. That close. However, calmer minds have prevailed, especially in light of your own mutation cures and this Third Invader colony of mutants you've just discovered. Plus, two other critical situations have just arisen, which we'll get to shortly.

"The Circle of Ambassadors has also ruled that all telepaths must be armless so they can be instantly identified as such. For obvious reasons. However, we have reviewed your unique situation, Mrs. Parkinson. You must remain as you are, since somehow you had telepathic abilities before you were mutated. Dr. Westby, you may make your presentation."

Isabella once explained how the place of articulation impacted the sounds people made. Senior Ambassador Le Blanc's giant upper lip disk obliterated all bilabial and labiodental sounds, such as the English sounds for p, b, m, w, f, and v. Yet, the language translation box around her waist did properly reproduce these sounds. I concluded her unit must have been fine tuned to the sounds she was able to make. I made a note to ask Piper Strawn about that when I returned.

The doctor said, "Yes, but first, let me ask this. These implants which Edyta gave the sixteen hundred colonists— they can't be undone? These people exhibit maniacal behavior?"

I sighed. "Yes, that's putting it mildly. She ran a continuous implant for the entire eight days the victims were in their mutation comas and then afterwards every night while they slept. Our mental technology simply cannot reach them, but we hope in a year or so, the implants will desensitize enough that we can erase them. "

"Okay then," Dr. Westby said. "The Federation would like to make a deal with Earth. First, carry out your mutation cures on the Earthmen. If more of these supposedly disposed of agents appear at some future date, ship them to my genetics Federation laboratory for safekeeping.

"In return for sparing Earth, we'd like to carry out some genetic mutation experiments on those sixteen hundred colonists, whose lives are pretty much already ruined. We have some ideas and theories that may truly help them and eventually the entire Federation. None are harmful. Successful experiments have been done on mice. No danger.

"Turn over that one colony to the Berktold Soros Group, who will run it humanely and carry out the experiments. Your world may colonize all the other domed towns on the planet. All we desire is this one domed town and its already mutated and implanted people. Give us this, and the Federation will sign a no-destroy agreement with Earth and the Sol Empire."

Senior Ambassador Le Blanc added, "Don't agree and I'm authorized to give Admiral Skaggs the order to destroy Earth, but we'll allow the recent giant and dwarven immigrants a chance to leave. It's your choice, Senior Judge of the Sol Empire."

"So you want us to sacrifice the sixteen hundred in order to save the world?" I spat out.

"That's about the size of it," she said. Her eyes bored into mine. "That's the best deal we could make. Remember, half the ambassadors voted to destroy Earth rather than risk those mutation agents spreading. They still want Earth gone, but we've gotten them to agree to allow the Berktold Soros Group to conduct their genetic research on that isolated, single colony. Take it or leave it."

"With no oversight from anyone in the Sol Empire?" I asked.

"Point taken," she said.

I sensed an extreme covert chill coming from her.

She added, "You may inspect the facilities as frequently as desired, but no one else. I'm authorized to appoint you to be the Governor of Domes, the name of the Sol Empire's new world on Iota Piscium-C. As Governor, you can run everything else on the world. You may visit and express your opinions on the experiment and even offer suggestions and assistance."

The weight of the world rested on my shoulders. All eyes focused on me. "Okay. I've no choice but to agree to this. Three billion versus sixteen hundred. Hardly a choice. Will you make the announcement to Earth? If something happens to me, can someone else become the Governor?"

I had to sign my name to the official documents. The aliens gaped as I used my foot to sign them. Eve stifled a laugh at their behavior.

That done, Admiral Skaggs and the two Federation representatives held a brief press conference, outlining the decision not to destroy Earth just yet. They presented the details: women would remain Galactic Dolls, men would be re-mutated as soon as possible back to what they'd become after the Third Invaders' mutation, any of the original mutation agents that remained would be confiscated, and the sixteen hundred members of the colony on Iota Piscium-C became guinea pigs for the experiments of the Berktold Soros Group, subject to oversight by me. They decided the name for this new world was Domes and that I became the Governor of Domes.

Suppertime came. Admiral Skaggs escorted us to the officer's mess. Always before, I ate in the crew's mess hall. Well, she was a Senior Ambassador and the President of the Circle of Ambassadors. Again, I endured both overt and covert stares as many watched how I could possibly deal with eating.

That handled, the Admiral put us up for the night. The Senior Ambassador wasn't ready to discuss the other two items on her agenda. "I expect they'll arrive tomorrow." That's all she said.

Once in our large state room, Lara said, "That ambassador is a veritable bitch! Runs the Circle with an iron fist. After I was implanted, she tried to have me terminated right away. I don't trust her to do what's fair, only what is lucrative. So are you really going to be the Governor of Domes?"

"I sure don't want to be."

"She can't do that and still be our Senior Judge," Ashley said. "I don't even see how she can be our Senior Investigator if she's always on Domes and not on Earth. I'm having a hard enough time juggling those two positions when she is on Earth."

Sherry's lower lip rose accompanying her attempt at a sad face. "She would have to leave all her sisters and close friends behind. It's almost as though someone wants her out of Earth's governing arena."

I appreciated the robot's thoughtfulness. "Damn. Sherry's got a point. Senior Ambassador Sanura Fenku hired the giant to kill Sam, Matt, and Nikita. She's been trying to get me to accept one of Earth's Senior Ambassador positions since we joined the Federation. I bet her reasoning suggested I'd be more likely to do that if my family were dead. And now this President of the Circle of Ambassadors appoints me to be Governor of Domes, many light years from Earth. I find this coincidence highly suspicious. But I can't figure out why these aliens want me away from Earth. As a telepath, I'd be more dangerous to them on Bela Prime."

I chuckled and added, "Bonita would probably say there's a conspiracy here."

Everyone laughed.

Ashley had the last word. "But you *have* saved Earth from being destroyed. Three billion of us owe you everything. Thank you. Maybe that's why—someone wants Earth destroyed. Well, I think there's a line forming for that."

Again, chuckles echoed.

"Still, I have to say, like Deanna, I found Domes fascinating. I love how the lights automatically turned on as you walked down halls or into rooms. Amazing technology in the domes."

"Very helpful for the sixteen hundred," Sherry said. "Whoever lived here set up amazing automated living environments. Perfect for those telepaths. Of course, I wonder how soon they'll tire of eating the blue goo—the raw synth food, which is all that automated system can produce."

Ashley said, "You ought to bring flavoring machines and supplies from Earth. The sixteen hundred will love you for that. Still, I've heard blue goo is often the only food on long duration exploration ships. Yucko."

Eve said, "I have to admit it's hard to tell the difference between a synth chicken dinner and a real one just by taste alone. Your Bernardo would disagree with me. Is he any closer to opening his own restaurant?"

We chatted about home things before turning in for the night.

Chapter 24 Valid Agent Uses

Senior Ambassador and President of the Circle of Ambassadors Heidi Le Blanc conducted the morning meeting, though Dr. Tye Westby, the Federation's top geneticist, joined us. She introduced us to Mari and Lippo Tulo who had arrived during the night.

"They are from the planet Jamo some four hundred light years from Sol and close to what your world knows as Pulsar 437."

Once more, my ignorance bothered me. I'm sure Sam would know what she was talking about. The two short aliens had brownish skin, but otherwise looked entirely human in their late fifties. Both also wore language translators. Their apparel appeared old-fashioned, like some of Leslie's costumes in her store.

"Their world is only now coming into its industrial age. They do not have spaceflight, for example. Jamo is part of the Federation, watched over by several other empires."

His black suit coat had twin tails and front buttons. The LED lights reflected off his shoes. Endless knots of embroidery highlighted her light blue cotton dress. Matching shoes peeked from the hem of her dress.

"The population of Jamo steadily declined during the last century. The Tulo family represents the youngest people on their world today. The problem: no new children have been born since the births of these two people. During the last century, birth rates fell off rapidly hitting zero about fifty years ago. The future of these people and their world is incredibly bleak. However, Jamo is incredibly rich in gold, silver, rare earths, iron, platinum. Even Uranium. They export shiploads of valuable minerals everyday. I'll let Dr. Westby explain their situation. Doctor…"

"Yes, it's simple really. The best theory to date is the pulsar's radiation has sterilized all males on Jamo. Astrophysicists backtracked the positions of Jamo's sun and the pulsar, correlating with observations recorded over a century ago by Jamo astronomers. Back then, the pulsar's orbit brought it close to Jamo, flooding their night sky with intense radiation which caused massive sunburns. Today, the pulsar is rapidly retreating from their sun, but the damage is done.

"We've conducted extensive studies and verified the initial findings. All males on Jamo are sterile. Their genetic makeup has been altered. Currently, geneticists are conducting experiments on surviving women, attempting to breed new babies. All females, of course. But that's a very slow process and is incapable of maintaining a survivable population. They have imported some dwarves to help carry on the extensive mining operations. However, unless another solution can be found, we're looking at the extinction of all humans on Jamo."

I spoke up. "Couldn't our Galactic Doll genetic mutations help them?"

Mari, Lippo, and Dr. Westby smiled.

"Precisely. That's the reason we're here today. I would like to try mutating Lippo using your Galactic Doll agent. If my theory is correct, not only will his biological clock be reset back to his early twenties, but it could well repair the genetic damage done by the pulsar."

Lippo said. "If it works, Jamo is prepared to pay you billions of credits, tons of gold or rare earths. Uranium. Name your price. We will pay it."

"Hey, if it works, you don't have to pay us anything. I'm just happy to help prevent the loss of all your people. Dr. Westby, are they compatible to us? Homo sapiens sapiens?"

"I believe they are close enough to risk the attempt. Yes, there is some chance Lippo could die, but unless a cure is found soon, the remaining billion on Jamo are going to perish within the next two decades."

"Have to try," Lippo said. "You don't want any payment?"

"No, of course not. If we can help, it's only right that we do so. How soon can we try it?"

Dr. Westby said, "As soon as we can get samples of the agents."

"I've got crates of the stuff in my spare bedroom.

Honestly, I'd suggest trying the original Galactic Doll agent first. The other one, the armless telepath Galactic Agent is much stronger, more potent, but you become handicapped, as I am."

I felt they needed to hear the truth. Both Lippo and Mari swallowed hard as I said that last. Few would want to face life without arms.

"Mind if Lara and I assist you, Dr. Westby? We are very familiar with these agents," Eve asked.

He wiped his brow. "I could use all the assistance you can provide. I've heard these agents are incredibly effective."

I didn't need telepathy to know how worried he was of accidentally mutating himself.

Sherry volunteered. "I can make a quick trip and bring back samples."

Before I could reply, Senior Ambassador Le Blanc said, "That will be acceptable, but wait until this meeting is finished. There's more. So, doctor, are we finished with the Jamo situation?"

"Yes. As soon as we get the agents, we'll inject Lippo with the original version and see what results. If it doesn't work, then we'll try the dominant telepath version. If either are successful, we'll need to acquire or manufacture enough for about five hundred million males."

"The mutation comas last about eight days for Earthlings," Lara said. "But we should be able to tell if they're working on his body within a day. Before the eight days are up, we should be able to see if his body is back to making sperm again."

Eve added, "We would like to have a small DNA sample to analyze because we might be able to predict outcomes, especially if there are significant deviations from Earthlings. Dr. Patricia Ann Baxter might be able to create an aerosol version of the agent so you can quickly reach everyone on Jamo. Sherry, see if you can bring her back with the samples."

"Okay then," Senior Ambassador Le Blanc said. "There is a second case. Empress Kalindi Amandani of Indrani-C in the Varouna Empire wishes to purchase a supply of the armless telepath agent for her own personal use. She has been the Empress of that empire for sixty years, bringing immense prosperity and peace to their thirty-nine worlds. The Varouna Empire is one of the most powerful and vital groups in the entire Federation of Planets. Her worlds supply nearly a hundred Senior Ambassadors. She is a beloved empress and plays a vital role in holding that empire together working toward common goals.

"She has asked me to bring you, your geneticists, and samples of that agent to Indrani-C. You can test her so see if the agent will work on her. If so, she, too, is prepared to offer you substantial payment for a small supply of the agent."

"Where is this Indrani-C?" I asked.

"In your star catalogues, it's listed as YBP1194. It's within an open cluster of yellow stars much like your Sol. Your catalogue lists it as Messier 67."

Again, I knew Sam would know precisely what she meant. I didn't. A glance at Admiral Rossi told me he didn't know that either. So I felt a tad better about it. But Admiral Skaggs did, naturally.

She continued, "Once we have the agents on board, we'll head to Indrani-C. It's just under three thousand light years from Sol. The trip will take about twenty days travel time at top speed through hyperspace. We'll use a heavy cruiser. So perhaps you should go with your assistants and arrange for such a long trip. Anticipate you'll be gone less than two months, unless we stop off on Jamo first. Eve and Lara should come with you, too. We'll need their genetics expertise."

Dr. Westby said, "We'll have a fully equipped genetics research lab on that ship. In case we need to make some changes."

As we boarded our shuttle back to Earth, Sherry commented. "Do you realize how fast she said we'd be going? That's sixty times faster than Deanna's Friendship travels in hyperspace."

"We can go faster," I said, "but we've always tried to conserve fuel. Still, it's not a heavy cruiser."

We chuckled. "Ashley, you're coming, too. Gotta have my assistant this time. You're my arms on this trip. I'm sure they won't let me bring our helpful machines."

"Thanks."

She looked pleased, I think. We landed late that afternoon. While Sherry arranged to have half of the crates delivered to the shuttle at New O'Hare, I outlined what had happened to my family, sisters, and friends. They'd come to welcome me home and to thank me for preventing the genocide of Earth.

"Can I come, too? Please? Pretty please? It's summer vacation. I won't be in the way," Nikita pleaded.

"Hey, Mom, that's not such a bad idea," Isabella said. "I'd like to learn these two new languages. They're not in our Sol database yet. It'd give Nikita a chance to see if she really wants to be a linguist. She and I can learn them together. Besides, Owen can watch after Maria for six weeks."

Sam rolled his eyes. I waited for Matt to beg to come, too, but he didn't.

"Mom, don't look at me. I'm not going to waste my summer vacation. Fritz and I have big plans," Matt said. Fritz Hugo nodded vigorously.

"Okay. Okay, my daughters can tag along."

"Yeah! Issi, we get to go. Coolest of cools!"

Nikita jumped about, while Isabella grinned. I wondered if they'd planed this in advance.

Celeste advised against trying to bring Patricia Ann Baxter. Heavily implanted to be one of the colonists on Domes, taking her away from there would likely cause a psychotic break. She decided to tag along with us.

She teased me. "You'll need a few more arms on this trip."

Thus, Ashley, Sherry, Nikita, Isabella, Eve, Lara, and Celeste joined me on this trip.

Oh, what of the proposed May Day empire-wide elections? Because of the situation on Earth and bickering among potential candidates, the elections were postponed until July. Many wanted more time to campaign.

On May 7, the eight of us and our many bags entered a transport to take us to the heavy cruiser, Blackbone.

"Wow!" Nikita exclaimed, when the Blackbone appeared outside the windows. The main body was hexagonal and dwarfed our transport. Wing decks flared out from the six sides. Each was as long as the main body, but narrowed to points at their tips. Weapons bristled along all surfaces, so many that I couldn't count them. This Bela Prime ship had to be as large as the Kanika battleship. Impressive.

"Nikita, we could put dozens and dozens of my exploration ship inside this thing. It's humongous," Isabella said.

A rear docking bay opened, again dwarfing our transport. As we docked, I spotted at least a dozen other transports moored to the bays. Walkways led forward. As we stepped out, a security squad met us.

"We're to carry your things and show you to your cabins," one said.

Sherry said, "Hey, treat those with great care. They hold those Galactic Doll mutation agents. You don't want to break any of those containers."

I watched all color drain from the men's faces. After that, they handled the crates as though new-born babies.

As we approached our cabins, Senior Ambassador Le Blanc stepped out. "Oh, there's more of you." Her eyes darted from Isabella to Nikita and to me.

I smiled. We three wore Leslie's fancy designer gowns, the kind that encased our empty shoulders. Isabella and I had long black hair, while Nikita's was brown.

"My daughters, Isabella and Nikita."

"Oh, the famous linguist. Well, this is an honor. Welcome on board the Blackbone."

Nikita bubbled with excitement. "Issi and I want to learn the Jamo language and the one on Indrani-C. I'm going to be a linguist, too. When I get older, of course. This is my first trip on a real spaceship. It's awfully big, isn't it? Mom said you're the President of the Circle of Ambassadors. Lots of people back home wanted Mom to be one of our Senior Ambassadors, too. Then, I'd get to come to Bela Prime with her. Oh, yeah. And this is my Aunt Celeste. Can you talk with that huge lip disk? Is it really heavy? How can you eat or do you have to take it out? I do love those earrings. If Mom becomes a Senior Ambassador, will she get them, too?"

I interrupted. "You'll have to excuse Nikita. She's quite excited about this trip."

"That's okay. I'm talking, but I have to always use this language translation unit. Otherwise my own people can't understand what I'm saying. It's good that you want to be a linguist, Nikita. The galaxy needs more people who can understand more than their own language. Here are your cabins. I've reserved these three in a row for you. Each holds three people. I'll let you decide who's with who. My cabin in next to yours. After you get settled, we'll meet in the Planning Room. Come get me when you're ready."

"Since we don't have our helpful machines with us," I said, "Celeste, why don't you bunk with me and Nikita. Eve, you take Isabella and Ashley. Sherry and Lara can share the third."

"But I want to bunk with Issi," Nikita protested. "She and I are going to be learning languages together. So we ought to be together."

Celeste laughed. "I'll take those two with me. Ashley and Eve can bunk with you."

The security guards kindly stowed our bags in the cabins and departed. Ashley unpacked for me. This time, I let her. The metal drawers posed a challenge for me, and I didn't want to waste time.

Senior Ambassador Le Blanc led us down the long hall. "This is the Talo's cabin. Dr. Westby's is next door. This hall leads to our private mess hall, rather one reserved for our use. On the left is their infirmary where the doctor has setup his genetics lab. Mari and Lippo are waiting for us in the mess hall."

Lara and Eve joined Dr. Westby, leaving us to meet the others.

Once introduced, Nikita said, "This is so cool. Isabella and I want to learn to speak your language. If you don't mind, that is. She's a famous linguist and I want to be one. When I grow up. You'll probably be in mutation comas though. We've all been in them. Is your people really dying off? I'm sure these mutations can fix things."

Isabella and Nikita joined Mari and Lippo. Both seemed

to be enjoying the linguistic distraction. The rest of us sat at the next table.

"So are they both telepaths, too?" asked Senior Ambassador Le Blanc. "She's quite precocious."

I jested. "Nine going on twenty-one."

"Well, if she comes to Bela Prime, I'll see she gets a set of these earrings. You and Isabella can also have a pair. They're not just limited to Senior Ambassadors, like the lip disks are. Honestly, I think you three would look positively stunning in them. Better yet, since you aren't accepting any payment for helping the entire world of Jamo avoid extinction, I'm going to get all three of you a set of these incredible earrings. I won't take no for an answer."

I wanted to protest they might well inhibit our freedom of motion. That we needed to carry things cradled between our heads and shoulders, but it seemed impolite to do so. Just then, Eve joined us.

"Okay, we're ready for the Talo family. Lara and I have verified their DNA are compatible with ours. First, we're going to try the least damaging mutation, the Galactic Doll agent. If that doesn't solve the problem, we'll try the telepath agent version."

I suspected Eve purposely avoided saying the armless telepath agent. While Mari and Lippo talked with Isabella and Nikita, Lippo stared at their empty shoulders, probably trying to imagine living like that. Well, it's not fun.

"We'll be with you all the way," Nikita chatted, as we followed Eve to the infirmary. "Don't worry. I'm sure the mutation will work."

I think the two enjoyed Nikita's constant chatter. It helped take the frightening future off their minds, at least a little bit.

Lara and Eve injected both with the agent.

"That's all?" asked Mari.

"Yes. It can be turned into an aerosol infecting an entire building. Or in even larger quantities, a whole city," Eve said. "A simple injection is vastly preferred, since you can count on receiving the proper dose. In a few minutes, you'll start to feel sleepy. That's to be expected."

"I am a bit tired," she replied.

Eve caught her as she slumped into the mutation coma. Lara handled Lippo. While they removed the two's clothing, Dr. Westby measured and weighed their bodies.

"So that's all there is to it? A simple injection?" he asked.

"Yes. This is the optimum method of delivery. Using an aerosol version is trickier. Some giants tried it outside Nikita's grade school, but got the dosage wrong, severely limiting those infected. Now we wait. We'll start seeing results in a day. The question is: will it restore his semen? Their biological ages should be reset to their early twenties. If all goes well, this should restart their entire civilization."

Lara added, "If this version doesn't, the telepath version is much stronger in its effects. Heck, that one brought Sam and Matt back to life after they were pronounced dead."

"What?" exclaimed Senior Ambassador Le Blanc.

I outlined what had happened. I couldn't resist adding, "We traced the funds back to Senior Ambassador Sanura Fenku. She hired the giant to kill Sam and Matt. We have no idea why she wanted my family dead."

All the while, Eve, Celeste, and I watched for any reaction from Senior Ambassador Le Blanc. Because of her giant lip disk, her face displayed little reactions. It's amazing how many facial expressions are in some way hinged upon one's mouth and lips.

"You should have your Senior Ambassadors launch a formal complaint against her. Have them bring their proof," she replied. "More importantly it shows how powerful this telepath agent is. Incredible."

Lara added, "It also brought Molly back from the dead. Sixth Invader shot her in her head, but the mutation agent kept her and her baby alive. It took a whole month for it to restore her body. So yes, the telepath agent is powerful. Trouble is, it's dominant. All offspring end up having the same mutation. Not so good. Still, that's one argument they've made for keeping it around. At least in syringe format. On a deep space exploration ship, its commander and doctor were killed by a poisonous plant. Both were injected with the agent and survived. I call it the Death Cheater. Of course, the side effects aren't to be taken lightly." She nodded towards me and my daughters.

"Still, they do seem to do okay. I remember Senior Ambassador Strawn. His wife had to assist him a quite lot as I recall. Still, he executed his duties admirably well," she said.

With little to do, Isabella and Nikita pestered her for linguistic details about languages spoken on Bela Prime. Thus, the day passed. I noticed we saw very little of the actual crew. I began to suspect their commander wanted nothing to do with three obvious telepaths. Boredom set in for me, but my daughters seemed enamored with Senior Ambassador Le Blanc.

Lara and Eve spent long hours monitoring changes in the Talos. At meals, they kept me informed. Mari's bosom continued to grow, but her feet hadn't altered. More importantly, Lippo's body showed marked changes as expected. On the eighth day, everyone gathered round the pair. Lippo's body morphed into that of a Galactic Doll with giant breasts, matching Mari's. Curiously, their feet remained normal while their hair had grown about eighteen inches.

Luppo woke first. "Did it work?" he said, before gasping.

His voice had risen into the soprano range. Eve wrapped a sheet around him.

Dr. Westby said, "So far, it's gone according to what they expected, except your feet and legs are normal. We need to take some samples."

"I feel so funny, so different. They're much too heavy!"

Mari woke and looked over at Lippo. "You look so different. Did it work? How soon can you tell? I feel more energetic. What do I look like? Oh, my clothes aren't going to fit, are they?"

Senior Ambassador Le Blanc held up a mirror.

Mari gasped. "I'm fifty years younger!"

I said, "More likely your biological age is around early twenties. At least that's what ours have always been. Show Lippo what he looks like. You're twenty-something, too."

He just stared into the mirror. Shocked. While others

helped them to their cabin and worked on finding apparel they could wear, the three geneticists set to work examining the DNA results.

"Incredible," Dr. Westby said. "I do believe it has worked. It's critical to see if Mari can now bear children from Lippo." He left to tell them the news and work out the next test: get Mari pregnant.

At supper the next day, Lippo gushed. "It worked. Mari is pregnant. We're about to have the first Jamo child in more than a half century! I know I look really weird, but to have babies again. It's worth it. How can we ever thank you enough?"

We congratulated the ecstatic couple. Then came serious talk about how best to deal with the remaining population of Jamo, just under a billion older people. Dr. Westby, the Talo couple, and a large amount of the mutation agent departed the Blackbone in a deep space transport, bound for their world. He arranged for a supply ship to meet there, bringing materials to allow him to manufacture more of the Galactic Doll agent. Me, I was thankful we didn't need to use the armless telepath version.

After they left, life became even more boring for me. Meanwhile, Nikita and Isabella pestered Senior Ambassador Le Blanc and any crew they could find, doing their best to learn the common language spoken on Bela Prime. Too slowly the days passed.

About halfway there, the Blackbone dropped out of hyperspace to refuel on some world. From the little we could see, it must have been nighttime. However, I did hear Senior Ambassador Le Blanc leaving the ship and then returning.

When we had lunch in the mess hall, Senior Ambassador Le Blanc had a surprise for us: three pairs of her fancy earrings!

"I had them rush shipped to that refueling station. It's not often I get to treat others like this."

"You shouldn't have. I ought to pay for them," I said.

"Accept a little thank you, Molly. You've just saved a whole planet. I've a set for each of you. Yes, Nikita, you're getting an identical set, too. Promise me you'll keep up with your linguistic studies."

"I will! Wow! Look at them. They're gorgeous! Thank you," Nikita bubbled.

Each earring draped down ten inches in five tiers, each about two inches tall. Gold and platinum filigrees housed the large gemstones, each about an inch and a half long. Each tier held four rows of the stones and their housings.

"The stones are manufactured diamonds. So don't worry, they're not unreasonably expensive," the ambassador explained as she set to work installing them. "The metal is gold covered platinum, so these setting are nearly unbreakable. I've never heard of any ambassador's earrings breaking."

"Now, because they are heavy, we pierce our ears and install these metal grommets. They allow the earrings to swing freely without harming earlobes. We always install them at the top of the lobes as close to the lower ear cartilage as possible. You'll fee a pinprick as I punch these grommets into your lobes. If you wear these for a number of years, you might need to get larger grommets. The lobe openings tend to get stretched in time, making the grommets quite loose. Not likely to happen for about five years."

"How do they come off?" I asked. I felt a pinprick in each ear along with a bit of noise. She closed a punch or pliers device that drove the grommet through my lobe and then flanged it out. I'd have to cut my ear to remove it. It reminded me of grommets attached to sails on boats on Lake Michigan.

She laughed. "They don't." The ambassador lifted up one earring and used another device to insert the top loop through the grommet, fusing the ends together. "There. They can't come off. You'd have to use tiny wire cutters to remove them. Since these are quite expensive, women don't wish to have them fall off or lose them. The lower tier rests on the top of your bosom. There. One lady done, two to go."

"They are terrible heavy. Can they rip our ears?" I asked.

She chuckled. At least that's what it sounded like through her giant lip disk.

"Hardly. With these, you can swing them around and feel your shoulders."

Later, Nikita said, "She's right. Now I have a way to feel my shoulders and chest. Way cool. Thank you ambassador. These are super. Look at me, Mom. You look great, too. Thank you. Thank you."

Again, I couldn't tell if the ambassador was smiling or not. I thought perhaps her eyes shone. Reading a Senior Ambassador was challenging.

"Nikita, you look so grown up," Isabella said. "Ouch. That's some pinprick."

My youngest daughter sat up very straight. Her eyes reflected how pleased and happy she felt. Already, though, their heavy weight annoyed me, and I'd only worn them a few minutes.

"Mom, come on. Let's go to our cabin and see what we look like in the mirror," Isabella said. "Thank you, Senior Ambassador. Thank you!"

I followed them down the hall to my cabin. Inside, we stood before the tall mirror admiring our new appearance. The glow on my daughters' faces told all. But would they still like them tomorrow? Would we even be able to sleep?

With days to go before we arrived on Indriani-C, I joined them in trying to learn the common language spoken on Bela Prime, Federation Common. Weird trying to emulate a metallic voice from a translation unit. Nikita did get her to turn it off once and speak what we'd been hearing from the box. The lip disk made her words incomprehensible.

"I can see why you need it," Nikita said. "Still, I think your disk looks fabulous. Maybe one day I can get one. You think so, Mom?"

Kids. Landing on Indrani-C didn't come soon enough for me.

Chapter 25 Empress Kalindi Amandani

We dropped out of hyperspace many hours before actually landing. Why? From viewports, we saw hundreds of ships in our vicinity. Dozens upon dozens of yellow stars very like our own Sol dotted the field of view. We were entering a star cluster, one whose stars were as old as Sol. The Senior Ambassador explained that an Indrani-C computer controlled our cruiser, guaranteeing no accidents.

"Remember," she said, "the Varouna Empire is one of the oldest in the Federation and one of the most important members, if not the largest. It's ruled by one woman, Empress Kalindi Amandani. That woman wields more power and respect than anyone I know.

"It's said she brought peace to thirty warring planets, but that was at least sixty years ago. Fortunately, she doesn't take any interest in Federation policies and actions. Her appointees handle such matters. Some say she's rich, the wealthiest woman in the Varouna Empire, but I tend to discount those rumors. Years ago, I tried to get her to become one of their Senior Ambassadors. She talks in riddles, sometimes."

"What did she say?" I asked.

"Something like 'be careful what you give up.' I probably had a blank look on my face, for she added, 'Without those language boxes, no one can understand what you say and yet you are an ambassador whose words are vital.' But I told her, look, on Bela Prime, absolutely everyone looks up to you; you get only the very best treatment, best food, best everything. She merely smiled. So I ought to warn you Kalindi can be infuriating."

"I've watch you at meal times. The disk makes eating and drinking pretty awkward for you."

"It's nothing, really. You get used to it. You would make a fabulous Senior Ambassador, Molly. Your late Aaron Strawn and his wife, Piper. I admit he had a difficult time for perhaps a week, but she helped him with such things. In your case, hundreds of young women would line up to be your assistant, helping you with dining and such."

"Piper did tell me they were treated like royalty on Bela Prime. That surprised them," I said.

"She's absolutely right. There isn't a better job on any world anywhere in the Federation than being a Senior Ambassador, unless you've a more war-like disposition. In that case, join the Admirals and Generals." She chuckled—at least I think that was the sound I heard from beneath her shiny giant disk.

"Molly, bring your whole family. On Bela Prime, Nikita can get the very best education the Federation has to offer. Honestly, there are no drawbacks. Not even financial. With the salaries the Federation pays Senior Ambassadors, you can live, as Piper said, like royalty."

"But I'm now supposed to be the Governor of Domes." I countered, feeling out just how tightly I was being held to that position which I didn't want.

"Oh, after you take the post, you can always assign someone else to relieve you. I'd love to have you with us on Bela Prime. Ah, we're finally landing. Honestly, the space traffic around Indrani-C is almost as bad as it is around Bela Prime. That's saying something. We're landing at Indus City. The empress is in the tallest spiral building. We'll take a shuttle from the spaceport, unless they land us closer."

"Wow. Mom, look! Those are some buildings!" Nikita interrupted us.

I'd never seen architecture quite like this. Spiral buildings soared upwards, needle points touching the clouds, or so it seemed. As I looked closer, their cross-sections were all hexagonal. Many buildings, like the skyscrapers of Chicago, occupied an entire city block at ground level, but their tops seemed tiny.

Senior Ambassador Le Blanc pointed out. "The Empress Kalindi Amandani holds court at the very top of the tallest spiral. That one there."

"Wow! Super coolest!" Nikita gushed.

"Where will we be staying?" asked Ashley.

"There are guest quarters on middle floors," she said.

"Kalindi will likely give us one whole floor for our use. Everything is automated. You'll see. Made for you and your daughters."

I wondered what she meant by that. Perhaps because the empress had no arms, they installed automatic features, like lights that turned on as you walked down a hallway. Surely, they didn't have the robot-like machines that we did to help us with our hair and dressing.

"I should warn you. The empress's spiral isn't all that fancy. It's not opulent, contrary to what I would expect. The accommodations are comfortable, but not plush. You'll have much nicer quarters on Bela Prime. Quite why someone as wealthy and powerful as Empress Amandani is chooses to dwell in such a plain habitat eludes me."

She probably didn't realize it, but she just told me quite a lot about herself.

"The food," she added, "is excellent. Real food. Not the flavored synthetic goo we're fed on the Blackbone."

An aide came and adjusted our language translation boxes.

Senior Ambassador Le Blanc said, "They set them to deal with the local language on Indrani-C. Empress Kalindi prides herself on speaking many languages. She does speak Federation Common. It's possible she's learned to speak your English dialect. She's an amazing woman. Okay. Here we go. My security men will transport our baggage and your crate with the mutation agent. Follow me."

As we stepped outside, I couldn't hear anything anyone was saying. Wisely no one spoke. An almost continuous roar of spaceships landing and departing drowned out everything. If I closed my eyes, the smell of tar, oil, and fumes convinced me I was at New O'Hare. I smiled.

The Blackbone parked close to a hexagonal spiral building. Giant letters arced over the gigantic entranceway. I presumed they were letters. Isabella tried to say something about them, but we couldn't hear her. Once inside, the only noise came from voices and countless language boxes. Sound dampening wiped out the outside noise. That I found amazing. We could use that at New O'Hare.

"There are thousands of landing ports across the planet. We're at the one next to the Empress Spire, as it's called. This way. Oh, millions of people visit the spire each year. Some are tourists; others have empire business here," Senior Ambassador Le Blanc said.

A man in a green uniform walked up. She told him, "Empress Kalindi Amandani is expecting us. We're the party from the Sol Empire."

"Ah, yes. This way," he said.

He stared long at Isabella, Nikita, and me. Surely he'd seen armless women before.

A long tunnel led us into the ground floor of the Empress Spire. Hundreds of people moved like giant ants heading toward or coming from elevators, banks of which lined the six sides. A hexagonal reception desk sat squarely in the center. Automated voices spoke in a continuous drone, indicating which elevator bank rose to which commerce levels. As we walked the long distance to our elevators, one thing struck me. No security guards. Not one. In fact, I hadn't seen anyone carrying a weapon. No blasters, no guns, no laser pistols.

As we waited for the elevator, I asked, "Aren't there any security guards? Boy, this sure isn't like our corporate offices in Chicago."

Again, I think Senior Ambassador Le Blanc chuckled. "Oh, there's security. Tight security. But it's all unseen. Cameras are everywhere. When we entered, cameras scanned us for weapons, bombs, and such. No need to be overt about security."

Ding. The elevator arrived. As we stepped inside, she added, "Going up two hundred floors in barely a minute. But you won't feel a thing. Marvelous elevators."

"Hello. I am Diti Tara, Empress Kalindi Amandani's personal assistant. Welcome to Indrani-C and the prosperous Varouna Empire."

She looked at the three of us. I spoke up, "I'm Molly Parkinson. My daughters, the linguist Isabella and Nikita."

I introduced the others, but I saw Diti relax once she'd figured out which one of us was me, the one she was expecting.

She was short with a light brown skin tone and black hair. She wore a loose fitting gown, rather professional looking in my opinion. Nothing fancy. Two gold rings adorned her hand, along with a golden wrist bracelet. A sun-burst gold pendant hung from her neck with a fiery ruby in its center. I later learned this was the empress's symbol. She wore sandals.

"This way. Empress Amandani is expecting you."

She waved her arm and led the way into the Royal Audience Room. A banner over the arched doorway said so, though Senior Ambassador Le Blanc read it for us as we walked through.

Sunlight filtered through hundreds of windows. The whole top floor consisted of windows set in hexagonal frames. Purple drapes hung on either side of the windows. Polished white marble with silver stripes covered the floor, which looked more like a ballroom floor. At the north side, a purple chair dominated. Dozens of smaller purple chairs rested against a back wall. However, several men quickly entered and slid enough of them out for us.

Just as soon as they arranged the chairs in a semi-circle around the larger one, they left. Empress Kalindi Amandani hobbled into the room, a bent, frail, eighty-nine-year-old woman. But we all knew we were in the presence of a goddess.

There aren't words to describe Kalindi. Holy. Intense presence. Instant total peace. Complete present time. No thoughts of any past. Serenity.

I think serenity best describes how I felt. It radiated from Empress Kalindi. As I discovered during the ensuing days, this was how everyone felt when she was in the same room. Incredibly amazing.

"Welcome, Mrs. Parkinson. Please have a seat. My body's too old to do much standing any longer. I see your daughters take after you. I'm told Isabella has become a famous linguist. One of my empire's linguists attended the conference on Earth in February. One learns much if one listens."

"Molly. Call me Molly. Yes, this is Isabella and Nikita. My personal assistant, Ashley, and my security person, Sherry. My sister and geneticist Eve and my dear friend Lara, also a top geneticist."

"Your buildings are so cool! It's amazing," Nikita said. "I'm very pleased to meet you, too. Do you really run this whole empire? Mom's been trying to bring some sanity back to our Sol Empire, but so many men keep trying to take over. And then some giants keep trying to kidnap our people, turn them into telepaths like us, and sell them. Then, they tried to kill Dad and Matt. And now the Federation wants to kill everyone on Earth to get rid of the mutations. But maybe Mom has stopped that from happening. Of course, it helped that she married Admiral Skaggs' niece. He's the one who was going to blow us up. And..."

"Nikita. Give her a chance. Sorry, Empress Kalindi. If you let her, she'll talk all day."

"Oh, I find her enthusiasm refreshing. Nikita, you and I will have a private talk later on. We have much to discuss, don't we?" She winked, bringing a broad smile to Nikita's face.

"My, you three have the most interesting dresses I've ever seen. I shall have to purchase some from your Earth for myself. And such earrings. I see Senior Ambassador Le Blanc has influenced you. And Isabella, we'll have a private chat as well. But first, Molly and I must discuss the mutation agent with Eve and Lara. Senior Ambassador, will you please take these two young ladies on a tour of this spiral? And take Ashley and Sherry with you. If we need arms, I'm sure we can manage for a short while."

For the first time, I saw Senior Ambassador Le Blanc do as she was told as though this was her own idea. Command presence. Empress Kalindi spoke in her soft, gentle voice, but the command power simply couldn't be disobeyed. I saw a slight strain line the ambassador's forehead as though she tried to resist the empress's request, but failing utterly. Gaily, Nikita headed for the doors, followed by Isabella. Sherry and Ashley followed, while the ambassador brought up the rear.

"Wait for me," she said.

When they left the huge room, Empress Kalindi tackled the reason we came.

"So, I believe you've brought a large supply of what your people call the armless telepath Galactic Doll agent."

"Yes, enough to treat perhaps a thousand people," Eve said.

"Good. Will it affect my DNA the same way it does yours? Is there a test for that?"

"If we had a sample of your DNA to study," Lara said, "we can make a good guess."

"Okay. I presumed you'd need that. Diti has a sample for you. She can show you to a lab I've had setup for your use. Return when you have completed your analysis."

I didn't see her ringing a bell, but Diti chose that precise moment to reenter the room. "This way."

That left me alone with Empress Kalindi. Further, I noticed that I was outside my body, several feet behind my head. How unusual, but I had clear perceptions. I felt incredibly powerful.

"Molly, it is so refreshing to meet someone as alive, aware, and able as I am. Are all people on Earth as aware and able as you are? Or is it because of your sister Celeste and her therapy? I've heard tales of it. Lara, the dwarf, was supposedly completely insane, or so my Senior Ambassadors tell me. Yet she appears as sane and alive as you or I."

I chuckled. "You don't miss a thing. Yes, I've had thousands of hours of Celeste's therapy. With it, we trace trauma and even unwanted emotions and attitudes and losses back to their original source: always something filled with pain and unconsciousness. We erase it. Usually those sessions have ended up with me erasing something bad that happened to me in earlier lifetimes.

"But to answer your question, no, they're not. Only a few of us have had much therapy. Some have had enough to realize they are more than their bodies and minds. And I didn't develop telepathy or my ability to glimpse possible future events until after thousands of hours and erasing hundreds upon hundreds of bad things either that I did or that were done to me. I came to see that I wasn't my body or mind. That I've lived countless lives before this one."

"I was afraid there weren't, Molly. I've not met a single person in the vast Varouna Empire that is as aware and able as you are. Person-mind-body. But I best tell you about myself.

No telling how soon Eve and Lara will return with the results.

"Like you, I've seen much of my past. I came to this star cluster because it held so much promise for habitable planets with human-like bodies and with space travel. Many suns just like your Sol. When I first picked up this body, most of these worlds were in contest with each other. Silly me. I hadn't observed the body lacked arms. Birth defect. Anyway, wars happened with alarming frequency. That's not a fun game to play, so I acted. One by one, I brought the worlds together forming the empire of thirty-nine worlds that it is today. I'm the glue that holds it together. Yes, it's taken me seventy-one years to get it this far.

"My biggest fear is that when I'm gone, they'll revert back to their old ways and break up this powerful empire. That is why I took note of what has been happening on your Earth. Rejuvenation. More than that, rejuvenation without regrowing arms. You see, my lack of arms has aided me in my quest. Others see me as being unable to abuse my position of power. I can't hold credits. I can't make use of most objects that others tend to covet or strive to acquire. Thus, I can't be bribed. Others have reported how skillful you are using your feet and toes. When I was a teen, I did too.

"However, I soon discovered others looked at me as very handicapped and thus not a threat to them in any way. So I took advantage of their blindness. Over these many years, that has helped me in my efforts to rule them. Most human vices are lost on me, since I've apparently no way to make any use of them. Greed, gluttony, envy, jealousy, vanity, arrogance, cowardice, sloth, recklessness, perversion. The list is endless. In their eyes, these don't apply to me, so I can't be corrupted. Vanity hardly applies to me. I can't dress myself or feed myself, so I've let them believe. Jewelry is lost on me. Who would want to marry an armless woman? They've never found any thread they could pull to unduly influence me. Long ago, they stopped trying to find a way to grow arms on this body. Had they succeeded, they could have used that to attempt to bribe me.

"My goal, Molly, is to be rejuvenated and continue to lead the Varouna Empire for another long period. When I'm convinced these worlds won't revert back to their warlike state, then I'll step down. That's why I've brought you and your mutation agents here. This empire is one of the strongest in the Federation. If it so chose, it could conquer the rest of the Federation and its minor empires. Alternatively, it could disintegrate and severely weaken the Federation. I can't let either happen."

"Wow. Now I understand, Empress Kalindi. I hope our mutation agent works on your body. But didn't you ever marry and have children?"

"Comparable magnitude. Would you be truly happy if your husband was a moron, a dope? I checked. You first married a man who had several university degrees and was brilliant in robotics and computers. Then, you married a man who, I'm told, can remember everything he studies, brilliant in other ways and is even a navigator.

"You see, when a person is as aware and as full of life as we are, it's nearly impossible to have a spouse who is not in some ways comparable. I've never met anyone, male or female, until your family today, who realizes they are an immortal being, not made of physical universe matter and energy—one who has and uses a mind, and one who for a brief time inhabits a specific human body.

"So no. I've never married. While I might have engineered a way for a child to succeed me, I've had none. Hence, I'm hoping your mutation agent will rejuvenate this body. Enough about me. I want to share some wisdom with you. Why?

"If the Sol Empire has any chance of survival as an empire, you must become its empress, just as I've done for the Varouna Empire. To lead it forward and be successful, consider this.

"Sanity and greatness stem from continuing to love your fellow people despite any and all reasons not to do so. Hatred of others leads to sorrow and despair, to say nothing of unhappiness. Yes, sometimes one does have to act for the safety of others, but one does not have to hate them—just remove the danger to others.

"I'm not talking about forgiving others either, for that

brands their acts as bad. Why would you want to accept the bad act, which is what forgiveness implies? Rather, just do what's necessary to maintain the safety of others and understand the perpetrator.

"That perpetrator is a person and is in the same universe as the rest of us, subject to all the betrayals and terrible pressures and forces and drives that this universe can dish out. Accordingly, some now act as their betrayers once did, while some have become oblivious to it all. Some have succumbed and now rant and rave, torture, and enslave like the demented, tortured souls they are.

"So do not change in the face of bad actions. Instead, handle the danger and go on doing your job. Your justice, your forgiveness, your mercy are not important when compared against your ability not to change just because of such provocations. Act, preserve order and decency, but don't give in to hate and vengeance. In this universe, it takes great strength to love your fellow people.

"Molly, I've looked into your background. Rather, I've heard the reports. You inherently strive to follow these principles. Take that Sixth Invader Captain who spend thirty years undermining your world and nearly conquering it, L'Grina. Instead of vengeance, you chose to run your therapy on her burned arm and helped her discover who and what she really is, an immortal being. That is greatness. That is why you will make a great empress of the Sol Empire."

"Wait. I just want to be a private investigator and help Celeste run her therapy on others. I want to help people like those the Third Invaders took to Domes and implanted," I said. Her suggestion I be the empress shocked me.

Empress Kalindi laughed. "What do you think I do? Seventy-five percent of my daily activities is detective work, your private investigator actions. I have to find out the real facts, not what others tell me. Only then can I make intelligent decisions. From what has been reported to me, you are already doing that. All you lack is the kind of personal presence that I have."

"Well, that's kind of a big lack, wouldn't you say? I've never met anyone quite like you."

Again, she chuckled. "True. But you've already taken the most important step to achieving that kind of presence. You're positioned above and behind your body's head, aren't you?"

I hadn't paid much attention to my location. "Well, now that you mention it, I am. Happens a lot when I erase a traumatic incident."

"I've found that collapsing my space down and sitting inside my head with tunnel vision through the body's eyes drastically impairs my abilities, my awareness."

That reminded me. "Is it like what happened to me when I woke up and found she'd cut off my arms? Before, I controlled the space about three feet around me, the reach of my arms. Afterwards, I felt as though my whole space had collapsed down to my nose and boobs. I've felt my space as condensed ever since. No, wait. Recently, it's been expanding back out. I'm sort of developing telekinesis. Enough to keep the body upright when it would otherwise take a spill."

She smiled. "Precisely. I couldn't have stated it better. When exterior to the body, your powers easily express themselves and grow. But when interior to the body, your powers collapse to only what a body can do. Plus, with the knowledge you have of the dark side of human minds—where the trauma resides—you can control that in others. Until now, you've probably only worked on erasing the pains, but as empress, when you need to handle some danger a person is causing, you can re-stimulate such trauma in them to get them to cease their destructive actions. A massive headache shuts almost anyone down."

"I'm not sure I'd want to do that. Anyway, I'm supposed to be the Governor of Domes. And I've promised Bonita I'd go with her to Bela Prime to uncover the rogue robots. But already I'm stuck with being the Senior Investigator and Senior Judge."

"I wondered why you brought a robot android with you. Security person?"

"Excellent security. Long story." I told her about the ten advanced human form robots, five of which followed the robot laws and aided us. "So the other five have no programming and disappeared. We believe one of them killed Senior Ambassador Aaron Strawn on Bela Prime because he discovered the robot was impersonating one of the admirals or generals. He was killed before he could expose that robot. So I need to track it down." I decided not to tell her that Bonita had been Ted last lifetime.

"The Sol Empire is at a critical junction. Empires are built upon a hierarchical bureaucracy of several potential types. Corporations are common. But as your people discovered, in a crisis, one individual must lead."

She smiled. "A standing joke on Indrani-C is how many committees does it take to change a light fixture? A dozen."

We chuckled.

"A beneficent monarch is desirable. A tyrant leader is disastrous. Senior Ambassador Le Blanc wants you installed as Governor of Domes. Alternatively, she wants you to be a Senior Ambassador on Bela Prime. What she apparently doesn't want is you to continue being the Senior Investigator and Senior Judge. I find that curious, because you would be my choice to be the Sol Empire's empress."

"Senior Ambassador Sanura Fenku wants me on Bela Prime, too."

"The Senior Ambassadors are always playing political games, particularly with fledgling empires and other new worlds."

"I suspect they have some kind of ulterior motives for wanting me off-world. But I've no idea what those may be."

"You are wise to suspect that. I do have substantial influence with the Circle of Ambassadors. Your current positions as investigator and judge puts you in the unique position to overrule any executive or legislative decisions the Sol Empire makes. Is that correct?"

"As it stands, yes. No one else wanted the job. They're interested in raw power. But I do need to find ways to help those on Domes and also Bonita."

She closed her eyes a moment. "Okay. I suggest we approach it this way. I'll see that the Federation insists you remain as the Senior Investigator and Senior Judge with total power to overrule any executive or legislative action the Sol

Empire and corporations make. But take a brief time off to attend to the needs of those on Domes. As part of that, install a replacement Governor of Domes. Meanwhile, I'll assist Bonita in tracking down the rogue robot on Bela Prime who killed Senior Ambassador Aaron Strawn. Is that acceptable?"

"Perfect."

"Ah, I believe Eve and Lara are returning. I hope with good news."

Right on cue, the pair walked in, led by an aide who promptly departed. From the smiles on their faces, I suspected good news.

Eve said, "Empress Kalindi, our armless telepath Galactic Doll mutation agent should work on your body. Of course, your appearance could be quite different. On Earth, the agent drastically reduced wide diversity of women's bodies."

"Excellent. How soon can we begin?"

"Whenever you are ready," she replied.

"Well, I should have my promised talks with Nikita and Isabella first. Let's do it after lunch. I believe they are returning shortly. Please let Diti show you to the dining area."

The others entered the room, but only Nikita and Isabella walked over to me, while Lara and Eve headed to the doors. Senior Ambassador Le Blanc looked quite confused, probably why her body wasn't allowed back into the room.

Diti said, "If you'll follow me, I'll take you to the dining area. Empress Kalindi will be along shortly, after a promised word with the daughters."

Isabella and I moved off to one side, giving Nikita and Empress Kalindi some privacy. Still, I overheard them.

"Wow, that was so cool! All those exhibits. I've never seen hexagonal spaceships and buildings and everything. Way cool," Nikita said.

"Thank you. I do like to look at them, too. Reminds me of where we've come. So, what do you really want to do with your life?"

"Oh. Well, I did want to be a linguist like Issi, but..."

"I gathered that much. You love your older sister and want to be like her."

"Yeah."

"But..."

"Well, I want to be like Mom, a telepath. I always have. She's so powerful."

"Is that why you don't want arms?"

"Yeah. But..."

"But?"

"Well, she never seems to use her telepathy much. She and Aunt Celeste are always helping others with therapy sessions. I have too. Given others therapy sessions. Like some of the kids at school. Falls, sprains, cuts. I have them erase those little traumas. Their bodies heal up like super-fast. That's what I really want to do."

"Do you need telepathy to do that?"

"No. Besides, I feel like I'm a cheater."

"How so?"

"Well, Mom earned her telepathy. Aunt Celeste gave her thousands of hours of therapy. Me, I just got it free from the mutation. Kinda cheating. But I really don't need telepathy, do I? I ought to earn it, like Mom did, don't you think?"

"That would be a very admirable thing to do. Earn it and help so many others."

"I'm glad you think so, too. It's probably the most important think in the world."

"You are right about that. Perhaps one day when you get older you can come to Indrani-C and give me some sessions."

"Can I? Really? You got a deal!"

"We best get lunch, don't you think?"

Nikita scampered over to me, explaining what they'd discussed, while Isabella sat across from Empress Kalindi.

"Such a fine young lady."

Isabella smiled. "You bet. Quite a little sister. She's torn between being a linguist like me and a therapist like Mom. Do you realize she's given her fellow classmates hours of therapy sessions? Amazing sister."

"That's impressive. And how about you? Now that you have a family, are you planning to return to an exploration ship in search of new habited worlds and languages to decipher?"

Isabella laughed. "Motherhood has changed me. Actually, no. It's a very dangerous proposition. You never know what poisonous plants and dangerous animals you'll encounter on a new world, to say nothing of people. Owen and I have enough funds that we can live our whole lives without ever working again."

"Makes sense. You don't see me flying about in spaceships. So are you still interested in deciphering ancient languages? Like that on this new world Domes?"

"Yes. I've not had the chance to talk to Mom yet. But Owen and I would like to go there and see if I can unravel that language. Learn the secrets of that world."

"I'm sure your mother would back you on that. But do you need telepathy to decipher ancient languages? Some of our linguists have asked me that. I promised to ask you."

Isabella laughed. "Hardly. Ancient languages—which I studied for my PhD—no, not at all. If you encounter a new people speaking a new language, then absolutely telepathy greatly helps. I can pick up concepts from them and work out the corresponding speech patterns. But for ancient ones, heck no."

"So, if you're going to now work on ancient languages and not go back out exploring for new worlds, you don't need telepathy."

Isabella brightened up. "You're right. Living life without arms is a real drag. I should get mine regrown. I'm not about to put Owen and Maria at risk by flying off ever again. Heck, recently, a commander and doctor got killed by a poisonous plant as they were leaving an uninhabited world. Thank heavens someone injected them with the mutation agent which brought them back. Apparently, they were dead only a couple minutes. Oh, I'm keeping you from lunch. Come on. The others are getting impatient."

We joined the others in the dining area. Whatever we ate, Eve said it tasted like roast duck, potatoes, gravy, and lettuce. Lara suggested it tasted more like gundrilla and luc, while the ambassador insisted it was roast pheasant and dill. Empress Kalindi made no comment, while Diti fed her.

Isabella, Nikita, and I were fed by the others.

Next, Eve and Lara followed Empress Kalindi to her bedroom, where they injected her with the mutation agent. When they returned, Eve explained she had already entered her mutation coma. Now we had eight days to kill.

As I waited, the fact that I'd been in the presence of a very able and powerful being struck me hard. Senior Ambassador Le Blanc resumed pestering me to join her on Bela Prime. I felt the constant serenity I'd had when around the empress slipping away. I realized if Celeste's therapy had gotten me to where I was, then perhaps even more might raise my abilities closer to that of Empress Kalindi Amandani.

At the moment though, I had no idea what other possible trauma I could have to erase. I'd developed telepathy as a result of thousands of hours of therapy. I'd earned it, as Nikita said. Had I earned my telekinesis or had it developed because my body had been mutated so many times? If nothing else, I had to continue to study Celeste's therapy. But...

Where had Empress Kalindi come from ninety years ago when she arrived on Indrani-C and took her current body after it was born? Were there others out there like her, able, powerful, and serene? A whole planet of gods? For a moment, I wanted to drop everything and go off exploring for such a world.

"Mom, as soon as we get back, Issi and I are getting our arms grown," Nikita said, bringing me back to the present.

Responsibilities. Such flights of fancy had to wait.

Right on time, the empress came out of her coma, a young woman in her early twenties once again.

"God, they're huge," she exclaimed while looking at her body in a full-length mirror.

"Glad your feet didn't mutate," I said.

Again, I wanted to bask in the serenity radiating from Empress Kalindi.

Quickly, we wrapped up our business. I arranged to have our style dresses sent to her. She solved one problem for me.

"Send Bonita here right away. I'll arrange for some of my detectives to accompany her and help her find this rogue robot. You take care of those poor people on Domes and then establish yourself as the Senior Judge. You're going to be their breath of sanity. Your role is vital, if the Sol Empire is to thrive."

Senior Ambassador Le Blanc said, "But I want her to be one of their Senior Ambassadors."

"Not going to happen," Empress Kalindi said. "That would be a total waste of her abilities. See that she continues to be their Senior Judge."

For an instant, I felt some sympathy for Le Blanc. She looked so downcast and had no choice but to accept the Empress's ruling.

That's when I realized another aspect of Empress Kalindi. She had total impingement. When she said something, her message arrived at the other person in such a way that it could not be shunted aside, protested, or disobeyed. Now, if I could do that...

Chapter 26 Recovery

We arrived home to many surprises on Tuesday, August 1, 2361. First shock. Matt and Sam looked masculine again! Their arms had grown significantly.

"Wow! What happened to you two?" I asked.

Beaming, Sam hugged me. "Eve and Lara's new mutation agent is working. Most of Chicago's men are male-looking again. GMed is working on other cities now. Those two are gonna be famous. There you are. Eve, Lara, thank you. Thank you." He gave them a hug, too.

"What happened to the elections?" I asked.

"They're scheduled for the fifteenth. Been quite a hubbub. I recorded some of the more important developments. You're still the Senior Investigator and Senior Judge. The Federation, Admiral Skaggs, and our Senior Ambassadors have been relaying the decisions, which if we follow them, will avoid the annihilation of Earth," Sam explained.

"Short version. Sol Empire has to have three governing bodies. The Senate must be reconstituted and will make the laws. The Office of President will enforce those laws and handle defense matters. The Senior Investigator and Senior Judge continue on just as they have been and can veto any Senate law or any action taken by the President. Your offices will remain on Earth, but the Office of the President will be on Pylon, Epsilon Eridani, while the Senate moves to Brussels, Tau Ceti. That compromise made those off-world happy. So tell us all about your trip," Sam said.

I barely started when Bonita arrived with all our relatives and friends, though Nikita had already dashed next door to find Veronica. I spent an hour briefing everyone.

Later, Nikita and Isabella accompanied Lara and Eve to the Med Center to being their arm regrow process, while Bonita and I discussed going after that rogue robot.

She said, "I can't believe you've gotten us some help in tracking it down. I was worried I'd have to go it alone. I know you're gonna be stuck here dealing with Domes and then the Senior Judge stuff. Those are important, and I don't dare pull you away from them. This'll be perfect. If that empire is as powerful as you say, I should be in good hands. Don't worry. This time, I'm gonna get that robot and put it out of business."

"Promise my you won't get yourself killed this time. I've gotten Empress Kalindi to promise me that if you do get blown up, she'll see you get back to Earth. I don't want to have to hunt all over the galaxy to find you again."

We laughed, but she seemed very relieved to hear that last. With that, she headed off to pack, because Senior Ambassador Le Blanc's heavy cruiser was headed back to Bela Prime and would drop her off on Indrani-C.

I watched the recordings Sam had made and reached a decision on who I was voting for in the coming elections.

While I wanted to go to Domes and see what had been done during the past almost three months, delays prevented my departure. Ashley had three court cases that couldn't wait. Then, Deanna asked for a further delay. She organized an exploration force of four ships with two hundred engineers and scientists. Already a huge list of potential colonists had signed up, many from Earth, which wasn't surprising.

Earth had very little news from Domes. Admiral Rossi kept two cruisers there just in case the Third Invaders returned. The Berktold Soros Group had arrived and unloaded substantial equipment, setting up their research office in one of the many empty homes in the dome where the sixteen hundred lived. Beyond that, our authorities heard little else. But we did hear Dr. Tye Westby, the Federation's top geneticist, arrived there from Jamo.

On election day, I cast my vote for Natalie Leonovich for President and her husband, Dimitri, as our Senator. As I walked out of the voting office, I felt wonderful. For the first time, I, Molly Parkinson, had a choice in who would be our leaders. I wondered how many other ordinary people around the Sol Empire had similar feelings.

Unfortunately, Dimitri won the presidency, but he did install Natalie as his Minister of Defense. He created six other ministers to help distribute the load of governing. Weeks of planning preceded their move to Pylon, Espilon Eridani.

At my last family meeting, I said, "Kids, I've been chosen to become Governor of Domes, our newest Sol Empire world on Iota Piscium-C. Already, the advertisements are out asking for colonists to immigrate there. Plus, I'm going to have to check on the sixteen hundred who'll be undergoing the experiments of the Berktold Soros Group. So, I've got to move there. But I hope to be gone only a few weeks."

"But what about us?" asked Nikita. "It's summer vacation. We could come, too. Issi and Owen are going. Why not us?"

"I know you could, but who knows what kind of experiments this group is doing to the sixteen hundred people. I have to prevent more atrocities, if I can. Plus, it might not be safe there. The Third Invaders could return at any time. Our cruisers couldn't protect us from even one of their flying saucers. They'd sell us into slavery faster than we can blink. I need Isabella to translate the language found on documents on Domes."

That chilled their desires to come with me.

Finally, September came, and the heavily loaded Friendship departed for Iota Piscium-C, the world of Domes. I promised to return as soon as possible.
***
"Welcome, Governor Parkinson."

Dr. Westby greeted me as the Friendship landed on the pad close to the igloo-like main doors. Three other ships landed to our left.

"This is Ashton Soros of the Berktold Soros Group. He's conducting the experiment on the sixteen hundred people, per the agreement to avoid destroying everyone on Earth."

I sensed he wanted to remind me this man had the rights to do whatever he wanted to our people. I had the distinct feeling I wasn't going to like what I was about to discover.

Ashton gave me one of those I'm about to stab you in the back smiles. He stood six feet and wore a suit. Not just an ordinary suit, but an immaculate one. A vacuum sweeper couldn't suck a speck of dust from his clothes. Instant dislike.

"He has several degrees in psychology and behavior modifications. Well suited to conduct the Berktold Soros Group's experiments."

"Deanna Cartwright and crew. I've brought two hundred engineers and scientists to evaluate and study Domes. My daughter, Isabella, is going to attempt to decipher the language of those who build these domed towns. Where do we stay? I'd like to see our people as soon as possible."

"I estimate ten thousand people once lived in this domed city. There's plenty of room for your people. We're housing you close to the experiment side of town, but your crew should be kept as far from the experiment zone as possible. We're putting them up on the south side of town. Your new home, Governor, is just south of the experimental zone," Dr. Westby said. "If you'll follow me, I'll take you there, while Ashton can lead your crew to their homes. We can't read the alien street signs, so they're pretty pointless. This place is huge. Easy to get lost."

"Ashley and Sherry will stay with me. Lead on. But I want to visit our people as soon as possible."

As we walked, he said, "Incredible technology. At night, the walls sense your movement and light the way. No home has a roof, so during the day, sunlight lights us. Plus, the dome filters out harmful UV rays. I swear the designers thought of everything."

Once at our new home, Sherry and Ashley headed back to the ship to cart our bags and equipment here. Meanwhile, when Ashton joined us, we three headed north into the experiment zone. I gasped.

We'd stepped into one home that had been converted into a classroom. Twenty men and women sat before computers with holo displays. A head set with microphone perched on their heads. All were immersed in their studies.

All wore Leslie's fancy gowns designed for we armless telepaths. I spotted the usual tall heels that accompanied massive bosoms. Males wore similar gowns, but in more earthy colors. I could tell women from men because the women's pregnancies definitely showed. I knew Edyta had impregnated all the females in the colony. Some who had been captured months before the thousand looked like they were in their last month.

A helper robot stood beside each of the twenty. No, they didn't look like Sherry. Rather, these had arm-like appendages and moved about on wheels, about as unhuman-like as possible.

"I'm glad you have them clothed." I tried to say something positive. Edyta kept everyone naked and working on food production.

Ashton said, "Yes. Civilized. Each is now spending all their hours studying university courses. I had your Galactic Robotics modify their maid robots to serve them. Each robot is programmed to respond to the needs of one human. The robots are the people's personal servants, dressing them, feeding them, bathing them—handling their every need, so they can focus their attention on learning all they can. I've installed other robotics to handle the town's agriculture and food production. Each home has one of Earth's dry cleaning machines, along with a dishwasher. Your sixteen hundred ten people have everything they need."

"Thank you for clothing them. But how? When I left here, Edyta had installed the most vicious implant I'd ever seen."

"That's the whole point of this experiment," Ashton said. "Yes, at first, I didn't think we could do anything for them. However, our research group found a way. We re-mutated them using your armless telepath Galactic Doll agent, but at triple strength. During their brief comas and for a week after that, we re-implanted them. Let me explain. This is quite an achievement.

"Initially, they were implanted with this:

```
I love myself just the way I am. I don't
want to change anything about my body. I just
love how I look. It may take me longer to do
things and sometimes it's much harder, but I'm
very pleased with myself and my abilities. I'm
strong, smart, beautiful, and powerful. I'm
always cheerful, totally happy and content,
though I have to learn new ways to do things.
```

My life is precious to me.

    I am very happy to be here. I am part of a wonderful group. The colonists are the very best people. I want to always do my part for the colony. I must help other colonists, just as they help me. I love being here. I'm honored to be a member of this colony. I never want to leave. I'd rather die than leave this colony. I must follow the orders of the Council. They know what's best for us.

    I must have many, many children and with as many fathers or mothers as I can to help promote genetic diversity. I must have sex when I wake and at night. I will only be sexually satisfied after I've had a child by everyone in the colony. Having many children is vital for the survival of our wonderful colony. I promise to do my part.

    I will never forget any of these words. I will repeat them several times each day.

    "The trouble is the implant isn't specific about what they are to do, other then follow the Council's orders. You see, our group wants these sixteen hundred ten people to make a difference in society. Edyta wanted them to breed more telepaths and to make their own food and such. To be an independent society. Probably because she didn't want to provide them with anything from Earth. Primitive living so when their children got the opportunity to move off-world as a telepath, they'd jump at the chance to get away from such a low subsistence life."

    "I believe that was her intention. Has she been reprogrammed, too?"

    "Hardly. We're not about to educate a Third Invader! No, she's still around naked and doing menial chores. She's on latrine duty." The men chuckled. I didn't.

    "So we merely added a few more lines to the implant," Ashton said. "I'll play them for you." He fiddled with his phone.

    My personal robot handles my physical

needs so I can spend every possible hour of each day studying and learning all that I can. I must earn many college degrees. I must become as smart as possible. The future of the colony depends on me knowing as much as I can. There is no limit to what I can learn. I must devote myself to studying and having children.

"And there are the results. All sixteen hundred ten have been studying and advancing rapidly. The Group brought in a state of the art computer network with every known online course your empire has to offer. Some need highschool refresher courses, though. Still the results we're getting exceed my expectations. In a few years, why, you'll have an incredible pool of highly educated, brilliant people."

"Then what?" I asked. I couldn't believe he'd added to their maniac implants. "They're programmed to be unable to leave Domes."

"Tisk. Tisk. First, let's see how far they progress in their educations," Ashton replied. "We believe some of their thirst for knowledge will be inherited by their many children. In a couple decades, we might have some of the smartest people in the galaxy who are also telepaths. These people could well be the most valuable people in your empire.

"I should also tell you the new automated agricultural and food production facilities can feed five thousand people. So you're not going to have to worry about that until other colonists come. Also, the Group has authorized me to make you an additional offer. We're prepared to fill this dome city up with similar colonists. We'll handle their mutations and the cost of additional computer equipment and robots. Just say the word. The dome city can house about ten thousand people. You could have ten thousand genius telepaths for your empire. Just say the word."

I wanted to scream, but bit my tongue instead. "We should wait and see how this group fares first. Their lives can't be undone once this has been done to them."

"Point taken. It can't be undone. That's kind of the whole point. The Berktold Soros Group wants to salvage what those Third Invaders did to these people. This is possibly the very best idea yet."

"If it works." I countered. "How do we know who lives where? I'd like to visit some I know."

"Well, none have expressed any interest in locating any specific person. But we have that information available. Check your phone. Wait, let me."

He brought up the registry. I asked about Lia Johnston. She was in home Twenty-three. Next, he showed me a map of the streets and homes on this northern end. He'd labeled the streets North One, North Two, and so on, while the cross streets were West One, West Two, for example. Her home was on North Seven and West Nine.

"All houses have their new numbers plainly visible. We've got temporary street signs installed, mostly so we can find our way around. They usually stay in their homes. At night their robots fetch any needed supplies while the humans sleep. Efficient."

"Okay. I'm going to wander around some. You don't need to accompany me."

"I've got reports to fill out and deal with street and home naming for your new two hundred. Take your time. Our offices are in Number One by the main north entrance by your spaceship. Drop by when you're done."

With that, he left. After watching these twenty for a few more minutes, I headed off to find Lia. I could tell a lot by how she was doing.

I wandered around for a time. Many of our new arrivals passed by lugging crates of equipment and baggage. Ashton was correct. Each home had a large sign posted beside its front door. I found Number Twenty-Three and slipped inside, being quiet.

Senator Bill Fennel, her husband, sat at a desk beside Lia, along with eighteen others and twenty motionless robots to the right of each person. All had headsets with microphones. All were intently studying. I moved beside Lia, who did notice me. She looked up and into my eyes.

Instantly, hers watered heavily. It looked like she was studying a physics lesson. She said, "Pause. Help me. I love myself just the way I am. I don't want to change anything

288

about my body..."

I said nothing as she continued reciting her implanted words. She ended with, "I have to study. Help. Resume."

The computer continued playing the falling ball example. I shifted my position so I could see her eyes. Glazed over. I felt sick at my stomach. Conclusion: only a minimal amount of her attention was on anything in the present other than what she supposedly studied. In a flash, I realized their education was actually being recorded on a mental circuit. The person wasn't learning anything. The knowledge would be useless to them; these were people, not robots.

"Ah, found you," Ashley said. "We've got the temporary living quarters setup. Isabella is off exploring along with the others. Sherry sent me to find you. I think she's worried about something. This way. Hope I don't get lost."

When we entered our new quarters, Sherry just finished her bug weeping. "Safe. No bugs..." She voice hesitated, replace by a flashing red light on her device. She placed a finger to her lips and waved it around us. It flashed more rapidly the closer it got to my giant earrings. She pointed to a chair, which I took.

Ashley sat beside me, the color drained from her face. While Sherry closely examined my earrings, I reflected on all I'd said since receiving these earrings. Had I disclosed anything that should have been a secret? By the time Sherry removed it, I decided I hadn't revealed anything important. I sent a telepathic message to Isabella warning her.

Sherry whipped out her phone and typed a text message but didn't send it, showing it to us instead.

`Going to track where its signal is going to.`

"Ashley, stupid me. I left my bag on the Friendship. Can you help me fetch it?"

A bit of pink returned to her face.

"Ah, sure. Let's get it now. Then, we've got much work to do."

Sherry nodded approval. We three left, Sherry going a different direction than us. Once safely inside the spaceship, Ashley relaxed.

"That's scary. Who is spying on you? And why? Senior Ambassador Le Blanc? Why would she do that? Maybe she didn't know the earrings were bugged."

"Help me setup a long distance call to Sam."

Eventually, the connection activated, though the time delay was fifteen minutes, hardly fit to hold a conversation. I had Ashley write out the warning on a paper, asking Sam to have Holly Ann see if she could find the bug in Nikita's earrings and remove it. He promised he would. That done, we headed back.

Sherry sat at our dining room table, a pad of paper in hand. I read: Traced the signal to Ashton Soros's room. Removed Isabella's bug. Should destroy them now?

After Ashley read the note, we three looked at each other, unsure the best route to take. I suspected Sherry couldn't compute the best action to take. Ashley looked spooked. So I decided for us.

"Break them," I said firmly.

Sherry crushed the four bugs between her fingers.

"I wasn't sure if we should confront Soros about this or not," Sherry said.

"This way, it'll look like we found them and destroyed them. And that we didn't bother tracing signals," I said. "I don't trust that man. What that Group is doing to our people is almost as bad as what Edyta was doing."

"But aren't they gaining tremendous educations?" Ashley asked. Lines formed on her forehead, as her brows rose.

"I visited Lia Johnston. All that supposed learning is merely building up mental circuits, rather like a recorder. None of it is reaching the person. They won't be able to use any of it. All they can do is play it back like one of Isabella's language tapes. It's a total waste of time. Ashton Soros must have some other motive in mind, because none of these people is getting any educational benefit from their studies."

"Just keeping them occupied?" Ashley asked, scratching her head.

"Yeah, think so. Likely a disguised telepath breeding group," I said.

Before the others could comment, a squeaking noise distracted us. Edyta arrived at the front door, pushing a janitor's cart.

Glassy-eyed, she said, "Clean toilet now."

She shuffled past us, pushing her cart along. Her hair was a tangled mess, and she wore no clothes. We watched in silence as she struggled to do the task with her feet and toes, all the while whispering the usual implant words. When she finished and rose to her feet, our eyes met. For the briefest moment, she recognized me, but then the fog of her implant returned. She pushed her cart on out of our new home.

"So that's the treacherous Third Invader that did all this to our colonists," Ashley said. "Serves her right. She gets to experience what she's done to our people."

"True," I said, "but Soros should show her some dignity. At least clothe her."

"Even though she had our people living naked?" Ashley asked, her hands on her hips. "I think not."

"We aren't the animal she is," I said, vowing to speak to Ashton about it.

"Hey, there you are. Been looking for you," Eve said. Lara continued to watch the receding form of Edyta.

"Hi, Eve, Lara."

"Hey, we've finished our genetic analysis of the sixteen hundred. They've used a slightly modified mutation agent on them," Eve said.

"Different than the original version the Third Invaders used?" I asked.

"Yes. During those months we've been gone, the Soros Group used a new agent on them. They're still manifesting the usual Galactic Doll mutations, giant breasts, mutated feet, and no arms."

Lara butted in, "But it's just enough different so our arm regrow cure won't work."

"And this mutation is highly dominant," Eve added, "more powerful than all the others used on Earth thus far."

"Plus, they've lost their telepathic abilities," Lara said, stamping her foot on the floor. "That's very nasty of them. Crippling these people with no benefits. Criminal, if you ask me."

"What? So they aren't trying to breed telepaths?" I asked, feeling my brows rising sharply, as did creases on my forehead. "What the hell's going on here? Time to get some answers from this Ashton fellow. Come on."

I stormed off to find Ashton Soros, the four others trailing me.

A grey cloud engulfed me. Coughing, I slowly collapsed onto the floor. As the body slipped into another mutation coma, I rose up and out of my body, intent on finding out what was happening. I spotted strangers in has-mat suits carrying bodies out of the dome. I followed along and watched them put them into a spaceship. I'd never see this kind before. Who were these people? I saw them carrying Ashley's body out and later Deanna's. No, this can't be happening. No. No. No.

Ashley's hand rested on my shoulder. "What's wrong? Now what?"

No grey cloud, only the sunshine-lit hallway. I swallowed and blinked.

"Had a vision. Another mutation attack on everyone here. Ashley, Sherry, go warn the others. Get everyone back to the ships and lift off, but hang around and see what happens next. I'll delay seeing Ashton Soros until everyone is out of the dome."

"What about you, boss?" Ashley asked. Her face lacked all color.

"I'll stay with her and protect her," Sherry said. "That's my job. Come on. We have to get others out of the dome."

While they dashed off, I wandered by Lia's home. There she sat mindlessly watching that education class. I decided to do some mind probing. Did she still have telepathy? A light touch told all. Quickly, I touched the other nineteen men and women. No telepathic abilities remained in any of them. I sent a telepathic "you're right" to Eve. Something very fishy was going on, but what? This made no sense. Telepathic skill was the only positive benefit of the armless mutation agent. Why would these people want to remove it? Were they sadistic?

Again, I lightly brushed Lia's mind. A whitish-grey cloud encased her and her mind. I saw what appeared to be a voice recorder playing in the background, rattling off the implanted words in a continuous loop. Out before her eyes, another voice recorder took in what she was hearing and seeing, the knowledge circuit. These studies wouldn't be useable by these people, just more recordings on a new mental circuit. I had to get this stopped.

Chapter 27 Reverse Engineering

"So I ask you again, Ashton, what the hell is going on here?"

The others had quietly departed, the four ships jumping into hyperspace at zero velocity. Then I found Ashton Soros and complained.

His covert demeanor escalated. With a sneer, he said, "They warned me about you, Parkinson. Seems they were right. You are a meddler. Well, I'm no fool. Prepared for this. I saw the ships leaving. So you're the only one left."

"I'm not about to let you mutate all those new arrivals. What kind of a beast are you?" I spat out.

"So you think you've outsmarted us, eh? Ruined our Plan A. I was supposed to gas everyone if you caused trouble. Ah, well. A wise man always has backups. You think you're so bright. Bah."

"Look, we've verified you've re-mutated all sixteen hundred, removing their telepathic ability. Making them live handicapped lives is bad enough, but wiping out their telepathic skill removes the sole aspect that allowed them to make a good living. All that supposed learning they're getting is wasted. They're only storing it on mental circuits. Won't do them the slightest good. What you're doing is inhumane."

"You really are quite observant. We know they aren't really learning anything. That isn't the point of this experiment. It's a known fact you can't educate via implants."

"I'll bite. So what's the whole point of this? These colonists were tricked by the Third Invaders, turned into armless telepath Galactic Dolls, and formed into a breeding colony. Several women are due to give birth any day, though most are only halfway through their pregnancies. Now instead of regrowing their arms and helping them restore their shattered lives, you've removed their telepathic abilities and have them mindlessly watching education courses all day long. I call that a betrayal on top of a betrayal."

"I can see why I was warned about you. Okay, I'll show you what we're doing with them. This way." His arm motioned me out of his office door.

I turned and headed outside to the long hallway, pleased that he would show me what the purpose of the experiment actually was. Perhaps, I thought, I'm getting somewhere.

I felt a pinprick on my neck and wished I had arms to swat it away. The world turned grey and then black. I did feel hands catching me, preventing my collapse onto the solid floor. Tendrils of a swirling grey cloud enclosed my mind like a spherical vice. By the time I computed I'd been drugged and backed out of my head to recover and see what was happening, significant time had passed.

As my native vision turned on, confusing me with its spherical vision—all directions at one time—I sensed a moving spaceship. One of those silly helper robots sat inert beside my body, which laid on a very narrow bed. Rows of beds. Rows of robots. Twenty of us in this room, while twenty robots had recharging wires attached to wall outlets. I sensed movement or vibrations. Conclusion: we're being flown somewhere. Voices. I drifted toward the sounds.

"Yeah, I tell you that Parkinson woman and her daughter had electronic bugs in those giant earrings."

I recognized the voice of Ashton Soros. "Yes, I searched. Found a LD Relay hidden in my office. No, I don't know how it got there. Someone is or rather was spying on them. She claims to have destroyed the bugs."

"Yeah, I know. But she gave me no choice but to move up the timetable. The results of Phase 1 are positive. I know it called for a full six months indoctrination, but four will have to do. All indicators are positive."

After a pause, he said, "We shouldn't have a problem with Phase 2. Yeah, I'll go ahead and do her now. Over and out."

A wash of aesthetic white energy swept over me, generating that wonderful serenity akin to what I felt when in the presence of Empress Kalindi Amandani. Only I heard words.

I love myself just the way I am. I don't want to change anything about my body. I just

love how I look. It may take me longer to do
things and sometimes it's much harder, but I'm
very pleased with myself and my abilities. I'm
strong, smart, beautiful, and powerful...

On it went. Of course I loved myself. I knew I was
strong and smart. Whoosh. I got sucked into the same implant
script the other sixteen hundred had. As I blacked out, I
realized the trigger had been my own agreement with the
opening lines. I vowed not to agree next time.

"Welcome, everyone, to the Soros University here in
Muscoda, Bela Prime, the most prestigious university in the
galaxy. You're in the married students' dormitory housing
complex of this sprawling campus. Your robots know where
everything is located, so just depend upon them."

I blinked rapidly, trying to focus and orientate myself. I
lay naked on a soft bed, my robot standing beside me, clothing
resting at the foot of the bed. The voice came from within the
wall overhead. I looked about and saw Lia and Bill Fennel
lying in the next bed across the room from me. A small dining-
kitchen area to my left looked vaguely familiar.

At this point, the implant words came flowing out of my
mouth, but I tried to focus on the disembodied voice, which
sounded vaguely familiar to me. Admittedly, I wasn't all there
at the moment.

"Congratulations to each and everyone of you. To be
selected to attend Soros University with full scholarships is a
very high honor. Kudos to all sixteen hundred eleven of you
who made it. All your physical needs are fully paid for. Your
only task is to study as hard as you have been back in your
colony. When you graduate, you can then return to your
colony as highly trained, competent men and women."

"Soros University does have a strict dress code. You've
been provided with acceptable school apparel. The campus is
home to fifty thousand students from many different worlds.
You should wear your language translators at all times.

"After you are dressed and fed, your class schedules are
on the dining room table. We've programmed the robots to
easily navigate you and your computers to the various
classrooms and on time, too. On behalf of Soros University, I'd

like to welcome each and everyone of you top scholars to our incredible school. Thank you."

"My name is Cleo. Please rise, Molly, so I can dress you," my robot said in its monotone.

I struggled to sit up, still reciting the implanted words. My feet wouldn't lie flat on the floor. I should know what that meant, but it eluded me just now. I did my best to follow the robot's commands as it dressed me.

Silky, smooth, polymer, black, seamed stockings encased my legs, held up by a garter belt. I vaguely recalled seeing something like this before. Okay, my mind wasn't functioning quite right. A white silk blouse with tiny sleeves fit my giant bosom so snugly the robot found buttoning it a challenge. A short, black skirt with belt came next, followed by shiny black tall spiked heels with an ankle strap. I tried to protest that I needed my feet and toes, that I couldn't undo the straps, but I just mumbled more of the implanted verbiage. Finally, Cleo tied a black, short tie around my neck and under the blouse's collar.

"Get up. Eat breakfast," it said, moving across the tiled floor to the small kitchen area.

Wobbling as I got my balance, I thought I hated wearing such tall heels. No, these were even taller than... Sorry, I couldn't recall what. I took careful, shuffling steps to the table. Lia and Bill were already there and being fed by their robots.

"Molly?" Lia said. A tear formed, but the robot stuffed another fork of eggs into her mouth.

I think we had a good breakfast. At the moment, thinking wasn't my strongest attribute. Cleo fed me. Actually, it did a good job of it, aware of my readiness for another bite. He produced a straw for my tea, adjusting it so it was within easy ready. While I sipped and read over my class schedule, he fetched my new computer and language translator, the latter of which he secured to my belt.

Economics 101 began at 9 a.m. in Room 110, Soros Econ Laboratory. Cleo picked up my schedule and stuffed it in my blouse pocket.

"Brush hair. Come," it said.

I followed the robot to the bathroom, but we handled necessities first before it brushed out my hair, tying it back in a ponytail.

"Students wear hair this way," it said. "We must walk to class now."

Lia, Bill, and I followed our robots out the door. I couldn't open it while dressed like this. We three looked nearly identical with our giant bosoms prominently on display in these tight blouses, long hair, and tall heels. An escalator affair took us to the ground floor. At least the outside doors opened automatically.

For a moment, we three just stood there gawking at the sight. Hundreds, thousands of young men and women all wearing identical apparel moved about the concrete walkways, a sea of white tops and black bottoms. Normal men wore white shirts and black pants, but our Galactic Doll men looked just like Lia and me. The normal women also wore equally tall heels with ankle straps, so we fit right in with the other women on campus. My giant earrings did get quite a few stares as did our cute, but empty sleeves.

Classroom buildings lined either side of the giant concrete walkway called the Rectangle. The single person's dorms lay at the far end of the Rectangle, a fact pointed out by the robots. I focused on not falling down, but slowly my mind regained some measure of normalcy, though the implanted words continued to bounce around my brain.

Men frequently dashed past women. For once, being handicapped didn't matter. All women moved both slowly and carefully, though they did stare at our empty shoulders. Most men, however, gawked at our bosoms.

The buildings were giant rectangles of red stone or brick with glass windows. Most housed at least ten floors. Ten signs in front of the Soros Econ Laboratory identified it in many languages. To my surprise, English was one of them. Four large entrance doors allowed many to enter at one time. Men preferred to rush and took the left-most doors, while slower moving women opted for the right doors. All were automatic, though.

As I entered, a young woman joined me. "Hey ya. Ya

must be one of dem Iota Piscium-C women. Gosh, you really don't have any arms. I'm Marki."

While she didn't speak English, my box translated her words, more or less.

"Hi. Molly." I did my utmost to not vocally recite the implanted words. Again. Not in front of her.

"Golly, you sure have whoppers. I do love your earrings and long hair," she said. Seeing her hazel eyes and smile allowed me to relax. "I've got Econ 101."

"Me, too. Kind of lost."

"We were told ta make ya'll feel at home. That they programmed your robots to know where t'all is at. But there's signs." She pointed upwards. Signs, again in ten languages, indicated room sequences and directions. "Beginning classes are on ground floor. But are escalators to upper floors. We best take ones on right. Guys are always late and rushing about and take ones to left. We canna rush at all. But these heels are **so** cool! Donna ya think? So sexy."

"I can't walk without them. Have to wear them." I managed to get two sentences out without spouting: I love myself just the way I am. I don't want to change…

Marki chuckled. "We all have ta wear them. If'en we wanna attend Soros U. Dress code, too. I love the stockings and blouse. Very expensive. Here we are. Wanna sit by me? I can help ya if'en the robot cain't."

"Sure. Thanks," I muttered, once more fighting from spouting the implant words.

Cleo got my computer out. It booted up in two seconds. Now I was impressed. To my left, Marki took out hers. I smiled. Identical computers. We fit in with the student body. Curious.

Her shoulder length hair was fiery orange. I wondered where she was from and if that was her natural hair color, but simply couldn't vocalize anything that lengthy. Damn implant! Heck, I probably never heard of her world; at least I didn't show my ignorance.

The holo display flashed a message: Say Record when lecture starts. Stop, when done.

My eyes opened wide. In walked the professor, a robot

at his side. Like us, he too lacked arms, but otherwise looked like ordinary men, probably in his late fifties. Both Marki and I said "record" at about the same time. So did forty other classmates, twenty of us from Earth.

Conveniently, the computer recorded his lecture and visuals, but translated them into English. I glanced at the words scrolling by on Marki's computer, but saw only weird symbols, her alphabet, I presumed.

When the lecture ended, Marki said, "You're in married dorm. Black tie. Mine tie's red. I'm over in the Single's Dorm. Room 1545. Come by some evening. We cain chat."

The Electronics Lab hosted my next class: Reverse Engineering 101. Section Z. My mind settled down a little during the long walk to this stainless steel and glass building. While I would have preferred a long walk to get a grip on my mind, Cleo kept hustling me along. While hundreds of men and women filed into the building, my lab was in Room 1510. I took the right side ramps, trying hard to remember what Marki told me. Yes, guys did rush up the escalators, two steps at a time. I wondered why they were in such a rush.

When Cleo and I stepped off on the fifteenth floor, so did Lia, Bill, and two others from the colony. We five and our robots entered the lab room, filled with electronic equipment. I wished Holly Ann could be here and see all this stuff of which I knew nothing. Imagine my surprise when Ashton Soros walked into the room wearing the same apparel as all other males did on campus, whether a student or faculty.

"Ah, Molly Parkinson. Good to see you're finding your way around our university. Is Cleo handling your needs okay?"

"What did? Yes." That's all I dared say, because I sensed the implant words about to burst out. Crap. They did anyway. "I love myself just the way I am. I don't want to change..." I bit down on my lips, stifling the rest of the litany which continued to replay in my mind.

He chuckled, adding to my disgust. Hearing me mutter the words caused Lia and Bill to recite them. In turn the other couple spoke theirs, too. Wisely, Ashton waited until we finished saying the words.

"As the Berktold Soros Group promised, we're here to

see if we can salvage what the Third Invaders did to the colonists. The first phase is complete, except for Molly, that is. We'd planned for you to work and study with your robots for six months. Why? To get you totally used to the robot handling your physical needs. Molly's intervention cut that short, but we're probably okay. Even Molly is doing well with Cleo's help.

"Your telepathic ability has been removed, genetically, that is. Why? That alone is just too great a temptation for the unethical to kidnap and sell you into telepath slavery."

"You unethical," I tried to counter, still struggling to keep from reciting the words all over again.

He ignored me. "In this phase, we are going to reverse engineer the Third Invader's implants you're suffering from. That's what all this equipment in this lab is for. Professor Heli will be here shortly to run the equipment, testing her theory. You are the first to have it done. Mind you, all this is still in the experimental stage, so you'll report here every other day for class. Professor Heli will test you and monitor your progress. We're confident we can now undo these electronic implants.

"In Phase 1, we proved a cleverly designed second implant can completely alter the initial electronic implant. Edyta had you all living naked and trying to run the colony using your feet and toes. Unbelievably crude. Our secondary modification had you dressed, dependent upon a robot helper, and studying from dawn to dusk. Quite a change, if I say so myself.

"But as Molly pointed out, that learning was merely a circuit. Heck, you probably don't follow what I'm saying even now. Doesn't matter. Here comes Professor Heli."

In walked another woman, dressed just as we were. She had long black hair akin to mine. What surprised me was she too had no arms. What the heck was going on? Crap. The implanted words rattled off in my mind once again. I just stared at her.

All her equipment was voice-activated, but she also had a helper robot.

Ashton said, "Begin with Molly. She should be the easiest case."

"How long was she under the implant?" Professor Heli

asked. My language translator converted her Federation Common into English.

Ashton answered, and she said, "Good. Yes, the easiest case. Molly, sit there, where Fel is pointing. My robot will rest the head harness on your skull. Fine. Power up. Level Nine. Activate."

She said additional words, but I didn't hear them. No, that unbelievable white aesthetic energy field obliterated all. Serenity. I felt something like an electric spark—the kind you get when you suddenly unplugged something that's on. Sparks. The device sucked mental energy out of my mind. I sensed the implanted words, the mental mass, the pain, the unconsciousness—all of it being sucked out of my mind. My instinctive reaction fought against that being ripped away from me. Yet, I couldn't prevent it from being stripped from my mind. And it hurt.

"How are you feeling?" Professor Heli asked. She'd turned the machine off. I'd lost track of time.

"Got a bad headache. Otherwise... What the hell did you do to me?" I asked. In spite of the throbbing head, I could think clearly again.

"The theory is," she said, "that with the right energy levels, one can extract those implanted memories from your mind and brain cells. Reverse polarization. Do you have any compulsion to recite those words?"

"Huh? Well, no. Magic. Yes, it's gone. I feel like I lost something, though. Kind of like someone stole something from me."

"Excellent. Ashton, I think this is going to work. Chat with Molly, please, while I work on the others," Professor Heli said.

She spent fifteen minutes on each, beginning with Lia.

"Why did you kidnap me and re-mutate me?" I asked, wishing I could rub my forehead.

"Because you were about to wreck everything. We had no idea if this new theory would work. We've erased the implant I gave you. Damned impressive. Perhaps we've no a way to undo the Third Invaders' implants. The Sixth Invaders are using that tech in your neck of the galaxy. Until Heli's invention, termination was the only answer, except for your miraculous cure of Senior Ambassador Lara Axe-head, that is."

"What happened to her arms? My Econ professor lacked arms, as well."

"We take only the brightest and ablest professors here at Soros U. We, in the Psych department, have discovered many of those without arms compensate for their disability in other ways. Some by becoming beyond brilliant, as many of the professors here have. When provided their own robot assistant, they are free to develop their mental facilities. The Berktold Soros Group scours all known worlds for the best and brightest people. We have a campus with fifty thousand incredible minds, learning all they can."

"Why us?" I asked.

"If Professor Heli can undo what the Third Invaders did to them and now that they're familiar with using their robot helpers, they'll be free to fully develop their minds. The Psych Department believes from these sixteen hundred, we may find at least half will become stellar individuals, excelling in their fields or even becoming great professors. Those who don't wish to study will be taken back to Domes. They'll then be your problem, though we'll send the robots along with them. It'd be cruel not to do that. All that stay will have full scholarships, costing them nothing for their advanced educations."

He chuckled. "Of course, within the Psych Department, there is a betting pool on how many of the sixteen hundred eleven will stay and become brilliant."

"Can I talk with Professor Heli later on? About what she's doing?"

"Of course. I hope you will choose to stay here at Soros U and develop your mind. If you do, I promise to see your family is brought here to join you. All expenses paid."

"Tell me, just how many armless teachers do you have? Are there other armless students? Not including us, of course," I asked. My curiosity roused and my mind working again.

"Half of our faculty or six hundred ten. All brilliant professors. Very able. We do have nine hundred six handicapped students out of our nearly fifty thousand. Not counting your new additions. As you attend classes while we're working on erasing your people's implants, notice just how able these professors are. They're geniuses. Those who are students like yourself show incredible potential or they wouldn't be here. This is a highly exclusive university. Perhaps the best in the galaxy."

Professor Heli finished working on Lia. Bill swapped places with her, while Lia sat beside me.

"My head. I've never had such a bad, throbbing headache. I'm almost nauseous. Molly! You're here. We got attacked by the Third Invaders. At least I think so. I think I'm missing a bunch of memories. I feel like I've lost something. Something huge. Important."

"You have," Ashton said. "You've lost all those implants." He explained what he'd already told me.

"I'm not reciting a bunch of words, whatever they were, so I guess that's something. So we were horribly mutated and implanted? The Third Invaders really did betray us. Well, they deserved what they got. I wish I could rub my head."

When Professor Heli finished the last one, she said, "Don't forget to be here same time in two days. Follow your class schedule. We've no idea if this treatment is permanent or not."

"So we could wake up tomorrow remembering everything?" asked Lia.

"We just don't know. Let's hope not," Ashton said. "Now, go get some lunch. Student cafeteria gets crowded about now. Robots will lead you."

"God, the air feels so good on my face," Lia said. "My mind feels like it's got cobwebs in it. I've lost something important." She sighed. "What a headache."

"I can't remember how you got here," she asked me. "Can you tell me or maybe you can't recall either?"

We had a long walk to the cafeteria located close to the Single's Dorm. Thousands of other students also headed there for lunch. Men dashed past women, except for a few who held hands.

Lia said, "Incredible. This blouse and these stockings feel fabulous against my skin. Never noticed that before."

Bill added, "You can say that again. I feel a hundred

pounds lighter, but it's as if someone stole something vital from me. What a crazy feeling. Does anyone remember what happened after we blacked out just after landing? My headache is a doozy."

No's echoed. So I brought them up to date. If nothing else, maybe it would trigger their recalls of the implants they'd endured. Maybe Professor Heli's engineering didn't work. It wouldn't do to have someone mention a trigger word only to have the whole implant return full-force.

As we entered the huge cafeteria building, Marki waved at me.

"Hi ya," she called out and joined us. "Hey, this way. Lane thirty-six is always less busy. More of your people?" she asked.

I introduced Lia and Bill.

"Whoa! So it is true. Some of your women be really men!" She stared at Lia and then Bill, until his face reddened. "Cain't tell any dif. You sure us's a man?"

"Yes, absolutely. Lia is expecting our first child in a few more months," he said. I sensed he wanted to deflect her attention. I noticed my telepathic ability still present.

"Lia shows, but med's got ways for women-women babies. Well, I tell'ya I heard some'o your'n are men, but didna believe it. He's just as hot as you two are. Good thing ya'll married. Guys might be all over ya, Bill. Ah, here we are. Cafeteria style. Pick and choose. It's free. Much as ya can eat."

Buffet style would be our term. Each dish had ten labels on them. We picked what we thought might be good to eat. Turns out, it was real food, not the synth stuff. Foreign tastes, though.

Later, I went to Calculus class. While getting my Gen Ed degree, I'd gotten my math skills somewhat improved. So Calc was my next step. The building looked like one of Earth's medieval fortresses. Quaint and picturesque, but tall with many windows. My professor was another armless woman. Three for three. Perhaps, Ashton had purposely chosen these professors for me.

She began by saying, "I was born without arms. The Federation makes incredible prostheses for missing feet, legs, and hands. But the whole arm ones are heavy and virtually useless, cosmetic only. So we use these robots as our hands. Calculus plays a vital role in the development of robots. Let's see how."

I began to believe Ashton had chosen these classes for me, when I attended my last class of the day, basic physics. The armless professor did a good job, and I became engrossed in his lecture. When the lecture ended, I was sure I had been setup by Ashton.

When we finally returned to our dorm room and could relax, my headache had pretty much vanished. However, both Lia and Bill felt bad. Lia began crying. I sat beside her.

"What's wrong?"

"I feel I lost something vitally important. Like its been stolen from me. Worse, I have this horrible ache in my stomach. Molly, we murdered ten thousand innocent Third Invaders. We thought we were getting justice for their massive betrayal of our men and the colonists. Not sure what happened to them; I still can't remember that part. I feel so guilty. I might throw up."

"I do too," Bill added. "I feel sick about what we did. We never should have murdered all those people. We boiled them alive while they slept. They never had a chance. Even children died."

The other two who shared our dorm headed down to find supper. They'd been original colonists. I stayed with Lia and Bill.

"Both of you, close your eyes. Okay. Now return to when you first had the idea to get revenge on the Third Invaders." They nodded. "Good. Go through that and tell me what you did."

Off I went, trying to run two therapy sessions at the same time. Not any real choice. If I chose to run Lia, Bill would have overheard and run his identical trauma. Rather, I should say they were running through trauma they'd given to others.

"The slate isn't balanced. Being handicapped like this is sort of making up for it, but it would be better if I was also implanted like you told us we were," Lia said. "I killed ten thousand people. Nothing can ever make up for that."

"She's right, Molly. Nothing can. When we set off to do it, I knew it was wrong. I stay in my cabin most of the time. Being helpless can only partially make up for what we did. I wish we'd stayed implanted or whatever had happened to us. I just can't remember."

Oh, god. What a mess. Still, I persevered and ran them through it several more times, making them be very specific about what they did, when, who, and where. At last, I asked if there was something they'd done that was similar and earlier in time. Both floundered saying, "No" several times, before they actually spotted blackish masses around their heads.

Many recountings later, I had the full story from each of them. Lia had shot and killed her husband during a domestic dispute in her last lifetime.

"They said it was an accident and justified, but I knew what I was doing in that moment," she said, finally relieved.

Bill, on the other hand, had been complicit in a robbery gone wrong in which his pal had killed the woman they were robbing. That had happened some three hundred years ago.

I ended the sessions and had our robots fix us a snack, since the supper hour had long passed. The other two joined us just as we sat down to eat. While I didn't pay too much attention to either, they didn't look happy. I admit I was too exhausted, falling asleep the moment Cleo tucked me into bed.

Coughing woke me in the morning.

"Time to get up, Molly," Cleo said. "Are you well?"

"Yeah, feeling lots better. No headache. What's with the others?"

"I believe they have what you call colds. Sit up. Time to dress."

"Another white silk blouse?"

Cleo attempted to chuckle. I think that was the proper interpretation of his noise.

"All apparel is identical. Your closet has a dozen white blouses and black skirts. Six leather heels. All the same. Every woman on the Soros U campus has identical blouses, skirts, stockings, and shoes. Only the tie color is different. Black for married people, red for singles. All men wear identical apparel, too. School policy."

By the time Cleo finished his explanation, he had me dressed. I felt alert and awake this morning, quite a change from yesterday. The silky blouse and stockings felt electrifying against my skin. Could it be their construction materials?

The robots made and fed us our breakfast: bacon, eggs, toast, butter, yogurt, and tea. That's what Cleo claimed the food was. The tastes were slightly off. The other four coughed occasionally while we ate. They sneezed and had runny noses. That reminded me Celeste once observed people often experienced a sudden or shocking loss right before getting ill. Hum.

This morning, I had a particularity long walk to my first class in the Language Lab, close to the Single's Dorm at the far end of the Rectangle. I met Marki coming my way and waited for her.

"Federation Common 100?" I asked.

She grinned. "Ya. Gotta learn it. Suppose'ta be common t'all worlds. Heard big push ta make it so. You look good today."

"I feel myself today. You look fine yourself. Say, do you know what material these blouses and stocking are made from? They feel..."

"Real sexy?" she finished with a giggle.

My face felt hot, but I nodded.

"Donna know. Gonna find out, though. Donna have anythin like it on my world. Come on. Donna wanna be late."

Professor Lakebottom, didn't surprise me. Not after yesterday. I was certain Ashton wanted to prove to me the validity of his position. She didn't need arms to have us practicing our Federation Common. First though, she instructed everyone to turn off the language translators, which Cleo did for me. For two hours, we recited simple sentences and questions. I felt like I was five years old again. So this was what Isabella and Bernardo endured learning new languages. Such was not for me, but learning Federation Common would be very useful for me. Two hours passed rapidly.

I did notice Marki continued to practice Federation Common while we walked out. On our way to lunch together, Marki asked, "So you must be very wealthy. Those earrings.

Usually worn by Senior Ambassadors."

"Nope, not really. Senior Ambassador Le Blanc, the President of the Circle of Ambassadors, gave them to me and a pair to my daughters, too."

Marki's eyes widened. "Wow. You must be important woman."

"She's trying to persuade me to become a Senior Ambassador."

"They're beautiful," Marki said. "Come by tonight. We chat."

"If I can. Say, my language unit translates your Fed Common words much better than it does your usual language."

Marki giggled. "I'm practicing it when I'm with you."

My last class was pilot training. I laughed. "Cleo, I could pilot very well when I could use my feet and toes. Dressed like this, it's gonna be a joke."

"I follow your commands. You pilot. Me, your arms."

I doubted that. This building looked somewhat like a grey rocket ship, the tallest building on campus. Our class Piloting 101 was on the first floor, but signs suggested this building had a hundred floors. Once inside, I saw why. The floor area was small compared to all other buildings I'd been in, only four classrooms per floor.

When I entered, I felt quite nervous and ill at ease. How could I be a pilot dressed like this? The outfit made me pretty much helpless to do more than walk very slowly. This time, I told myself, we're going to have a person with arms conducting the class.

I looked around the classroom. Six of us lacked arms, but several were our people, perhaps pilots originally chosen to be colonists.

In walked a middle aged woman with her robot.

"Welcome to Piloting 101. I'm Commander Kalos and pilot of the Bela Prime light cruiser, Windsong. Lost my arms when I was four. That didn't stop me, and it damn well better not stop you. I saw many of you staring at the six students who don't have arms. Well, you can stare at me, too. Now before I begin, how many of you already have a pilot's license for some form of spaceship? Please stand if you are a licensed pilot."

Several men stood. Not to be outdone, I stood, too. Commander Kalos smiled at me. I heard murmurs and inhales.

"What do you pilot?" she asked me.

"Transports up to but not including light cruisers," I said.

"So that bit of business is settled. Let's get down to real piloting. But I should warn you six, your robot assistants don't think. They only obey your commands. So if you tell them to steer the ship into a sun, it will do so. You can't depend on them to think an original thought. Enough said.

"Class, when I'm done with you, you'll be able to pilot all craft including a light cruiser. In subsequent courses, you can increase your competency levels all the way to piloting a battleship. Let's begin."

For once, I knew most of what she had to tell us. Today, anyway. I felt cheerful while walking back to the dorm. As I neared, I heard others coughing. I had a hunch colds were going to be commonplace among our people.

Once in our room, I discovered Lia and Bill ran fevers. These robots could sense body temperatures.

Lia coughed and said, "Molly, it's funny. All day, I've been seeing memories of what happened to us after the Bolt landed on Iota Piscium-C. Even the implant words are there, but none of it bothers me in the slightest. Kind of like recalling what I had for supper. How weird is that? This cold is getting us both down."

Their robots spoke up. "We take you to infirmary now. Can walk?"

I watched them wobble out of our room. Wisely, the robots put steadying arm appendages around their waists. Either that, I thought, or carry them.

I laid back on my bed. I finally had time for myself. First, I tested my telepathy. Whoa! In fact, my telepathic ability had increased noticeably. *I'm not telling a soul that I still have it!* I checked and found I still had memories of what happened to me after Ashton had knocked me out. Lia's observations proved correct. The memories had returned, but had no importance or effect on me. Somehow Professor Heli's process had stripped the energy out of the incident. That meant trauma energy was *real* electricity . That will interest Celeste and Holly Ann back home.

Bored, I decided to take Marki up on her suggestion I visit her. I'd forgotten what room she'd said she was in, and I didn't have her contact number. So I placed the concept to have her call me into her mind. Minutes later, my new computer beeped. Cleo opened it for me, and I took her call.

"Hi ya. Wanna come over?" Marki said.

"You bet. What's your room number?"

Although full dark had come, the sky had so many stars shining down on us that it was nearly daytime. No need for campus night lights! Bela Prime is close to the center axis of the galaxy. A barred spiral, Sam used to tell me. The bar covered the night sky.

Cool nighttime air only increased the wonderful sensations coming from the stockings and my blouse. But I had to walk the entire length of the Rectangle. I hadn't thought of that. The stockings constantly massaged my legs and knees. Interesting. I felt invigorated when the doors to the Single's Dorm opened and I entered, Cleo at my side. He seemed to know the route so I let him lead.

When we reached her door, I couldn't knock, but Cleo did.

"Hi ya! Come on in. Ignore the mess. Mates are in the game room."

I didn't need telepathy to sense she was very happy to have me over. Her dorm room housed five, just like ours did, identical layouts. Several open closet doors revealed dozens of identical white blouses and black skirts.

"Sorry about the long walk. Forgot about the heels. Are you used to them yet? Can you imagine? Heels seven nuks tall? Oh, a nuks is about this much." She showed a length with her fingers, about an inch. "I'm gonna try to speak in Fed Com as much as I can. My translator does okay with your words."

"Thanks. Yes, I'm used to them."

"Well, we never had such tall heels before. I spent all orientation week just trying to get used to them and not fall down. Most do. Everyone says it just takes getting used to. Anyway, every woman on Bela Prime wears them. Professional looks. You weren't here during orientation, were you?"

"No, I just arrived Monday."

"Well, they explained we should always wear a professional outfit, unless a job requires a uniform. 'A professional appearance promotes self-worth and instills confidence in others.' That's what they drilled into our heads. We've been here a couple weeks; every woman we've seen has the professional look and these tall heels, though they have some variety in styles, which we don't. So have you been out into the city yet?"

"No, I haven't. I always try to look professional, though on my world dress gowns have replaced this blouse-skirt look."

"Well, you're gonna have to go out with us on Saturday. We'll make a day of it. Saturdays are supposed to be our socializing day. No studying allowed, but Pektor seems to ignore it. He's one of my roommates. Casti and Lori are the other two. We three women had an awful time getting used to the heels. Thank stars for orientation week. Come on. Let's go meet them. They wanna meet you. Someone said they saw you in pilot's class. That right?"

"Yes, I already am licensed to pilot smaller ships, like transports."

"I can't imagine how. But then I suppose your robot handles the controls for you. Anyway, come on. The others are in the game room playing Detective."

I followed her, Cleo behind me. "What's Detective?"

"Only the hottest game in the dorm. We're from Snaggard-C. That's in the Sagittarius Arm. We have full scholarships to Soros U. Either that or you gotta be very rich to afford to come here. This place costs a fortune, but our scholarships pay for everything. Even gives us a hundred credits to spend in town each Saturday."

"Do they give out many scholarships?"

"I think a third of the campus has one. Maybe more. Honestly, this university has a reputation of being the best one in the whole Federation. People come here from everywhere. Those that can afford it, that is. The rest of us can, only if we get a scholarship. I'm majoring in aeronautics. Want to help my world build better spaceships. And get rich, too." She laughed.

We entered a large room filled with game tables and lots of people. She led me to her mates.

"Molly, this is Pektor."

A young man about five inches shorter than me in my heels rose, his eyes darting from my bosom, to my earrings, to my empty blouse sleeves.

"Oh, we should speak Fed Com, cause her translator box doesn't handle our language very well."

"Wow! Welcome, Molly. Gosh, you're something else. Kinda didn't believe Marki when she told us about you. Are you really a spaceship pilot?"

"Yes, licensed to fly ships up to a light cruiser."

"I can't believe it. But then, I can't believe many things I've seen this first week of class. Have a seat. Join us. We're playing Detective."

He pulled out a chair for me while the others scooted to make room for Marki and me.

"Casti and Lori," Marki said, pointing each in turn.

I concluded her race, though completely human looking, were shorter than us. He had brownish hair and a tan complexion. Casti and Lori were twins with curly auburn hair and pixie-like faces.

"Hi ya, Molly," Casti said. "You look beautiful, just like all the others from your world. But Marki says some of them are men. That can't be true."

I chuckled. "But it is. Male Galactic Dolls. The Sixth Invaders developed these mutation agents to try to turn my world's entire population into something akin to theirs. So how does this game go?"

"You can't tell the men apart?" Casti persisted.

"Only when they remove their panties. Otherwise, nope."

All three women giggled.

Pektor changed the subject. "So there's a dozen personas, a dozen possible weapons, and two dozen locations. At the start, each group of cards gets randomized and one from each is chosen. That'll be the who did it, with what, and where. It's kept secret. On the board are all the locations. Those bits represents the weapons, like a blaster. These tokens represent the personas. We each choose one and put it in our start position. All the others are shuffled and dealt out to the players. Oh, Cleo can roll the dice for you. Whatever comes up is how many spaces you can move. When you get into a location, you can ask the person on your right a who, what, and where. If they have one of those cards, they have to show you one. If they don't have even one, then the next person has to show you one, if they have one. Your challenge is to play detective and deduce the who, what, where. When you announce it, you get to peek at the secret cards. If you're right, flip them over. You win. If you're wrong, you lose and are out of the game. Your cards get displayed to all the remaining players. Got it?"

I laughed. "We have a similar game on Earth called Clue. I loved it and played it often. I have to warn you. In real life, I am a private investigator, and I'm also the Sol Empire's Senior Investigator. Prepare to have your butts kicked."

All four roared. The challenge was accepted. Hours flew by. I hadn't had this much fun since grade school days. Had it been that long? I did win one game and came close to a second, before we had to quit.

Marki asked, "So, will you come into the city with us on Saturday? Please?"

"Yeah, you gotta come," Casti insisted.

"Sure. Where do I meet you and when?"

"Maybe we should meet at her dorm so she doesn't have so far to walk in the heels," Lori said. "It's a bear walking in them. I'm still not very used to them. We don't have heels on our world."

"There's three of you. So I'll walk here," I insisted.

Marki showed me out, giving me a hug as we parted. Cleo moved to my side as we began our long walk back to the Married Dorm. Again, the chilly air and my apparel sent marvelous sensations throughout my body. Plus, I felt like a kid again. What an evening.

The next day, I got pulled out of my Econ class by

Professor Heli, who sounded very worried.

"Something's gone wrong. Everyone I've erased the implants from, except you, has gotten sick. Lia and Bill ended up with pneumonia, but they're doing fine now. Their robots caught it in time. Others have various types of colds. You don't. So we need to find out what's going on before I erase more implants."

Her robot led us into her lab where she conducted her implant removal. Ashton joined us, a worried look on his face.

"Have you figured out what's going on?" he asked Professor Heli.

"No, my procedure is definitely erasing the implants, but..."

"They're getting ill," he finished her thought. "Why?"

"You're not really erasing the implants," I said, hesitant to get into an argument.

"I certainly *am* erasing them," Professor Heli barked. "You've stopped reciting your implanted words. So have all those I have treated. It's erased. Gone. No longer forcing a behavioral pattern on them. I can tell. Just look at these energy readings. I've sucked vast quantities of implant energy from their minds. Meters don't lie. Anyone can see just how much energy I've removed. Here, look. This is the energy sucked out of your mind. It's the lowest amount, since you had the smallest implant. Here are Lia and Bill's levels, much larger. And here at two of the original colonists who underwent even more extensive implants. It's as clear as the nose on my face. My procedure is sucking the harmful energies out of the implants, erasing them."

How fascinating. Celeste would love to study her results. But she was fundamentally wrong. "What about the being, the person themselves?"

"Don't be silly. We're competent psychologists. No such thing as ghosts. Balderdash."

"So what are we?" I asked. I got rather argumentative.

"You have a body there. It's obvious. I can see it. Feel it," she said. Ashton nodded. "You have a mind. We all do. We think with it. Implants install behavior patterns in minds."

"Through the use of pain, drugs, and electric shocks," I

added, spitting out the words.

"Precisely. All that energy is stored in the mind. My revolutionary device reverses the flow. I suck all that stored harmful energy back out of the minds."

"But what about the person?"

"What do you mean by person?" Ashton asked. "She just said you have a body and a mind. That's all there is."

"You're blind to the third part of man, the person, the being. Look, what you've done is *steal* memories and the energy stored in them from a person's mind without their consent. When you're done, they feel as though they've lost something vitally important. Haven't you noticed people often get ill after they've suffered a shocking loss of some kind? That's why so many are getting colds. Instinctively, they believe they've lost something highly valuable and can't get it back.

"But in fact, it's still there. You claim the implants are erased. They aren't. I ran a therapy session on Lia and Bill. Both were able to view and erase why they felt so guilty and so deserved being implanted in the first place. When you removed the implant's force, you took away what they were using to balance their ethics scales. I checked with them yesterday. All those memories of what happened on Domes has returned to Lia and Bill, but—and this is a big but—those events are now as important to them as what they had for breakfast last year. Utterly trivial. So yes, you removed the harmful electrical charge from the implants, but they got colds because they instinctively felt they'd lost something. They were holding onto all that implant trauma which you ripped away from them without their consent."

"Are you saying we should ask permission to erase their implants?" Professor Heli asked. From her tone, I sensed her utter disbelief.

"Okay, Molly. What happened to you after I came up behind you and injected your neck with the knockout drug? Professor, you've erased all this from her mind. She won't be able to remember anything until I wore her up during the trip here."

"Well, how much detail do you want?" I proceeded to

describe all that I could from the vague, now insignificant images, including the behavior pattern verbiage.

His pale face spoke loudly when I finished.

Professor Heli said, "So all we need to do is ask their permission first? Then, they won't get sick?"

"It's worth a try. No guarantees, but that's what I'd do. Then, it isn't so much a theft."

Ashton said, "Professor Heli, give that a try. We can't have sixteen hundred students running around with colds and pneumonia."

"So you're reversed engineered the implant technology. As I recall, it uses energies in the kilo-yattahertz range, which we perceive as the most aesthetic thing ever, serenely beautiful and irresistible."

She chuckled. "Perceptive. You know more than you let on, Mrs. Parkinson."

"Does your technique sort of reverse the polarity of the energy beams? Anyway, considering how debilitating these implants are on our people, it's invaluable to have the harmful energies sucked out of them. Long term, though, I wonder if those memories can be reactivated."

Professor Heli said, "And if I boost the energy even higher, can I suck away the person's actual memories, which you claim are still there? Now that's worth exploring next, Ashton. I'll submit another grant request for that."

He nodded. She then asked, "So you and your therapy aren't able to erase these implants? Ashton told me that. Is that the case? We know you did so with that implanted dwarf Senior Ambassador, what's her name."

"Yes, I could reach Lara and help her erase it. But honestly, I spent over a week at it. With our colonists, the implants were just too strong to reach the person, the being. They're completely at the mercy of the implanted behavior. Our best guess was that after a year, perhaps we might have been able to finally reach the being and begin to erase the incidents."

I added, "At least now they have a chance at life again. Time will tell if these implants will recharge up and affect their lives again. For now, you're saving them from a hell."

She smiled. I thought it best to keep on these two people's good side. Even Ashton seemed relieved.

I headed back to the dorm to check on Lia and Bill. Both were in bed. Their breathing had returned to normal. Their robots fed them light soup while I watched.

Bill said, "They have powerful antibiotics. Knocked this infection in short order. I still feel like I lost something, but like Lia said, the memories I thought were stolen are back. They don't seem to bother me. Molly, how can we possibly make up for what we've done? Do we dare tell the Third Invaders what we did? That could start a war with Earth."

"Can I get back to you on that? I think I have an answer for you, but I want to check further."

Lia said, "That's fine. We're still recovering. Say, more bad news. I ran into Dr. Patricia Ann Baxter on Tuesday. She's already completed a genetic study of our bodies. Seems none of our existing cures will make any changes to our bodies. We're stuck being this way for now. Still, she told me not to lose all hope. Maybe a cure will be found. You know those geneticists. Always the optimists."

Crap. That's not what I was hoping for. I so wanted normal feet again.

Chapter 28 A Visit to the City

By Saturday, I'd grown comfortable with Cleo handling my physical needs. A tad clumsy at times, but it got the task done. In this outfit, I couldn't be independent. No access to my feet and toes. Right now, that didn't bother me so much. The tactile sensations from the stockings and blouse were amazing. I just hoped my feet and knees could handle a visit into the city.

During the week, I'd become fond of Marki and her three roommates. At twenty years old, their age appeared to match my biological age of twenty-two. I keep having my bio clock reset by these mutations. Their frankness and love of life filled me with real hope for the future. I hadn't realized how much "bad" stuff I have had to endure these past many years. Yes, I missed my family, but for the moment, I felt invigorated. I put off requesting a call home to let them know what was happening. Partly because I wanted to be certain of my analysis. We'd seen too much treachery. What nasty surprises were in store for us here?

During the slow, long walk down the Rectangle, many other students nodded or said hi to me, especially women, who in their tall heels walked as carefully as I did. My legs felt wonderful in the cool breeze.

The attitudes of others toward me surprised me. I expected buckets of sympathy coming from those I met. "Oh, you poor thing. How awful your life must be." I'd gotten tons of that back on Earth from strangers I'd met. Here, the most I'd received had been a few mumbles and breath intakes in Piloting 101, probably disbelief more than anything else. If Ashton was right and half the faculty at Soros U were handicapped as I was, that alone must have changed people's opinions of us from a sympathetic pity to one of respect and probably awe in the case of the professors. Refreshing.

My fellow students treated me as just another one of them. So far, not one had shown me any deferential treatment because of my handicap. Now if this was the norm here, our sixteen hundred had a real chance at a life. Or was there some kind of nefarious undercurrent at work? In part, that's why I had to "see" the city.

"Hi, Marki. Casti. Lori. Pektor. Lead on. What's the name of the city we're in?"

Pektor chuckled. "You need geography 101. It's Muscoda. Bela Prime is twenty-five percent city. Some suggest it'll be fifty percent in a couple decades. Muscoda is the college city. Hoffdorf, where the ruling bodies have their offices, is about five hundred gelds from here. Crap. You don't know what a geld is. A long way," he said, flushing.

Marki said, "That's why we gotta learn to think in Fed Com. So we can communicate to others. That's what our professor says. Okay, so what's on the agenda?"

"I want to get my nails done," Casti said.

"Yeah, and we should have Molly get her hair done while we're getting the manicures," Marki said.

"And I'll visit the arcades while you four do that. Meet up for izzi and ale. Brown Bottle?"

"Okay. Brown Bottle. Say around noon," Casti said.

That settled, Pektor dashed off, leaving us in the dust. It seemed that way to those of us taking perhaps four-inch steps at a time.

"We're like *so* lucky to have gotten these scholarships," Marki said. "With degrees from here, why, we can go almost anywhere and get great paying jobs."

"We gotta graduate first," Lori stated.

"Party pooper," Marki retorted playfully.

We left the outer perimeter of the campus behind us. Many people traveled about using shuttle air cars that darted about some hundreds of feet up. Avenues of what my great-grandparents might have called streets connected everything. At least twenty-five people could walk abreast down them and did so in places. All kinds of buildings lined the sides of the street, here called Main West Two. I learned they used a directional numbering scheme for these giant foot paths. Evidently, Ashton had copied this scheme for us on Domes.

Some buildings housed shops on the lower floors with studios and apartments above them.

"That's a grocery store," Marki pointed out. "We went in there once. Couldn't read any of the labels, though. Gotta learn more Fed Com."

Her girlfriends giggled. I saw men usually preferred to walk down the left side of these pedestrian avenues, though the women would have said they raced. Women preferred the right side. Students from the university were recognizable by our blouses and ties. However, most of the women I saw today were locals.

While they all wore a professional woman's outfit, some had pleated black skirts, for example. I saw dozens of different white blouse designs, some with long sleeves. However, every women I saw wore the same black stockings and very tall heels, but in many different styles than ours. While the population wore black and white apparel, their shops displayed vibrant colors, perhaps overdone.

I couldn't read the shops' signs, but Cleo, my robot, could. Soon, the others kept having me ask Cleo what this sign said and then that one. Cleo got a workout.

Finally, we entered what obviously was a hair and nail salon, given the pictures painted on its front walls. Thankfully, Marki handled the arrangements. The women here wore similar professional women's outfits in black and white with equally tall heels.

"Molly wants her hair done and trimmed a little so it doesn't drag the ground. We all want our nails done," she said.

For the next hour, I got pampered. Well, my hair did. When she finished, my hair looked very shiny with a luxurious smell. It slipped around almost as if I'd just used my hair and nail machine on it back home. Marki insisted I not tie it into its usual ponytail until we returned.

"It looks so full and shiny black," she said. "How about these?"

She held up her nails, which were now about an inch longer and painted a bright orange to match her hair. Lori's new nails were a deep crimson, while Casti's were more of a cherry red.

That done, we headed on down the pedestrian avenue. Marki suggested we head for the open air restaurant where we planned to meet Pektor. My guess is that it was a mile on down the avenue. Periodically, benches and potted shade trees provided a respite, which the women insisted on taking. Their feet and knees weren't used to this much walking. Mine either. Often I saw local women sitting on benches, along with university students.

Pektor waved to us, running up and out of breath. "Just on time," he said. "Wow. Molly looks different. Good job with her."

"Like our nails?" Marki asked, flashing her now long shiny orange talons.

Not to be out done, Casti and Lori displayed theirs. I suspected he really didn't know what to say.

"Looks good. Let's eat."

I let them order for me, trusting them because I couldn't read a thing on the menu. It seemed awkward to ask Cleo to read it for me. Imagine my surprise when the waiter delivered what could only be described as a pizza to our table, along with mugs of brown ale. We sat on ornate iron chairs with a sun canopy over our heads. She too wore the usual black and white professional woman's outfit, but she had a Brown Bottle apron over it. She moved gracefully in her tall heels, so I surmised she'd been a waitress for months if not years.

As we ate, I watched the local people go by. Shoe styles and the type of skirts and blouses varied but not the color scheme. Hair styles differed, perhaps more so than in Chicago. I picked up relaxed vibes from the thong.

After eating, Pektor headed to a gaming store to check out the latest board games. We four strolled along the avenue. I spotted what had to be a shoe store.

"If that's a shoe shop, can we visit it?" I asked.

"Viroqua Heels, it says," Marki said slowly sounding out the strange syllables.

Inside, a vast array of heels greeted our eyes. I had no idea of the cost of any pair. Speechless describes how I felt. At least a hundred different styles sat on display shelves. Everyone had spiked heels as tall as the ones we wore. I looked in vain for anything lower and found nothing at all. The smell of leather assaulted my nose. I liked one set of pumps which were similar to those I wore back home, the kind I could slip off so I could use my toes. I almost bought them, but didn't because Casti pointed out we weren't allowed to wear anything but school sanctioned apparel while on campus.

She said, "If you buy other stuff, the U gives you an off-campus locker where you can store them, picking them up on your way off the campus."

It wasn't worth the hassle. We continued shopping but were grateful for the many benches along the avenue.

"I'm soaking my feet for hours when we get back," Marki declared.

"Not unless I get there first," Casti said.

"Come on. We don't want to miss supper," Lori added. "Molly, you're staying for supper with us, right? Can't say no."

I grinned. "Don't I get to soak my feet?"

We all laughed. When we entered their room, Pektor had already returned and set up his new board game for us—right in the middle of the dining room table, I should add.

"It's called Castles. There are up to four players, each of which starts their army on one side. It sounded an awful lot like a multi-player chess game. While eating, we had to try it out. To their amazement, I won the game.

"How'd you do that?" Pektor asked.

"The best defense is a strong offence," I said. "Plus, it helps that I used to carry a gun and have had to terminate a man who was trying to kill me and my sisters."

"What? You've actually shot a gun-thing?" Marki asked, wide-eyed.

Long after dark, I headed back down the long Rectangle to the Married Dorms, Cleo at my side. I think my feet had gone numb, but I felt like a teenager again.

I spent Sunday doing homework and visiting others from the colony and from the Bolt. I did give four sessions to some of the Bolt's crew who, like Lia and Bill, felt they'd committed a horrible atrocity.

On Monday as I headed off to class, Ashton caught up to me. He had the luxury of being able to dash about. Okay, bit cynical.

"Glad I caught you. How would you like a tour of Hoffdorf from which the Federation is run? I can show you the Circle of Ambassadors and much more. There's ballets, orchestral concerts—much to see and do."

"Okay with me. I visited the local city here with some student friends on Saturday. I'd like to see more. Aren't there any slums on Bela Prime? Where's the seedier part of town? Surely, you have one."

Ashton laughed. "Hardly. This is the very center of the Federation of Planets. The manufacturing plants are down in South Continent. That's about as low-brow as it gets on this world."

"So you're telling me our people have the best chance for a productive, happy life by living here on Bela Prime? Unless an arm regrow cure is found."

He cocked his head. "Yes, I guess I am at that. We set this experiment up in phases. Professor Heli's electronic removal of the implanted behavior patterns is working. Now we have to wait and see how well the sixteen hundred adapt to university life. Can they learn sufficient skills to become productive members of Bela Prime life? That's Phase 4. We'll have to see."

"What happens if they don't?"

"We'll send them home, but with their robot helpers, as promised. Now if they succeed, well, you've seen how brilliant some have become. Not all do, mind you. Still..."

He led me towards the faculty parking lot, where countless shuttles rested in their slots. Imagine a giant bookshelf with slots for a group of books. Each slot held a shuttle. Stacked twenty high, stairs led down from them.

"We'll take my shuttle. I'm picking up my wife on the way."

As we walked towards them, he continued, "Now then, I should explain further. You see, on Bela Prime, we teach our children properly from the very beginning. Starting at age five when the girls begin wearing normal tall heels and proper outfits and when boys begin wearing proper male apparel, they're taught the Three Bests: Look your best. Feel your best. Be your best. Later when they're ten, we add the motto: A professional appearance promotes self-worth and instills confidence in others. These are drilled into their heads. These principles are ingrained into anyone raised on Bela Prime; they come as naturally as the air we breath. It's second nature to us all."

"What happens to those who don't want to follow them?" I asked.

"They move to other worlds within the Federation of Planets, a world where they'll fit in. As the center of the entire Federation, we have to uphold the very best. We have to adhere to a professional appearance promotes self-worth and instills confidence in others. We're being held to a higher standard than most other worlds."

We halted near one shelf of shuttles. "I'll bring it down. While you can climb the stairs, your robot can't. Back in a flicker."

Every shuttle was light blue. With a pointed nose and cockpit with two seats, each had a rectangular passenger area and could carry six people. The engine made no noise as Ashton backed it out of his parking stall and gently set it down not far from me. A side door opened, and he waved for us to enter. Cleo simply rolled on inside. I took the left side seat because there was an empty space where Cleo could park at my side. I picked up a flash image from Ashton's mind. He often gave shuttle rides to handicapped faculty.

I could barely feel motion as it lifted off. He soon joined me.

"Computer controlled. It'll fly us to my home so we can pick up Didrika. Before that, I should explain something else about our society. Like most, we have an aristocratic class, who can trace their ancestry back to the dawn of civilization. Most aristocrats dwell in Hoffdorf, naturally. That's were most of the Fine Arts are located."

"The wealthy, too?" I hinted, not caring for the direction this headed.

"Well, yes. Aristocratic men wear thousand credit suits, black of course. Aristocratic women must set themselves off from commoners. Thus, they pride themselves on having tiny waists. They wear tight-laced corsets to achieve their special look. My Didrika is an aristocratic woman, high bred, though I'm technically not an aristocratic man. That tag isn't gained by marriage. However, I have gained substantial prestige by marrying her. Perception is key on Bela Prime. A professional appearance promotes self-worth and instills confidence in others. Didrika insists on showing you the sights of Hoffdorf. So you are about to see the other side of Bela Prime."

He opened the side door. I hadn't even realized we'd traveled; I could love this shuttle.

"Oh, Ashton! Call it by it's right name. For Zelda's sake. It's Cass-C. Not Bela Prime. You must be Mrs. Molly Parkinson. I'm Didrika Reiner. Ashton's my husband. The Reiner family. One of the original seven families. Founded this Federation of Planets."

She walked into the shuttle and sat opposite me. Didrika wore her jet black hair up in a fancy do, held in place by many jeweled pins. She sat stiffly erect, though her tiny waist caught my eyes at once. Her corset must be cutting her in half. Her low-cut blouse revealed ample cleavage, highlighted by the large gold pendant holding a giant red ruby. She wore stockings and tall heels quite similar to mine. Petticoats puffed her skirt which ended at her knees. Eight large gold rings set with a variety of gemstones adorned her fingers. Her crimson nails stretched out six inches. Two gold arm bands accentuated her upper arms.

"The Reiners. The Stroebels. The Kaufmanns. The Auerbachs. The Kleins. The Nussbaums. The Schmidts. We made the Federation of Planets. Forgive my husband. He's an educator. Has no feel for history. This world is Cass-C. Been so forever. Someone's wild idea—this Bela Prime. Makes no sense. It's time things change, Ashton. Not soon enough for me. Now, let's look at you, dearie." She turned to me, while Ashton meekly headed to the pilot's seat.

"Pleased to meet you," I said.

"My, dearie, you are a sight. Such a bosom. Ought not be hidden under that blouse. Men. You could be stunning. With proper corset training. Ashton's right, dearie. Rescuing your people. Cass-C makes excellent prosthetics. But not whole arm replacements. Tell me, dearie, does that robot help you enough?"

"Yes. It takes getting used to. Back home, I do everything with my feet and toes."

"How ghastly. Uncivilized. I'm convinced Ashton did right. Bringing your people here. Giving them the robots. We have many handicapped people. Birth defects. Accidents. So on. Gave them the robots. Instead of cosmetic prosthetics. Some became university professors. Some hold top designer positions."

I realized that her corset was so tight that she could barely breathe. Hence, she could only speak in short sentences before having to take another breath. Curious.

"Not all are geniuses. What happens to them? Ashton says they're sent elsewhere."

"To their home worlds. Or down south to our industrial complexes. We're humane, dearie. I want to show you Hoffdorf. The 'creme von creme' city. As we say. Best of the best in the galaxy. Unfortunately, can't get you inside some. You aren't properly attired. Must wear corset. Ashton says you're being a student. If you change your mind, dearie. I know the best corset store in Hoffdorf. They make mine. Won't trust any other maker. Not with something this important."

"Ashton said we can see some of the sights. Right?"

"Yes, dearie. I'd love to take you to the symphony. But they'd not allow you in. Not properly attired. You know. Look your best. Feel your best. Be your best. Professional appearance promotes self-worth. Instills confidence in others. Never truer than in Hoffdorf. Ah, on right is Reich Spaceport. Finest on Cass-C. But not largest. Those are found in down south. The industrial continent."

The spaceport dwarfed New O'Hare. I saw other shuttles like ours darting about the skies, mad gnats on a hot summer night. I couldn't count the number of spaceships, let alone tell their world of origin.

"Ashton, land us in the Fine Arts Sector. We'll walk some. Best to see these on foot, dearie. See that complex? That's Symphony Hall. Looks kind of like a band shell. Next to it is the Fine Arts Museum. Yes, set us down there, Ashton."

Again, wide pedestrian avenues separated the

buildings. He sat us down in the center of one. After Didrika, my robot, and I stepped onto the avenue, she ordered Ashton.

"You may leave us now, Ashton."

"Good. I've a meeting on campus. Bye you two," he said.

Potted trees and benches lined the avenues. She led me down the right side of the avenue, pointing out the various sights. Every block or so, she sat on bench to catch her breath.

"So why do all women on Cass-C wear these really tall heels? The mutation distorted my feet, so I've no choice but to wear them."

"Well, dearie, it's simple. We walk slow. To enjoy the world. Take time to appreciate life around us. We bring new life into the world. Makes men pay attention to us. If a man can't match your pace. He'll never have patience to treat you right. We control all men this way. He must treat us right or else. All Cass-C women know that. Look your best. Feel your best. Be your best. Professional appearance promotes self-worth. Instills confidence in others. Controls men. Ashton probably didn't tell you that. The last part of our motto. Dearie, ours is a matriarchal society."

"I didn't know that. So men don't run things here?" I asked. "It looked like Ashton was in control of a lot of things."

She laughed. "We let them rush about. Do their things. When a woman dies. All her fortune goes to her daughters. Though the husband and sons get a small stipend. No man ever inherits his wife's fortune. Believe me, dearie. We aristocratic women have large fortunes. Just look at the wondrous form of our Symphony Hall. Designed by a woman. Fabulous."

I gazed on the architectural marvel. Many women ambled along the avenue, often sitting a spell on the benches, just as we did. Their stiffly erect postures told all. Men also walked the avenues, but they moved quite swiftly, compared to us.

"What about crime? I've not seen any police officer or security guards."

Didrika chuckled. "Penalties are too stiff. Crimes against women on Cass-C are the worst. If convicted, their arms are removed at their elbows. If you see anyone with hooks, they've harmed women. If they commit another, their legs are removed at knees. But we give them prosthetics, though. If it's severe, we execute them. We have hardly any crime on Cass-C."

"Wow. We throw ours in prisons."

"In ancient times, we did, too. Cost prohibitive. Changed to this and no crime to speak of."

"Back home, I'm in charge of key investigations and handling judgements. The Sol Empire's Senior Investigator and Senior Judge."

"You should be in our ID. That's the Intelligence Division. They do all of those things. Behind the scenes, dearie. If you see an ID person, you're in bad trouble. They wear all black clothing. Can't miss them. Probably wish you had, though. Here's the museum. I can take you in here. This way."

"This is huge!" I thought we entered a cavern.

"Impressive. Art displays to our right. Space displays to the center. Cultural displays to our left. Natural History—plants and animals—is in another building."

"I hate to admit this, Didrika, but I've seen almost nothing of the galaxy beyond my home world and a little of the new Domes world."

"To our left, then. Cultural museum. Nearly every world in the Fed sends us samples. Even the more primitive cultures. Don't worry. There's benches in here, too."

"Why the uncomfortable corsets? They made me wear one during the filming of our Miss Galaxy beauty pageant. That was really hard for me."

"Purpose for everything. Our stockings massage the whole leg. Makes walking in the heels pleasurable. So we can slow down. Observe the world around us. Corsets enhance our curves. Quite why we need that is lost in time. Cass-C aristocratic women have worn them for centuries. You'd look fabulous in one. What with your bosom. I want to show you something."

We walked past all kinds of dioramas with various peoples wearing their native costumes. Most looked like normal humans, but with varying heights, skin colors, and facial structures. Apparel varied from robe-like clothing to loin cloths. Painted backdrops represented typical images of that world, which helped place them in their cultural settings. Unfortunately, I couldn't read any of the tags or plaques.

"Here you go. Origins of the Senior Ambassadors and their lip disks."

I saw a dark skin group of natives in leather skirts all sporting giant lip disks, perhaps made of bronze or copper.

"One of the first worlds added to the Fed is Bestial-D here. We sent ambassadors to them. They sent some here. All ended up with the disks. Since then, all Senior Ambassadors wear them."

We rose from the bench on which we'd rested while I studied the diorama. I heard heels clicking on the tiled floor and turned to see Senior Ambassador Heidi Le Blanc coming our way.

She called out. "Hey there. Been looking for you, Mrs. Parkinson. Heard you were on Cass-C. Ah, Mrs. Didrika Reiner. May I have a word with you?"

The ambassador now wore heels as tall as ours, but she was uncomfortable in them, walking as though fighting their restriction to her pace. Evidently, she had to wear these when in public, too.

"Madam President," Didrika said, coldly. "Here to recruit Mrs. Parkinson, are you?"

"Yes. No. Well, yes, I can always keep trying. Molly would make a fabulous Senior Ambassador from the Sol Empire. I've been after her for some time. When you are finished visiting her, Molly, I can show you the Circle of Ambassadors and other sights, such as our living quarters. The more you know about living here, the more informed your decision can be."

"I'll have to see. Right now, I'm staying at Soros U."

"Give me a call. Better yet, I'll call you later. Mrs. Reiner, what's all this we've been hearing about a disbanding of the Circle of Ambassadors? The generals are being sent home. A Circle of Seven? What's going on? As President of the Circle of Ambassadors, I should have been notified of these changes. We are charged with making the Federation laws.

What's going on?"

"Didn't you read the official memo? I know you received it. I sent it to you days before the implementation."

"Well, yes, but what's really going on? How can they change what we ambassadors do? We're in charge of making the Federation laws."

"Not any longer. The Seven have long disapproved. Of the way the Circle of Ambassadors operates. Besides, by definition, an ambassador is a diplomat. Sent by a world as its representative. To a foreign world. Doesn't say to make laws."

"But who are these Seven? What gives them the right to undo this?"

"Seven aristocratic families founded the Federation. Centuries ago. Brought peace to this side of the galaxy. They've decided that you are diplomats. No ground wars have been fought. Not in centuries. Generals aren't needed. They've been sent home. The Seven are back at the top of the new organizational chart. Below them, are the Admiralty Roundtable and the ID. The Admiralty enforces the laws of the Seven. The ID handles all investigations and jurisprudence. The Circle of Ambassadors now reports to the Admiralty Roundtable. You are to relay and enforce Fed rules. You remain the main diplomats. So get used to doing your job, Madam President."

"We'll see about this. Just who are these Seven men? There's nothing in the document that tells me how to contact them. The entire Circle of Ambassadors wants to launch a protest."

"They are anonymous. Their identities are secret. The admirals can only directly contact Seven. Seven can contact Six. So on up the line to One, who controls everything. You can submit your protest to your admiral. He can send it up to Seven. Won't do you any good. I speak as an aristocrat. The Seven are done with you making crazy laws. This is Cass-C. Not Bela Prime. Come, Molly. Let's get lunch."

Senior Ambassador Le Blanc stomped off, purposely pounding her steel heel tips onto the tiles. Didrika mumbled something, but led the way to an exit. Once outside and breathing in the fresh air, Didrika calmed down. More people walked on the avenues, and we joined the lunchtime crowds.

"See that?" She pointed to a tall needle-like building. "We're eating up there on the top floor. From there, you can see all Hoffdorf. You'll have to excuse Le Blanc. She isn't taking the Fed reorganization well. The more I think about it. The more I can see you in our ID. You'd make a great agent."

Why did I feel like I was being recruited by everyone I met?

Chapter 29 ID

No one stared at me while I ate atop the Needle, the best restaurant in Hoffdorf, according to Didrika. Yes, many glanced at me as the woman led us to our table against the windows. The robot following me gave it away. How different from my experiences around Chicago. With those like me teaching at the university, probably we were a common sight. Didrika didn't pay any attention to Cleo feeding me. Rather, she chatted and pointed out key landmarks. I did notice the portion sizes: small.

As we rose to leave, I said, "Thank you for showing me around. I've learned tons about Cass-C."

"You're so welcome, dearie. It's not often I have such fun."

As we stepped out of the Needle onto the wide avenue, a man in black stepped up to us. He'd been leaning in a niche at the side of the towering spire. He wore a black shirt, black pants, black shoes, black gloves, with a black mask covering his face. Oh, and he carried a black weapon in a black holder on his belt.

A man's voice said, "Parkinson. Come with me. Reiner, I'll see she's returned to the university."

He pointed off to the right where I saw one of the shuttles parked, its side door open. The craft was entirely black, rather ominous.

"Not so fast." I protested, as he tried to hurry me. "These heels are a bitch."

Impatience. Disgust. I read his surface thoughts and didn't ask questions. Rather, I focused on not taking a tumble while hurrying as much as possible, which wasn't much at all. After I stepped in with Cleo following, the man shut the door and headed up front without saying anything further. I took a seat. No windows. I decided to play along. For now.

I had no way to judge time, but my guess is we flew for no more than ten minutes. I did sense us descending a considerable distance during the last moments of the flight.

The masked man joined me and opened the side door.

"Out," he barked.

A parking garage? No, some kind of hangar. But heavy tarps rippled slightly. Wherever we were, they wanted to keep it secret. My heels clicked on the concrete floor, announcing my arrival. I spotted video cameras following me as I moved alongside the masked man. We stopped at the door to a room. He flipped a switch. Cleo, which had been following along behind me, ceased all motion.

"Robot stays here. Inside."

His gruff voice grated my nerves. He did open the door for me. When I entered, I blinked. Bright lights startled me for a second. I spotted an empty chair on one side of a steel table. Two others sat on the other side. The man motioned for me to sit. Both wore totally black outfits. I paid more attention to the woman, though. Black blouse, black pants, and black soft-soled, comfortable shoes. So not every woman had to wear these tall heels.

I sat down and stared back at their piercing eyes. Sober faces threatened me, as if I'd committed some heinous crime. Well, two can play that game. I returned their stone-faced glares. The man spoke first.

"I'm Commander Klaus Ziegler of the Intelligence Division. Squad 19. This is my psych-profiler Mina Gerhardt. Seven has ordered us to interview you for a position with the ID. Frankly, we don't take handicapped personnel in the ID. Ever. But Seven gave me the order, so I had you brought here."

His tone: gruff. His emotion: disgust. He glanced down at a computer screen I couldn't see.

"I see you are the Sol Empire's Senior Investigator and Senior Judge. No wonder Earth is in such a mess."

I'd heard all I cared to hear. I spoke with the coldest tone I could muster. "Good. Now take me back to the university. I'm done here. I thought the ID was supposed to be a crack outfit. Obviously, Mrs. Didrika Reiner must have exaggerated. Considerably."

I stood up, debating whether to try to open the door myself or wait on them.

"Sit down. I'm not finished," Commander Zeigler

ordered.

"As far as I'm concerned, you are!" But I did sit down. "Earth is in such a mess because for over thirty years the Sixth Invaders infiltrated our top leaders using their body swap machines. They invented these nasty mutation agents in an attempt to turn Earth's population into a society like their own, where their men are the domestics. I played a major role in uncovering and defeating their plans. Rather it's your damned Federation that is threatening the genocide of our people."

"That is in the records I have. Impossible to believe it," he barked. "Says you also are a licensed transport pilot. You've programmed a robot to do that for you. Clever, I suppose."

"Bull shit! We don't have any robots like Cleo. Manufacturing robots and helpful machines, yes. I fly using my feet and toes, stupid."

The muscles on his temples tightened. Something Empress Kalindi Amandani told me popped into my mind. I sent out calming vibes before I said, "Perhaps, we're getting off on the wrong foot, commander. I still have two of them."

I grinned. That broke the ice. A fleeting smile flashed before he installed his stern countenance.

"All right. The ID is charged with gathering intelligence on crimes and any threats to any world of the Federation of Planets. We report directly to the Seven. After we acquire the evidence and apprehend the guilty parties, we deliver the requisite justice."

"You must be doing a good job of that. On Earth, corporations have security guards everywhere, plus there are local police forces, and even a Local Defense Force, which is a militia to help out when needed. I've seen no police, no security forces anywhere I've been, but then I've not been many places on Cass-C yet."

"That shows us the Sol Empire is still in its infancy. Barbaric, perhaps. No, you'll see none of those on Cass-C. Yet, the ID forces are where we're needed. I presume Mrs. Reiner told you something about crime on our world."

"Yes, she did. While giving me the tour. She said if I see a person with no lower arms, that person is a convicted criminal."

"Precisely. Petty crimes: lose dominant lower arm. Significant crime: lose them both. Severe crime: termination. With those unvarying penalties, we've eliminated crime on Cass-C. We've made it safe for the aristocrats to walk the streets of any city. In order to do that, the ID has instant response teams. Crack agents. Highest possible readiness to respond to anything. Rough physical training surpasses anything in any army or spacer's guild. That's why we can't accept a handicapped person in our ranks. Hell, Mrs. Parkinson, you can't even walk fast, let alone run. That's wholly ignoring being able to protect yourself. Forget protecting fellow agents or the public. You can understand that."

I grinned. "I can't speak for your agents and their training. And yes, thanks to this latest genetic mutation, I have no choice but to wear these tall heels. As for the rest, you might be surprised. Now, are we done?"

"Hardly. I presume you can't handle weapons, such as blasters."

"On Earth, only our soldiers carry blasters. Too dangerous. We still utilize ancient projectile weapons call guns. They fire—"

"We know what a gun is. We have them, too."

"Well, I carry a 9mm Glock when situations warrant it." There, let him stew on that one. "I'm also a private investigator. Over the years, I've found using your brains often produces more rapid results."

At this point, the psych-profiler spoke up. Mina Gerhardt said, "Commander, she has a point." Looking at me, she said, "Seven asked us to look into you. We have. Got quite a dossier on you. I think you can agree because of your severe physical limitations you're not qualified to be in the ID. But we'd like your input on a situation, if you have any information."

"What's the situation?" I asked.

"The murder of your Senior Ambassador Aaron Strawn. We've acquired footage of the shooter firing a blasters at him. Our techs cleaned up the quite dark video, enough for us to get a good facial image. At first, we believed he was a giant, but from the improved video, it's clear the shooter was a human male. Unfortunately, we've hit a dead end. We've the best facial recognition software anywhere in the Federation. He remains an unidentified male. No match in any Cass-C database. No match on anyone arriving or departing any of our many spaceports. The man just vanished. We don't tolerate cold cases. My assumption is that Seven believes you might have some additional data on this case that may help us. Do you?"

"Well, actually, I do. I've been investigating Aaron's murder, too. I'm not surprised that you can't match the perp's face. In fact, that's what I would have predicted."

Both straightened up and stared directly at me.

"Long story. Got a few minutes?" They nodded. I had to be very careful about what I divulged.

"Seven years ago when we were fighting that battle to throw off the Sixth Invaders, unknown to us, some personnel, perhaps Sixth Invaders in disguise, in our Galactic Robotics corporation developed five human-form robots. These things are completely indistinguishable from real humans. They fit in perfectly, but are quite strong. They have the ability to alter their outward form, even their gender. The trouble is they vanished from Earth before they could have the usual robot laws introduced into their programming. Thus, they're rogue robots. My first husband was killed by one as he tried to track them down.

"Piper Strawn brought back his laptop. I had people crack his security measures and retrieved his daily journal. He kept a day by day record of his time here on Bela Prime, I mean Cass-C. His last entry suggested he discovered one of these missing human-like robots was disguised as someone in the Admiralty Roundtable. He intended to expose the robot to the other Senior Ambassadors the next day. My conclusion is the robot found out Aaron had discovered him and terminated Aaron before he could reveal the robot's identity."

"That's quite a story, Mrs. Parkinson," Mina said, clearly disbelieving it.

"Molly, please."

"Not so fast, Mina," Commander Ziegler interrupted. "How could such a handicapped person detect this robot? If it can change its appearance, as you say."

"Telepathy. Aaron was a telepath. That was a side-effect of the armless Galactic Doll mutation agent. Robots don't have minds like ours. I was a telepath, too, before Ashton got to me and undid everything. We can sense human minds all around us. But the robot had no thoughts, only circuitry. I'm sure that's what Aaron sensed and why it got him killed.

"Since his murder is still unsolved, Admiral Skaggs's niece, Bonita Valdez, is coming to Cass-C soon, along with detectives from Indrani-C, to see if they can find this rogue robot and solve the crime. She has the full support of Empress Kalindi Amandani."

Commander Ziegler grinned and exhaled. "Now Seven's orders with Mrs. Parkinson make sense. If Amandani is involved, shit's going to fly. There were five of these robots?"

"Yes, five who didn't have the robot laws installed in them. You know, a robot can't harm a human. I've searched Earth pretty well. None of them seems to have stayed. Quite why one came here is unknown. I suppose I'm not allowed to ask about any secret robot development programs you might have."

"You got that right. We'll look into it."

"Say, can I ask you something, Mina?" She nodded. "How come you don't have to wear these tall heels? Every woman I've seen wears them. Until I saw you, that is."

She flashed a brief smile. "Oh, I do have to. Whenever I go out in public not wearing black. Something I try to avoid." I smiled back.

"You probably don't know this," the commander said, "but do you know what kind of brain or control circuits these human-like robots have?"

"Positronic brains. That's what my husband Ted said."

"Shit. We *do* have a problem. Well, thank you for your assistance, Mrs. Parkinson. We'll take it from here. If you have any influence with this Bonita Valdez, please convince her to let us handle the matter. Mina, see her out. Now I see why Seven wanted us to talk to her."

With that, he rose and rapidly dashed out of the room. Mina rose and escorted me to the door, where Cleo sat waiting. "Return her to the university," she ordered the still masked man who'd brought me here.

Later, I walked out onto the Rectangle, though many students glanced my way. Seeing an ID ship got everyone's attention. That evening half the student body heard I got off an ID shuttle. Marki insisted I tell them all about my afternoon.

When I finished, she said, "See, I told you Molly hadn't committed any crimes."

Ashton interrupted us. He'd found me in their dorm room.

"Molly. Please come with me right now. We've encountered a serious problem with some of your people."

I tried to walk as fast as I could, fearing some dire emergency. I almost fell but I managed to use a bit of telekinetic force to keep upright. I slowed down. Now walking across the Rectangle and away from prying ears, he said more.

"Professor Heidi has erased more of the colonists implants. However, many of those are begging for us to kill them. That they don't want to live like this."

"That's your big emergency?" I asked and stopped walking.

"Well, yes. I can't understand it. We've provided everything they need to be able to live a most productive life."

"Imagine you woke up tomorrow to discover you had no arms, looked like a woman, and found you were on a strange planet with people who didn't even speak your own language. Ignoring the implants and mistreatment they've already endured, how do you suppose you'd react?"

"That accounts for the screams, I suppose. How was this handled on Earth?"

I sighed. "In some of the worst cases, we honored those who requested to be terminated. When we had a lot of therapy givers available, we did our best to erase their trauma and give them a willingness to continue to live by showing them they could use their feet and toes to do the things in life. That the Sixth Invaders also made hair machines and dressing machines helped a lot. Usually it took eight days of constant therapy to get them to a point where they'd at least give living a try."

"So we need to provide counseling for these people."

"You'll have to do something. I could try running our therapy on one person, but allow at least eight days to get them anywhere near stable. If they were all on Earth, Celeste might be able to organize enough therapy givers to handle them, maybe. These are going to be tough cases."

When we arrived in Professor Heli's lab, four of the colonists sat sobbing on chairs. I recognized Patricia Ann Baxter and her husband, Vernon, the medical doctor. Their baby rested in a baby sack slung over his shoulder.

Patricia Ann saw me. "Molly? You, too? Please, tell them to terminate us. I can't undo this genetic mutation. All is lost. Forever."

"Patricia Ann, Vernon. You're looking well."

"But we're not," she wailed. "We've lost our telepathy, too."

"I know. I've lost it, too. But Patricia Ann, we need you."

I could see reasoning wouldn't work. A good night's sleep might. With Ashton's help, I got them back to their dorm. The robots whipped up dinner, while I kept the pair calm. After eating, they relaxed a little.

"Why can't we remember anything?" Patricia Ann asked. "We remember being selected for the colony and getting onto the ship with our many crates of stuff. Then, we woke up here in that strange lab. Their arms were gone. Our telepathy vanished. I vaguely remember analyzing our new DNA alterations in some lab."

"By tomorrow or the next day at the latest, you'll find your memories back, but all the heavy charge on them will be gone. Not as good as our therapy sessions. In short, we were betrayed by the Third Invaders." I proceeded to tell them what had happened on Earth and on Domes.

"We're now on Cass-C or Bela Prime. The university seems to be top notch. I'm hoping you'll be able to study all they know about genetics so you can help us find a way to regrow our arms again. If anyone can do it, it's you, Pat. I'll come by in the morning and give you a session to help you and

Vernon recover. We've got to find ways to help sixteen hundred eleven of us."

They accepted that, and I returned to my room. Ashton followed.

"So they are completely disoriented," he said, after we sat at the dining room table.

"That's an understatement. The last thing they remember is getting on the Third Invader's flying saucer. They wake up here missing their arms and telepathy, can't speak the language, and have no idea where they're at. That's enough of a shock for anyone."

"Okay then. That gives me enough data to act. I'll arrange for social workers to be present when each person has their implants erased. Have them help orientate the people. I'll give that a try. Oh, I do hope my wife didn't bore you."

I laughed. "Oh, no. She's quite a woman. I just wish she wouldn't keep calling me dearie."

Ashton laughed. "I won't tell you what she calls me." With that, he left.

The next morning, I visited Pat and Vernon. The night's sleep calmed them.

Pat said, "My memories are coming back. Not too clearly, but they're there. These robots do help us more than I expected. Still, we're so disoriented."

"I figured that. Let's see what a therapy session can do."

I spent the morning working on Pat and did Vernon in the afternoon.

When I finished, he said, "Thanks, Molly. I do feel more relaxed and not so freaked out."

Pat said, "I've been doing a lot of thinking while you two were going at it. Bela Prime is the heart or center of the Federation of Planets. It stands to reason the best geneticists and labs are here. If we're ever to find a way to regrow our arms, Vernon, I think we have the best chance of discovering that here. We should see what all this university has to offer. If we don't like it, she says we can return to Earth."

I relaxed. With Eve and Lara working on cures back home and Pat exploring options here, I felt hopeful. Also hopeful the sixteen hundred could be salvage and not killed.

Time to check with Ashton and see how he and Professor Heli fared today.

"That's working somewhat," Ashton said. "Counseling is helping a little. No more screaming. No more immediate death wishes. Mind you, they aren't pleased, but are giving university life and the robots a chance. That's all we can ask. As I said, this whole operation is an experiment. We do want to save lives in the pursuit of scientific knowledge."

Chapter 30 Endings

"I need to return home," I said. "It's been nearly two months. Besides, your people seem to have a handle on the recovery of the sixteen hundred people."

Ashton agreed. "I'll arrange a transport to take you back."

"Will Cleo be coming with me? Can I bring back my university wardrobe? Maybe some additional samples. My sister would love to see if she can copy some of the designs."

He agreed and arranged for the trip back tomorrow. Meanwhile, I spent time with my new friend Marki.

"If I can get back here, I'll look you up for sure," I said as we hugged.

Two crates contained all my current university clothing, but Ashton sent along a spare robot and four extra crates of university apparel. He also sent along a liter of the mutation agent he used on us, the one that removed telepathic skills but redid the Galactic Doll mutations. He wanted our geneticists to have samples to study. Whether he desired an arm regrow cure I couldn't tell. He had far too many vested interests, and I refused to probe his mind. So far, everyone remained convinced I no longer had telepathic abilities, just like the other sixteen hundred.

The long trip back took twenty long, boring days. Since this was a commercial flight, I continued wearing my university clothing and allowed Cleo to deal with my needs. I maintained the appearance these people expected to see. In truth, I found it relaxing to have the robot handling some of my needs for me. Late October, 2361, I arrived home, security men carting my many crates to my house for me.

"Matt! Come see. Mom's got a robot," Nikita said when I walked in.

"It's name is Cleo. It handles my personal needs like Ashley used to. But what happened to you? You've grown inches. Where's your regrowing arms?"

Something had happened. Her face flushed. She wore

our usual style dress that encased our empty shoulders. Plus, she again wore her tall heels.

Matt and Sam joined us. Hugs and kisses followed.

"Okay. What's happened to Nikita? One of you going to explain?" This wasn't what I expected.

"I still have my telepathy, but Aunt Celeste says I'm not supposed to tell anyone that I do." Nikita hedged, putting a spin on what happened.

Sam looked at her. I swear she looked years older, not just taller. Her breasts had grown substantially, but years before I thought they should.

"Mom, I wanted to see Issi and the colony. So I snuck onboard a supply ship. It was easy to sneak into the dome city. I wandered around a while before I found Lia. I started talking to her—sort of. She talked crazy-like. A yellowish gas floated down from pipes overhead. And we all passed out. Sherry put on a gas mask and rescued me. We hid in the basement until they carted everyone away, including you, mom. Sherry told me all this. When the gas went away, I woke up. Hours later. Aunt Celeste says I got mutated again. Now I'm like you and the other colonists. But she and Lara are working on new cures. And I look so much older, don't I? But they're awfully heavy and hurt each morning. Aunt Celeste says that's because they're growing so fast. My dress size keeps changing each week. Anyway, I'm fine, really I am. Sorry about sneaking off like that. But I really wanted to see the colony and Issi."

Sam shrugged his shoulders. "Sorry. We didn't miss her for almost two days. She claimed she was spending the weekend with the Hugos. My bad, honey."

"Forgiven. I hope you learned from that, Nikita. Now you're stuck like me and the rest of the colonists. Come here. Hug."

She and Matt headed off, leaving Sam and me alone.

"Sam, I have really missed you. Another hug. You really look like a man now."

I buried my head into his shoulders.

"Hope you like me looking more or less like I used to. They say it'll be a year before our arms grow enough to not look so out of place."

We talked and kissed. It was all that I could do not to push him into our bedroom and onto the bed. Only the arrival of Ashley and Sherry chilled our passions, at least until nighttime. They dropped by with news.

Ashley said, "Most of your sisters and their families are on Domes now. A lot of dwarves have also gone there. Ten deep space ships left with a number of families fleeing the potential destruction of Earth. Calling themselves Space Gypsies. Eve and Lara's cures for men are still being duplicated and used. We've restored about a quarter of the men so far. Dimitri wants to see you as soon as possible. I think he wants to replace you so you can deal with Domes. There, that about does it. So what happened? We want all the details. Sherry managed to hide out and avoid being mutated and captured, but she didn't know what actually happened."

Sam brought me a brown ale. He knew this would be a long tale. Two hours later, I finished up. "So where's Bonita?"

Sherry said, "She got impatient and left for Indrani-C. She told me, 'Molly's going to be tied up with Domes for a while, so I'm going on ahead. I've talked with Empress Amandani. She's providing me with two of her top investigators. So I'll stop there first. Tell Molly not to worry and to find me when she gets done with Domes.' I've verified she reached Indrani-C and picked up the two investigators. My guess is that she should be on Cass-C or Bela Prime about now."

"She always was impatient," I said. "I guess I should pay Dimitri a visit soon."

The next morning with Cleo following me, I met Dimitri and Natalie at Barnaby's for breakfast, their treat. I continued to wear my new university outfit. I really liked how the stockings and blouse felt on my skin.

"This is Cleo, my helper robot. I suppose I should bring you up to date first." I spent an hour relating the news and how I hoped Patricia Ann would one day find a new arm regrow agent.

"So you and all sixteen hundred have lost their telepathic abilities?" Natalie asked. "That's awful. But I do see Ashton's reason. No way will anyone want to kidnap them now. Still..."

"Awful price to pay," I added. Both nodded.

"Well, Admiral Skaggs is still around, verifying we're getting the mutations rectified," Dimitri said. "I think he'll leave soon. Thankfully. We've given your situation considerable thought. Molly, it's not fair to you to make you have to be the governor of Domes and be the Senior Investigator and be the Senior Judge. Especially handicapped as you are."

My ire swelled. But she had a point. But not the handicapped one, though.

"So we looked at what we thought was the most vital position and decided it was Domes. There is so much that can be learned from that world. We want you to oversee it as the Senior Ambassador suggested. Well, as she ordered. Ashley can come with you, if you wish. Between us, she's a good candidate for Senior Judge. We'd like to get more women in top positions. Jie and Ward have been running the investigations while you were gone. Either would be good for the position of Senior Investigator. What do you think?"

Outed. Politely, but outed none the less. It simplified things.

"Jie is a bit insecure. Ward would be my pick. I think Ashley will make a fine Senior Judge. At least she'll be on time, unlike me."

That brought some chuckles.

"When I head to Domes, I'll take Sherry with me as my personal security guard. I'll have to arrange things with my family before I can go."

"Deanna left a ship for you to use. One of her new copies of the Friendship. It's parked at New O'Hare and called The Parkinson."

My turn to laugh. Now closer to lunch, I headed home to talk with Sam. Was it fair to move the kids to Domes? They'd leave behind all their friends. I forgot his wishes. He worked at the UC library. Would he want to move? What would he do there? Would the kids want to move? Nikita likely would, if only to be closer to her big sister, Isabella. Matt was another story.

He came home for lunch. While he prepared our meal, we discussed the situation. He knew I'd probably have to go to live on Domes.

"The kids and I have discussed the possibility you'd be needed on Domes. Matt doesn't want to go but Nikita does. But hon, there's something else you should know. Since about August, some people are ranting against the corruption and failures of Earth's corporations and leaders. These past weeks, Web postings argue for a revolt. I've a feeling we're going to see more violence, only I can't predict where. I've talked with the Hugos about this, but they think it's unlikely to amount to much. After all, the corporations still pay everyone's monthly allowances. The amounts are definitely much larger since we entered the Federation, but people are still dependent on those handouts."

"So Helen thinks this will blow over?"

"Yeah. That's her thinking. Why chew off the hand that feeds you? She said if GD stops paying monthly salaries, all those they sponsor are going to starve to death. She thinks these protests will eventually die out. Anyway, I was thinking I really haven't any business going to Domes. What's a librarian gonna do there? It's not like our daughter has uncovered a vast collection of books for me to catalogue."

"But I'll miss you."

"Same here. Matt really likes his school and friends. I feel like a heel taking him out of there and moving to Domes. He likes all his buddies. Nikita is another story. She's not told you about how school's going for her, has she?"

"No. I thought she was enjoying it. Cheerleading and all that."

"Male kids' bodies have been restored, and the cures applied to the girls, so all their classmates are pretty much normal. As they grow older, the girls' bodies will become Galactic Dolls, but with Eve and Lara's cures. Since Nikita's return with her body re-mutated and somehow growing rapidly, she's become something of an outcast, different from all the other girls. Their feet are normal. Hers aren't. She's now the only student who lacks arms. It's been really bothering her. I'm glad you're back. Talk with her tonight."

"We best have a family meeting. I've got to go to Domes soon. Maybe I can find someone to take over as governor for me. Have to see. And why couldn't Bonita wait for me?"

Sam laughed. "When has she been patient? I'd be really upset if a robot killed me and I sure would go after it as fast as possible. I think she felt encouraged because Empress Amandani is supporting her investigation and sending along help. I tried to get her to wait a while, but she had a bee in her bonnet as we say."

That evening over supper, the kids got to watch Cleo feeding me. I could see Nikita wishing she could have a robot helper, as she bent over reaching for another bite on her fork held between her right toes. While many actions were awkward for us, the important thing is that we found ways to do them. Still, she was envious.

"Nikita, I'm going to see if we can program that spare robot Ashton sent back with me to be your assistant some of the time."

Her eyes opened wide and shone. Before she could chat away on that, I focused our attention on the Domes situation.

"I've got to move to Domes soon. How long I'll be gone is unknown."

"We know, Mom," Nikita said. "Can't I go with you?"

I smiled. "I was just coming to that. If you want to come, that's fine with me. Dad tells me Matt doesn't want to move."

"Right. Please don't make me move," he begged. "Please. I'll lose all my friends."

"And there's no library on Domes for Dad," I said. "So, gang. What do you think of Dad and Matt staying here, while Nikita and I go to Domes. Our family will be apart a lot, but they can come for a visit during the summer. I don't know how long I'll have to be the governor of Domes, so I can't promise how long our family will be apart."

"Yippee! Fine with me, right Dad?" Matt said.

Sam smiled. "I agree with your mother. This is probably the smartest move we can make. You and I would be miserable on Domes. Nikita and Isabella are close. Besides Nikita wants to maybe be a linguist, so it's perfect for her. We'll miss you both, though."

Later that night when I went in to Nikita's bedroom to tuck her in—I couldn't do any actual tucking with heels strapped on my feet—I told her I knew about her school troubles.

"Dad told me how your other classmates have turned against you."

"I'm not even on the cheerleader squad anymore. Just because they all got the cures and those don't work on me now. Even Veronica stopped being my best friend. How soon can we go?"

"We'll start packing tomorrow. Deal?"

She smiled. "Deal!"

Sherry, Ashley, and Celeste dropped by just as we finished breakfast.

Sam said, "Can't join you for lunch. It's Dad's Day at the school. I get to have lunch with Matt here."

Matt cracked a sheepish smile. I kissed both goodbye, as they walked out past the three women.

"Love you both," I called out.

They waved, and Sam blew me a kiss. Now to the business at hand.

"Thank you! Thank you!" Ashley said. "I can't imagine why you chose me as the new Senior Judge."

"You'll make a good one. Congratulations."

She hugged me and hastily left to start her new job. No chance of being late.

"I'm coming with you to Domes," Celeste said. "I've done all I can do here. People just never learn. My therapy is wasted on them. On Domes, I hope to make a real difference."

"I can help. Imagine a whole world where everyone had all the therapy they needed. Where everyone is healthy and happy," I said. "I should tell you about Empress Amandani."

Sherry said, "We should pack first. Talk on breaks."

We laughed. Nikita eagerly packed some of her possessions, though slow going. Still wearing one of the university outfits, I did little more than make suggestions where this and that should be packed. Five crates of the confiscated mutation agents sat in one corner of a spare bedroom. While I wanted it destroyed, I took Sherry's suggestion to pile it in a corner of the basement out of the way of everything. Sam could deal with its destruction later on.

By noon, workers arrived to cart one EMAC full of things to the new spaceship, The Parkinson. Sherry went with them, while Celeste, Nikita, and I headed out to eat lunch at my older son's new restaurant. Bernardo's.

"Hi, Mom. Aunt Celeste. Nikita. Is that your new robot thing?" Bernardo said.

"Yes, Cleo. I can't get over how good you look. All the mutations have been undone. You look like a male again."

He chuckled. "No kidding. So many of us are back to being normal. And we have Aunt Celeste, Aunt Eve, and Lara to thank for that. So are you really moving to Domes? We heard you have to be their governor."

In my opinion, he'd become an excellent chef. Mouth-watering food presented in aesthetic manners under candle light—I thought Bernardo's was destined for five stars.

Boom! A huge explosion somewhere in Chicago rocked the building and our floor. Teacups rattled. Water sloshed about in our glasses.

"What the hell was that?" I asked.

"I bet the rioters finally did it. That has to be a really big bomb, Mom," Bernardo said.

He dashed from table to table telling his many wealthy customers everything was okay here. Not to worry. But I worried. I had a sickening feeling in my stomach. I looked at Nikita. Her face looked ghastly white.

"M-m-mom, Matt's gone. I can't reach Dad either. Or anyone at school."

Bernardo turned on his giant monitor, switching to the news. Everyone in the restaurant stared in utter disbelief at the drone images being relayed. Even the reporter could barely speak, so horrified by the carnage. The kid's school, wealthy mansions—everything vanished into one giant crater covering ten blocks across. The screen split and the rioters' manifesto scrolled by. They demanded an end to corporation rule or expect more bombings. The view split again. Images of other bombings in four other major cities scrolled by.

We watched as emergency responders arrived, but they just stood there looking down into the gaping crater. There weren't any bodies to recover. At least I couldn't see any. This time I knew I'd lost Sam and Matt for good. No mutation agent could save them.

"Why didn't I see this coming?" I wailed. "Have I lost some of my abilities? I should have seen this and prevented them from going to school."

"Molly, you've only been back here a couple days. A lot has been going on during the more than two months you've been gone," Celeste said.

Sherry came racing into the restaurant. Spotting us, she ignored the staff and darted to us.

"Okay. Molly, Celeste, Nikita, come with me. Now. Got to get you to safety," Sherry said.

"You go, Mom. I'll be safe. I'm not leaving my restaurant."

Bernardo hugged me. Quietly, we followed Sherry while the other patrons continued to stare at the monitors.

"Sam and Matt are gone," I said.

Sherry said, "I know. They and hundreds of school kids and many of the wealthier corporation owners and their families. Roughly ten square blocks. Massive EMAC bomb. Helen's studying surveillance video that shows men landing it close to the school and pretending to have a breakdown."

"Dear god. The Hugos will be devastated. Both their kids," I said.

"Casper was late getting to the school for Dad's Day. So he's shaken up but alive. Veronica had lunch with her mother. Take your daughter to work day," Sherry said.

I exhaled deeply, relieved for my friends. I guessed Sherry felt annoyed at our incredibly slow pace getting to the MTES. We had to take a round-about route to get home. Part of the direct route to our home wasn't there any longer.

When Nikita and I plopped down on our couch, the terrible loss hit. Together, we sobbed. Sherry stood guard, just in case, while Celeste sat with us and didn't say a word. When I finally wiped my eyes and face on my blouse, Celeste acted.

"Nikita, I'm doing your mom first."

My loss was real and acute. I'd lost them once before, but the mutation agents had brought them back from death. This time there was no return. I shed buckets of tears as I ran through the loss trauma. When I hit a stable point, Celeste ended with me and worked with Nikita, who in turn cried her heart out, even going so far as blaming herself. An hour later, my daughter relaxed, though we both knew we had more to handle.

Cleo and Sherry prepared supper. We ate in silence. As we finished up, the Hugo family came over. Helen's bloodshot eyes told all. Wet spots dotted Veronica's school dress. Casper looked positively distraught.

Without a word, Celeste ran her therapy on Casper, while I took Helen aside to help her. Nikita assisted Veronica to deal with the loss of her younger brother, Fritz. I did hear Casper wailing, "I should have been there with him in his last minutes. I was late, damn it." I knew he blamed himself.

Hours later, the heavily charged loss lessened, they headed home. Cleo fixed some cocoa for us, and we held a family meeting.

Sherry said, "I want you off this planet as soon as possible. How quickly can you make arrangements?"

"We'll need to box up their things. Donate them to the needy," I said. "I'll have to arrange for a caretaker to keep our home up."

Celeste said, "Sherry, we'll make the arrangements in the morning. Let's leave by early afternoon."

That satisfied the robot.

Celeste had long ago arranged for workers to care for their apartments and Leslie's Costumes R Us store. She had that setup in less than an hour. However, I had trouble dealing with Sam and Matt's things. Every time I saw another shirt, toy, or even shoe, it reminded me of them. Acutely. Thus, we wound up merely boxing every thing up, storing it in the basement. Many boxes hid the mutation agent crates. I figured I'd see to their destruction another time.

We made our departure time, though we stopped to say farewell to the Hugo family first. I let Sherry handle the controls of The Parkinson, content to be a passenger this trip.

"Fifteen hours before arrival," she reported after dropping into hyperspace.

***

"Oh, Mom! We heard about Dad," Isabella said.

We landed on time. She and Owen were there to meet us, but inside the igloo doors, all my sisters and friends waited, ready to welcome me to Domes. Mixed, but strong emotions, greeted our arrival on Domes.

Deanna said, "We're giving you Home 1 as the governor's mansion. Thanks to Isabella and many others, we're learning a lot about this place. Can you believe there's hardly any metals on this world. Iron is very rare. It's all silicon and germanium. Literally everywhere. We're already beginning to market them to the rest of the empire."

"Wow. Has everyone here had the cures?" I asked. Deanna's giant bosom was gone, and she wore sneakers. Only Nikita and I wore the tall heels.

"Look at us," Felix, Leslie's husband. "We're men again."

Hank, Janine's husband, and Deanna's husband, Russell Godwyn, also wore male clothing and had had the cures. I soon learned everyone on Domes had all the known cures. We had a "normal human" population, though at least half were dwarves with a scattering of giants.

After they led us to our new home, Bev brought out a keg of brown ale. We partied, while I related all that had happened to me. Many eager ears listened attentively. I finished by complimenting Eve and Lara, who looked very pleased to be acknowledged for their genetics work.

For a week, Deanna continued to bring me up to date on all the activities on Domes. The population currently stood at a little over a hundred thousand, but more arrived each week. Survey crews mapped the geological resources of the world, while also mapping the locations of the many domed towns and cities. Others worked on identifying the flora and fauna. The fiercest animal, akin to a tiger, could rip a human in half, but these were rare and never entered a domed city.

Deanna discovered tunnel transportation tubes connected the cities. Her task: figure out how they worked and get them operational again. She had also installed a global defense shield to prevent Third Invader flying saucers from landing on the planet. So I'd been right in letting Sherry bring us down, for she knew the access code. Thus, I felt secure at night. After the bombing on Earth, really secure.

She also got George, a duplicate of Cleo, activated and attuned to Nikita's voice. That pleased my daughter, who liked having the robot helper. Maybe this would work out.

After a full week, I discovered Nikita silently crying in her room.

"What's wrong, honey?" I sat down beside her on her new bed.

"I don't fit in. There's no one here like me or you. We're the freaks of Domes. There's no one to play with or that will play with me. 'You can't play; you don't have arms.' So I sit here just studying all the time. But I don't want to go back to Earth either."

I sighed. "Honey, I don't fit in here either. Everyone's got their vital work to do. I'm mostly in their way or move too slowly."

She pressed her head into my chest. "What're we going to do?"

"I don't know yet."

The next day, Sherry ushered me to the radio shack, the home in which they'd installed all the communications equipment. "There's a long distance message coming in for you. It's from Bela Prime. Ashton Soros. Nearly an hour time delay between here and there. So no rush. When you're ready."

I followed her to the home. The radio operator had me sit and positioned a mike for me. A clock displayed a count down before the next transmission would arrive. At last, the set crackled. Voice only. No video.

"Mrs. Molly Parkinson. I hope you're on the line now. There's no easy way to tell you this, but it's about Bonita Valdez and her two Indrani-C detectives. They've been murdered."

Stunned. I sat there in a daze before my mind kicked in.

"...arrived safely last week. We put them up on campus at the request of Seven via our Senior Ambassador. It

354

happened last evening. No witnesses. Blaster shots to the head at close range. ID is on it. This has become intergalactic incident. Empress Kalindi Amandani is furious. I'll check back in two hours to see if there's a reply. We've handled their funerals already. Over."

The message ended. Silence. I sat there a moment. I'd lost Ted twice now. I'd only just gotten to know Bonita. Why hadn't she waited for me?

Celeste quietly joined us. "I'll take her back to her home, Sherry. Session time. Send the appropriate reply."

"Mom, what's wrong?" Nikita said when we returned home.

"Bonita. She's been murdered," I said.

Celeste led me straight into my new bedroom for another therapy session to handle this shocking loss.

Later and feeling better, I headed back to the LD radio shack. I had to place a call to Admiral Skaggs to tell him the news. Better for him to hear it from me than from someone on Cass-C.

"I'm so sorry, Molly. I can't thank you enough. But, yeah, I heard the news from an ID investigator on Bela Prime. Murdered. Why would anyone want to murder Bonita? Makes no sense. If you weren't the Governor of Domes, I'd ask you to investigate."

His words hit me like a puff of fresh air. Go to Cass-C. That was the answer for me and for Nikita. At the university, we wouldn't be freaks. We'd fit right in with all the others.

"I'll assign a new person to be the governor. Sir, I'm going there to investigate and get justice for Bonita. You can count on me to do that."

I heard a sharp exhale. "Thank you. I will owe you a very big favor. Anytime, anywhere. Do you have transportation arranged? Over."

"Not yet. Just found out about it. Over."

"Okay, I'll send a high speed transport to pick you up tomorrow. It'll get you there in about fifteen days, stopping to refuel several times. Pulling out the stops here. Remember, I owe you for this. Thank you. Over and out."

I walked back to my new home. Slowly compared to all

the others who seemed to dash about, scurrying ants on urgent business. No, I didn't fit in here.

"Nikita, we're going to move to Cass-C. We'll stay at the fancy university with all the others like us. We fit in there. You'll see."

"Wow! Perfect, Mom. Yahoo. When do we go? How long will it take? I'll get Issi to help me pack."

Others joined me. Eve said, "Sherry just told us. Molly, Lara and I are going with you. There's nothing more we need to do here. But there's sixteen hundred of you on Cass-C that need cures. Count us in. When do we leave?"

"Thanks. Tomorrow."

"Hey, I'm coming, too," Celeste said. "Sherry, as well. You best get a new governor appointed soon."

Deanna joined us. "I just heard..."

"Yes, I'm heading for Bela Prime or Cass-C tomorrow. Deanna, I hereby appoint you to be the new governor of Domes. Congratulations!"

The others clapped, but Nikita and I couldn't.

Isabella rushed in. "Mom, is it true you're leaving us?"

"Yes, tomorrow. Help Nikita pack, will you? I'm going to miss you and my granddaughter, but I'm needed there. I have to find Bonita's killers."

A breathless General Bev rushed in. "Heard ya going to Bela Prime. Want me to go help you blast those murderers?"

"No, you're needed here, Bev."

Her face fell slightly. "Yeah, I know. I'm providing security for this whole world. Tall order. Gail and I are up to it. If you need me, give a holler. We'll come as fast as we can. How long is the flight anyway?"

I chuckled. "Bev, you won't like it. Admiral Skaggs said it takes fifteen days at max speed, stopping to refuel several times."

Russell, who just arrived, said, "That's because Cass-C is close to the center of the galaxy, about as far from us as you can get. Molly, so sorry to hear about Bonita. You need us, you call. We'll come."

That night, my clone sisters threw a farewell party for Nikita and me. I got a little drunk on the brown ale. But I knew this was the right decision. Whether or not I could find the murderers, probably the human-like robots, the university life on Cass-C was what I desperately needed right now. And Nikita, too. This was the right decision for us. I had no reservations. Earth and its constant squabbles and fights had taken their toll on me. Many of my remaining relations and friends were safe on Domes. Now I could relax, be myself, and enjoy a second chance at being twenty-two again. Maybe learn new things as well.

The End.

Vic Broquard

A Favor to Other Readers

How about helping other readers? Many readers rely on reviews to make the decision whether to buy a book. You can help them make their decision by leaving your opinions and viewpoint in a short review of the positive things of this book. Writing the review and expressing your opinion only takes a few minutes, and other readers will appreciate your efforts.

Click this link: Sol Empire Volume 4 Power Moves
https://www.amazon.com/dp/B07BQ5JVTM/
scroll down to Customer Reviews; click on Write a Review, and enter your review. Thank you.

Author Information

Visit My Amazon.com Author Page
Vic Broquard Author Page

Follow My Blog
Vic Broquard's Blog

Follow Me on Social Media
Facebook
Google+
LinkedIn
YouTube

Other Books by Vic Broquard

Without Warning (fantasy)

The Trident Series: (fantasy)
    Volume 1 The Trident and the Book
    Volume 2 The Trident and the Scepter
    Volume 3 The Trident and the Resurrection

The Adventures of Elizabeth Stanton Series: (science fiction)
    Volume 1 The Evolution of the Path
    Volume 2 The Great Messiah
    Volume 3 Of Kings and Queens and Troubadours
    Volume 4 Chaos in the Aftermath
    Volume 5 Power Plays
    Volume 6 Age of Exploration
    Volume 7 Abducted
    Volume 8 The Emperor and Empress
    Volume 9 A Job Worth Doing
    Volume 10 Degradation
    Volume 11 The Second Crusade
    Volume 12 When Worlds Collide
    Volume 13 Dark Ages

The Lindsey Barron Series: (fantasy)
    Volume 1 The Rod of the Apocalypse
    Volume 2 The Board of Governors
    Volume 3 The Crown of Moses
    Volume 4 Dominus for President
    Volume 5 The National Health Care Program
    Volume 6 States Justice
    Volume 7 Cross and Double-cross
    Volume 8 Down the Dragon Hole

Zoran Chronicles Series: (fantasy)
    Volume 1 A Dragon in Our Town
    Volume 2 Dragons, Power, Courts, and War

Planet of the Orange-red Sun Series: (science fiction)

Volume 1 When Kingdoms Fall
Volume 2 Dark Ages
Volume 3 Age of the Towers
Volume 4 Difficillis Exitus
Volume 5 Age of the Lords
Volume 6 The Renegade Tower
Volume 7 Rebellions
Volume 8 The Aliens Return
Volume 9 Power Struggles
Volume 10 Guilds, Genetics, and Gods
Volume 11 Magi, Witches, Swords, and Superstitions
Volume 12 The Voyage of the Eagle's Seed
Volume 13 Eagle's Seed and Origins
Volume 14 Justifications
Volume 15 Responsibilities

The Return of the Wizards: Twelve Companions – The Making of Wizards (fantasy)

Slow Comes the Dark Series: (science fiction)
Volume 1 Creeping Darkness
Volume 2 Serendipity
Volume 3 Darkness Descends
Volume 4 Perversion Incarnate
Volume 5 Extermination Wars

Reclamation Series (science fiction)
Volume 1 For the Want of a Pill
Volume 2 Organ Donors

Dragons, Magic, and Me (fantasy)
Volume 1 The Box

The Sol Empire (science fiction)
Volume 1 For the Want of Humanity
Volume 2 Fear
Volume 3 Greed
Volume 4 Power Moves

www.ingramcontent.com/pod-product-compliance
Lightning Source LLC
Chambersburg PA
CBHW072115250626
47159CB00007B/2456